Jane Thynne was born in Venezuela and educated in London. She graduated from Oxford University with a degree in English Literature and joined the BBC as a journalist. She has also worked at *The Sunday Times*, *The Daily Telegraph* and *The Independent*, as well as a broadcaster on Radio 4.

She is married with three children and lives in London. Her previous novels are *Patrimony* and *The Shell House*.

THE WEIGHING OF THE HEART

A NOVEL
JANE THYNNE

First published in Great Britain in 2010 by
Byline Books, PO Box 64990
London SW19 9DD

ISBN 978-1-907560-00-2

Printed in Great Britain by Lightning Source, Chapter House, Pitfield, Kiln Farm, Milton
Keynes, MK11 3LW, United Kingdom

Ancient Egyptians believed that the heart recorded all the good and bad deeds of a person's life. After death the heart was weighed in the scales against the feather of truth and if the scales balanced that person would be welcomed into the afterlife.

O my heart which I had from my mother! O my heart of different ages! Do not stand up as a witness against me, do not be opposed to me in the tribunal, do not be hostile to me in the presence of the keeper of the balance."
Spell taken from the Egyptian Book of the Dead
to persuade the heart not to give away its owner's secrets

"I see wonderful things."
Howard Carter

"Golden shrine for statuettes (?two)"
Caption beneath empty cabinet in Howard Carter's inventory of Tutankhamen tomb

Before

Samuel had kept a photograph of himself and Carter. The Valley of the Kings, November 1922. Himself, with his head tilted and smiling, squinting into the sun, and beside him Howard Carter his hero, dapper with his bow-tie and ebony cigarette holder, already impatient, already looking slightly away. Behind them, like a great gash in the earth, was the tomb.

The night before they had entered the burial chamber. A small group of them, all sworn to secrecy, had gathered to undertake an excavation that everyone afterwards would agree had never taken place. Under cover of darkness they would pass through Tutankhamen's opened antechamber and using a hammer and chisel, break through the sealed wall of his burial chamber, the deepest recess of the boy king's sepulchre.

By day the Valley was a sweltering cauldron of searing rock, but at night the desolate desert chasm had a peculiar, unearthly atmosphere and a strange stillness, riven only by the harsh cry of a raven and the odd jackal's call. It was a long, dusty trudge through the winding path of the Valley, threading between the gullies and gorges of that harsh, inhospitable landscape which the ancients had chosen for their necropolis, the City of the Dead.

When they reached the place they stopped to pass round a hip-flask. He let the whisky burn down his throat and started as behind them an owl swooped with sudden precision on its prey. Checking his wristwatch by the faint moonlight he could just discern the time - two am. The very dead of night. Appropriate for such a trespass. Without speaking, one by one they silently descended the sixteen shallow steps to the mouth of the tomb steps, and opened the thick steel gates.

Who could forget, as they stepped down into the blind

gape of the tomb, that they were being received into a place of death? Who could not picture the moment when the pharaoh's body was drawn into the tomb, escorted by musicians and priests who would touch the lips of the mummy with spells so that the boy king might speak and defend himself in the Hall of the Dead? Who could not imagine his descent to the underworld, past the twelve gates guarded by flame-eyed serpents and caverns inhabited by jackal-headed gods feeding on rotted corpses? Who could not hear the hurried curses cast by the ancient priests to deter anyone from disturbing the king as they sealed up the door of death against men unwise enough to enter?

Samuel wasn't superstitious. He believed in no supernatural forces, good or ill, but still he needed to stiffen himself against a sense of violation as he groped his way in the blackness and felt the freezing air on his flesh.

They were in a narrow, sloping tunnel, about twenty five feet long and just high enough to stand in. Guiding themselves with their hands along the smooth limestone walls they passed in single file until the passage opened into a cavern of around twelve feet by twenty. This was the antechamber, still crammed with the funeral furniture and other effects of the dead king. There were benches, couches, statuettes and chests, stacked up in random disarray. And there, though he could barely see it, on the right hand wall, Samuel discerned the glimmering outline of two black and gold life sized sentinel statues of the king guarding a sealed door, stamped with the royal cartouche.

Despite the cold, and the thick linen jacket which all the excavators wore, sweat dribbled down his scalp, plastering strands of ginger hair against his forehead. His entire body was clammy with fear. The darkness in the antechamber was as thick as a wall and his throat constricted. He tried to remain calm but he could not help picturing the air clogged with the dust of long decayed flesh, as though the must of thousands of years was entering his body and becoming

3

part of it, transubstantiating the dead to life again. The dank smell of earth filled his nostrils and every cold breath caught in his gullet, as though he were sucking in a ghost.

They waited, shifting anxiously, as Carter, stripped down to his vest and braces, began chipping away at the plasterwork with a chisel, laboriously forcing a hole at the base of the sealed door. He issued soft, impatient grunts as he worked, raising a cloud of dust that settled like ash on their clothes. Using a crowbar he eased the stones loose and placed them one by one on the ground beside him. Once he had gouged out a space of about a foot high, they dropped to their knees one by one in the pitch blackness and crawled through.

When Samuel's turn came, his heart was racing with claustrophobic terror as he squeezed through the splintered cranny with effort and looked up to see what no earthly eyes had seen for the past three thousand years. There, within a yard of the doorway, spasmodically revealed by the flashes of Carter's torch, was what seemed like a solid wall of gold. As he pulled himself to standing he saw it was an immense shrine of gold-blue faience, every part of it inscribed with intricate patterns. Magical symbols, he guessed, to protect the royal body within. Ahead of him Carter had bent down to retrieve a small wick lamp, whose mud base was covered in hieroglyphics. Holding it up to the light he read aloud: "It is I who hinder the sand from choking the secret chamber. I am for the protection of the deceased."

For a while they all remained still, too cramped to move much in the tiny vault, until Carter finally moved a few steps further towards the door of the shrine. With infinite delicacy he drew back the ebony bolts to reveal a diaphanous linen veil spangled with tiny daisies of gilded bronze. As he touched it, one golden flower fell into his hand, so he put it in his pocket, then pushing back the hanging uncovered the doors to another gilded shrine, covered in hieroglyphics. Inside, enfolded in further shrines, Samuel knew would lie the sarcophagus of the boy king.

It was deathly quiet. The tomb seemed to suck back sound into itself. The only noise was the soft cracking and snapping of the wooden tomb furniture as it was exposed to the air after so long, and the faint scuttle of scorpions in the corners of the antechamber. The torchlight sent shadows shuddering up the walls. Suddenly Carter, who was ahead of them all, edging towards the north east corner beyond the shrine, let out a gasp. Straining to see in the darkness Samuel glimpsed a low opening to another chamber, piled high with glistening objects. Carter's voice was reduced to a choked whisper: "The Holy of Holies...".

Impatiently they peered over Carter's shoulder to see. The small chamber was the Treasury, containing all the most precious items of the pharaoh's funeral rites. Jewels, scarabs, amulets and a magnificent painted shrine guarded by the figures of four protective goddesses and containing the canopic urns for the organs of the dead king. There were gold and silver perfume flasks, and dozens of shabti figures to serve him in the afterlife. Exquisite colours stood out against the soft brown of the limestone walls; yellow, blue, amber, russet, black. Jerkily Carter's torch explored the contents of the room, its beam alighting on each new discovery excitedly - a games set, statuettes wrapped in linen, an ostrich feather fan, a majestic statue of Anubis - returning and picking them out with its dancing finger of light. Carter uttered little sporadic cries of astonishment. Everywhere was lapis lazuli, amethyst, turquoise, cornelian, obsidian and red jasper. Hushed, and reverent, they shifted around the glinting cavern, silent with wonder. Carter's face was shining with sweat in the torchlight, his hair matted with dust. His eyes gleamed in amazement. He alone in that cramped boy's room, amid the jumble of his cherished possessions, dared to pick up the objects and scrutinise them.

Samuel was the last to approach the Treasury chamber. As he squeezed alongside the shrine towards the doorway, groping his way carefully, he saw Carter's torch alight on something so brilliant, so exquisite, that even though he saw it for a split-second, its image was forever seared on his retina. It was a face, but a face of such serene beauty that it seemed poised between the human and the divine. Its gaze was intense and disturbing. It appeared to stare straight at him and for that moment, suspended in the torch's beam, it seemed to Samuel that the face was questioning him, judging him, probing the deepest recesses of his mind. Then the light moved on, and it was gone.

Yet even while the image faded, he had the feeling of something nameless but palpable beside him. Something had taken shape from the darkness and decay and was suffocating him. His legs felt weak, as if the tomb itself was draining him of life, and for an instant he sensed he was about to cross an invisible barrier, stepping over a crack between the present and the past, between the living world and the dead. His skin crawled and a feeling of hopelessness descended on him. There was no way to explain it, but he recognised it was Death he felt there. It was Death, malevolent and yet impersonal, intangible yet as real as any of the people standing beside him. Yet this death was not in the past, but in the future. It was a death yet to come and his heart hammered with premonitory dread.

Seized by a rush of panic, he turned back, sank to his knees to force himself out of the hole into the antechamber, ripping his trousers against the shards of rock and gashing his leg as he did so, before stumbling up the steps to the surface. Behind him he heard his companions calling after him but he ignored them, as he half-walked, half-ran, with the blood trickling down his calf, miles back along the deep gorge between the bone dry Theban hills.

Perhaps because they should not have been there that night, perhaps because they were all sworn to secrecy, no-one commented on Samuel's flight from the tomb when they met at the site early the next day. Nor did they discuss

6

among themselves what powers those ancient priests might have invoked to protect their dead. Perhaps they should never have set eyes on the objects that were meant for gods not men. Perhaps they should have heeded the Egyptian who claimed to have read an invocation inscribed on the burial chamber wall, the last duty of the priest who sealed up the dead king in his most sacred precinct: "Death Shall Come On Swift Wings To Whoever Disturbs the Sleep Of The Pharaoh." Where had it come from, that moment of icy fear? Samuel had no answer. All he could think was that if he had not been there that night, then the terrible things that followed might never have happened.

All he had left now was the photograph. He imagined himself putting that picture in an album someday, an album that would grow musty and spotted with age, and how beside the place and date he would write a neat caption in a deceptively modest hand, "Myself and Howard Carter before the tomb of Tutankhamun". How people would ask him questions and how he would tell them lies.

Chapter One

It was a foggy evening in March 1924 when Samuel Dux began his life again. He came up out of the gloomy vault of Victoria station, hailed a cab and took a letter from his inside pocket. He glanced again at the address on the envelope, though he knew it by heart, and drew his coat more closely around him, hoping his ancient suit wouldn't appear too creased by the journey.

Leaning back against the cab's cracked leather, he felt a slight griping in his guts. That was hardly a surprise - a lingering stomach ache was one souvenir of Egypt that everyone brought home - but it could equally have been a quiver of excitement. Because this was a fresh step for him, and apart from twenty pounds in his wallet, a change of clothes and some books in his case, he came possessed of nothing but his past.

He only had a mile to travel, but the journey was exaggeratedly slow. He'd almost forgotten fog could be like this, hanging dense and clammy on the skin, blanketing the senses and muffling the car horns and early evening bustle. Through the murk office workers hurried home with their briefcases under their arms and shop girls marched along to the tube, their lean coats with collars ruffled up against the evening air, the taste of acrid smog at the back of their throats. The newspaper stands advertised the latest move in a celebrated murder case. There was something about an actress he didn't recognise whose play was a triumph in New York. The new government was having a crisis. It was two years since he'd left, but behind the fog London was still stoically the same, staid and long suffering, enduring winter like a bad cold it might never shake off.

Elmer Barrington's house, on the corner of one of the

smarter London squares, was even grander than he'd pictured it. Tall and majestic, it loomed like the prow of a huge ship, pale stucco gleaming in the dusk. When he went up the steps the light of a lamp above the black door reflected his face back at him in the paint's shine. It was a narrow, high-cheekboned, clever looking face, with a thin-lipped mouth. His skin was burnt to a coppery brown, and the ginger hair under the hat was bleached blond by the sun.

Practically as soon as he had rung the bell the door opened and a butler stood looking at him impassively.

"Good evening. I'm Mr Dux…I think Mr Barrington.."

"Of course Sir. You are expected..."

The man swept the door open and motioned Samuel into a hall with a floor of chequered black and white marble. There was a side table, with cut flowers and a silver card tray. A smell of vacancy and furniture polish hung in the air. A series of oak panelled doors led off the hall and directly opposite the front door, facing the incoming visitor, was a portrait of a young man with a weak chin, widely spaced eyes and an unworldly expression. He wore an officer's uniform and had pale hair beneath his cap.

Once the butler had taken his coat Samuel stood still. In the distance he heard a dog's high pitched bark.

It seemed that no-one would be coming to greet him.

"Is this all your luggage, Sir?" Both men looked down at the single case which was shiny in patches and frayed at the edges.

"Er. Yes."

"Then allow me to see Sir to his room."

The butler moved off, up the wide marble staircase, to the second floor where he led Samuel into a bedroom of palatial proportions, with tall windows giving onto the square. There was a wide bed covered in a damson coloured quilt, heavy mahogany furniture and a cluster of silver-framed photographs on the chest of drawers, a couple of the same boy in uniform, staring blankly ahead of him. Perhaps this was his room, then. On the marble-topped dressing table stood a ship in a bottle and a chess board, with the pieces laid out, ready to play. In a bookcase to one side of the bed was a range of books with fraying, coloured spines, *The War Of The Worlds, She, Twenty Thousand Leagues Under The Sea*. As Samuel looked around him, the butler twitched at the door.

"Dinner is at eight, Sir. Mr Barrington will expect you in the drawing room before then. If there is anything you need.."

"No. No nothing, thank you."

Samuel waited until the butler had glided away and peered into the bathroom right next to the bedroom. It was lined in deep green Doulton tiles, with a bath encased in mahogany and, he was gratified to find, a shower cabinet installed with chrome attachments. Undressing swiftly he stepped in and hot water spurted from the circular head, coursing in rivulets down the ladder of ribs right to the small tidemarks of dirt between his toes, accumulated from days of travelling. He noticed a few grains of sand still stuck in his bellybutton. The soap smelt of musk and bergamot. He stood there for a while, the hot water planing down his body, feeling every muscle soften and relax. Before he changed back into the suit he flung himself flat out on the bed, in what the Egyptians called the corpse position, and exhaled. For a moment he was transported back to his small room in Luxor, with fat, bristly flies circling overhead and outside the shouts of the native workers in their guttural Arabic, getting drunk and fighting, and at night the incessant screams from the streets as though the entire country was engaged in ceaseless physical conflict. He pictured the little sun-baked houses, their insides thick with shadow, and the traders who sat there, regarding the passing strangers with a gaze that was at once acquisitive and indifferent. The distinctive stink of the city came sharply back to him, a mix of sweat and urine, dung and dust.

Sitting up, he shuddered. Just thinking about it brought anxiety creeping over him again and the familiar sickening sense of dread like a sour taste in his mouth. He took a silver hip flask from his case and drained it. He had to forget about that now. He had a new job after all, even if he hadn't yet the faintest idea why he had been given it, or what that job was supposed to be.

* * *

Elmer Barrington liked the monumental style. Being dwarfed by his furniture did not, despite popular aesthetic notions, make him feel at all insignificant. Instead it enhanced his considerable significance, in his own eyes at least, to surround himself with Doric columns, bulging chesterfields, enormous glass bookshelves and titanic chairs specially sculpted to accommodate his girth. He was not the kind of man to feel apologetic about his size. He had sharp little eyes buried in a puffy face. His flesh had a solid, mountainous quality about it as though it was more than mere muscle and fat sheathed inside its layers of linen, flannel and silk. Partly this was down to a whalebone corset that he wore for a back problem. The pain was continual but in a strange way he was grateful for it. It evinced a constant grimace which proved very useful in business transactions.

His first business had been confectionery. Back in Chicago, where he was born, his father had a firm, not a large concern, just a single factory and a couple of dozen workers, and the young Elmer's destiny had never been expected to stray far beyond winegums, pear drops and sherbet dips. Marshmallows, butterscotch, fruit cups and liquorice had formed the boundaries of the business until the day that Barrington's Candy Cake, a little bar in silver paper and a red wrapper was born and became the favourite brand in the state. It sold across the country, sold and sold, the millions of squares of candy amassing like glutinous bullion, quietly consolidating the Barrington fortune. By the time Elmer Barrington was twenty-five he was able to explore his ambitions in many different spheres, and few people in England connected the Barrington name with something as simple or pleasure-giving as candy. Sugar may have been the bedrock of his wealth, but upon it he had stacked a fortune made from commodities and property, from shares and the stock market as well as other, less regular ventures. Almost nothing pleased him as much as the opportunity to make a deal, and there was almost nothing he would not make a deal in. With his fortune grew a desire for all the things money can buy - social position, political influence and power – and as he had grown more successful he had come to believe that nothing was quite beyond his grasp, nothing could not be rightfully his, if he only wanted it enough. That was how he felt about the business with the young man before him.

His back was nagging him, so he leant against the mottled marble fireplace for support and drank a glass of whisky.

"Good journey?" he asked, in a tone which did not convey undue solicitude for Samuel's comfort.

"Very good, Sir. The crossing was very calm from Alexandria to Trieste. Then I went on to Venice and took the Transcontinental Express up to Boulogne. In fact apart from fog in the channel …"

"I expect you want to know why I've invited you here," he interrupted. The tone was bored and impatient. His voice was a low, American growl which deterred dissent.

"I do rather."

"Well you'll have to wait until tomorrow, I'm afraid. My daughter will be joining us for dinner, and I don't think we need to discuss it with her." He looked at his watch. "She's late, damn her."

Unlike most people, Samuel was not especially offended by Barrington's curtness. It reminded him of his classics master at school and he found the lack of small talk rather a relief. They stood together in silence, bathed in two yellow pools of light either side of the fireplace until above them, a door slammed.

"Here she is at last."

There was the clacking of heels, and a girl in a duck-egg-blue dress walked into the room. She was accompanied by a hairy white dog on a lead, with a pink bow on its head, claws skittering on the polished floor.

"Iris, this is Samuel Dux. He's come to help with my project."

His first impression was that she was as unlike her father as a human being could be. Where he was solid, she was ethereal, the chiffon of her dress and the translucence of her skin adding to the impression that she might blow away altogether, if not anchored by the dog. She was tiny where he was tall, with blonde hair cut in a heavy golden bell that framed an elegant face, just a little too angular to be called pretty, with high cheekbones and a sharp nose. But on closer inspection he saw the resemblance. She had her father's strong chin, and blue, intelligent eyes with a watchful, birdlike quality which made her look as though nothing would escape her attention. She gave Samuel a swift curious glance, which seemed to take in at once his suit (sagging), his shoes (scuffed) and the patches where his soft collar was worn threadbare. He proffered his hand and for a fraction of a second, her hand rested in his, cool and silky.

"Iris has quite a social life. Parties every night. Quite a whirl of excitement. She'll be more than capable of entertaining you while you stay, if you've a taste for such things. Won't you Iris?"

Iris gave him a glance. It did not signal unfettered excitement. She stuck her chin out, small and stubborn.

"Maybe. The thing is, Daddy, there's been a mistake. I'm afraid he'll have to move."

The geniality which had softened Barrington's face with the arrival of his daughter clouded again. "What are you talking about?"

"Somebody, Cairns I suppose, has put him in Charles's room."

Barrington's eyes did not flicker. Without further comment, he turned on his heel and led the way to the table.

Some hours later, back in the boy's bedroom, where he guessed he would be staying because his paltry belongings had been unpacked in the wide, mahogany drawers, he laughed at the strangeness of it all. What a way to spend his first night back in London.

The dinner had been good - the best food he'd had in ages – watercress soup swirled with cream, lemon sole and then duck, and you could tell all the ingredients were of the highest quality because everything tasted rich, dense with flavour. But the girl Iris just toyed with her food. That must be what kept her skinny as a rake. She had sat through dinner saying practically nothing and answering any enquiries just fully enough to pass as polite. She paid no obvious attention to anything Samuel said though she was listening to everything, he could tell. Across the polished expanse of table, through the branches of the handsome, silver epergne, he detected the occasional, subliminal flicker of interest cross her face.

It was a shame, really. A little social interaction wouldn't have gone amiss after his journey and it was a long time since he'd even talked to a girl of his own age. She shot him curious glances when she thought he wasn't looking. Samuel didn't know much about women, but he recognised a sulk when he saw it. If he was to stay here for any time, he only hoped her mood would improve.

* * *

The next morning, lacking any particular instruction, he hovered outside Barrington's study, smoking a cigarette and waiting for the man to appear. Relieved though he was to have left Egypt behind him, Samuel was mystified by what Barrington could want with him. What talent could he possibly possess that this man might use?

He had grown up in a village outside Nottingham where his father owned a printing firm. His parents were Methodist people who valued decency and hard work and whose unfaltering devotion to him was accompanied by a marked aversion to emotional gesture. Love was expressed by the fleeting touch of a hand on the head or the occasional offer of a lean maternal cheek to be kissed. At moments of great affection his father shook hands. Embracing Rose, his mother, was a frigid, twitchy affair, and not lightly attempted.

As a young man Eric Dux had borrowed money and established himself in business and from the day his son was born Samuel's only destiny was to carry on the painstaking task of building up the firm. That was the natural order of things and undoubtedly what God ordained.

The first signs that God's plan might not run entirely smoothly came when Samuel showed a flair for drawing at grammar school. When he was sixteen, Mr Hennessy the art teacher came to see Eric and Rose and informed them that their son possessed real talent, which was something to be cherished and developed, rather than crushed in the mundane environment of - what was it? - a commercial printworks. Samuel was the first pupil in decades who had shown such ability, and the teacher wanted assurances that it would not be stunted. Mr Hennessy, who drained several cups of tea during this one-sided encounter, was an eccentric figure, who wore hair slightly longer on his collar than was approved of, and told his pupils about Modernism. Sitting in the Duxs' front parlour he talked with much gesticulation about art school, in London maybe. Eric and Rose received him with the habitual attitude they adopted towards those they considered their slight social superior, rigidly polite, with tight smiles and poker straight. But when the man left, they made it clear to their son that any sort of art school nonsense was out of the question.

Samuel didn't protest. He knew very little of what art school entailed but it didn't stop him drawing. What started off as a skill for sketching nature, birds and still-lifes, began to show signs of developing into a mature, idiosyncratic artistic style and in the final summer of school he won a competition. The prize was awarded at the village fête by Lady Horrocks, the châtelaine of the local manor house, which had been taken over as a military convalescent home. Lady Horrocks was much taken with Samuel. Perhaps the eager, fresh-faced boy seemed more appealing than the dead-eyed, wounded soldiers who shuffled around her home or perhaps it was that with her husband, Sir David, away in Whitehall working for the War Office, she was simply lonely. Either way, the result was that he spent the whole of that summer roaming her house – with its walnut-panelled rooms laid with kashmiri rugs, floor to ceiling glass cases stuffed with ethnographic artefacts collected by Sir David and its library converted to an officers' mess. Sometimes, in the conservatory amid the palm trees and exotic plants, Samuel would be required to take tea, entailing piles of sandwiches and cakes and a conversation with the soldiers, which was never an easy affair. The ones who were not physically impaired could seem at first glance normal, but on closer inspection there was something about the angular faces, the imperfectly fitting clothes and imprecise haircuts, the tics and spasms, which made him think of reject toys on a shelf, whose button eyes or ears deviate just slightly from the norm. One man stared ahead of him, his book clutched to his chest like an old lady clasping her bag on the bus. Another argued with an invisible visitor in a low conversational tone. "They would really be far better off dead," Lady Horrocks would proclaim quite audibly. "Kinder you know."

The chief pleasure of these visits was exploring her husband's collection of antiquities, standing in the long, airy passage where they were piled up haphazardly, in no sort of order, almost as if they had been abandoned and he was there to exhume them. There were statues, some with features blurred and vague, others acute as though listening to silent music. Little blue Egyptian funerary figures, a piece of a mummy case with delicate painting in pale gold and ochre, unguent jars and vases and fragments of stone carved with the images of Thoth and Horus and Osiris and Isis. Samuel had never seen objects like them. Their dignity and restraint, the purity of the lines, the power of their dimensions and their severe simplicity.

He turned eighteen just as the war ended, escaping the fighting by the skin of his teeth. It might have been the sight of so many families in the village whose sons returned crippled from the front, but Samuel's parents abruptly rejected predestination, abandoned their protests and decided that he should, if he wanted, pursue an artistic career. In Nottingham preferably, but ultimately, and if it were absolutely necessary, they would not object to him going to art school in London.

Given this sudden, unlooked-for escape from the world of commercial printing, it did appear absolutely, overwhelmingly necessary to Samuel that he should move to London immediately. But once he arrived in the capital it became obvious that the whole art-school idea might be a little ambitious. For a start he would need to pay for it, and the fees seemed to be vastly more than the sum his father had pressed meaningfully in his hand "for contingency purposes". For a few weeks he flirted with the notion of moving to Paris and finding a garret to paint in, during which time he frittered away what reserves he had on exploring the city, until finally, driven by hunger and a reluctance to return home, he enlisted in a studio to learn draughtsmanship.

It was a mistake, and he knew it at once. Life as an apprentice draughtsman was unimaginably monotonous. He was put to work in a grey, high- windowed basement in Holborn, surrounded by serious, silent men much older than himself who had sat out the war at their desks. The time he would have to serve until he had earned enough to pay for his artistic studies seemed to stretch indefinitely before him. There was just one other apprentice, a passionate left-wing Welshman called Alan Collins, who had failed the medical during the war and driven an ambulance in France. After the fighting ended he'd been keen to study economics at the LSE but his family was too poor to send him. Together they would share a pint after work - Alan railing at the injustices of the world while Samuel contemplated the wrong turn his life had taken.

His only escape came in the lunch-hours when he would frequent the British Museum, drifting through the galleries, staring into the glass cases, imagining he was back at the Horrocks' home fingering the antiquities at his leisure.

One day, hanging on the fringes of a lunchtime talk, he heard of an archaeological survey of Egypt that was in need of volunteers. A body called the Egypt Exploration Society wanted draughtsmen to chart and record the work they were engaged on in the deserts outside Luxor. On that drizzly London day, Egypt sounded as exotic to Samuel as London once had. In one impulsive gesture he spent the whole of what he had earned thus far, plus the tiny sum his mother had sent for emergencies, on a ticket to Cairo.

And it was perfect timing, as it turned out. Four years after Europe's youth sank into the Flanders mud, Howard Carter brought up the boy king with the dazzling golden face, and the world went mad.

The atmosphere was exhilarating. Momentous. Suddenly Egypt was the centre of the earth. And Samuel was right in the centre of it.

The society had entrusted him to the care of a Dr Fellowes, a tiny, kindly gentleman in a white pith helmet who was involved in an excavation just the other side of the hills from the tomb. He was exploring some twentieth-dynasty tombs which had been comprehensively looted by robbers thousands of years before. The work was dull and unrewarding. Dr Fellowes, an archaeologist of the old school, spurned modern comforts and liked his helpers to erect their own tents on site, rather than take houses locally. He had dug at Giza, and the early dynastic necroplis at Nag'ed Der and at Lisht, but he had been here for twenty years now and had very little to show for it.

Despite his training as a draughtsman, Samuel was put to work excavating, sorting through shards of limestone chips day after day, sweating and cursing in the coruscating heat.

One morning, alerted by a native runner as he was taking his tea on a camp table laid with starched linen cloth, Dr Fellowes called Samuel over. His normally spry, sun-wizened countenance was pink with excitement.

"You, dear boy, are about to witness something very exciting. Something you will be able to tell your grandchildren."

Samuel was momentarily confused. Talk of grandchildren evoked the fleeting image of himself here forever, as the years reeled away behind him. He tried to question Dr Fellowes but the man seemed to want to preserve the surprise, as though Samuel were a child himself. Not that Samuel, or anyone digging in those valleys could have had any doubt what the find was, as they walked across the cliffs and climbed up the limestone terrace of the escarpment where everyone believed the boy king Tutankhamun's tomb was situated.

Dr Fellowes impressed upon Samuel that he occupied a very privileged position. One indeed that he would fill only until more experienced people could get there to help. But as soon as Carter met Samuel he seemed to take a liking to him. Once he found out about Samuel's skill at sketching there was no more talk of him being there in a temporary capacity.

"I think I can use you, Mr Dux," Carter said, with a momentary look of keen scrutiny.

He was put to work copying the objects in the ante chamber. Sketching them was a vital exercise because things that looked perfectly solid had an unsettling tendency to crumble into dust within minutes of exposure to air. Even standing in that space he was almost afraid to move. The tiny chamber was crammed like the props department of a touring opera company, the objects encrusted with gold and semi-precious stones. The work was intricate and time-consuming and it was almost too dark to see in the tomb until a photographer arrived and fixed up a system of mirrors and silver paper reflectors so that shafts of sunlight were thrown into the depths.

There was something about these figures, and their serene inscrutability, that felt comfortable to Samuel. Their demeanour seemed unconnected with the earthy squalor of humanity around them, as though they were sprung from a different race entirely. Their expressions were devoid of human nuance. The artists who made them spoke not of love, or envy or regret but empire and dominion and posterity. Who would not feel foreign in this place, surrounded by indecipherable symbols and a culture so distant and estranging? Which meant that Samuel, with his habitual sense of dislocation, was somehow at home.

It was soon after he arrived that he met Violet Esterhazy, a well-born Englishwoman in her forties with an aristocratic bearing but no income to match. Her absentee husband had taken work on another dig but she remained at Luxor for the social life, one of a crowd of ladies, including the wives of visiting dignitaries and friends of Lord Carnarvon's daughter, Lady Evelyn, who clustered round the site, getting

their silk dresses and cotton parasols coated with dust.
Sometimes they'd even take lunch with Howard Carter
and his colleagues in one of the Valley's empty tombs, on
a table set with spotless linen and crystal glasses. Samuel
remembered one such lunch, trying to remain composed
and negotiate his poached fish while Violet pressed her knee
against his thigh beneath the tablecloth.

It was down to Violet, in the end, that he had fetched up
here. The day the letter arrived they were at her home –
events had forced him to stay in as much as possible – and
she was languidly stroking his hair in a maternal manner
that was intensely disconcerting. She sat up, so that the flesh
on her stomach ruched in little rolls, and lit a cigarette.

"Oh Elmer Barrington. He's a darling. A great friend of
mine back in London. Didn't I mention that I'd had a word
with him?"

"No. You mentioned nothing about arranging my career for
me. Anyway what does he want? He doesn't say."

"Oh it'll be something perfectly pleasant. I told him how
clever you were. Besides, he's ridiculously rich." She
paused to exhale and smile down at him through the smoke.
"Samuel, don't look so fierce! I thought you'd be pleased!
It's probably a little consultancy work for him. He's a terrific
collector. He probably wants you to ferret things out and tell
him exactly where to *pounce*."

She made a little feline gesture of entrapment, but he
moved away.

"He wants me to go to England to see him. He's offering to
pay the fare."

"Don't be miffed darling. I shall miss you frightfully, I
will absolutely pine every day, but the digging season's
practically over and besides, you know, I think it's really
about time you left."

How much did she know? Violet was always hard to read.
Her true beliefs and motivations were a mystery to him. She
might care for him, but equally, she might long to be rid of

him. Either way, even as he sat there, frowning at the letter, he knew that this was his escape.

The heavy tread of Elmer Barrington down the corridor cut short these reflections. He ushered Samuel into his study, a comfortable, opulent place, with an Aubusson rug on the floor, Watteaus and Fragonards on the walls and shelf upon shelf of Egyptian pieces. Barrington's collecting craze had been through many phases - from paintings, illustrated prayer books, tapestries and musical instruments, right through to mediaeval weaponry and roman marbles. Once he had shipped back from France an entire staircase with balustrade which had been affixed, with anachronistic panache, to the front of his Jacobean country house. There was a room in his house which the maids fought among themselves not to dust because every surface was crammed with priceless porcelain from the Ming dynasty. Many a hillside chapel in Tuscany had born the brunt of his flirtation with Italian altarpieces. Greek ruins had been rifled for their statuary. But right now the full blast of his passion was concentrated on ancient Egypt.

"You know, Mr Dux," he began, pouring coffee from a silver pot. "I envy you."

He paused for a chuckle at this preposterous notion.

"Yes it's true. Listening to you last night, I reflected that you have had an experience that I myself have never had, and can never have."

"You can visit Egypt can't you?"

"Oh yes. Of course, and I intend to, whenever my business permits me. I will see the pyramids and sail down the Nile and visit the tomb and fulfil the entire *'touristic'* agenda, though I flatter myself I'll be a little better informed than the average traveller. I was a personal friend of Carnarvon for years - he had me down to see his furniture collection at Highclere. I can't tell you the splendour of the things he had there. To sit at the desk of Napoleon taken from Elba and see where the chair's arms have been scratched by the imperial fingernails. Can you imagine that? Hmm? Nothing one can get from pictures compares to the sense of history one has from actual contact with the authentic item."

He ran his sausagey fingers along the arm of his chair as he spoke, as if making his own historical indentations, and fixed his small eyes on Samuel intently.

"But even though I will be exceptionally, *formidably* well prepared, I will still never achieve what you have. Because you were there at the moment of discovery. You saw those wonderful things untouched, exactly as they had been left by the funeral priests thousands of years ago."

Samuel flinched. The next thing he would be asking about was the curse.

Was it true that secret poisons had been released when the seals of the tomb were breached? Had not Lord Carnarvon himself fallen victim to the curse? Even the esteemed author, Sir Arthur Conan Doyle, said the Earl was killed by an elemental. Was he not, like other famous explorers before him, like Frankenstein and Faustus and Dr Jekyll, destroyed by the results of his own explorations? How else could anyone explain the fact that Carnarvon - a man in apparent good health - had died so suddenly after the discovery? Not to mention that at the moment he had expired, on the night of the 5th April 1923, all the lights in Cairo had gone out and his little terrier bitch back in England had keeled over too, and died? Because after all these were facts and indisputable.

Anticipating Barrington's next line of enquiry, Samuel said: "I expect you want to ask about the curse."

"Heck." Barrington shot him a sceptical look. "You don't believe in that, do you?"

If he hesitated, it was so slight that Barrington didn't even notice it.

"No, actually."

"Good to hear it. It's a heap of superstitious nonsense."

Samuel shifted in his seat. Misjudging Barrington made him look foolish. He began to worry about this proposed new job. Surely the idea wasn't that he would simply sit here and talk about his years in Egypt? What kind of job was that?

"You said, Sir, you would explain what employment you had in mind for me."

"Ah yes." Barrington relaxed his posture. "It's to do with a building I've been planning."

"A building?"

"Well," he laughed deprecatingly. "More of a monument really."

Sitting back in his mammoth chair and steepling his fingers beneath his chin, Barrington began to outline his vision. He had decided to build a vast headquarters for his company, to be established on a piece of land he had already purchased in the east of the City. In design it was to be elegant, absolutely of the moment, yet, in the quality of its construction, a landmark for posterity.

"It sounds very impressive. But- I don't mean to sound dense - I still don't see how exactly it involves me."

Barrington stood up abruptly, signalling that the meeting was at an end.

"I've a very special role in mind for you, Mr Dux. But I suggest we discuss the details at the site tomorrow. In the meantime, I hope we have the pleasure of your company for an extended stay, so settle in. Enjoy yourself. I've told Iris you may be available to escort her tonight. As I said, she's out almost every evening, at parties, balls and that sort of thing. She doesn't stop."

"Must be tiring." Samuel felt ill-disposed towards Iris after her behaviour the previous evening.

Barrington seemed to understand the inference. "Perhaps my daughter seemed a little…, unforthcoming last night. She's not used to visitors. And she was badly struck, we all were, by what happened to her brother."

That must be the boy in the uniform. So he was dead then.

"May I ask what happened?"

"Charles? It was the Somme. 1916."

"I'm sorry."

Barrington's small eyes, glinting sharp in the folds of his face, fixed on him. "Sure. I take it you were too young to fight..."

Samuel dug his hands in his pockets.

"Yes, Sir. I was born too late."

Barrington glowered at him. From disbelief, or disdain, it was hard to tell, and for just a moment he seemed locked in private thought, until he turned away and said: "I expect your father's grateful."

As they went out into the hall they passed Iris just coming in, the little dog tethered on a plaited leather leash, her skin tinged with a rosy glow. She wore a grey chinchilla collar which framed her face in a cloud of fur and she trailed a light, floral perfume.

"I've told Mr Dux that you may be in need of an escort tonight, Iris."

There was a slight, rebellious purse to her lips. Without looking at Samuel she said lightly: "Oh not tonight, Daddy. I'm afraid I'm going out with Dolly."

"Another time perhaps then?"

"Yes, I'm sure there'll be another time."

She passed them dreamily on her way upstairs, but Samuel caught her eye and thought he detected in it the faintest glint of mockery. It was enigmatic, that face, but he couldn't help feeling it was a face set against him. Why? For some reason she seemed intent on being deliberately antagonistic towards him. What had he ever done to her?

Barrington, however, did not appear dismayed. His composure restored, he turned to Samuel and rubbed his hands.

"Well then Mr Dux, it seems we have the evening to

ourselves. And I have to say I'm keen to hear more of your experiences. I want you to tell me everything that happened."

* * *

So he wanted to know everything that happened, did he? Just the thought of it made Samuel quail. Could it really be that he was going to have to relive the time he so dearly wanted to forget? To recall the events that he wanted to obliterate from his memory as thoroughly as the priests of the nineteenth dynasty pharaoh Horemheb had obliterated the memory of his predecessor Tutankhamun, toppling every statue, defacing every relief, chiselling out every cartouche of his name? Where could he even begin?

At the start, he supposed, because when he thought about it, that was where things had begun to go wrong.

The first hint of it came one evening a few days after the opening of the tomb in November 1922. Carter had invited him for a drink to his house at Elwat El Diban, but when he arrived Samuel found him hunched in his chair on the verandah, drinking whisky and soda and gazing blankly into the distance as a flock of slow-winged birds passed, black against the violet sky.

The British liked to joke that Howard Carter had made this particular part of Egypt his own. The Valley was Carter's Colony and the house was known to everybody as Castle Carter. It was a squat, brick construction, set in a striking situation on the hill at the entrance to the Valley with a spectacular view of the boats on the Nile and beyond them, the far hills melting into the dusk. Carter had designed it himself with an Arabic-style domed central hall, set with low sofas and cushions, and high, arched windows. The bricks had been shipped all the way from Lord Carnarvon's English estates and Carter had each one stamped, just like a pharaoh, with his own name and date.

Samuel knew all this because people were always talking about Howard Carter. It was a curious fascination given that Carter did not exactly exude charisma. He was said to model himself on his patron Lord Carnarvon, to the extent of using identical toilet water and the same tailor in Savile Row and taking elocution lessons to round his flat Suffolk vowels. On the dig he cut a dapper and immaculate figure in his tweed three piece suit, homburg, and blue spotted bowtie, but in conversation he was graceless and by nature he was a loner.

Now, looking across at his host, frowning and abstracted, Samuel was puzzled. This should have been the best time of Howard Carter's life. Each day the excavation rendered up new excitements and Carter's celebrity spread further round the globe, yet the man seemed listless and preoccupied.

As he cast around awkwardly for something to jolt Carter from his reverie, the pet canary let out a stream of song from its cage up in the bougainvillea and Samuel was reminded how Abdel Al, Carter's servant, had called it a "bird of gold", presaging the discovery of the tomb.

"Perhaps the natives were right about that bird," he commented. "I mean Sir, you'd not had much luck until now."

There had been some jars and a yellow limestone statuette and some cracked alabaster vessels that bore the name Amenophis I. One season they dug up a mummified cat. But there was nothing really major. Nothing to make up for the desolate landscape with its brutal cliffs rising each side of a dry plateau and the heat which seared down on the arid gravel like a furnace, accompanied by a hideous wind that whipped up out of nowhere and flung scalding sand in the face, leaving a bitter aftertaste of clay in the mouth. People said the east valley was empty. Three thousand years of robbers filleting through the layers of sand and rock ensured there was nothing left but more sand and rock. But finally Howard Carter had proved them wrong.

Carter shook himself from his thoughts, tipped his glass to Samuel and said with the ghost of a smile,

"So you call this luck do you, Mr Dux?"

"I didn't mean - that is, Sir, I wouldn't ever underestimate your achievements…"

He fixed Samuel with a steely stare, then smiled.

"No, of course not. It was the war that inspired me actually. A grid system I heard about for mapping out artillery barrages in the trenches."

He'd divided the triangle of ground in the middle of the valley on this grid, ensuring in his meticulous way that not an inch of the rock face would be left unexamined. From 1917 onwards he made a systematic search beneath all the rock chippings and debris thrown out by previous excavations until that season there was just one small section left. This little area had been deliberately untouched before, so as not to impede access to the popular tomb of Rameses VI. Carter decided to clear the debris of some ancient workmen's huts and dig down to the bedrock though he thought it unlikely there would be any other tomb so near.

When the find came, he was alerted because the usual babble of the men's voices had fallen silent. Then there was a shout. Carter's water boy, struggling to set up the communal zeer, the water jar for the men, had laid bare a stone slab, which when it was cleared proved to be a flight of 16 steps, leading into a passage cut from the rock, sloping downwards and just high enough to stand upright in. At the bottom was a sealed doorway, quite evidently, by its size and shape, in the style of the eighteenth dynasty. Above this doorway were seal impressions of the Royal Necropolis, Anubis the jackal, seated over nine foes. The seal of a king.

Carter managed to contain his excitement for two weeks, until Lord Carnarvon arrived from England and together they prepared to open the sealed door. Carter inserted a candle at first, and the hot air escaping from the tomb caused it to flicker. He replaced it with a torch, peered inside and was struck dumb in amazement at the sight of strange animals, statues and sacred objects within. There were massive gilded wooden funerary couches, giant statues, caskets, boxes and chariots. Monstrous creatures, part hippo, part crocodile, loomed out of the darkness and their shadows reared up on the wall. Works of art were stacked seemingly at random, resting on thrones. And everything, on every surface, was gilded. Carter gasped at the gorgeous, sumptuous splendour of it all. "Do you see anything?" demanded Carnarvon, beside himself. "Oh yes," said Carter eventually. "I see wonderful things."

Once Carter had stepped into the antechamber, where no-one had trodden for three thousand years, they couldn't get him back. They heard him exclaiming in the darkness and saw the flash of his torch as it passed from one group of objects to another. "There's enough stuff here to fill the whole Egyptian section of the British Museum!" he exclaimed. And then, against the right wall, sandwiched by two black sentinel statues, he saw a sealed doorway stamped with the seals of the royal necropolis and realisation dawned. Surely just feet away from them, untouched by robbers, lay the sepulchral chamber of Tutankhamun, where the sealed sarcophagus and the choicest treasures would lie. This had to be the greatest body of archaeological material ever found. The only intact tomb of a king of Ancient Egypt. It was wonderful, Carter said.

But it didn't stay wonderful for long.

Chapter Two

Iris pulled the turquoise silk shift dress over her head and thanked heaven that she didn't need one of those elastic bust-flatteners that Dolly wore. They made you feel quite faint and liable to black out at the most inopportune moments. She adjusted the tassels of her dress to float at mid calf and turned sideways to see her reflection in the mirror. Even to someone as critical as her, it was a satisfying sight. She was as sleek as a seal. It was as though her very body was striving to emulate the boyishness that had been so desired in her by her parents.

Iris had been born seven years after her brother Charles - a sickly, premature little baby only just alive. As he looked down at the baby, squalling like a boiled lobster in the froth of her cot, Elmer Barrington could not help wondering why he and his wife Margaret, so amply furnished with money, breeding, talent and looks, should have been denied something so straightforward as fecundity. Why his simple desire for a long line of sons, an achievement that was elementary to the poorest inhabitant of the slum areas of London, should be thwarted. Iris was all they had managed after six years of trying, rather than the brother that Charles - already a little milksop with a penchant for quiet games - so badly needed. It was infuriating.

It was down to his wife of course. Margaret had always been frail. They had met on his first visit to England, at a time when he had no ambition beyond sampling the requisite high points of European culture before returning to Chicago to continue the family work of making Barrington's Candy Cake into America's biggest brand. But the petite young debutante he met at a house party undid all his plans. Despite her physical weakness, she possessed the intelligence and confidence to question and challenge him. She could see beneath his bullying and bluster and Barrington, who was used to people wilting beneath his assaults, found this a novel experience. It went without saying that the Plunket family, who came over with the conquest but were down on their luck, represented all the worst aspects of the European culture he was here to absorb – they were decayed, run down, and badly in need of an injection of American cash. But Margaret, he decided, was a find. When he proposed, he expected she would agree quickly and they would move back to Chicago together but instead she took her time to consider him and even when she did accept, she refused point blank to leave England. No one had ever stood in Barrington's way before, but it became perfectly evident that if he was to have the wife he wanted then his future would have to be built here. And after all he wouldn't be the first American to come over and prop up the impoverished English upper classes.

So he branched out from the confectionery trade and turned his attention to speculation. He wheeled and dealed. Stocks and shares were his skill, though he bought property and land, too. For recreation he joined forces with Arthur Vickers, a benevolent publishing millionaire who became the closest thing he had to a friend. A few racehorses here, several properties there and slowly the digits of his invisible wealth multiplied, as seemingly secure as the place Barrington had carved for himself in London society.

Having stayed and built his new business up, it was a bitter blow to Barrington when her fragility killed Margaret well before time. She died of septicaemia at the start of the war. The only mercy was that she didn't live to see what happened to her son. In a short space of time Barrington's family, small enough as it was God knew, had been effectively halved, reduced to its tiny square root. And family was the kind of stock that took generations to recover.

For Iris, as a young teenager, the loss of her mother was devastating. When she was a child, in the tiny, circumscribed world of the nursery, she had longed for her mother's evening visits, bringing with them lavish kisses, a sweet gust of perfume, Guerlain's Muguet or Chez Poiret, and sometimes a smuggled violet or peppermint cream. After she died, it fell to Charles, when he was home, to replace this affection, and being gentle and sensitive he became more than a brother to Iris. The siblings acknowledged the qualities in each other that both lacked in themselves, Iris was restless and energetic and loved riding, swimming, squash and tennis, whereas Charles preferred to stay inside and read. He had a slight speech impediment and could not properly pronounce his "r"s. He kept a teddy bear in his inside pocket, for which he was brutally tortured at school. Until his father discovered and outlawed the practice, he had enjoyed collecting wild flowers.

But what their father never saw, and somehow couldn't see, was that Charles was always laughing. Iris remembered him lanky and comical, making up plays for her with their French puppet theatre or singing funny songs with her name inserted, or at bedtime reading the series of short stories he had composed, *The Awful Adventures of Iris*, in which she roamed the world with her pet parrot, naughty and bold. Whether they were kicking the leaves in Kensington Gardens or on an improving outing to the National Gallery, he was always excellent company.

He collected knowledge the way other boys collected stamps or shells and taught her far more than she ever learnt in the classes of Miss Moore's Academy in South Kensington which she attended from the age of eight. He knew about things like coats of arms, lions rampant and couchant, about sheepshank and slipknots, about how to make owl hoots from your cupped hands and skim stones across a pond. He read their tarot cards and made her shiver when he drew the hanged man, though he explained it signified not death but life suspended. He cured her fear of arithmetic with his tale of the algebra zoo where Pi lived with the mysterious hypotenuse. He taught her bits of ancient Greek and invented a code with rude words for some of their father's business associates. He painted a series of magical maps that she still kept, deep in a drawer, charting her imaginary adventures. In all these things he made a personality for Iris that was braver and more brilliant than she felt she was. He made a world for her, of which she was the clever, subversive centre, triumphing over all disasters. Her friends adored him too and unlike their older brothers, who were large and distant and always off playing rugby, Charles was never too busy or too grown up to have fun with them.

Yet in his father's presence Charles seemed to shrink. He hunched his lanky form as though by physically diminishing he might attract less of his father's attention. Iris remembered glimpsing him in his room one day before an interview with their father, gasping with asthma, clutching at the air with hoarse, rattling breaths, and she hung behind the door, digging her nails into her hands, as though she could share some of the pain.

Barrington in turn appeared to resent his son for reminding him of his wife. He spent longer and longer away shooting, fishing and hunting, and he invited Selina Vickers, Arthur's wife, to induct Iris into the rituals of London society. Iris would get on well with Mrs Vickers, whose daughter Dolly was Iris's age herself and needed to be brought out, so could share a season and a dance. She was with Dolly on the day she last saw Charles, standing in the hall newly kitted out in his officer's uniform with his brass buttons and Sam Browne belt. The dressing up aspect of soldiering had excited her and she spent her last minutes with him poking at his outfit and wanting to know where he kept his sword.

After the war there was not a day of her life when Iris did not ache for the loss of her brother and rage at the brutal god who snatched away the person dearest to her and a part of herself in the process. Yet she was never sure what her father actually felt. If it was grief, it was evidently so deep and bitter that he was unable to give it expression. Then again, it could have been indifference. They never discussed it. Silence settled and solidified between Barrington and his awkward daughter. In the halls of the huge house, her mother and Charles lingered between them like weighted air, their names rarely uttered. If she did mention Charles, the word sliced the atmosphere like a knife, an act of violence out of all proportion to the mild-mannered figure he had been. Her mother's name, like the most precious of jewels, was not for public use.

For years she had been terrified that her father would marry again, provide himself with a new young family and edge her out, but when that threat materialised in the shape of Edwina Glencoe, his silly, shingle-haired mistress, it became clear that her father had no inclination to remarry or replace the family he had lost.

Iris glanced at her watch, looked again at the shimmering dress and decided it would do. She was only going out with Dolly after all, who as well as being plain, having inherited her father's broad jaw, his bent nose and her mother's large build, was quite impervious to clothes. She pulled a velvet coat with a silver fox collar round her shoulders, then remembered the motto: "minimum clothes, maximum cosmetics" and shrugged it off, re-applying a slick of Autumn Flame to her lips. A few further tweaks and she was ready to leave.

One thing she was certain of. She would not be taking Samuel Dux with them, tonight at least. Father had asked her, so in the end she supposed she would have to drag him somewhere, though she didn't see why he couldn't make his own arrangements. After all, he must *know* people, though she was sure as anything they wouldn't be her sort of people. She simply couldn't understand why she was expected to be responsible for his social life.

Still she lingered at her dressing table, shifting round her collection of cut glass perfume bottles. Who was he really? An archaeologist, or an architect? It was mystifying why anyone would want to leave Egypt to come and live with a man he barely knew and his daughter. Iris had overheard something her father had said to Edwina, something about "the chap had no choice but to come" but of course he hadn't bothered to explain anything to her.

There was something instinctively disturbing about Samuel Dux. Was it his air of self-sufficiency, or his faint provincial accent? He was good looking, she supposed, despite his ginger hair. He had sharp, green eyes, a straight nose and a clever, judgmental face, which made her perversely determined to give nothing away when he probed and tried to draw her out about her life. She knew, of course, that she was being horribly rude in refusing to answer his questions, but father didn't notice, or if he did, he didn't care. He was too busy quizzing Samuel himself. Yes, perhaps it was that which annoyed Iris about Samuel Dux - the way her father found him so engaging. Her father was not the sort to tolerate anyone out of idle friendship but she had watched them talking, ensconced comfortably in his study as if they had known each other all their lives, the amber whisky in their glasses glinting in the light of the fire. Father had never, never talked like that with Charles. To Iris it was almost as if Samuel was the son her father would have preferred. And that was quite enough for her entirely to detest him.

"I just can't wait to get down to Woodstanton! Lady's had nine puppies and Seraphina's in foal. I'm longing for the weekend. I suppose you don't want to come?"

"No thanks Dolly."

"You should, you know. The puppies are absolutely

adorable apparently. You could have one to take home. A
friend for Paw-Paw."

"Paw-Paw doesn't like other dogs."

"He doesn't seem to like anyone."

"He only likes me."

Iris glanced across the Café de Paris to where their escorts
for the evening were standing at the bar. Boringly both
men had spent their time so far competing for her attention,
though Dolly, in her excitement over the puppies, seemed
wholly oblivious to it. Iris looked away and tried to catch
sight of her reflection in the mirrored panelling on the wall.

There was nothing so restful as being in Dolly's company.
It was like revisiting childhood, not that Iris's childhood
was the kind you'd especially want to revisit, but at least
there was no need for artifice or good manners or any
sort of effort at all. Iris could continue to smoke and stare
around her while Dolly rhapsodised about the livestock
at her parents' Gloucestershire home. Just hearing about
Woodstanton made Iris grateful she was no longer forced
to visit it. It was a squat, square-faced Georgian edifice
which had withstood a series of architectural interventions
by ambitious occupants for the past three hundred years
without any significant improvement. Cupped in a hollow of
misty hills surrounded by parkland of champing sheep and
distant villages, it was the most archetypal English spot Iris
could imagine. A bit like Dolly herself in a way. Stolid and
dependable and utterly without pretention.

The fact that the two girls were as unalike as could be
was what made it work really. Dolly admired Iris's slender
elegance and Iris was glad that Dolly didn't see her as a
rival, the way other girls did. Dolly had a penchant for
practical jokes which complemented Iris's natural daring. As
they grew up they became inseparable, sharing everything.
Throughout their adolescence they had been taught together
at Miss Moore's, learnt the piano together and got drunk
on gin and vermouth together. They had compared breasts

together, taunted their French tutor together, and discussed men together. At least they had always had, until now.

"Something's the matter, isn't it?" Dolly interrupted. "You look awfully…."

"Inscrutable?" suggested Iris, mildly interested. That was what she had been called in last month's *Bystander*.

"No. Irritable really. As though you had indigestion. Or the curse. Do you?"

"No."

"Is it Edwina?"

"No, for a change."

"Your father then?"

Iris paused a moment, then lit another Sobranie.

"It's nothing really. Promise."

"Well I wish you'd cheer up. Angus and Henry already think you're bored to tears. And you're actually going to have such fun this evening. It's not every night we get invited to parties with American art dealers in Grovesnor Square."

Chapter Three

Esther Hartley jiggled her cup of weak tea in its saucer and tried to maintain an expression of intelligent interest, whilst wondering how long the woman was likely to go on for. She supposed she ought to take notes, indeed she had her notebook open right there on her lap, but by the time the speaker was half way through the bit about "the socialist woman of the future" and how she would be a true equal, freed of servitude to her fellow men, Esther's concentration had strayed. Around her a dozen other women and a couple of men sat attentively. *They* were taking notes.

Esther had been flattered at the invitation to join the Vanguard Club. It had been set up by a group of socialist women, most of them members of Beatrice Webb's Fabian Society, in the wake of the election of Britain's first ever Labour government, with the aim of embracing the new chapter that had opened in British political life.

The Labour government was a wonderful thing, even if it had come as a bit of a shock to everyone. Stanley Baldwin had gambled on an election in 1923, shortly after he had come to power, but he had miscalculated. Both Labour and the Liberals saw huge increases in their seats, the Conservatives lost their overall majority and that January, after a vote of No Confidence, the government fell. After which Asquith, the Liberal leader, gave his support to a minority Labour government with the result that the King sent for Ramsay MacDonald, the Labour leader, and what everyone was calling the Great New Era In British Politics began.

Idly Esther allowed herself to imagine her father's face should he know she was here. He viewed the Socialist government like one of the marauding tribes that besieged the promised land in the dull bits of the Bible. The ones who were reliably obliterated by a vengeful God. And though she did care very much about freedom, justice and equal opportunity for all and about the development of socialism in China which was to be the subject of next week's talk by Mr Bertrand Russell, she didn't see why everyone had to be so serious about it. They sat, poised slightly forward in their chairs, like seals waiting to catch a fish.

Absently Esther stretched out one foot and turned a slight ankle to admire her new shoes with their square diamanté buckle. Despite how much she cared about Socialism, the main reason she was here was that her Aunt Ettie, Lady Atwood, had joined the Labour cause and although she was a little too busy to attend the club itself, had lent her London house for meetings. Only it was the house that was the problem.

Esther glanced around her. The room was unashamedly grand, stuffed with antique chairs with gilded legs and pale blue shot silk upholstery, hung with great, glinting rococo mirrors and looking out on one of the best squares in London. The air was scented with enormous vases of lilies, grown in the Atwoods' own hot house at the country house in Kent and brought up daily. Tea was provided in a grand silver teapot, on a tray piled high with expensive porcelain and plates of specially made ginger cake and delicately cut cucumber sandwiches. It was all appallingly wrong. Everyone knew that Beatrice Webb hated luxury. She fretted about Labour people being seen in the midst of too much grandeur. There had already been an embarrassing problem with Euston Lodge, the home of the Countess of Warwick in Essex, which had been used for a conference, only to meet with Mrs Webb's disdain on account of there being "too many grand rooms." Mrs Webb wasn't even very keen on Ramsay MacDonald, who was said to have no proletarian sympathies at all and derived far too much enjoyment from fine wines, furniture, paintings and elegant society. Not to mention weekends at Windsor Castle. The King, it was said, had taken a warm liking to Mr MacDonald. Despite one man coming from a Scottish croft and the other a castle, they had found common ground together in their love of the Highlands and ancient Celtic stories. That was all very well but it was seriously letting the side down.

"If the party's out of power by the summer, it'll do them good," one of the older women had remarked sourly to Esther. She had wide yellow pony's teeth to which a ridge of lipstick clung. "All these parties at Buckingham Palace, and invitations from royalty. Lady Londonderry and what have you. It's gone to his head."

"But didn't the Prime Minister say everyone must lower their expectations until he gets real power? In a majority government. We can't expect a revolution overnight."

"Revolution? The only revolution happening in this party is that it's turning into a tribe of Tories. Even Oswald Mosley is joining the party now. And he's married to Lord Curzon's daughter."

Across the room she caught Alan Collins frowning. She bent her head to her notebook and began scribbling. Alan was an impressive figure to her and she craved his approval. It had been Alan after all, who first gave her proper paid work when he took her tentatively proffered cartoon, laughed obligingly and agreed to print it in the magazine. He was short, with a narrow pinched face, a little reddish goatee and small, round glasses. He had sat at his crowded desk without getting up, pushed a hand through his frizzy hair and said "Fine. We'll print this Miss Hartley, though I'm afraid we don't pay too well."

That was a while ago, when Esther was in her second year at art school. The art school was full of girls like her who didn't actually want to be there. During the war women had happily taken on munitions work and all the jobs like engineering, printing and transport, but now the men had returned the clock had been turned back, and working women were labelled irresponsible, as though they were wilfully depriving men of jobs. Teaching hospitals and other institutions which had previously welcomed female students, now closed their doors. So women who might have had decent occupations were instead obliged to do pointless things like attending art school, even if like Esther they had not the remotest chance of becoming professional artists.

Until a friend had first urged her to submit her work to *The Watching World* she had never heard of it, let alone bought a copy. It came out every fortnight priced at sixpence and dedicated to changing the face of modern Britain. The pages were filled with pieces about the classless society and economic equality, though this aspirational air was slightly offset by the advertisements for laxatives, trusses and kitchen appliances which the publication was unfortunately obliged to take just like any other magazine.

Alan was the only Bolshevik Esther had ever met. A couple of months ago, when Lenin died, you would think it was his own father the way Alan had actually wept and explained that Lenin was one of the greatest men in history, whose thoughts and actions would change the world forever. He had devoted an entire issue of *The Watching World* to Lenin, with a photograph of the mummified body laid out in state on the front page under the headline: 'The Last Pharaoh'.

The only point on which Esther's father and Alan might ever agree was that they both, passionately, wanted the Labour party out of power. In Alan's view this was necessary to give the party time to organise a purer, truer socialist regime. Though sometimes, he had confided to Esther, he genuinely feared that world revolution would never materialise.

When she mentioned that she had been invited to join the Vanguard club Alan had been enthusiastic. "Write all about it," he said. "I'll come too, and take a look."

Esther was obliged to agree, hoping fervently that Aunt Ettie would not be at home.

Now she got to her feet and took the silver teapot round.

The club didn't approve of servants and thought domestic service was degrading so Lady Atwood's maids had been told to wait in the kitchen, though they were to come up and clear everything away the moment the people had left.

The group was discussing the accommodation of some miners' wives who were to be coming down from the north to lobby parliament about their husbands' working conditions.

"We had some miners' wives staying with us before," said the horse woman approvingly. "They had lovely manners."

There were general murmurs of agreement about mining-community etiquette and in the event several offers of accommodation made, which meant Esther could keep quiet. She was relieved. Though she was looking for a place of her own, currently she was still living with her parents and five siblings. The idea of bringing a flock of miners' wives home to Chalcott Street didn't really bear thinking about. What on earth would they make of her father? And what would the miners' wives say if they discovered that Uncle Frederick, Ettie Atwoods' own husband, owned a coalmine?

"Mind if I accompany you?" Alan Collins held an umbrella over her grey cloche against the spitting rain. "We could find some tea if you're not in a hurry."

"Well.." She hesitated awkwardly, "That's very kind of you, but I'm just off to look at a flat."

His face closed immediately. "Sure. I've got a lot of work to catch up with as it is. I'm starting work on this special issue I told you about – the Forgotten of the War – remember?"

"I think so."

"It's for this autumn, in time for the anniversary. Ten years since the outbreak of war and thousands of invalids are still waiting for just treatment from a society that ignores them. We commemorate the dead but what about those who are still living?"

"Oh yes. Of course. I remember."

"I'm writing to Rudyard Kipling. Since he lost his son he's done a tremendous lot of work on the war graves. I'm hoping he might do a piece for us on the neglected survivors."

"That would be a terrific draw."

"It should be." He looked at her with disappointment. "Well I suppose you'd better borrow this."

He passed her his umbrella and trudged quickly off, his flimsy jacket drawn round him and his shoulders stooped against the rain.

Esther waited for the bus. The idea of leaving home, like most other things about her life, had not initially met with approval from her family. They had refused at first, quite adamantly. Young, single girls did not go around renting flats on their own heaven knows where. The way her mother saw it, a bachelor girl flat was one step away from the white slave trade and certainly far from respectable. But Esther's petitioning, along with the extremely cramped conditions of Chalcott Street had eventually prompted her father to recall aloud that there was a flat, in a house owned by an army friend he had known, that might just be suitable.

"Frank Stevens – the doctor you know - lives in a great museum of a place, and he said to me just the other day that he was thinking of letting the top floor. It might be perfect. Frank would keep an eye on her. Let us know how she's doing."

Her mother, with the reassuring predictability that was her forté, issued a categorical refusal. "How tremendously unsuitable, John. How could you?" But within a day her adamantine opposition had mutated to "Where exactly is this flat?", and after a week, the final, concessionary, almost throw away remark. "I shall have to see it first of course."

Esther imagined the flat as a hushed, dingy place smelling of cough medicine and disinfectant. The idea of living with an army friend of her father's was not appealing, but her interest grew when he returned with more details. It was a furnished flat in Bayswater with its own bathroom. Frank Stevens would charge her £100 a year, heating and lighting included. Her mother complained that Bayswater was "not a place we know", referring to its location on an idiosyncratic social map of her own devising. But as she peered from the window of the bus that evening up a wide, tree-lined avenue, Esther thought it quite handsome. Number 54 Waverley Gardens was in the middle of a tall, dignified terrace which had mostly been divided up into flats and boarding houses. She stood on the doorstep, taming her damp hair behind her ears, and rang the bell.

In the event Dr Stevens was out but the woman who did for him was happy to show her the top floor. The doctor himself inhabited the downstairs floor, she said. "He keeps himself to himself, Dr Stevens."

The flat was glorious. It was up in the eves of the house, light and airy with two rooms, the bedroom with a simple chest of draws with a mirror on the top, and a comfortable armchair on top of an ochre rug, then a tiny kitchen, containing not much more than a gas ring, and a narrow bathroom. Esther opened the stiff window as far as she could and gazed out. It was very near Paddington. She could hear the screech of metal and the high wail of wheels grating on the rail. The hot, acrid smell of coal-fired trains drifted over from the station on the damp air. She wondered what it would be like to live on her own and felt a moment's lurch of terror, though she instantly quelled it.

"It's perfect. I'd love to take it."

Chapter Four

"So. Mr Howard Carter," said Barrington, in another of their evening talks, as they sat together in his study before the fire, settled deep within the capacious leather armchairs. "He must have been pretty pleased with himself, I imagine."

Within two weeks Carter was behaving like a man on the verge of a nervous breakdown. What should have been the most exhilarating find in history, ensuring for its discoverers glory and fame in posterity, had become bedevilled with hitches and disputations. *Bedevilled.* That was the word Carter used.

Samuel found him one morning, arguing loudly with a group of journalists. They were constantly complaining about their restricted access to the tomb and now a row had arisen concerning quite spurious suggestions that Carter wanted to take Tutankhamen's mummy off to England. There was a virulent attack in that day's local Egyptian newspaper and Carter exploded with fury and stalked off, motioning Samuel to walk beside him.

"Bradstreet of the *Morning Post* has behaved disgracefully. I shall refuse to speak to him. Let him get his gossip from the bar of the Winter Palace Hotel," he said breathlessly. "Those cads and swine have nothing better to do than prop up the bar and spread their lying and their calumnies."

Already the news of the find had spread like wildfire. Visitors swarmed there in their thousands. They steamed down the Nile from Cairo and booked themselves into the Luxor Hotel or the Winter Palace. Then they would buy a whole day's excursion ticket from Cooks Tourist Office and set off at 6am, crossing the river and toiling along on donkeys up the five mile road to the Valley, where they would set up camp with their parasols and picnic baskets.

Some even brought knitting. Every day was like Derby day. Alongside the cars, animals and pedestrians, a throng of locals ran in their tarbooshes and turbans, selling lemonade and fake antiquities. Each day the train from Cairo off-loaded more journalists, sightseers, antiquarians, would-be film-makers and every kind of commercial adventurer to join the crowd, shouting and jostling, all wanting to go down and look at the wall bearing the royal names, all wanting the frisson of fear and excitement from entering a tomb that had been sealed for so many thousand years.

Carter's plan was that everything from the antechamber be cleared to another empty tomb, that of Seti the second, situated at the extreme end of the valley, which he would use as his "laboratory". There it would all be noted and catalogued, repaired and restored before eventually being transported by ground railway to the river, from where it would be taken by steamer to Cairo. But every time he entered the tomb the crowd surged forward shouting their questions and requests, begging to be shown around. And every day he got

ruder and crosser.

"It's bad enough that I have to show all the ladies and the wives and hangers-on around the treasures like a glorified tour guide. Now the sightseers and journalists expect the same treatment," he raged at Samuel. As if they had not sacrificed enough for the convenience of the tourists! The Valley's cliffs and gullies, once the hiding place of treasures beyond imagining, were now dotted with the square openings of tombs which had been fitted with electric lights. The sandy paths of the wadi were smoothed for the benefit of visitors. The secret necropolis inaugurated by Thutmose the First at the start of the 18th dynasty to protect the bodies of dead kings with a series of false trails, hidden passages and disguised entrances, had been stripped of its mystery for twentieth century eyes.

Ordinary tourists could at least be put off. But it was not so simple with the VIPs wanting to be shown around the site, asking too many questions and wasting everyone's time. There were endless visits from the Queen of the Belgians, the Mayor of New York, and flocks of Lords and Sirs and Honourables. Every time visitors came the delicate objects had to be removed or protected, tools put away, and the electric wiring altered. It meant hours of work lost every day and now the Egyptian Antiquities Service had weighed in, demanding a full list of those authorised to work on the site.

Samuel hurried alongside Carter, trying to keep up with the older man's brisk march. It was only nine, but already it was unbearably hot and the Valley felt like a barren cauldron clenched in a fist of savage, rugged cliffs. A dust storm was blowing and sand smarted constantly in their eyes.

He rattled out his exasperations as they walked. The Egyptian government had set its own native inspectors to watch over him. The idea that he was being monitored for potential theft infuriated him.

"Considering these fellows are all descended from notorious grave robbers, it's certainly amusing," he remarked acidly. Then it was the Hollywood people.

"Could I please help Mr Archibald Wilson? He seems to think that he would like to make a motion picture about us. All he requires is for us to clear these bothersome artefacts out of the way as soon as possible so he can install his cameras."

Then it was the unfairness of it all.

"Arthur Evans had none of this nonsense at Knossos. There was nothing like this for Sir Flinders Petrie at Ur of the Chaldees. I am an excavator, not a holiday company. Why must I suffer these odious people with their incessant demands?"

He stopped and rested on a rock, taking off his hat and putting his great, awkward head in his hands.

"I'm afraid all these visitors, Mr Dux, have left my nerves in an extremely ragged state."

At that moment the water boy approached. The water boy, who had found the first step of the tomb, was Carter's favourite. He would be there every day at Carter's side, serving his drink, his goatskin container with its rope of water twisting and fracturing in the sun, a handsome lad with soft, expressive eyes. Either because of his youth, or his unflaggingly cheerful demeanour, he was generally thought to have a way with Howard Carter and was often sent to mollify him when things got difficult. Now he approached with his water and knelt at Carter's feet, but Carter only ran his hand over the boy's curly head despondently and waved him away.

As they watched the boy trot off, Carter said quietly: "There's something wrong."

Samuel hunted for some emollient words. "Perhaps Sir, you're tired. You should consider taking a rest. A few days break away. Maybe a trip to Cairo."

Carter glanced up at Samuel with his bloodshot eyes.

"It's not rest I need." He wiped the drops of sweat from his brow.

"I am not ill. It's not the tribulations of the newspapermen that have prompted my malaise. There is something else wrong here." He stared at the searing sand beneath his feet and then drew out of his pocket a scrap of paper. In a quieter voice he said,

"Are you familiar Mr Dux, with the Egyptian Book of the Dead?"

"Of course sir."

After all, what excavator could be ignorant of it? The Egyptian Book of the Dead was the most ancient human work of religious literature, older than the Bible by hundreds of years. *Katab-al-Mayyit*, the book of the dead man, was the name was given by Egyptian tomb-robbers to the magical writings they found in every burial place to protect the soul against the hideous and terrifying shapes of the powers of darkness. It was a collection of spells, incantations and charms to help the dead in the afterlife, with elaborate rituals and words of power given by the god Thoth, by which the soul would negotiate the hazardous journey to the underworld. For thousands of years these magical words had been found in coffin texts – that is, writings on coffins and papyrus rolls, or inscribed on the walls of tombs, sarcophagi and amulets. But it was only very recently that they had been gathered together and even more recently that they had been published in a book by Dr Wallis Budge, keeper of Egyptian Antiquities of the British Museum, and a man Carter knew of old.

Samuel craned his neck to see what was written on the paper Carter held, but he could barely decipher it. From what he could make out Carter had scribbled a line of hieroglyphics – an ibis, he thought, an arm and an *ab* – the heart - signified by a small canopic jar. Samuel had not yet learned enough to decode the syllabics and determinatives, the phonograms and logograms that made up what Egyptians called "the words of God" and Carter, it seemed, had no inclination to show him. He tried prompting him further.

"I met Dr Wallis Budge once," he volunteered. "At the British Museum."

"Did you?" Carter flicked him a look of sudden interest. "Budge believes it all you know. The paranormal. Ghosts and hauntings. Ridiculous stuff. All that research into ancient religion must have gone to his head. You can't fault his scholarship though. I've been reading his treatise on Egyptian magic. It's very thorough."

Samuel was intrigued. He still couldn't see what a line of hieroglyphics could have to do with the disputations around the tomb.

"Why did you ask me Sir? About the Book of The Dead?"

For a moment it seemed as though Carter was about to say something more, then he gazed away, shoved the scrap of paper back in his pocket and hauled himself to his feet.

"Oh, it's nothing that can't wait. There are just some coffin texts that I would like you to work on. Now, let us get back to the site."

On their return he seemed to recover himself and when they passed a fresh batch of sweating tourists labouring up the road with their picnics and parasols, he was provoked only to low-level grumbling.

"What kind of frenzy is this Mr Dux? Can you understand why the whole world should want to camp on my doorstep? What power do these objects have to provoke such madness?"

"And could you Samuel?" Barrington's little eyes were fixed like gimlets on him. "Could you understand the power of those objects?"

For a moment it seemed there was an inflection in Barrington's voice, a layer of meaning that he could not quite catch. Samuel looked down at his whisky and laughed. "Oh, they were just work to me. It was fascinating work of course, though it was a little solitary, I suppose, being down in the tomb. But the social life at night made up for that. And of course I was pretty honoured that Mr Carter had taken me on at all. Everything was fine until…"

"Until?"

"Until I left, I mean."

Until the night that things veered so suddenly out of control, so precipitately and without warning, that it seemed his entire life had lost its footing. As though his life had simply slipped and skittered off its course like a stone falling from the Valley's red, desolate cliffs.

* * *

"Now you'll need to use your imagination here," Barrington let his arms describe a sweeping circle. "But this will be the central hall. The beating heart of Barrington House."

They were standing in a muddy, rubble-filled yard in the midst of the City of London, dwarfed by the tightly packed office blocks around them, gazed at curiously by people sitting on the top decks of passing buses and trams. Not that there was anything new about building work - palatial new department stores and office blocks were going up everywhere you looked, any niche that was empty one month would be filled the next, and the whole City breathed an air of confident prosperity. Muffled against the cold in a borrowed overcoat, Samuel side-stepped the puddles and tried to keep up with his employer. Barrington strode ahead through the vacant lot wearing his bowler, pin-striped trousers and an expensive coat with Astrakhan collar, his face alight with enthusiasm and pride, as though in his mind's eye he was already transported into the proud and shining lobby of the headquarters itself.

When Elmer Barrington said this was his monument he meant it. When complete it would tower over all its city surroundings, the offices and shops, the churches with their pale, bone-coloured spires, and the slender, mediaeval houses sandwiched between banks and offices of busy Victorian brick. The design would be distinctive, the total impact unforgettable.

"I still don't understand," Samuel hesitated. "What exactly you want me for?"

Barrington laughed again, apparently delighted by the young man's confusion. "Remind me where you've just been."

"Egypt?"

"Precisely." Barrington clapped him on the back with a painful thud.

"The greatest and most intelligent civilisation that ever lived until our own. Probably even greater, considering they never sunk into the decadence that Europe is witnessing today. The Egyptians are an inspiration to us, and I want that inspiration to be reflected in Barrington House. I want *you* to bring Egypt right here to London."

Samuel quailed. "But I know very little about architecture. I trained as a draughtsman."

"Architecture? I'm not asking you to be an architect. I've got one of those. Two in fact. What I want is your experience. I want the feel of it. I want you to take all those emotions you had in the Valley, the excitement, the wonder, the joy, and embody them in this building. You, Mr Dux, have witnessed at first hand a style that signifies permanence, quality and perfection and above all lasting opulence. Mr Holmes over there is the architect. Work with him. Give him a sense of what you saw out there. You will be our guide. Our touchstone."

Samuel considered for a moment, then remembered how limited his options were.

"Well, Sir, I can try."

In the event, any fears Samuel may have had about the job were unfounded. Holmes, a lugubrious figure with a handlebar moustache who looked up apprehensively when Barrington entered his office, took no offence at having a "touchstone" foisted upon him. And Samuel's interest grew as he saw, from the rough sketches that lay before them, just how the Egyptian influences would take shape.

The frontage of Barrington House would be panels of black mirrored glass divided by marble pillars, a temple to the wealth and energy of Barrington's life. Beyond it the motifs of Ancient Egypt would be incorporated into a design of bold modernism. Elevator doors would be etched with lotus flowers, the eye of Horus would be imprinted on the brass plates of the doors and a mosaic of entwined serpents worked into the marble lobby floor. The hushed and carpeted top-floor suite which Barrington himself planned to occupy would be decorated like a sumptuous transatlantic liner, with carved wooden panelling, lacquered insets covered in Egyptian-style bas reliefs and gilded faux Egyptian chairs.

He turned to Samuel, his small eyes alight.

"Think you might enjoy it Mr Dux?"

He did, rather. It was strangely exhilarating to find himself back in London, and the job was intriguing, even if it did mean living with this man and his hostile, uncommunicative daughter.

He had tried to talk to her again that morning. He had been loitering in his room - Charles' room – while he waited for Barrington and his car. The room intrigued Samuel, whose own bedroom at home had been a cramped, functional space, looking out onto potato fields. This was huge and chilly, with damask wallpaper the colour of old blood, heavy cream drapes, a desk like a bank manager's and a leather chair that might have come straight from a gentleman's club. It was more the sort of room you would associate with an elderly relative than a growing boy, but Charles had done his best to establish his possessions there and they remained in place untouched - the ship in the bottle, the collection of butterflies, a stuffed owl, a telescope, and above all books, rows of them, with his name, Charles Barrington, inscribed on each flyleaf in black ink with the date when they were acquired.

Samuel picked out one - Conan Doyle's *The Final Problem* – and was looking at the looping copperplate of its dedication "*To Charles From Mama, Christmas 1910*" when he sensed a stirring in the air behind him and glancing around saw Iris, staring at him from the door. She was wearing a pale blue chiffon dress and her hair was pulled back in a chignon. He felt momentarily embarrassed, as though he had been caught stealing, the book still in his hand.

"That's my brother's book."

"Yes, I'm sorry, I was just looking." Unnerved by her stony gaze, he added: "Look I'm sorry if...I mean I know this must be hard for you, me being in his room."

"It is," she said flatly.

"You'd probably prefer I moved."

"Yes," she said, with barely a flicker. "I would."

"Perhaps I should ask your father then? I mean I really didn't want to cause any…"

"He wouldn't listen."

"I'm sure if I spoke to him …I don't know if he realised.."

"He knows."

He gestured to the book still in his hand.

"Sherlock Holmes. I'm rather a fan of his actually and I've not read this one. I suppose your brother was keen on him too…"

Just for one moment she looked as though she was tempted. Tempted to discuss the brother she so sorely missed and whose name was never mentioned with the only person who had bothered to ask about him. But then she seemed to change her mind.

"My brother's life is not some ancient history waiting to be unearthed thank you very much, Mr Dux. You don't need to dig around here. You're not in Egypt now."

She turned on her heel, dignified and erect. Hot with annoyance, for a moment he wanted to march after her small retreating form and demand an apology for such a melodramatic little speech, but in the end he decided to take the compassionate view. It must be hard enough being Barrington's daughter, let alone having no mother, then losing her only brother in the war. Quite besides having to live in this great tomb of a house. It was a smooth-running, richly furnished, impeccably decorated tomb all right, but it was a tomb all the same, in whose echoing halls two people who failed to communicate went through the motions of living together. Grief hung in the corridors like stale air. The great grandfather clock in the hall stitched out the seconds into emptiness which had once been drowned by children's laughter and shouts. The hoards of pictures and sculptures and possessions were gathered in the vacant rooms as if to compensate for the absence of living occupants. This house was like some mausoleum where those who had died were never mentioned, and the space they left was filled with ornaments from other places of the dead.

Chapter Five

Having no clear memory of Dr Stevens, Esther had cast him in her mind as an elderly man with a leather briefcase and an ancient gold fob watch such as her doctor at home had always flourished when people needed their pulses taken. So the actual sight of him on the first Saturday morning was a surprise. He was tall and thin with sandy, rumpled hair, and not nearly as old as she had imagined, in fact probably only in his thirties. He was shabbily dressed in a battered brown tweed jacket, and had a high-browed, intelligent face with a wide, thin-lipped mouth that seemed determined to compress any smile that might escape. Apologising briskly for his absence and business over the past few days, he had taken her into his sitting room which was filled with piles upon piles of books and papers, towering on all the surfaces including the chairs, so that she had to clear a place to sit, and sized her up, as though she were presenting herself for a job interview.

"Well well. You've grown."

Esther stiffened. "I suppose it's been a while since you last saw me."

He leant against the mantelpiece, plunged his hands in his pockets and smiled fleetingly. "Yes. Of course. The last time I saw you, you must have been about thirteen years old. You were on your way out to tennis. You were wearing a tennis skirt and you caught me a hefty bruise on my shin with your racquet."

"Oh. I'm sorry."

"Apology accepted. You were ticked off pretty fiercely at the time, but when you went out of the room I saw you laughing about it with your sister."

Dr Stevens wasn't laughing. The eyes that he fixed upon her through his round spectacles were grey and appraising.

He paused in his interrogation to move a stack of papers from one surface to another.

"It's very kind of you to let me the flat," she volunteered.

"Not at all. I was about to rent it out anyway. By the way, though your father is a friend of mine, I intend to conduct our business on an entirely commercial basis. I take it that's how you would prefer it?"

"Yes, of course."

"Your father asked me to keep an eye on you, but I'm not here to act as your guardian. For one thing, I'm far too busy and for another, you're old enough to run your own life."

"Quite."

"So if your parents look to me for reports of your activities, I shall have to disappoint them."

"Yes of course."

"There are, however, a few rules of the household."

Was it really necessary, this attitude, which made her feel so uncomfortable, as though she was appearing before a headmaster, rather than a landlord? It must be because he was a doctor, but how unpleasant for his patients.

"My clinic is some way away, but I do occasionally see patients here so I'd be grateful if you'd pass quietly when you come in. What else? No male guests and no pets. The rent, as you know, is £100 a year. Mrs Bennett will look after your cleaning and washing if you like."

He continued with a sort of rapid interrogation which she assumed was intended as polite chat. She was at art school, and she had some sort of job also? Yes, he had heard of *The Watching World*, though no, he didn't read it. He suspected it was not his sort of magazine. How was her father? They had not seen much of each other recently, because he'd been so busy. Damp, cold weather like this always made more work for doctors.

"How did you meet my father?"

"We knew each other in France," he replied, as though that was explanation enough.

"And you were a doctor there?"

"Royal Army Medical Corps."

His words seemed bitten off, as though he could hardly bear to impart the information. Esther couldn't help sensing that he disapproved of her efforts at conversation, though it may have been mere impatience. She was glad when the telephone interrupted with a call from a patient and she could escape up the stairs to her own territory. There would, she hoped, be little reason for their paths to cross.

As far as its opening hours were concerned, art college was gloriously liberal. But though she tried her best in the classes, and could execute a very competent still life or landscape, Esther was not really satisfied. Her favourite thing, though it barely counted as art, was cartoons. She had taken to illustrating the big stories and characters of the day - the Prime Minister, the King and the Kaiser - which was how she had come to the attention of Alice Cohen, and subsequently discovered *The Watching World.*

Alice Cohen, with her fur stole and amber beads as big as birds' eggs, was the centre of attention at their college. She accepted the glances and turned heads and admiring whispers as her due. She was the acknowledged star of their year, the one whom everyone knew would go far. She was the only child of a well-known bohemian family who were acquainted with most of the famous artists of the day. Augustus John came to the Cohens for dinner. Millais had painted Alice as a child. Her mother, Sidonie, had been a suffragette and now held regular salons at which writers, artists, politicians and actors could mingle, secure in the knowledge that they were all people of considerable talent and influence. Alice had precociously attended these salons for years, lisping her pronouncements on opera and ballet from a tender age, yet to the chagrin of many she emerged from such advantages entirely unspoiled and possessing an idiosyncratic talent of her own. At a time when so much was stylised, there was an uncomfortable realism in her art. She liked to focus on figures at the margins of society, down and outs, milkmen, coalmen, the bird lady in Trafalgar Square, whose portraits, with their pasty, enquiring faces, were unforgettable. She saw every nick and flaw in the flesh and her figures had a peculiar dignity because of it. Like the bold, vibrant shades in her canvases, she dressed in a rabble of colour, in dramatic patterned velvets and glowing silks. She had a large, bustling body, a mass of springy chestnut hair which stuck out wildly and a no-nonsense approach. Esther, whose family had always favoured conservative shades of navy and brown in their clothing, as though the use of more vibrant colours was morally as well as aesthetically reprehensible, had admired Alice Cohen from a distance but when Alice first approached her, and scrutinised some of her cartoons, Esther found herself quite abashed.

"They're fairly good those drawings. You could sell those, you know. To a magazine."

"Oh, I don't know. I don't know if I'd want to…"

"Why not? You could make good money."

"Do you think so?"

"Certainly. And economic independence is everything. You don't want to have to depend on a man do you?"

"No," said Esther, as hastily as she could. "Of course not."

"So it's vital that you make a living, not compromise yourself. You'll need to assert yourself if you're going to succeed."

Everything militated against a woman making a success in the art world, Alice explained. Even in her own background, she had detected a lingering belief that women could not really paint or write as well as men.

"It makes my blood boil. Why can't they see that it's circumstance, not talent, that's the issue? It's because women have spent their lives ordering lamb chops and doing the washing and having babies and making sure that nothing gets in the way of the men that they haven't been turning out the plays and the portraits with quite the same regularity."

"What about the Brontë sisters?" ventured Esther. "They had to run the parsonage and they still wrote quite a lot. And Jane Austen."

Alice paused midflow and looked furiously at Esther, before breaking into her deep, throaty laugh.

"Well they didn't have children. That's the key. Children sabotage art. I know for a fact that I'm never going to breed."

Esther was spellbound by such certainty. And Alice seemed just as certain that the two of them should be friends.

As expected, she saw little of Dr Stevens at Waverley Gardens and when they did meet it was invariably in the hall, as he was either coming in or leaving, always with his scuffed leather bag and a faint air of distraction.

His greetings, clipped monosyllables muttered beneath his breath, seemed a deliberate deterrent to the kind of polite conversation which Esther would have immediately struck up. Once when she was wearing a new, peacock-blue Jaeger evening coat, on her way out to meet Alice, he had scrutinised her with puzzlement, as though he didn't even recognise her. He was old before his time, she thought uncharitably.

Chapter Six

"It must be terrific fun, digging things up."

Samuel looked down into the little, glittering eyes of the face before him. Sheathed in a shimmering dress the colour of lapis lazuli, from which extruded tiny, bony legs in silk stockings, she resembled a very thin tropical insect clutching a glass of champagne. Her eyes were outlined heavily in kohl and she wore a long rope of pearls and a jewelled band around her forehead. The idea that Samuel had actually been present at the unearthing of Tutankhamen appeared to excite her terribly.

"It's not exactly fun. It's a science."

"A science. Really?"

"Certainly. Nowadays Archaeology is seen as any other branch of scientific research. Like Medicine or Psychology. Or Economics."

"Oh don't be silly. It's far more thrilling than all those. Finding all those treasures…the treasures of King Tut. All that gold hidden away in a little cave. It's magical."

"Certainly it's thrilling when you find something. But it's nothing like magic when you're there. It's hard, meticulous work, excavation. After your preliminary research you make a systematic plan for working through the rock layers…"

But this level of analysis was not what the girl had in mind.

"I just can't believe you've actually been there! And there's one thing I have to ask you."

He knew what was coming. Most people in England saw the discovery of the tomb as some kind of fairytale, as though a magic wand, rather than sweaty, gritty, backbreaking work, had prised open the door and revealed its contents in a blaze of light. Anyone who'd not been there seemed to treat the whole affair as a cross between a detective story and Aladdin's cave, with a bit of the Greek myth of Nemesis mixed in.

The nemesis being the curse of course. He steeled himself. "What do you think of the curse? Do you believe in it? I do. Isn't it true that everyone who dares to set foot in the tomb will be struck dead?"

"I'm standing here, aren't I?"

"Yes, but you're looking awfully pale old chap."

The intervention came from a huge hearty man, with a face spattered by freckles and a head of orange hair, convulsed at his own wit.

Samuel looked around for Iris. She had kept him waiting that evening, kicking his heels in the drawing room, for a full half hour after they were supposed to leave. He felt sure Barrington had finally put his foot down and positively instructed Iris to take Samuel out. This she had agreed to without varying the faintly bored expression that was her habitual demeanour. As for himself, Samuel had no particular desire to accompany this mute girl to a party, except for an idle curiosity to see if, once alone, her manners might improve.

They hadn't. When she had finally appeared that evening, looking exquisite in a mink-trimmed cape and under it a drop-waisted emerald dress, she made no apology for being late, merely preceded him to the car where she sat in silence and answered his questions monosyllabically, the small, blonde helmet of hair turned slightly away from him, as though the architecture of twentieth century Belgravia held a special fascination for her. He tried very hard not to let it bother him but eventually, couldn't help himself.

"Tell me Iris. Exactly why did you ask me tonight?"

"Why? Well it's an Egyptian party, so I suppose you're the perfect person," she replied, though his being perfect was scarcely what her expression suggested.

"What do you mean Egyptian?"

"You know… fancy dress. People wear costumes and head-dresses, and pretend they're goddesses or mummies. You must have seen it. It's all the craze."

"Oh that."

It was a craze he could hardly have failed to notice. Having physically left Egypt, Samuel had found it perverse to discover it replicated everywhere about him. A welter of ersatz antiquity had sprung up all over London in the wake of the discovery of the tomb. The papers were gripped by a fascination with all things Egyptian and the excitement was even given a name - Tutmania. Tut's face began to appear in theatres, steamships, furniture and fashions. Huntley and Palmers biscuit tins came in the shape of funeral urns, perfume bottles were designed like mummies. There were Egyptian sandals and dresses *à l'Egyptienne.* There was the Tutankhamen hat, the Luxora frock, the Nile Style. The shapes and emblems of Egyptian art, so old, sacred and traditional, had become new, secular and fashionable. And in the process they had entirely lost the taste and elegance of the originals.

He scrutinised her own outfit. "Well you're not in costume."

"God no. I hate all that Egyptian stuff." She gave him a cool glance. "I think it's a tremendous bore."

No one else did though. Iris's friends adored dressing up. They would drape themselves in wigs and togas and knee breeches and crinolines at the slightest excuse. The men loved it as much as the girls, if not more, and were only too ready to pile on the make-up of a regency dandy or a roman emperor. Everyone at that evening's party, held in honour of a pair of newlyweds, Baffy and Maud Simonson, at Maud's parents' home, had plunged into the Egyptian theme with gusto. One guest had even arrived encased entirely in a wooden mummy, which had to be hefted by two men from the taxi to the door. Several of the women were carrying ostrich-feather fans and most wore draped and pleated dresses decorated with pyramid and scarab motifs. Round their brows were jewelled and tasselled headbands. In the ballroom lilies rose from giant oriental vases and on tables at each end were plaster table lamps in the shape of lotuses.

"Wedding presents," someone murmured, "aren't they ghastly?"

The chandelier threw little prisms of light around the room. In one corner there was a jazz quintet of anxious looking black men and between the guests waiters in turbans circulated with trays of Egyptian cocktails and little tin cigarette cases in the shape of Pharaoh's heads containing real Egyptian cigarettes.

Iris had made a token attempt to introduce Samuel around. She hailed a man called Johnny who had just returned from a fishing trip and was keen to share the tiniest details of each catch. After Iris vanished he directed his narrative exclusively at Samuel.

"On the second day I took my first salmon and he was a monster. A twenty pounder. Plucky old thing he was though and clever too. He thought he had me at first. It was a real battle of wits between us, but I had him in the end."

It was easy to see how a fish might pose an intellectual challenge for Johnny. Drifting away Samuel loitered on the fringes of conversations, catching only snatches in busy, loud, confident voices.

"I hear the Simonsons are moving to Putney."

"... People do live in the most odd places nowadays."

"And what about old Alex? No inclination for marriage there, I take it. Do you think he's …you know?"

"Darling, he invented it."

"…He's said to be the natural grandson of Edward VII."

"Oh, isn't everyone."

Samuel hovered, swallowing canapés. He had no objection to his position on the fringes. He was perfectly used to being alone. In fact he never expected it to be any other way.

At dinner he found himself seated next to a man who described himself as an inventor.

"What do you invent then?"

"Well I've had a huge success with a special kind of soap

for dogs and now I'm working on a collar stud that goes ping when you drop it, so you can always find it, y'see?"

"Ingenious."

"In fact I've got an awful lot of other ideas up my sleeve. Would you like to hear them?"

"Absolutely. Tell me all."

So for the next half hour the man chatted on and Samuel was free to nod intermittently and keep a close watch on Iris.

She was sitting far across the room, engaged in animated conversation with a tall, burly man. He had a red, meaty face beneath energetically sprouting dark hair and a protuberant moustache. As he moved his hand to rest proprietorially on her back, Samuel felt his distaste quicken.

"Who's that?"

"Bunny Devine. He's an American."

"What does he do?"

A woman with a hard face and a Cleopatra bob leaned over.

"He buys up art."

"Is there that much art to be bought up then?"

"Oh as much as you want. And it's not just here, it's Paris too. Montparnasse is swarming with Americans. Everything's so cheap to them, and since the war there's an awful lot of people who need to sell. Bunny buys up the modern stuff for rich collectors and if he's very lucky he meets some impoverished lord who wants to flog an old master to an American museum. Cigarette?"

Together they watched Bunny steer Iris away into the ballroom, his hand huge on her bird-like shoulder blade.

"Anything that's worth a lot, Bunny likes," she added with a sniff. "And with a name like Barrington, who's to say how much she could be worth. If you're happy not to ask too many questions."

"Why?" began Samuel, but the woman had already reached across the table and rapped her fan smartly on the shoulder of a fey young man in a white linen shift wearing the double crown of Upper and Lower Egypt.

"Rupert! Sweetie! Dance." It was more a command than a question and it was clear Rupert didn't have much choice.

Samuel wandered out into the garden. It was a cold, clear night and the bright snatches of sound and laughter from the house only seemed to intensify the darkness around it. Some people were dancing on the blue-black lawn, whose perfectly manicured surface was as smooth as a ballroom floor. He looked up at the lighted windows and the figures moving randomly about within them and imagined he was a scientist viewing a slide of Iris's life. Because this must be her life. A succession of balls, dances, dinners and parties, sometimes two or three a night, at the Savoy and the Ritz and Claridges and smart London addresses. The Season, then summering in the south of France, Cannes or Monte Carlo, shooting in Scotland. They had a packed timetable of pleasure these people, as though everyone was still trying to make up for being cheated of four years of leisure by the war. There was a frenzied quality to their partying, to the frantic jerk of their Charlestons and Bunny Hugs and Black Bottoms and Kickaboos, a frenzy to forget the past and to enjoy the present. Samuel fantasised for a moment that the ghosts of the war dead really did drift amongst them, as was popularly imagined, in a cloud of ethereal ectoplasm. All those Georges and Fredericks and Archies and Charleses, their faces still bloodied and bandaged but their hearts purified by life on the celestial plane. What would they make of them here, their living relations, dressed up as ancient Egyptians?

He lifted up his champagne glass and peered through it. The people before him became concave, swirling in a circle. He searched the crowd for Iris's face until he found her, dancing with Bunny. Samuel was no dancer himself, but he could see from the way her body swayed and swirled in syncopation that she was good. She arched her back to bend into Bunny's arms, their faces close together, then the music made her twist and bend towards him as if in submission. Watching her, Samuel was reminded of a painting on the back of Tutankhamun's gold-plated throne, in which the young queen Ankhesenamun put the finishing touches to the king's toilet, bending gently before her husband, pouring perfume on his hands. Out in Egypt there were always local girls keen to please the European men, but they had never interested him. The idea of submissiveness in Iris though had quite a different effect on him. Provocative, exciting even. Uncomfortably he turned away.

Further down the garden was a curious sight. A tent had been erected with a large, painted cardboard facade made to resemble the front of a pyramid, with rich, blue velvet hangings across the door. Across the front, in mock hieroglyphics, was spelt out the words Madame Coco. It was the fortune-teller's tent, every smart party had one now, or a palm-reader, tarot teller or medium. The fortune tellers wore gypsy clothes and had unplaceable, exotic accents. They would foresee your future for a piece of silver, afterwards pressing on you a business card bearing an anonymous suburban address for private consultations. The readings were always optimistic, and invariably brought a message from a loved one which depended more heavily on the amount of information volunteered by the subject than on the efficacy of the spirit world. In Egypt they were mad on fortune-tellers too. At the lowest rung old men would tell your future by staring at the sand, but the more upmarket proffered preposterous and badly spelled testimonials from English dignitaries such as the British High Commissioner Lord Allenby - "*This man very correct in foretelling*". Their forecasts were still vague and non-committal. Samuel bet himself he could predict almost everything Madame Coco would say.

But as he stood hesitating he had to steady himself for a moment, gripped by a peculiar sensation of dread. For a minute the tent and the house and gardens seemed to spin and in a queer rush of vertigo it was as though he was watching himself from a long way away. Then the moment passed as quickly as it had come, and the girl in the lapis lazuli dress emerged giggling from the tent and pushed him tipsily through the doorway.

It was dim inside the stuffy little cavern. Madame Coco, sitting upright beneath the folds of tented silk, had a narrow neck, jet-black hair and prim mouth that reminded him of a Modigliani. There was something about her entirely expressionless eyes that made his flesh creep.

Her voice was sexless, monotoned, a touch of Brixton.

"Cross my palm with silver and I will see what lies ahead for you."

He fished into his pocket and found a sixpence. She reached over and took his hand, circling her thumb round his palm in a way that made his senses tingle.

"You are a lonely man."

Defensiveness jumped in him like a bodily reflex.

"I wouldn't say so."

"You are alone in the world."

"Almost, I suppose."

This was different from the fortune tellers in Egypt, whose predictions focused swiftly and almost exclusively on money. He decided to accelerate the proceedings.

"So am I going to be rich then?"

"There is much that lies ahead for you."

"Not very specific, if you don't mind me saying."

Evidently the woman felt secure in the wide, misty world of the abstract. Samuel decided to force her back into the gritty realm of fact.

"What about my future. Will I marry? Have children? Work in a bank?"

She looked at him, her face utterly indifferent. "Your hand does not speak of those things."

"How convenient."

"When I look at your hand I see a darkness."

"What sort of darkness?"

Her eyes narrowed. "It is more like a dark place."

He had to give her credit for her acting. He looked down at his palm and its familiar, feathery lines.

"A place of death."

"Death?"

"Yes… but it is not your death. The line here, you see, doesn't stop." She lifted her blank, heavy-lashed eyes to his. "And I see a face there."

"Oh. What's her name then?"

He tried joshing, though he was beginning to feel sick.

"It is a face that weighs down your heart."

Suddenly he felt physically constrained, as though the lines on his hand were ties of invincible strength, binding him to their own, indecipherable dénouement. For a moment the tent receded and he saw again the gaping mouth of the tomb which had seemed to suck the life from him. He smelt its dank breath and his skin prickled against its chill. That beautiful face filled his mind, no matter how hard he tried to blot it out, and he felt again the urgent desire to flee. His heart was beating against his chest like a fist. He had to get out and get away. He stood up giddily, his legs weak beneath him and blundered off, feeling blindly for the gap in the tent and lurching out into the evening air.

It was getting late. From what he could tell, posses of people were arranging to move on to a night-club. With shaking hands he lit a cigarette and searched through the house for Iris. Downstairs, where maids were serving coffee from a silver urn, there was no sign of her. He ran up to the ballroom, which was emptying and found only a few dancers swaying and the band crooning *"It had to be you…"* He looked out of the window, down into the street below and his attention was caught by the shiny, red nose of a Bugatti, into which the large figure of Bunny was descending. In the passenger seat he saw only a gleam of blonde hair.

Chapter Seven

Esther rather liked the idea of visiting Tutankhamun's tomb, even though it was quite a way to travel, being in Wembley. The tomb was part of the Empire Exhibition, an enormous collection of pavilions and displays representing all the different dominions and colonies. It was an attempt to celebrate all the grandeur and magnitude of the British Empire and there were exhibits to commemorate all the agriculture, engineering, arts, crafts of the different countries as well as a miniature railway and a 50-acre amusement park. The precise reproduction of the tomb in the Valley of the Kings had occupied twelve sculptors for eight months and contained gilded beds, thrones, chariots, figures, stools, boxes and shrines, not to mention the sarcophagus itself, all done under the supervision of an Egyptologist called Arthur Weigall, using photographs he had taken himself when he was out at the site by Luxor. It was said that nearly £1000 worth of gilding had been used to recreate it and Alan, of course, disapproved.

They were discussing it at the office of *The Watching World,* where Esther had dropped in at Alan's request. For some reason she couldn't explain to herself she had removed before entering the office a new burnt-orange velvet jacket with fox-fur trim, chosen on Alice's urging. Underneath she had a perfectly plain linen dress.

She had bought them both coffee from a stall outside and was relishing drinking it, bitter and hot, as Alan outlined her first reporting assignment. He peered at her anxiously through his horn-rimmed spectacles.

"If the idea interests you, that is. Sounds a grotesque spectacle to me."

In principle, Alan explained, he was against the whole idea of the exhibition. As well as being a reckless waste of public funds, he opposed the Empire per se, being a big supporter of nationalist movements in the colonies, and had already voiced support for a strike amongst the construction workers. But even a magazine like *The Watching World* could not hope that its readership would entirely ignore such a large-scale event on purely ideological grounds. The virtue of sending Esther to report on it was that she could not only describe the exhibits on offer, she could also illustrate them. "And you at least will be able to provide our readers with an informed choice."

Esther admired Alan, but she wondered why he had to see everything in political terms, rather than in terms of just having a good day out. He talked about how dangerous it was that people should become sentimental about the British Empire at this point in history. He even objected to Tutankhamun's tomb being seen as an imperial achievement at all, on the grounds that it was properly part of Egypt's heritage and she was a newly independent nation. All this glorification of the Empire was just another way of shoring up a hierarchical society and consolidating class divisions. Besides which, the Empire was on the way out, everyone sensible recognised that.

"But when you think of the achievements…." Esther began, but Alan had moved on. He was flicking through the *Daily Express's* Londoner's Log, a diary detailing the exclusive exploits of duchesses and debutantes, their love affairs, their dinner parties and outings. There was an item about the sugar tycoon Mr Elmer Barrington accompanied by Miss Edwina Glencoe meeting Ivor Novello at the Prince of Wales Theatre.

"Look at their bovine, imbecilic faces," he expostulated. "They're enough to make you sick! I mean why would anyone want to read about the rich and their degeneracy? Why, as we hurtle towards yet another international crisis, does anyone need to know about so-called Society people? What about the interests and the social conditions of ninety-nine per cent of the population? What about the housing shortage? What about the more than million people who are unemployed? Why can't we read about them? These repulsive plutocrats don't see any connection between the working classes and themselves. Look at the way they treat their servants. They might as well be another species."

Esther couldn't help reflecting on yesterday's visit to Chalcott Street, where her mother had been complaining at the defection of the latest housemaid, a whey-faced girl with a limp. "Not a word of thanks for all I'd done for her. After all our kindness to her, she just ups and leaves. Said she wanted to work in a shop, would you believe it! Dreadful girl."

Everyone was losing staff at that time - people left domestic service during the war and had chosen not to return - but from the Hartley home in particular they left in droves.

"So I'll see you Saturday then," said Alan.

"You mean you're coming too?"

"Didn't I mention that?" He smiled. "Why not mix business with pleasure? There's a train which goes on the Metropolitan Line from Baker Street. We can get a combined rail and entrance ticket for 2s and 6d which takes us third class all the way. I'll call for you on Saturday at eight."

It was a date of sorts, and as realisation dawned Esther turned away from him to hide an infuriating blush. She wondered if Alan was attractive. Not conventionally, she supposed. He had an earnest face with a beaky nose and red hair and a prominent Adam's apple that jiggled disturbingly in his throat. Then again, she liked the way he never patronised her, or made intellectual concessions to her and she admired his confidence that what they and the magazine said actually mattered, as though it could change things and affect lives.

Certainly her own life was changing beyond all recognition. She was independent now, free to go where she pleased under nobody's scrutiny. Her old life was still there of course, but alongside it existed an entire realm of people and ideas which were sophisticated and unfamiliar, and most of it was down to Alice. Some time after she moved into the flat, Alice had said:

"We're having a party at home. Would you like to come? There are some people you should meet."

Esther loved that word "*should*". It was as though Alice had taken upon herself the burden of some sort of cultural education for her new friend, and although Esther was quite capable of conducting her own education, it was exhilarating to think that someone else was taking the trouble. She was longing to meet all the writers and artists, playwrights and poets Alice talked about. She already got on well with Alice's mother Sidonie, with her heavy lidded eyes and her way of treating everyone with reverent attention, which was irresistibly flattering.

The party was in honour of a new play by George Bernard Shaw called St Joan, with Sybil Thorndyke in the lead role. It was held in Sidonie's drawing room, whose walls writhed with William Morris leaves and roses and were crowded with paintings, many of them featuring Sidonie or members of the family, all of them by people she knew. The room was on the first floor, with a wide window overlooking the embankment, and the last traces of a crimson sunset slipping over the housetops. The family's numerous cats were camped with proprietorial ease on many of the available chairs and sofas.

Into the room swung a sudden crowd of tall, loud voiced people who all seemed to know each other, divesting themselves of coats and umbrellas at the door without any interruption in their conversation.

"A magical evening."

"She was just perfect."

"Where's Sidonie?"

"Oh darling, how lovely."

"A present? Oh I've heard about this. But where on earth did you get hold
of it?"

"Fresh from Paris."

Into Sidonie's hands someone had pressed a book called *Ulysses* and almost immediately Esther found herself in the midst of a group of people arguing about it. Though no-one appeared to have read it, everyone had an opinion. The book seemed to arouse the most extraordinary passions. Debate eventually distilled between two men, who stood to Esther's left and right and talked across her, so she remained for some time, silently sandwiched, hoping no-one would inveigle her into the discussion. The two men seemed very wound up about it.

"Someone was saying he's the new Tolstoy, but I fear there's something dreadfully low bred about it."

"Quite wrong. Joyce is a genius. This work has effectively ended the nineteenth century. He is the new, and we should all take note."

"Oh come on. From what I've heard most of it's incomprehensible gibberish. Just trying to impress, like a silly boy. The writing is all over the place. Actually I would say he despoils the English language."

Esther felt a rising sense of panic. Surely, out of mere good manners, someone would very soon solicit her opinion. Her eyes fixed on the chin of the Joyce man, where a mole sprouted hairs.

"I despair of such utter nonsense. Joyce has rewritten the rules. It is an awesome achievement. As I said in my review, he has rewritten the novel."

"So now we all have to write novels about men sitting on lavatories."

"There's no need to be deliberately dense."

The argument appeared to be getting more personal. Eventually the man who thought Joyce ill-bred turned to her as if for support. He had an aggressive manner and smelt of stale sweat.

"You look like more of an Eliot girl to me."

By sheer chance, she knew about T.S. Eliot, a poet who worked in a bank. Alan had read her Eliot's latest poem, which he said was the new manifesto for a godless generation.

"I did like *The Waste Land*."

"Marvellous, isn't it. Utterly unrelenting. The way I see it Eliot is the lightning flash which shows us the whole of the modern world. There is the old world lying in broken desolation on the field of battle and here we have a new world, in fragments."

Though he claimed to admire Eliot, the man seemed rather irked about it all, as though he had a lot to get off his chest.

"Everything now's in flux and disintegration. Even Eliot admits that contemporary history is a panorama of futility. You know Einstein?"

"I don't think so," said Esther, hoping she wasn't about to be introduced to him.

"The scientist. In his field, he says the same. He even thinks that space is warped. And that the instruments we use to measure space are warped too. So we can never get the true picture, d'you see?"

Surreptitiously Esther looked around her. Everyone else appeared engrossed in gossipy discussions punctuated by shrieks and gales of laughter. She and the angry man were the only people not party to the general hilarity. In the corner by the window, engaged in animated conversation, was a tall, intense looking girl. She wore a square collared blouse and a long blue dress. She gesticulated a lot as she talked, which made her seem to radiate nervous energy. The evening light appeared to curve round her head, firing up the bronze spirals of her hair and Esther was just wondering if it was coloured, when, to her slight alarm, the girl caught her eye, broke off her conversation and came towards her smiling, her hand outstretched.

"I'm Ursula Davis. Alice has told me all about you."

As it happened, Alice had done the same for Esther. Indeed she had listened to the story of Ursula Davis with such fascination, she felt she already knew her intimately.

Ursula was 23 and came from Leeds, the child of poor, but ambitious parents who recognised the fierce intelligence of their three daughters and poured all their energy into their education. All three had done well, and Ursula had repaid her parents' efforts handsomely by gaining a scholarship place to read Classics at Cambridge. While she was there she completed her first novel, *Little Lives*, which had been accepted by a London publishing house and came out to admiring reviews, just as she came down. But it was that point at which Ursula's parents' gratification in their daughter had ceased. *Little Lives* told the story of an oppressive northern childhood in a dour industrial town, where affection was scant and an imperious father ruled with psychological violence. The young woman went on to have an illicit affair and an abortion. Shortly after the book appeared Ursula's parents severed all contact with her and relations with her sisters became strained.

Some reviews condemned the novel for its bold treatment of unmarried sex and abortion. But others were glowing, and Ursula was accepted warmly into London society. The fact that she was young, beautiful and unmarried guaranteed her invitations to parties. Alice had also mentioned that Ursula had a "complicated private life", though she had not elaborated.

Despite this daunting reputation, Esther could not help warming instantly to Ursula. She had expressive eyes, a husky voice, which seemed to give everything she said an ironic lilt and she was appealingly curious about the details of Esther's work and family. But it was not until she turned slightly, so that her figure was framed against the light, that Esther noticed something else about Ursula. She was so tall and slender that it was impossible to disguise, nor had she many any attempt to conceal, the protruding bump of pregnancy.

Chapter Eight

*"Everyone's most curious to hear how you're getting on.
There was marvellous bridge last night at Hetty's and
after that we went on a midnight tride to see Karnak by
moonlight. Not much on today except a little tennis party.
The season's winding down now. I think a trip to Aswan
might be in order. We all miss you frightfully Samuel, though
I don't, of course, think it would be appropriate for you to
come back. On which subject I hope you can be of use to my
old friend Elmer. It would be for the best, I think, to help him
in any way he wants...."*

The letter, in Violet's distinctive hand, had been brought in
to him at breakfast, but he couldn't read it there, not under
the silent observation of Iris, inscrutably sipping coffee.
Time and again he felt her eyes on him, assessing him, and
it was hard to resist the desire to meet her gaze full on.
Could it be that she felt the same stirrings of interest in him,
or was she merely wondering when he would leave? These
musings vanished, however, when he saw Violet's letter. He
had taken it straight to the morning room and read it over to
himself with a rising sense of unease. Those thoughts which
most of the time he managed to damp down came surging
back. *"I hope you can be of use to my old friend Elmer.."*.
What did Violet mean by that? Was it some kind of threat?

It was on Christmas Day 1922 that he first met Violet
Esterhazy at the American house near Deir-El-Bahri. The
American contigent had by far the best time of it out there.
Their house, built in the Coptic style, had beautiful hanging
lamps and intricate wooden screens against the whitewashed
walls, rich Egyptian carpets on the floor and embroidered
cushions to rest on. It was also big enough to accommodate

several families. The American wives, with their husbands out at the excavations, spent their time planning numerous dinner parties and amateur dramatics to which they invited the British, and Samuel received frequent invitations. On Christmas day they laid on a dinner with crackers and plum pudding and paper hats, all served by waiters in white gowns and crimson sashes. Afterwards everyone relaxed with whisky and sodas, reading aloud pieces from *The Sphinx*, the illustrated paper for expatriates and chatting to Arthur Mace, a cousin of Flinders Petrie who had arrived to join the excavating team. Violet, who had twisted her ankle, was lying to one side on a sofa propped up by cushions, wearing a grey satin dress. She had a cat nestled beside her and was trawling her fingers through its tawny fur.

Samuel had heard about Violet. She was a well-born and childless English woman in her forties who was generally believed to have married beneath her. Her husband, a jobbing archaeologist who was finding it hard to make ends meet, had departed for another dig up the Nile at Abu Simbel leaving his wife to manage by herself. This she did, people said, through the illicit supply of antiquities to rich European collectors.

Reports of her attractions varied. She was tall and rather beaky, with misty, myopic blue eyes and a pale face above a long neck that made her look like a beautiful white bloom about to drop from its stem. Yet there was an energy about her that belied her milky-skinned languor. From the moment he arrived that evening he saw her eyeing him, though being immobilised she was unable to escape the elderly man who bent over her, boring her about the Amarna heresy.

Then Lucy Twill, the wife of one of the chemists who had been hired to observe the restoration process, introduced Samuel and Violet extended a cool hand.

"I saw you at the tomb the other day, didn't I?"

"Yes." He had spent the day sketching the wall paintings.

"But I didn't see you."

"Mr Carter sent his donkey over for me. I do think he's awfully sweet."

"Lucky someone does."

Given his undistinguished background, most people took Howard Carter's abruptness as a sign of low breeding, rather than eccentricity. As the son of a water colour painter his precise class status was ambiguous, yet he was a frequent target of sniping and snobbery.

"Carter's not a bad little chap. His father was my grandfather's gamekeeper. Extraordinary, don't you think?"

"It probably accounts for his awfully odd way with animals. He keeps a pet donkey, did you know, in the house! It wanders quite freely around the place and brays when it sees him."

"That's a country upbringing for you."

It was true, Carter loved animals – his home was a proper menagerie with dogs and pet gazelles, as well as his canary, and he had created a donkey park at the dig, where the numerous donkeys who were required to trek miles to the Valley with their human cargo could rest while their passengers visited the tombs.

But as for people, they were different. The English he tolerated, the local officials he disliked, the French he mostly despised. Some people thought he had an affection for Carnarvon's daughter, Lady Evelyn. They seemed very friendly - he called her Eve – and they posed for photographs arm in arm. But her father disapproved and in the end nothing came of it.

He was friendly with some of Luxor's antiquity dealers, and would spend evenings with them, drinking thick Turkish coffee. He was kind to the Arab boys who did the digging, filling their baskets with shards of earth hundreds of times a day, and he made a favourite of the water boy. But apart from that there was no-one.

"Oh I don't blame Mr Carter in the least for getting tetchy

with people," said Violet. "It's the journalists mainly who upset him. He says they're swine and I'm sure he's right. They are a dreadful nuisance."

"Well if he will make perverse arrangements with newspapers, what does he expect?" interposed Lucy Twill. "As an American I think it's downright unjust that Lord Carnarvon is making this agreement with the London *Times*. Mr Arthur Merton is getting exclusive access to the tomb, and all the other newspapermen have to wait around with no news. I think it's dreadfully unfair. I like Mr Merton but I really don't see why he should have priority. Isn't this find just as exciting for the rest of the world?"

"But is that any excuse for them to behave in such a fashion?" asked Violet. "They just seem to devote all their efforts to badgering poor Mr Carter."

"The local journalists are far worse," said Lucy staunchly. "They assume they should take precedence over everyone."

"Ah, but there I think they have a point."

"Just because they're Egyptian? The cheek of it! Who's done all the work? Who's invested the money and provided employment to hundreds of natives?"

Violet raised her face to Samuel. "What about you, Mr Dux?" she said, in a suggestively husky voice. "Do you think the Egyptians are being tiresomely possessive about their antiquities?"

Samuel hesitated. For someone who spent his days poring over ancient Egyptians, Samuel rarely thought about the rights of the modern variety. He had very little acquaintance with them, unless one counted bearers, guards and camel drivers, and generally they appeared either devious or obstructive, like the ministry officials who turned up from time to time to harass Carter. Not to mention the waiter across the other side of the room who seemed to be stubbornly refusing to pass this way with his tray of cocktails.

He shrugged. "You do have to ask who's putting in the

time and money on the excavation work."

Violet smiled equally. "Of course you do. Quite. Tell me, how are you finding it down at the coalface?"

She patted a spot on the sofa beside her and he sat down.

"It's incredible of course. I shall never see anything like it again." He accepted a drink from the waiter who had approached them at a single glance from Violet. "I mean, having the chance to examine things which no-one has looked at for three thousand years gives one a peculiar sense of trespass, but also…" he searched for the correct word, "of intimacy."

"Intimacy? Really?" Her eyes fastened on his. She gave a slow, crimson smile. "I would like to hear more about that."

He faltered. "Well yes. In fact if it wasn't for the heat…"

"My dear. You don't know what real heat is like until you've been to Ur. Ninevah and Mesopotamia are an absolute furnace. Now where are you staying?"

"I'm up with Dr Fellowes."

"That *is* a cause for discomfort."

"It's fine, though the bedding is a little hit and miss."

"I tell you what. I've just had some linen sent over from Harrods. I could easily spare some."

"Oh, don't worry about me."

"Darling, the pleasure would be all mine."

Sure enough the following day, which was Sunday, a donkey laden with a heavy, brown paper package toiled up the dusty track to the Fellowes house, its narrow hooves picking the way through the rocks, as Violet followed on behind. Once the package was disposed of, she waved at the unburdened donkey.

"I think my beast will be awfully envious if his friend has no passenger. Why don't you come back to dinner at my place?"

And that was how it started. He hadn't sought it, indeed would never have sought out Violet, but his reservations about her husband swiftly passed. To start with he simply could not understand what Violet wanted him for but in the end he decided he must be a recreation to her, like tennis or bridge, and she taught him so perfectly the separation of sex from emotion, it was hard to imagine it any other way. Violet's own lofty, aristocratic demeanour and her absolute refusal to care about the opinions of others, seemed to exempt them from the gossip their liaison might have attracted as they sought out all the diversions that Luxor had to offer.

In his free time they visited local festivals where they saw jugglers and singers and pipe players and ate lentil soup, Nile fish and lamb stuffed with tomatoes. They picnicked on flat Egyptian bread crammed with meat and herbs and sampled the sweet apple and aniseed smoke of the sheesha. They took sketching trips to local tourist sites, played tennis at the British Club and cards and mah jong at the Winter Palace. Sometimes Violet cooked for him with quantities of food shipped from England - sardines and pâté, tinned strawberries and peaches and jams.

She was English to her backbone yet it was Violet, more than anyone, who really showed Egypt to Samuel. Violet had trekked through the desert and drunk sour camel milk with the Bedouin. She had met and negotiated with members of the notorious tomb robbing family, the al-Rasuls, and visited their homes beside the Theban necropolis quite unchaperoned. The only Arabic most of the Europeans knew were commands and curses, but Violet had learnt enough to converse freely. When the other British women dwelt on the inferiority of the Egyptian race and the civilising effects that a British presence might have on their industry or government or justice system, Violet would merely look thoughtful. With Samuel she would venture out to the jostling streets to the bazaar, past the little mules scarcely visible beneath their huge burdens of vegetables and palms. They would stroll along the Corniche in Luxor, watching the horse drawn calèches drive tourists round the town and gaze across the Nile to the west bank as the sun dropped beneath the Theban hills. And it was in Luxor one evening as they were sitting in a café drinking the sweet, gritty Arab coffee, alongside old men playing chess, watching a sinuous belly dancer, her belly slick with oil and sweat, that she laid a languid hand on his arm and said:

"Very soon Samuel, you must meet my friend Husni."

Samuel folded the letter and placed it deep in his trouser pocket. He made his way back to the dining room but Iris had vanished. He took a piece of toast from the rack, buttered it and applied marmalade, but after one bite he abandoned it. For some reason his appetite had entirely deserted him.

Chapter Nine

Most people, Iris knew, assumed her interests to be music, dancing, fashion, make-up and the company of men. After all choosing clothes, going to cocktail parties, watching the motor-racing at Brooklands, visiting the theatre, dancing in night-clubs whenever possible, riding in Rotten Row and staying with friends in the country were all the sort of things girls like Iris enjoyed. In fact she could not have cared less. Sometimes she felt she was living someone else's life entirely.

What she did regret more than anything was that she was not born a boy. She didn't want to *be* a boy - there was nothing unfeminine about her - but she had enough insight to realise that her own nature, with its ingrained love of risk-taking and novelty, could be used to far greater advantage in a man's life. There was something within her - some kind of mental adrenaline - that seemed to energise her. She knew that the same traits which in the life of a rich, leisured young woman led only to fast cars, dangerous horses, and partying for as hard and long as possible, might prove an immense advantage in the world of business. Her character came from her father after all, and she knew, if she had been able to work in his world, that she would be just as successful as him. Right now she could be working alongside him, earning his confidence, learning the skills with which she could one day take over the running of his business empire, instead of simmering with resentment and an angry desire to defy him in some shocking and unspecified way.

She remembered when she was tiny he would have her climb in bed with him and share his breakfast. He'd doted on her openly then, readily indulging her demands for riding lessons or a bicycle or a puppy. But as she grew up his affections became more mercurial and the emotion he showed towards her was more often anger than delight. She would never forget a chance remark he made one day when she and Charles were small children playing with their parents in a sunlit drawing room. Turning aside to their mother he said:

"She is just like me unfortunately, and the boy, I'm afraid, is just like you."

What was unfortunate about that? Surely side-stepping her assets, rather than making best use of them, contradicted everything about her father's business practice. Yet instead of speculating that she might come into his business and follow in his footsteps, her father only expressed dissatisfaction. His acts of generosity were outweighed by vindictiveness. Her pony, Mint, had been sent away the day after she had failed to memorise some elementary facts about American history - Barrington was insistent that the children know their heritage; Who was the first president of the United States? What happened at the Boston Tea Party? Most of Iris's childhood had been one long process of toughening herself against him and recovering from her mother's death. By now the carapace she had constructed around herself was as hard as the barnacled diamond tiara she had been left by her mother to be worn on her wedding day, nestling in its vault at Coutts.

It was that wedding day which was to be the apogee of her career. It was clear that her father's sole ambition for her was to make a good marriage, which meant at the very least a titled one. Iris knew she was a commodity, just like all the other commodities Elmer Barrington dealt in - a deb on the marriage market. The only thing she and her father agreed on was that none of the men she had met so far was remotely satisfactory. Any young men who did take an interest in her were dismissed by her father as "gold-diggers" who assumed that they could live off the fortune Iris would inherit.

Perversely, that was what she liked about Bunny Devine.

He didn't seem to be very interested in her at all, or her money. The great, unfolding drama of Bunny's own existence was far too absorbing for him to concern himself with the details of other people's lives. He was never censorious with her, never talked about the future, never tried to influence her in any way at all, if you didn't count offering to teach her to pilot his little twin-engined plane, and that was so that she would be able to fly him back from Le Touquet where he liked to go gambling. He was a hopeless gambler. She had already been to clubs in London with him and watched him lose hundreds on backgammon and roulette. But he never allowed it to affect him. He greeted his loss with an insouciant grin and walked away to order more champagne and lobster. The guiding principle in Bunny's life was the pursuit of pleasure, though he was also serious about acquiring art treasures which he would ship back to America to sell. Everyone loved Bunny - actresses, shop girls and night-club hostesses. Everyone loved him, except Iris's father.

That evening they would be off to a night-club again. It might be the Embassy in Old Bond Street, the Café de Paris off Leicester Square or the 400, or the Kitkat Club, or several in succession. And she would need her stamina because in the early hours there might also be a "treasure hunt" during which everyone in their set would tear around the deserted, echoey streets of central London in their cars searching for a list of eclectic objects - a doorman's hat from the Embassy, a knife and fork from the Ritz, a camellia from a certain tree in St James's Park. Once they had even broken into Buckingham Palace but the captain of the guards had rung the police in a panic. In truth Iris thought this game was babyish but everyone else took treasure hunting terrifically seriously. They liked the idea of having a purpose in their pleasure. Still, at least Dolly would be there, the gayest and loudest girl in their group, setting the pace and determined to keep them up until dawn.

She was just on her way out when she passed Samuel Dux, heading up the wide marble stairs.

"Hello Iris."

She quickened her pace as she passed him, and he halted courteously to one side. He always seemed to be coming in just as she went out. She wondered if he planned it that way. No doubt, with his watchful, puritanical gaze he was privately criticising her for having fun. She felt a surge of rebellious feeling. What exactly *was* he doing here? He wasn't really a guest, was he? He was her father's employee. He didn't know any of the people they knew, indeed she had no idea what kind of people he did mix with, partly because she had refused to ask him. There was a strange, indeterminate neutrality about Samuel Dux which made her think that whatever mileu he was in he would never obtrude, but nor, like a perfectly schooled foreigner, would he ever entirely fit in.

The worst of it was he kept trying to draw her into conversation. People didn't have conversations in this house. First he tried to talk to her about Charles and she answered as tersely as possible, indicating that Charles was not a subject for idle chat. Then he attempted to tell her all about Egypt, even after she had made it clear she found all those antiquities a tremendous bore. Little terracotta heads with the nose knocked off, or the odd cracked jar which was supposed to be revered simply for being ancient. They weren't beautiful most of them, or art. She thought it was all just a great conspiracy got up by people who liked things simply because they were old and she had told him so. But now he seemed to have learnt his lesson. Generally he contented himself with wishing her a pleasant evening when he saw her going out, rather than asking her right out where she was off to, as though he expected an itinerary. Yet still, he was an intrusion, Samuel Dux, chipping away at her anger and loneliness, digging and delving into her life, just when she'd got used to things the way they were.

It was a chill night, and there were even tiny flakes of snow circling under the glow of the street lamps. Bunny had drawn up outside and was drumming his fingers on the walnut dashboard. He jumped out and opened the door.

"Hello baby. Fancy a little jazz?"

It wasn't the night-club first of course. There was a show, Clemence Dane's new play, and then dinner at Quaglino's, and it was not until past two in the morning that they found themselves in front of an anonymous basement just off Golden Square. Even clattering down the narrow metal steps gave one the feeling of exclusivity, as though entering a secret world. A man in a shiny buttoned uniform nodded at them, the black door opened, as if by sorcery, and before them in the dimly lit hall stood Madame Amber, the owner. Madame Amber was a tall, imposing woman, caked in make up, swathed in a dark green velvet evening dress, which displayed to full advantage her deep cleavage. Her knuckles blazed with jewels. In repose her face was flinty, betraying the difficulties of the life that had brought her here, and her eyes were hawk-like, alert both for the needs of her guests and for the prospect of trouble. Another hostess in town had recently been arrested for sale of alcohol without a licence, and although Madame Amber felt the occasional presence of the royal princes at her own establishment gave her a certain immunity against the indignity of police raids, one could never be complacent. By its very nature her clientele, encompassing artists and actors and so many of the more sensitive types, was liable to be unpredictable, but when she saw Iris she beamed.

"Miss Barrington and Mr Devine! How marvellous to see you. Your friends are here already."

She led them through a corridor to the main room of the club. It was dim and womblike, with mirrored walls, deep red plush banquettes and each table lit with a candle in a little pink shade. In one corner was a polished parquet dancefloor and beside it someone was playing the piano.

It wasn't hard to spot Dolly. She was holding court amid a crowd of young men, towering above most of them, a magnum of champagne in a silver ice bucket placed beside her. Dolly was never normally clever with clothes - she wore pleated tweed skirts which bulged over her midsection and dresses which made her look twice her age. But tonight she looked her wholesome best, in a dress of gold silk, speckled all over with silver glass beads and a simple ruby necklace at her throat. Her mousy hair was held with a diamond clip, and her wide features were softened by the candlelight. Iris felt a rush of pleasure to see her. At least things were never dull when Dolly was around. A man with fair wavy hair stood up tipsily, gestured towards Iris and Bunny and said that the drinks were on him.

"Drinks are in him, more likely," murmured Bunny, accepting a glass.

Dolly drew Iris down to kiss her and whispered in her ear: "We simply have to talk."

"What is it? A treasure hunt?"

"No. It's much, much more exciting than that. I'll tell you later."

One of the men was urging Dolly up on the dance floor. Bunny poured her some champagne, then melted away. Iris joined in the general gossip.

The talk among Iris's friends was always light, witty and brittle. Who was having an affair with whom, who had seen the latest revue, where they would be hunting that weekend, and who was lucky enough to be going out to the Riviera, where people had villas in the little fishing villages or perched above the pine-fringed bays. Occasionally they would discuss the latest theatrical productions or even art and music, but one thing no one discussed was politics. That was too dull. Nor would anyone mention the war. That was beyond the pale. Once Iris had asked one of the young men she was with if he regretted missing out on the war and he had replied languidly:

"Why should I? It was not really *our* war, was it? Besides, another one's bound to come along soon."

After a while, flushed and smiling, Dolly re-appeared at Iris's side.

"So what's this you need to tell me?"

"Have a guess!"

"You've found a new hunter." Dolly was always boring Iris with details of her favourite horses, how they were eating and performing, or if one was lame. She repeatedly pestered Iris to come and inspect Seraphina's new foal and was generally as enthusiastic about her horses as Iris had been about her pony at the age of eight, except Dolly was twenty-one. In truth Iris didn't really mind Dolly's rambling because she lacked the artifice the rest of them were trying so hard to acquire. Dolly's conversation was never sophisticated or brittle or clever and it didn't require very much that was clever in response.

"No, no, nothing like that. You'll never guess so I'll have to tell you. I'm engaged."

Iris looked at her friend with astonishment, then followed her gaze to the man now seated at the roulette table. Hector Monroe was tall and fair, with angular features, a narrow mouth and eyes as washed out as a grey Scottish sky. He had a shaved pink neck and a little brush moustache. His body was as lean and hard as a rod of steel. Iris had met him once or twice in the round of debutante balls after they had come out, but he seemed to have no interest at all in debs, and spent most of the time drinking. He was the son of a landed family, but it was going to be a long time before he inherited and in the meantime he had decided to stay in London having all the fun he would miss when he was exiled to the Highlands. But while he was admired as a good, all round sportsman and for a time looked as if he might try his hand as a Conservative MP, he soon lost interest, as he did in every other occupation, except the pleasurable pastimes of drinking, gambling and partying.

From the time they had first met, one of Dolly and Iris's favourite games was to discuss their precise requirements in a potential suitor. While Iris's requirements in a man were changeable and quixotic, such as knowing seven languages fluently, or having travelled to every continent, or being descended from Turkish royalty, Dolly's demands remained simple and unwavering.

"I don't care about anything else in a husband," she would declare, "just as long as he adores horses, dogs and children. In that order."

Now Iris looked over with dismay at the angular figure poised over the roulette wheel with glittering eyes, a balloon of brandy at his side. If Hector Monroe had a soft spot for puppies and babies, he was certainly hiding it well.

Dolly fingered the intricate knot of rubies and diamonds round her neck.

"He gave me this as an engagement present."

"It's beautiful," said Iris flatly. "What do your parents think?"

"They're thrilled of course."

"Are they?"

"Why shouldn't they be? I'm of age. And though it's a bit sudden, it's not as if Hector's nobody. He'll have the castle and the title in time. And all those…..glens."

"But when did you…? I mean I didn't even realise you liked him."

"Well nor did I actually. I mean I always liked him, of course, but I didn't realise he felt the same way about me until last week." Dolly's eyes glistened with excitement and she pulled down Iris to the seat beside her.

"I've been longing to tell you! It was terribly romantic. It was that night at the Johnson's party, you know, out at Heston Park. We just found ourselves thrown together. It was awfully hot in the ballroom and I'd gone out onto the terrace to cool down and I saw him standing there. He'd had a losing streak at backgammon and he was just sort of staring moodily out at the lawn so I leant on the balcony and stared chatting, you know, to be friendly. He told me about what frightfully bad luck he'd been having, and then he said, 'But you know, I think my luck is about to change,' and without any warning he leaned over and kissed me!

"Oh Iris it was so romantic in the darkness, hardly able to see each other's faces! He seemed….desperate almost. He said he'd been thinking about me for some time."

Seeing the mounting alarm on Iris's face she gave her a little, excited hug.

"Don't look like that! I know it seems a shock now and I should have told you before, but you'll love him once you get to know him properly, you really will."

Iris clasped her tightly back, as though Dolly was already being torn from her grasp.

She knew they should be raising their glasses and calling congratulations, but she felt utterly incapable of it. How could Dolly's parents allow their only daughter to make a mistake like this? How could they not see beyond the title and the possessions to the person within? The Monroe family, with their assumption of superiority based only on the rampages of some baron ancestor in the Scottish glens a few hundred years ago, were everything her own father despised. And even though Hector had been to Eton and Christ Church, his idea of cultural debate was throwing friends into fountains for reading a book.

Desperately she looked around for Bunny. He was exactly the sort of person who could greet such news with the requisite joie de vivre. He was over by the piano, bending down towards a woman she didn't recognise, a small woman wearing a dark coloured sheath with diamante shoulder straps.

"Who's Bunny talking to?"

Dolly looked over. The girl was exceptionally pretty, with a little heart shaped face and huge eyes, her hair falling in soft, lustrous waves.

"Don't you know? That's Tippy Pleasance. She often comes here after the show."

So that was her. Iris had heard of Tippy Pleasance of course. Along with everyone else in London. Tippy's story, of working her way up from Blackpool dance halls and end-of-pier shows to top of the bill in London's West End, abandoning her morals and her northern vowels along the way, had been reproduced in numerous newspapers and magazines. Noel Coward and Somerset Maugham had begged her to appear in their plays. Ivor Novello had written a song especially for her. The rumour was that she was after an English aristocrat, like so many other actresses before her, and no one doubted that there were several of whom she could have her pick. Despite the sweet modesty of her looks, she was said to be sexually voracious. She was said to need pills to get to sleep and different pills to keep awake. She kept cocaine in a powder compact set into the buckle of her shoe.

Bunny caught Iris's eye and came over. He squeezed her hand.

"Just telling Tippy how much I enjoyed her performance in Carnival."

When he heard Dolly's news Bunny was reliably jovial and called for drinks all round. Dolly sat, as though in a stupor of happiness, occasionally resting her head against Hector's shoulder. Hector, like Iris, appeared thoughtful. Eventually Iris could stand it no longer.

"I think we'd better leave, Bunny."

"We've barely arrived."

"I know. But I've got a terrible headache." It was true. The tension stretched a tight band across her temples. She suddenly felt very tired.

Bunny's car was a cocoon of walnut and buttery leather. She lay back in the seat as they drove back through the Mayfair streets, allowing the fresh air to cool and soothe her face. The pelt of her fur wrap ruffled in the wind. She was silent with shock over Dolly's engagement. How could her parents not see what was plain to Iris and everyone else who loved her? That giving Dolly to someone like Hector Monroe with his savage laugh and ice-cold eyes, was like placing your Lalique vase in the hands of a vandal. Parents were supposed to want what was best for their child but it was impossible to see how Hector Monroe could be the best thing for Dolly, no matter how many Scottish glens he came with.

There was also, Iris admitted to herself, another, more selfish reason for her distress. It might well be that she and Dolly would still spend time together after her marriage, but it would never be the same. Never again would it be the two of them against the world, their friendship a defiant, united front against the loneliness of life.

At the corner of the square Bunny stopped the car and flicked a glowing butt out of the window. He leant over, reeking of cigar smoke and placed her hand in his lap. The material of his trousers felt expensively soft. He shifted closer towards her and with one hand pressed her fingers down.

"No, Bunny."

"It's all right."

He began kissing her aggressively, so hard she could scarcely breathe, caressing her breasts and thighs. His moustache scratched her face. Beneath the cloth of his trousers she felt something move, and snatched her hand away, repulsed. She felt very small beneath his weight, and in her powerlessness she felt a sudden jolt of fear. She tried to push him off.

"Please Bunny. Not now. Just don't."

He was never usually like this. Normally he was what Iris and her friends called "a gentleman" and contented himself with a lingering kiss. He never lost his composure, his slow drawl or his smooth charm. Tonight, however, he was insistent, as though he had already been stirred and could

not stop himself. His entire body was hot and roused.
Iris made herself as chill and inflexible as she could and
eventually he sat back in his seat and relit a cigar.

"Sorry sweetheart. You're just so irresistible tonight."
He looked sideways at her. "You have no right to be so
preposterously beautiful."

She said nothing, so he added: "Good news about your
friend Dolly."

"Is it? Do you like Hector?"

"Like him? I certainly do. Good man."

"But do you think they're suited?"

"Suited? They sure seem happy enough."

"I don't know…."

"Sure you're not jealous darling?" He regarded her
bemusedly.

"What on earth do you mean?"

"Well most of the girls seem to like Hector."

"Not me."

He stroked her cheek. "I'm delighted to hear it. I want to
keep you entirely to myself."

She wondered if this conversation was leading somewhere
but knowing Bunny it was probably not. She yawned.
Unlike her friends she never took anything to help her stay
up all night. "I'd better go."

"Just before you do darling, I had something to ask you.
I'm off to Paris next week. I have a little business to take
care of. Will you come?"

"To Paris?" Bunny had frequently talked of them
summering down in the south of France. The prospect
sounded delightful, but it was also comfortably in the distant
future.

"I couldn't. Not so soon. My father would never allow
me."

"Aw come on. Just for a couple of days. There's a whole
group going. It would hardly be us alone. Surely you could
talk the old man round. I could show you Montparnasse.

And you'd get to meet a lot of interesting people. Artists. We could have a ball."

"Bunny, I'm afraid he would simply forbid it. There's no point in even thinking about it."

"Sure thing." Apart from a slight tightening of his lips, you would almost not detect Bunny's annoyance. She got out of the car.

"Well goodnight darling. Sleep well. And if you change your mind, be sure to let me know."

Chapter Ten

He was going down to that place again. Down where the dark huddled waiting for him. It was cold and he was gasping for air, but the dank breath of the tomb coiled into his lungs and seemed to choke him. It was so black he could barely see his hand in front of his face and he moved with the heavy tread of a swimmer wading through damp sand. He struggled to escape yet his body was paralysed. Gradually he became aware of someone near him. It was Howard Carter's water boy gesturing to him. His heart raced as he realised the entrance to the tomb was closing slowly over them. Soon the two of them would be trapped together for ever. A door slammed and he jerked awake.

It was the sound of Iris coming in that woke Samuel up. Peering out of the window, he saw Bunny's red car disappearing round the square. It was practically morning. The moon hung wan, with no colour. The first grey glimmering of dawn was in the sky and the ghost of dew lay on the grass in the garden square. He got back into bed, and tried not to think about his dream, but there was little chance of drifting back to sleep now. Ahead of him lay another exhausting day at Barrington House.

He heard the soft movement of Iris passing on the stairs and in the distance, a door closing. She was like some sleek, nocturnal creature, whose rhythms were wholly different from the dull, daytime crowd. He thought of her sitting at her mirrored dressing table, removing her jewellery, delicately, routinely, unclasping the long earrings and loosing the heavy pearls from her neck. He listened for the faint click of her watch as she laid it in the cut glass container, the soft rasp of the hairbrush. He imagined the gentle slippage of her clothes, the dress cast to one side, the stockings rolled off and discarded, until she stood naked and then, probably without washing, would simply fall into bed and sleep just as he and the rest of the world were bracing themselves for another day.

Stirred by these thoughts, he stretched and ran his fingers lightly down the ribs and muscles of his own torso. He felt alone without a woman in his bed. He craved the touch of bare skin against his own. At that moment he even felt an intense yearning for Violet, sleeping in her crêpe de Chine underwear that smelt of perfume and old cigarette smoke, or sitting naked beside him, laughing her gravelly laugh with her pendulous breasts and the wrinkled, triangular wedge of tan at her throat. It was Violet who had started it all, he supposed.

By March it was a hundred degrees in the shade and everyone's nerves were on edge. The Queen of the Belgians was visiting for the second time and had insisted on being given a private view of the burial chamber, while her son Prince Leopold, bored, lolled in the shade with a cigarette. Violet and Lucy Twill were supervising a cold buffet which they had set up beside the tomb of Seti the second with tinned meat and crackers from Fortnum and Mason. It was laid out on a table set with a white cloth, large silver punchbowl and fine china and a number of tables and chairs had been arranged beside it.

Samuel smiled to himself at the incongruity of the scene. The men in their three piece suits, the sandwiches, the silver and bone china and the whole transitory flotsam of Britishness against the harsh, indomitable backdrop of the Valley. Which didn't mean that he wasn't prepared to join them. He had spent the whole morning on his knees sketching the effigy of a cheetah in heat so strong it threatened to scorch the paper on the block - his calves ached from crouching, the muscles of his shoulders were tense and he had a raging thirst. He came upon the two women whispering animatedly.

"He's really over-stepped the mark this time," said Violet, her eyes alight with conspiracy.

"Who? What's happened?" he asked.

"Mr Carter. There's been a furious row. With Porch."

Everyone liked Carnarvon, who was known affectionately as Porch on account of his previous title, Lord Porchester. George Edward Stanhope Molyneux Herbert, the 5th Earl Carnarvon, owner of Highclere Castle, estates in Somerset and Nottinghamshire and several London town houses, was a tall, stooped man with a drooping moustache and an irrepressible, boyish enthusiasm. He loved cars – he had owned the second ever motor car in Britain – and had brought his favourite Ford over to Egypt with him. Every day he would motor up the road to the Valley to moon about the site, getting under people's feet, taking photographs and inviting titled friends to visit at the most inconvenient moments.

Though they made an unlikely pair, his relationship with Howard Carter had always been close. Together, and against the odds, the two of them had been excavating in Egypt for more than 14 years. It seemed incredible that on top of the journalists and the tourists, Carter had chosen this moment to pick a quarrel with his patron and oldest friend.

Violet leant against the shade of the granite doorway, her pale linen shift and kohl-rimmed eyes making her resemble, briefly, one of the handmaids painted on the walls deep inside the tomb. She sipped her lemonade thoughtfully.

"It's very curious. It seems Porch wanted something from Carter last night. He went to Castle Carter to fetch it, but Carter refused to give it up and they quarrelled over it. It was a terrible row. Carter was screaming apparently. It set all the dogs off."

Samuel was continually astonished at the speed with which Violet accumulated information.

"How did you find all this out?"

She smiled, aware of the quality of her gossip.

"Oh, secrets don't last long here Samuel! My servant's a friend of Abdel Al. He met him this morning buying tomatoes at the souk."

"But what could possibly cause such an argument?"

"I don't know. But whatever Porch wanted, Carter obviously refused to give him. Anyway, the row was so bad that Carter ordered Porch never to set foot in his house again. Can you believe it? Banning his own patron from his home! The man who has funded his every move for years!"

"It sounds hot-headed."

"I'd say! Especially when Porch has been feeling so unwell. It seems the poor chap was bitten by a mosquito and the bite has become infected."

"Where is he now?"

"Oh he's upped and left. He's gone down to Cairo."

A moment later, when Lucy Twill was distracted by pouring tea for the Queen's maid, Violet said more quietly.

"In fact, I have a little business of my own in Cairo, Samuel. Would you like to accompany me? A few days away from the Valley might do us both some good."

Violet was right. It was a relief to take the rattling Express down from Luxor to Cairo shortly afterwards. All night a cooling breeze blew through the plaited cane walls of the sleeping car and in the morning a steward brought them coffee and rolls. They disembarked at the Central station and tipped a native porter to haul their bags into a horse-drawn cab.

Violet had booked a room at the famous Shepheard's hotel, where they sat on the terrace beneath the palms watching the tourists go by. Up the scarlet-carpeted steps and through the great Moorish hall with its marble pillars and impressive sweeping staircase, a constant stream of people moved, speaking in loud English voices, pink, sun-burnt men and exhausted-looking wives, followed by arab guides in their red tarbooshes, hefting piles of crocodile leather suitcases.

Violet accepted a glass of champagne from a safragi with a tray. She was wearing her most seductive low cut dress of emerald green silk, but as she reached across to smooth his thigh, Samuel flinched.

"Not in public darling?" she said calmly, masking her surprise.

He grunted noncommittally. The truth was, it was not just the public nature of her affection he recoiled from. He was beginning to grow uncomfortable with Violet altogether. Though he could see no easy way out of it, he preferred their liaison to remain within the narrow confines of Luxor society.

Perhaps she understood this because she continued:

"Are you desperate to come with me tonight? Only I think you might find Sir Reginald a bit of a bore."

She was dining at the Sporting Club, a former British officer's club in a residential area of Cairo favoured by Europeans and Americans for its lush green gardens, leafy streets white stucco houses with balconies and vaguely Parisian air.

Samuel prevaricated with a cigarette. Sir Reginald certainly sounded boring. Might he be a former lover, or merely a business associate? He supposed that Violet must be discussing some kind of deal, but he realised he didn't really want to know.

"You go alone. I think I'd like to take a look around."

He walked for a while through streets filled with ornate apartment blocks, government buildings and grand houses with their wrought iron balustrades, past the Ezbekiyah Gardens bursting with brightly flowered trees, towards the labyrinth of streets that led to the Khan al Khalili bazaar. After months of the claustrophobic intensity of the Valley, Cairo, with its anonymity and sheer press of bodies was exhilarating. Muski Street was like plunging into a human river. At the borders of the bazaar the teeming streets were bordered by the open doorways of shops where craftsmen sat cross-legged, tooling leather, weaving rugs, and working metal. Peddlers selling sweets and souvenirs called out to passers-by. Everything was for sale, from used razor blades and fly whisks to postcards and old newspapers.

The scent of sandalwood and cumin mingled with the smell of gasoline and dung, sweat and tobacco. He dodged sad-eyed donkeys, almost invisible beneath their dreadful burdens, urged along with bamboo sticks, and carts loaded with purple olives, shrunken lemons and roasted yams. Stalls spilled over with sacks bulging with caraway seed, sage, mint, fennel, lurid powders and spices and the pale beige beans for making the ubiquitous fuul that every Egyptian ate. Toothless old men regarded him, from the small tin tables where they took sheeshas of apple-scented tofah tobacco.

"You buy Mummy sir? Papyrus?"

It was a swarthy man in a filthy, white gelabiya and a red scarf.

"Genuine mummy sir. From tomb. Magical. Four piastres."

Samuel smiled and looked around at the antiquities stalls, offering row upon row of relics, most of which had no doubt been manufactured in some backroom or factory the week before. The sellers had all sorts of tricks for tourists. They would pull a scarab through a turkey gizzard to age it, grind it with sand or simply soak it in tea.

He deliberated for a while over a carnelian amulet of the heart, in the shape of a scarab. It was an original - genuine amulets were fairly easy to come across – inscribed always with words of protective power and by custom placed on the chest of the dead. The *ab,* or heart, represented the conscience for ancient Egyptians, and it held a special power because it could determine the soul's passage to the afterlife. Several chapters of the Book Of the Dead, he recalled, were devoted to protecting and defending the heart and ensuring that it did not betray its owner in the Hall of

Judgement.

He turned the small smooth stone over in his hand, tried and failed to read the hieroglyphics. The stallholder leaned over and translated.

"This heart belongs to him of many names…"

Who was that? He tried to remember. It was Thoth, wasn't it? –

"Speak not against me, my heart. Protect me from the Devourer."

From what he recalled The Devourer was the frightening, crococdile faced monster, ready to consume those whose heart spoke against them.

"Special magic," concluded the stallholder encouragingly, placing his right hand across his chest to indicate his heart. "It will protect you."

For a moment, Samuel was seized by a curious urge to buy the thing. Although there was no reason for it, these amulets could be readily found in Luxor, and probably for far less than this man was charging, it sat warm and heavy in his hand as though it was fixed there, by some invisible charge. He longed to slip it into his pocket and keep it with him. Yet the presence of the man hanging over him made him feel like a gullible sightseer and with an effort of will he replaced it.

Undeterred the man reached across and plucked at his sleeve.

"Take it sir! To protect you!" He smiled repellently.

"I have no need for protection, thank you," said Samuel, annoyed, turning deliberately to another stall where he spent his last piastres on a wooden box inlaid with mother of pearl which he planned to give to Violet as an apology for not accompanying her.

 By now, it was dark, and as he wandered further into the bazaar he realised he was lost. Cursing himself for thoughtlessly coming out without a guidebook, or enough money, he went further, turning again and again through the

maze of streets, past the ancient overhanging houses, whose
harem quarters had fretted shutters which allowed women to
peer out without being seen. He passed along streets where
plumbing and sewerage were clearly non-existent, into
cul de sacs and dead ends. Women in long, black burkhas
hurried past him and watchmen began to bed down on mats
outside the shops which they were paid to protect for the
night.

 He tried to orient himself. Surely if he turned here he would
come out at the towering walls of the Al Azhar mosque,
which Napoleon had once charged. Was this not the road
back to Muski street, approached from another angle? He
wanted to savour being in the ancient centre of Arabic Cairo,
but instead he felt a rising anxiety as the buildings became
poorer and filthier, the shop fronts barred with steel shutters,
the wooden doors studded with heavy nails. Each lane he
passed through became narrower and more labyrinthine until
he was squeezing himself through stinking mediaeval alleys,
peering through grilles into dim rooms where men squatted
on the ground beneath brass lamps.

  He started as a face lurched at him out of the shadows
at his feet, arm outstretched, eyes white with blindness.
Most of the beggars were blind in Cairo, eye disease was
endemic, but this was a young child – a boy no more than
ten - squatting on a pile of rags. *Ya Mohannin ya rabb*” he
cried, “Have pity master!” but Samuel shook his head and
hurried on.

  As he moved deeper into the heart of the maze, along
between the crumbling walls so close they were almost
leaning against each other, some of them entirely covered
with awnings, he began to feel a growing sense of dread.
He told himself this was merely a normal, touristic panic at
being too far from his hotel. It was just claustrophobia he
felt as he squeezed down streets just wide enough for one
person to pass. Yet the night air was like breath on the back
of his neck and he had the striking impression that he was

not alone. Though he glanced behind him and saw no-one, he felt a presence like a choking mist pressing in upon him and with it a sensation presaging horror. It was a feeling he had had only once before. A sense of the nearness of death.

He hurried on further, his heart galloping and the blood rushing in his ears, telling himself that he was allowing his imagination to run wild, glancing repeatedly behind him. The words of the stallholder, urging him to take the amulet, came back to him and he dismissed them angrily from his mind. Sweat prickled on his skin as he turned down streets and doubled back on himself, cursing himself for losing all sense of direction. The stench of these dimly lit streets was becoming oppressive. For a moment he saw himself as if from above, scurrying like an animal in a trap trying to escape impending doom.

The next second, and with no warning, the night engulfed him entirely. Blackness closed over him and the street was plunged into pitch darkness. He felt the cold clutch of fear. The lights in the shops and houses around him had receded into the night. The dark was heavy, like a blanket, and it swaddled his every sense. Groping his way with one hand against the wall he blundered on.

Then he rounded a corner and with a shock came face to face with Howard Carter. He almost wept.

"Mr Carter! Thank God!"

The surprise of running into Carter was compounded by shock at his appearance. Though they were both in shadow, he perceived that Carter's face was haggard and drawn. There were rings beneath his eyes and he was badly in need of a shave. His lightweight linen suit hung from him, grubby and creased. Samuel took him by the arm and shook his hand forcefully.

"You've no idea how pleased I am to see you! I have to confess I'm entirely lost. What on earth is happening here? What's wrong with the street lights?"

"Electricity failure," murmured Carter. "It happens all the

time."

His manner was peculiar. He evinced no surprise at all at encountering Samuel on this anonymous Cairo street corner. Indeed he was almost like a sleepwalker in a waking daze. Samuel hoped he had some idea of where they were.

"Are you heading for your hotel, Mr Carter? Can I accompany you?"

In response he drew Samuel closer and jerked his head as if he feared they may be overhead.

"I've been visiting Porch, Mr Dux. I'm afraid he's very seedy indeed. Eve is suffering agonies. Pray God he will pull through."

"I'm sorry to hear that. I hadn't realised his lordship was so ill. *The Times* said he was recovering well. Is there anything I can do to help? I mean I'd heard…"

"It was sudden. This bite seems to have set off a blood poisoning and now he has pneumonia. I had a telegram late this afternoon from the Continental Hotel to say he was going down very fast."

"But surely here in the city, there are doctors? He has access to proper British medicine. If his daughter is here…"

Carter seemed hardly to hear what he was saying. It was almost as if he was talking to himself.

"If only we had not argued! If only I had not allowed cupidity to come between us! After all we have been through together. Fourteen years it must be. And he has been a true friend. The dearest of friends."

Samuel hunted around for anything to assuage his feelings.

"It was fortunate that you happened to be in Cairo tonight."

"It was sheer fate. I needed to consult a man in the Cairo Museum about some coffin texts. There was something I needed to understand."

"And did you? Understand I mean?"

"Oh yes." Carter's face had a ghostly pallor and had lost all of its usual animation. He looked utterly desolate.

"I think I understand all too well."

They walked back to the hotel district in silence. The next morning news came from the Continental hotel that despite a message of support from the King of England, Lord Carnarvon had not survived the night.

* * *

The judder of the plumbing began, prompting Samuel to climb out of bed, run some hot water and begin shaving. Thinking about Egypt made him turn with relief to the day ahead and the mental abstraction it brought him. The work at Barrington House was so absorbing that he forgot everything else, even thoughts of his employer's daughter.

The job was demanding, he was there from early in the morning until around six each night, and sometimes far later, yet the intense, unremitting labour was relaxing for him. Far from being a mere advisor on Egyptian style, he had been invited to contribute his own designs to the project, and had done so with growing enthusiasm. He had used some of the sketches he had taken from the Valley of the Kings, the wall drawings and inscriptions, and reproduced them in a blue and gold mural in the lobby. He had sketched doors with corbelled openings, glass panels inlaid with highly coloured geometric designs and prepared a plinth for the middle of the lobby to support what Barrington referred to obliquely as the "centrepiece" though Samuel had not gathered what that would be.

The architect Holmes not only tolerated his presence without rancour, but had taken to forcing Samuel out to lunch, to join him in a jar of beer and a pie. Holmes tended to defer to Samuel on the subject of their employer's Egyptology jag.

"I like the stuff of course. Very impressive," Holmes pulled on his moustache, anxious not to give offence. "But it doesn't do much for me. My wife now, she's the one. She loves Tutankhamun. Reads all about him in her magazines.

The fellow might as well be a cinema star as far as she's concerned. She wants to know everything about him. But then, having been out there yourself, of course you'd understand that."

In fact the general fascination with Tutankhamun mystified most archaeologists. The men out on the dig would have described the boy king as a minor Pharaoh of the New Kingdom period, who ruled from just 1333 to 1323 BC and died between the ages of seventeen and twenty, having restored to Egypt the religion of the god Amun after the heretical era of his predecessor Akenaten, who swept away the traditional religion of Egypt, with its plurality of gods, in favour of the single, all-powerful sun god, Aten. That was about the sum of it.

But here in England Tutankhamun was a celebrity. Popular magazines dwelt on his relationship with his wife and family. He was considered wise and sensitive, and an unusually doting father. The pathos of the young man, cut down in his prime, evoked universal pity and his glorious resurrection inspired a near religious fervour. It seemed highly unlikely that any of these people knew the first thing about the thoughts, values or concerns of the ancient Egyptian culture, but to hear them talk, it was as though the Pharaoh and his short life had some powerful relevance to them. Sometimes Samuel thought the whole thing was more about Europe than Egypt. As though the tomb itself had become a great gaping hole to be filled with the pre-occupations of the day.

He was thinking about this as he set out that evening, on his way to meet the only old friend he had any inclination to revisit. He caught a bus and sat on the top deck, looking out at the passing streets with voracious interest. There were car showrooms opening up, the department stores were bursting with goods, the shops looked smarter. London seemed fresher now. The stunned sense that hung over from the war had dissipated a little and there was a tide of optimism abroad. On advertisement billboards people were drinking Horlicks or eating Cadbury's chocolate or smoking Gold Flake cigarettes, as happy, fulfilled and well fed as if a war had never happened. Though when the bus passed the new Cenotaph Samuel noticed all the men on the top deck doffed their hats in respect.

A familiar regret crept across him as he hurriedly followed suit. He had never thought he minded missing out on the war. Who would? But those who were born too late faced a different struggle.

He recalled one day in Egypt when a number of large statues were being removed from the tomb where they had been packaged, ready to be transported on rail tracks out of the Valley. Each figure had been carefully wrapped in bandages and placed on a stretcher to be ferried out of the tomb. As one by one a supine mummified figure was disgorged, it suddenly became impossible not to see how much the stretchered figures trailing their bandages resembled the casualties transported out of the trenches in France. With her unfailing ability to read his mind, Violet had reached forward to caress his shoulders and said: "I'm so glad you missed the war."

Samuel shook her hand off and moved away. He too had thought he was glad to miss the war. But at that moment he was struck with a sense of futility. For young men like him there remained only a drifting emptiness, a lack of purpose, a restless searching for meaning. What good would he ever do with his life? By what brave gesture would he ever find fulfilment?

He had sent a note to the address he had kept and was delighted when he received a letter back saying that Alan Collins was still living there. Alan too had abandoned draughtsmanship and was now, of all things, a journalist.

The house was in a cramped terrace in one of the narrow

Georgian streets of Bloomsbury. As Samuel looked up at the first floor window he felt a momentary spasm of nostalgia, recalling the evenings he had spent there with Alan and a group of his friends, putting the world to rights and doing justice to a great deal of beer.

Alan flung open the door with his old urgency and seized Samuel in a delighted handshake. He looked gaunter and had gained a little goatee beard and a pair of round spectacles, which enhanced his professorial appearance, though his clothes made Samuel self-conscious of the new trilby, tweed jacket and flannels in which he had invested his earnings.

"My God! You do look the part."

Alan pulled on his ancient army greatcoat and they set off for the local pub. Settled in a comfortable corner, with their pints before them, they caught up with each other's lives and within an hour it was as though he had never been away. Alan knew all about the political situation in Egypt and instead of endlessly talking about the treasures or the curse, he asked the kind of questions no one else ever thought to ask.

"What do the natives think about their treasure being parcelled up by English imperialists?"

"Well they're not. Not any more. There's a new regime. The treasures are going to the Cairo Museum."

"That's what they say."

"It's regulated and the situation is very closely monitored."

"But do we believe it? I wonder how much of it goes missing."

"You're talking about stealing?"

"Exactly."

"Well historically it's the Arabs who've been the ones to steal from tombs. They've always stolen to order whenever collectors require it."

"That's inevitable. They're the pawns in a system propped up by the collectors in Europe."

"America, more like. I'd say the bulk of anything sold has been going to America since the war. The British Museum can't compete any more."

Samuel fidgeted with his glass and answered tersely but Alan was not to be put off.

"What about the nationalist tensions? Did you see much of it out there? The resentment is riding high, I heard. And there's anger over the occupation of the Sudan. How did your people on the dig get on with the Arabs?"

"The British don't have much to do with Arabs apart from give them orders. They don't exactly get invited to cocktail parties."

"No fraternising with the natives?"

"Something like that."

Alan leant back and scrutinised him quizzically.

"So that doesn't explain it then."

"Explain what?"

"Why you came back of course! You decide on the spur of the moment to become an archaeologist and have the luck to find yourself working on the most significant archaeological find for decades. You're taken on by Howard Carter himself. You're right in the centre of the action. Anyone else would give their eye teeth to be in your shoes. But you up sticks right in the middle of the proceedings, before they've even opened the mummy case and take a job with Elmer Barrington of all people. Why?"

Samuel kept his eyes on his beer, fighting a sudden compulsion to tell his friend everything that had happened.

"I was offered this job, and it seemed the right thing to do."

"Well it might be a useful thing for me. Barrington's an interesting character. Ripe for a little journalistic scrutiny, I suspect. But what on earth does he want with you?"

It was a question Samuel had repeatedly asked himself over the past few weeks, but now he was irked at Alan's tone and answered a little stiffly,

"I'm working on his new building."

"Ah! Barrington's Pandemonium! I've heard about this. What's it like?"

"Incredible. No expense spared."

"What is it about these plutocrats that they want to leave monuments to themselves? As if posterity will overlook their other deeds."

Samuel felt obscurely disloyal discussing Barrington like this. He decided to change the subject.

"So how about you? Not married yet, I see."

"Huh." Alan gave an embarrassed cough.

"Too busy for all that?"

"Yes and no. There is someone. At the magazine."

"Ah ha! You were keeping her secret. What's she like?" Now it was Alan's turn to appear evasive.

"She has a good mind."

"A good mind!" Samuel repeated.

"Well *fairly* good." Alan frowned. "But anyway, I'm too busy for much of a social life right now. It's a great responsibility being a journalist when your country is standing at a cross-roads."

From there he went smoothly on to the pressing subject of Labour relations and the trade unions. He'd recently joined the British Communist party. To Alan, Communism looked like the only hope now that Britain was becoming ever more divided.

"It's a class war we have now, no doubt about it. Between the workers and the capitalists. Society is divided, morally and economically, between the producers and the non-producers. It's a terrible situation."

"Terrible?" Samuel was bemused. "But everything's going swimmingly from your point of view, isn't it? I mean a Labour government and so on."

Alan pulled at his little goatee beard and pursed his lips.

"Oh that. It won't last. You wouldn't believe the forces out to destroy it. Look at the upper classes. The war's already forced them to sell their land and their country houses and their art. They already feel impoverished and frightened. Now they're genuinely terrified of the overthrow of the existing social order by revolutionaries. They'll do anything to bring down the socialist cause. You've heard all these scare stories they're putting round about a financial crash? The upper classes will engineer one if they have to."

"A crash? Now that I really can't believe. The economy's better than it's ever been."

Samuel regarded Alan's earnest face. The conspiracies he saw around him – whether about Barrington, or the English upper classes, were just as murky and far-fetched as the occult doings people ascribed to the Egyptian tomb. And they were wrong, weren't they? Surely they were wrong.

"Either a crash or another war. As soon as we've forgotten the last one."

Samuel lit a cigarette and said mildly: "I really can't imagine anyone is likely to forget the war."

"Oh no?" Alan gave a bitter, little laugh. "Well we've already forgotten the wounded. Thousands of them in asylums and special hospitals, tucked out of sight and abandoned. Ruined by shell-shock. Sitting there with injuries which no one can see and no one really knows how to treat. They're not the dead, they're the undead and they frighten us so we bury them and try to forget, while they rot their lives away. I'm doing a piece about them actually. A special issue. We're going to call it The Forgotten."

He broke off emotionally and they both stared at their beer for a while, before Alan said in brighter tones: "So where are you living?"

"With Mr Barrington actually, in his home."

"You're living with him?" Alan was incredulous.

"Well yes."

"But God. How awful for you. Permanently?"

"Oh no, it's entirely temporary. I'm supposed to be looking for digs."

He knew he ought to move. By now he should have been

looking around for a room to rent, somewhere cheap, in the suburban fringes of London. But so far he had made no effort. Why did he stay? Was it to luxuriate in the comfort of Barrington's hospitality after the strictures of Egypt? Or was it to indulge a growing curiosity in his daughter?

"You're living cheek by jowl with the man?"

"Him and Iris, yes. But it's not exactly cheek by jowl. It's a huge great place for just the two of them."

"Well we can't leave you there." Alan raked his hands through his hair distractedly. "Look I've got the answer. You can move in with me."

"That's a kind offer."

"There's plenty of room."

He thought of the airless attic space which served as a spare bedroom in Alan's flat. Sometimes, after an evening of drinking, he had collapsed there, trying hard not to topple the haphazard stacks of books and packing cases.

"Well I appreciate the offer. Do you mind if I don't give you an answer now?"

"Of course. There are no other takers at the moment."

No, he thought, he didn't suppose there were.

Chapter Eleven

It was Saturday morning and he was sitting in the morning room reading the newspaper in a slice of warm sunshine when he saw a headline that made his heart miss a beat. "*Mr Carter's Bombshell*" the report said. Looking closer he found that Carter, who had just departed for a lecture tour of America, had issued a writ issued against the great Empire Exhibition at Wembley for its exhibit of Tutankhamun's tomb. There was no way, Carter said, that his excavation could ever be accurately recreated. Nobody, let alone an exhibition, could ever properly record what they had found when they opened the tomb.

Samuel put the paper down and breathed slowly to calm himself. Only he and Carter knew just how true that was.

* * *

By the end of April Carnarvon's body had been shipped to England for burial and a pall of gloom hung over the dig. Carter came back to Luxor but he made no further reference to having encountered Samuel in Cairo. Nor did he mention again anything to do with coffin texts. He still raged at the tourists, and had fresh invective for those who now muttered that the excavation had been cursed. Any naïve sightseer unwise enough to mention such an idea in his hearing was treated to a torrent of withering disdain. Everyone kept their heads down, trying to accomplish as much as they could in the debilitating heat. So it was a relief when Violet said: "Do you remember that friend I was telling you about? Well he's invited us to dinner."

Rather than the Winter Palace or one of the places in Luxor the expatriates frequented, she gave him the address of a local house and he followed her directions down the narrow, dirt streets at the heart of the city. The alleys, which in the daytime lay quiet as sleeping cats in the sun, came alive in the evenings with music, lamps and people. At the address he had been given he pushed open a door of wrought iron entwined with jasmine vines and stepped into a courtyard filled with mango trees and palms. Violet was sitting at a table in the company of a handsome, dark-eyed man in a spotless gelabiyah.

"Samuel, I want you to meet a dear friend of mine. This is Husni."

The Egyptian stood and bowed graciously. His English was almost unaccented. His face was solemn and oval, the mouth framed by a moustache. It was the most ancient kind of Egyptian face, with the straight nose, full lips and pale skin of the earliest natives, markedly different from the darker Sudanese or those of Turkish and Syrian descent. He seemed not much older than Samuel himself.

"Violet has told me about you."

At a flick of his hand, the houseboy stepped forward to offer them glasses of lime juice. When it was time to eat they went into the house, a dark space full of antique silver and oriental rugs, with gleaming woodwork and the scent of rich, indefinable perfumes. The dishes were spiced with flavours both familiar and strange - cardamom, cumin, jasmine, almond and coriander. There was fried fish with anchovy sauce, red lentil stew, grilled pigeon and bitter little cucumbers followed by dishes of apricots, sweet pastries and coffee.

Quickly they found themselves talking politics. Samuel had always enjoyed political debate, but this was very different from Alan Collins's angry rhetoric in the pub. Husni's politics seemed urgent and practical and rooted in the possibility of real change. For the first time Samuel began to see the world from a different perspective, one in which ordinary people could make a difference simply through what they believed. He saw a different Egypt from the three thousand year old version he sketched every day in the Valley. The Egypt Husni represented was a country waking up from its own history.

Husni was a fervent nationalist, a follower of the popular leader Said Zaghul Pasha, who had led demonstrations in the streets for the country's independence. He talked animatedly of old empires crumbling and new ones rising in their place, of his hopes for the new independent state and the ancient dignity of his people reasserting itself. His voice was low and dignified but his plans were violent - one day soon a Muslim brotherhood would rise to purge his country of foreigners "always excepting," he said with a deferential wave towards Samuel and Violet, "our honoured guests. For to Muslims hospitality is a religious duty."

Husni was especially exercised about his neighbours in the Sudan and their anger that the country should remain under British control. Husni had friends there who had been inspired by Egyptian nationalism to demand their own self-determination. They had no interest in the continuation of British rule, Husni said. British policy in the Sudan was based on divide and rule, and all the best land was appropriated for British companies.

"But is the Sudan ready for self-rule?" asked Violet languidly. "Their own government doesn't seem to think so."

"All I say is that if the Sudanese need to be guided to independence then they should be able to choose their own guide, be it the British or the Egyptians. We Egyptians have spent too much of our history under the yoke of a foreign oppressor not to help a brother nation which seeks self-determination."

Samuel was mystified by the precise nature of Violet's relationship with Husni. They appeared to know each other well, yet her naturally demonstrative physical gestures, her habit of stroking and petting the men she liked, seemed notably restrained towards him. He decided that Husni was no sexual escapade but more an example of her astute opportunism. Husni and his colleagues surely represented the future of Egypt and it was becoming clear that any Europeans who intended to stay and do business may need to ingratiate themselves with an entirely new political establishment. If Violet was to carry on any kind of trade in antiquities, her best hope lay in cultivating Egyptians. For his part Husni seemed to regard Violet with a kind of amused tolerance.

"How about you Violet? How have you been occupying yourself?"

"I went to Castle Carter just the other day. He showed me the King's cup. You must have seen it Samuel? I told you Husni, Samuel is one of Mr Carter's favourites."

Samuel had seen the cup some months ago, when he had visited Carter's home to deliver a sketch of a small statue of Bes, the dwarf god with his knife and his musical instrument. The Wishing Cup, as some called it was an alabaster goblet of remarkable thinness, inscribed in exquisite detail with the maker's dedication to the young king. *"May your spirit live, may you spend millions of years, you who love Thebes, in the cool winds of the north with your eyes beholding happiness."* It was one of the most beautiful things he had ever seen.

"I did see it, yes. Carter had it in his house for closer inspection."

"Closer inspection?" said Husni sourly. "Is that what he calls it? And how much else has he taken home from the tomb?"

Violet laughed. "Oh, who can say? Everyone has a different rumour. Have you heard the one about the three aeroplanes which landed in the valley and took off loaded with treasure?"

"I have, and I've heard the one about the ladies who have left the tomb with parcels of jewels hidden under their skirts. And the king's head concealed in a crate of Fortnum and Mason red wine."

Violet gave her gravelly laugh and reached across the table to touch his hand lightly with her fingertips.

"Husni! You sound as though you believe those stories. You look so serious."

"I am serious. And I do believe it. This country - not to mention the whole of the ancient world - has been systematically robbed by excavators. The Europeans and Americans think nothing of plundering our sacred sites for their pleasure and with no respect for their hosts. Look at Schliemann's excavation of Troy. He allowed his wife to wear the famous jewels of Priam as if they were her own. The Germans were just as bad in 1913 when they found the head of Queen Nefertiti at Tell-el-Amarna. They had it back to Berlin like a shot, without telling anyone. Anyone would think the whole world exists merely for its treasures to be brought back to the *civilised* nations of Europe."

"But," Samuel protested limply, "things *are* different since the war. The law has changed. Excavators no longer have the same rights to keep their finds. There are all sorts of arrangements and safeguards in place."

"Oh yes." Husni's tone had become more heavily sardonic. "Perhaps the law has changed. Perhaps excavators are no longer unlicensed treasure seekers with a right to a share of the spoils. But unfortunately the finer points of our antiquities law seem to be lost on your Mr Carter. After all he's been doing a roaring trade in selling antiquities for years now. Cups, statues, jewellery. Where do they all come from? I suppose he doesn't see the difference. Nor does he question those notorious tomb robbers with whom he has quite openly done business."

Samuel was taken aback by his anger.

"He was a dealer in antiquities, yes, but he has also spent years of his time and quite a fortune actually finding the tomb," he volunteered.

"Who asked him to?" said Husni. "He thinks he can fool us

all. Look at that farcical opening of the burial chamber."

The official opening of the burial chamber in February had been a grand affair. Huge energy was expended on the protocol and seating arrangements and the narrow track to the Valley was crammed with Egyptian notables in red tarbouches, eunuchs in frock coats and dragomans in bright silk robes. All the dignitaries sat fanning themselves on cane chairs in the heat, like an audience gathered to witness the appearance of a theatrical star, who would not, of course, be appearing.

Husni gave a mirthless laugh. "Does anyone actually believe that was the first time Carter had actually been in there?"

Samuel busied himself with his sheesha pipe. "What do you mean?"

"Well you don't honestly think these men waited months to see the most important part of their discovery, the Holy of Holies? That after they discovered the tomb, they simply failed to look in the burial chamber straight away? My God, no-one could believe that. Carter and Carnarvon accessed that chamber almost as soon as they opened the tomb. I have it on good authority. Everyone knows that the best, most precious treasures will lie next to the body of the king. Are they just going to leave it there, unopened or unexplored, while they go off to sleep a sound night in their beds? Is that really credible? Or is it more likely that they come back at nightfall, when everyone else has gone, and explore the innermost secrets of the burial chamber at leisure?"

For a moment Samuel could not speak. A rush of nausea had brought the memory of that moonless night back to him. He saw again the solemn swearing to secrecy as Howard Carter took a hammer and chisel to the sealed door, and how the air in the narrow chamber was so still and thick that he felt it might ripple as he moved his hand. Holding his breath, afraid to inhale the spirit of the long dead boy, as though the atoms of evaporated flesh might dance again in the suspended dust. He saw himself hesitate at the doorway to the Treasury chamber and he felt again the brush of something malign, inexplicable, which reared up and sucked the life from him. He remembered his panicky flight, stumbling back up the Valley, leaving the others to pore over the treasures of the dead king.

"Why would they do that?" he asked.

"Because Carter and co. wanted to help themselves to the choicest treasures within."

"That's not true!" Samuel exclaimed.

"Oh, of course they did! Perhaps only a few things, just those things that took their fancy, that were small enough to carry. The odd jewel box. A pendant. Rings. Perhaps Mr Carter was asked to look after them, merely, for his patron Lord Carnarvon. Who has, as you so rightly pointed out, spent a fortune on the tomb and would like a return. Here is the perfect opportunity. Who will miss these little objects? No one. Because no one knows what was there."

Violet stretched her arms above her luxuriantly, so that a cascade of silver bangles slid down her white wrists.

"I was rather hoping he'd find a little keepsake for me actually. I remember everyone who visited Leonard Woolley's excavations at Ur went home with a little something. A going home present. Really Husni, is that so bad?"

"It's bad because these treasures are our own. They're our patrimony. You people have to understand that the world doesn't exist for the benefit of Europe. Our treasures should not be brought to light for Europe's entertainment. We're on the cusp of a fresh beginning here."

It was late when they finally made their way home, Violet's tall figure shrouded in flapping, crumpled linen and her long feet shod in sturdy boots. She gave Samuel a piercing look and said:

"So what did you make of Husni then? He's over emotional of course, that's the way of his people, but rather a…

magnetic personality, don't you think?"

Samuel merely grunted noncommittally. Stirred and excited by the meeting, he was still puzzling out the effect it had had on him. That void within him, that lacked any purpose or passion, was now filled with Husni's words. His mind buzzed with the force of Husni's argument. If he was right, if the British were shamefully and illicitly plundering the treasures of the Egyptian nation for themselves, then what was Samuel doing here at all?

By May the season was over and the Valley was left to its dead. Nothing would be done until autumn when the digging began again. The swarms of newspapermen departed the terrace of the Winter Palace Hotel and the deluge of wealthy tourists in sun hats and dark glasses with their hectic circuit of balls and dances and sports, were gone. The boats on the Nile sailed away with their American flags, and the whole raucous, excitable atmosphere evaporated in the searing summer heat. Husni took to inviting Samuel on his own.

It was impossible to express how much Samuel enjoyed being welcomed for an evening into the peace of a traditional Arab home, to eat and then play chess, or smoke in the cooling garden, sometimes with some of Husni's brothers and friends, sometimes alone.

Yet instinctively he also knew to keep these visits quiet, even from Violet herself. Once she arrived while Samuel was in the garden and he and Husni watched shaking with suppressed laughter as the Nubian servant sent her away.

"I think I will wait for Mr al-Khalid," she told him in her commanding tones. Weakly the Nubian flapped her away.

"Meeeses Esterhazy. I tell you. Master is out."

"No. I am absolutely certain he would like to see me. If you would just let me in."

"Master say no-one must come in."

Samuel felt flattered and gratified that Husni preferred his company alone.

These times with Husni were the most precious he spent in Egypt and they excited and unsettled him in equal proportions. Although the two men were about the same age, and could talk for hours without stopping, Husni seemed infinitely more mature and purposeful. He felt intimately involved in the future of his country, and was endlessly engineering activities like rallies and market-place talks and private meetings with a small cabal of nationalists from which Samuel was politely excluded. Beside him Samuel felt louche and immature, idling away his life waiting for events to over-take him.

One day Husni said: "Why don't you stay here, Samuel, and make Egypt your home? I mean it. It's a serious proposal. There is nothing to keep you in England, is there? And you could help in our great struggle."

Samuel laughed. "How could I help the cause of Egyptian nationalism?"

"Oh we would find a way," smiled Husni, clapping him on the back.

* * *

These thoughts were interrupted by a soft voice behind him and he turned hastily.

"Your evenings have been very full lately."

Iris had come up behind him so softly that he'd noticed nothing, but at the sound of her voice he jumped as if he'd been stung. Folding the newspaper to conceal the report about Carter, he stood up, swiftly regaining his composure.

"Hello. Yes, I've been quite busy."

Judging by her demeanour it would have been impossible to tell that Iris had not once addressed him, other than in sullen response to a direct question, since the evening of the Simonsons' party. She came across the room and perched on the green silk arm of a chair, crossing her legs. She looked unusually pretty. She was wearing a peach dress with a schoolgirl collar and looked at him from beneath her lashes in a way that signalled to Samuel immediately that she wanted something of him. His senses tingled at the sight of her.

"Are you enjoying your stay here?"

"Very much. It's very kind of your father."

He looked at her curiously, challenging her to tell him what she really wanted, but Iris continued as if for all the world the two of them were in the habit of indulging in the normal friendly chat between guest and hostess. She bent down and ruffled her little dog, which had followed her in and was sniffing adenoidally at his feet. Then she pulled out a cigarette from her bag. He leant forward with his silver lighter. If Iris wanted to play games with him, then he was only too happy to oblige her.

"I suppose you're meeting up with all your old friends. I expect there are loads of people you need to catch up with."

He smiled. "Well your father keeps me working pretty hard, most of the time."

"All the more reason for you to be able to relax here. You've really made yourself at home, haven't you? Shall I ring for more coffee?" She looked pointedly down at the tray the maid had brought in for him, with its silver coffee pot and a plate of biscuits.

"I'm fine thank you."

He looked at her expectantly, forcing her to come out with it. She wanted something, of that he was sure. He didn't fool himself that she had suddenly succumbed to a desire for his conversation.

She hesitated, picked up a magazine and riffled it, and then:

"Considering you're so busy, I suppose you'll be all booked up next weekend?"

"I'll have to check. Why do you ask?"

"There's something I'm going to. A ball, which might be fun. My father did ask me to find some events to distract

you. Introduce you to people, that sort of thing."
He leant against the mantelpiece with his hands in his pockets and smiled at her.

"Well that's just another example of your father's extreme consideration, but he doesn't need to worry. I'm quite capable of looking after my social life by myself."

"I didn't doubt it," she said tartly. "Someone like you. I'm sure you're hugely in demand."

"Oh I am."

"Well I'm sorry if I presumed…." A frown puckered the perfect surface of her face and she turned suddenly as if to leave the room. Aware that he was losing her, he came quickly across the room to her and reached out a hand to her shoulder.

"Wait a minute. You might as well tell me what this ball is that you're going to."

She lingered. "It's the Heart of the Empire ball. For the Empire Exhibition, you know."

He did know. The ball was to be a showpiece event at the Albert Hall, attended by the cream of society, a gathering that did not normally include himself.

"Sounds exciting."

"It might be."

Suddenly, he wanted to laugh. To restrain himself, he bent down and petted the odious little dog. "Hello old chap." The animal reciprocated by baring its yellow teeth.

"The thing is…" Iris was getting impatient. She had not imagined this would take so long. "I was wondering if you'd like to escort me?"

Samuel stood up again and hesitated. Iris was so close to him he was aware of her warmth, and the sweet, musky scent of her perfume. He could see a tiny mole on her neck and a scatter of freckles at the base of her throat. For a second he allowed himself to savour the surprising vision of Iris importuning him, before saying:

"Well it's very kind of you to think of me and I'd be

honoured."

"Good," she said shortly. "It's on Saturday night. Shall we leave at about eight?"

And with that she walked quickly from the room, leaving the glow of Samuel's little psychological victory to fade as he wondered exactly what she wanted of him.

Chapter Twelve

"What is it about Ursula Davis? You realise you've been pestering me about her for the past half hour?"

"I'm curious, that's all," said Esther, resting her arm along the window sill and looking into the street below.

The meeting with Ursula Davis had had the most peculiar effect on Esther. She couldn't get the woman out of her mind. Even Alice, who had originally suggested that the two might get along, was beginning to bridle at her endless questions. Who was Ursula's lover? What did her family think of the prospect of their daughter becoming an unmarried mother? Was she planning to marry the father? Could Alice lend Esther a copy of Ursula's book? The intensity of her friend's interest produced a graceless disgruntlement in Alice, which she did little to disguise.

Esther had taken a packet of digestive biscuits to the Chelsea studio, where Alice was painting her in three quarter profile as part of a large canvas which she planned to submit for her finals. The studio was a large, light-filled room, with no furniture except a plum velvet sofa but every wall crammed with an array of paintings and sketches. Some of them were Alice's preparatory pen and ink sketches of Esther, a display that might once have made her self-conscious, but by now her only thought was that whereas Alice was eating biscuits, she herself had been forced to sit on the window seat completely motionless for half an hour, despite a rumbling stomach.

Alice continued: "The thing about Ursula is, she may be very sophisticated intellectually but in many ways, she's rather immature. That's what's landed her in this situation. I mean free love is all very well, but there are other people to be considered."

Ursula's present predicament arose from her meeting

with William Fogerty, a well known man of letters, a good twenty years older than she was, with whom she had fallen passionately in love.

"So it was love at first sight?" For Esther that condition was an article of faith. She herself had never herself fallen in love, due to the shortage of suitable candidates, but was sure that when the man she would marry arrived in her life, she would know it instantly. Love at first sight was obvious. A person's qualities would surely need to be very well hidden for you to discover them only after time.

"Yes. A *coup de foudre* was how Ursula described it," said Alice mordantly. "More *fou* than *foudre* I would have said where Fogerty is concerned."

Certainly Fogerty was an unlikely seducer. He was short and portly, with a round, florid face, thick glasses and a dithering, mole-like demeanour. A narrow fringe of moustache skimmed his upper lip and he had a curious, nervous habit of clearing his throat, which swiftly grated on the nerves. Yet the liaison did not entirely astound onlookers, partly because Fogerty was daring and brilliant and seductive on the page, and partly because he had already enjoyed a series of affairs with younger women.

"So how did it start?" asked Esther, taking a bite of biscuit and trying to crumble it without moving her jaw.

"If you'll stay still for long enough, I'll tell you."

Fogerty admired Ursula's writing, and she his. Their mutual admiration led to a number of expeditions of an entirely respectable nature, culminating in a morning spent enthusiastically touring the National Gallery, at which, in a room devoted to Renaissance Madonnas, Ursula declared her passion. Fogerty did, to his credit, explain that he was and intended to remain happily married, but the reason for that happiness was the fact that his ageing, undemanding wife, a comfortably non-intellectual woman, tended to object very little to his affairs. Quickly and predictably he and Ursula became lovers, and soon afterwards Ursula discovered she was pregnant.

"Weren't they taking any….precautions?" asked Esther, for whom the intricacies of prophylactics, pessaries and gels was a grey area.

"He usually did, but Ursula says that passion overcame them. They'd been in his study, reading through some of his past book reviews, which must have been quite an aphrodisiac, as you can imagine," said Alice dryly. "But neither of them wanted a child, you can be sure of that."

"When is the child.. I mean is it quite advanced?"

"Oh yes. She's concealed it very well. There are only a few weeks to go."

"And what will she do then? I mean, how will she cope? How will people treat her?"

"With their usual heartfelt narrow mindedness, I suppose. Fogerty's renting her a place, a house in south London, and she's supposed to be hiding out there until after the baby's born to avoid more scandal. Coming here the other night was an exception. She knew my mother is not the sort to indulge in meaningless hypocrisy."

"Poor Ursula. She must be so worried. I mean I'd be distraught."

"Ah, but Ursula's not you. She's not distraught at all. She's tremendously high minded and really doesn't care too much what people think about her. She also has a huge faith in her capacity to cope. She says she'll get along quite comfortably with her writing and she's been asked to do some pieces for the wireless. Besides, she'll have the child adopted, so really, it's only a problem in the short term."

"But could she really bear the have the baby taken away?" asked Esther, in wonder.

"Oh, I don't know," snapped Alice, erasing an errant line on her sketch just a little too roughly. "Why don't you ask her yourself? She's coming here in a few days' time. I want to paint her while she is so fantastically bulbous. I'm sure she wouldn't mind if you came along."

In the time that she had been living at the flat, Esther had managed quite successfully to avoid meeting Dr Stevens. He was nearly always out and when he was in, he had absolutely no visitors, other than the odd patient. He appeared to be devoid of family and friends. From her conversations with Mrs Bennett, Esther had discovered that the doctor worked in the East End of London, which was why he left so early, before she stirred from bed, and didn't return until eight o'clock.

But that Friday he knocked on her door and asked if she would like to join him for supper, and the element of surprise meant she was too flustered to refuse. She was used to having supper out, or on a tray in the comfort of her flat. She was still relishing the bliss of her own privacy, away from the churning bustle of Chalcott Street. Instead, he led her into the narrow little dining room, its dark green wallpaper hung with murky Victorian landscapes and pictures of cattle and ships. The greenish glow of the lamp enhanced the sense of subterranean gloom. Dr Stevens brought in a dish of steaming macaroni cheese, served her, and proceeded to eat in silence, so Esther, whose nature abhorred a vacuum of conversation, launched into an account of the Noël Coward play *The Vortex* she had seen the previous night. She was in the midst of detailing pretty much the entire plot, when he interrupted.

"Your father asked me to keep an eye on you, but I don't believe your private life is any business of mine and I told him so." Stevens sighed. "But we're due to be dining at his club next week, so I really should have something to say. How's your art work? Keeping you busy?"

It wasn't thankfully. Esther had just spent the afternoon drifting in and out of Peter Robinson and Marshall and Snelgrove, admiring hats and gloves and scarves. The hat she had finally committed to, thirty shillings' worth of pink felt with two ostrich feathers springing from the side, sat upstairs in its box. She had been about to try it on again when Dr Stevens had knocked on her door.

"I've been very busy, yes. It's the final year, so we're all working on the area that interests us most."

"And what interests you most?"

"Well my choice is rather unusual. I'm preparing a series of cartoons."

He raised an eyebrow.

"They're based on political affairs."

He smiled thinly. "Somehow I'd never seen you as a political animal."

Esther's cheeks flushed with annoyance.

"Well perhaps you don't know me well enough."

"I'm sure I don't." He continued eating, then with somewhat exaggerated politeness enquired: "And which particular political affairs have you been illustrating?"

She hesitated. The other evening at Alice's home had brought a number of ideas to her mind. In particular the angry conversation about the two writers, Eliot and Joyce, and their respective rights to be regarded as geniuses, had inspired her to a cartoon in which T.S. Eliot and James Joyce held a boxing match, Eliot tall and proper in his pin-striped suit and homburg, Joyce short and shabby, with his sleeves rolled up. When she described it Dr Stevens was less derisive than she expected.

"Interesting idea. Personally I think Joyce's writing is incomparable, but I can understand some people may find it shocking. Perhaps in my field of work I'm used to seeing humanity in the raw. I haven't got hold of this latest book yet but I've read the rest of his work and I don't find it degrading. Not in the least. I find it dignifying. But what… you look surprised?"

Esther had been regarding him, startled. "Somehow I hadn't seen you as a literary animal."

He looked irritated for a moment, then his expression softened and he laughed. "Touché. I do try to keep up. So tell me about this magazine you contribute to. What sort of thing does it contain?"

"Political articles mainly. And a lot about international events."

"Do you get a lot of readers?"

"Not really. The editor, Alan, says we shouldn't focus primarily on the number of readers we have. Our chief focus should be the integrity of our ideas," said Esther, watching regretfully as Stevens finished up the macaroni. "He's keen to revolutionise society."

"Is he now? Oh well, never mind." Stevens yawned and pinched the bridge of his nose in a gesture of fatigue. "You must forgive me. It's been a long day. But Mrs Bennett's cooking goes some way to making up for it. Let's see what we have for pudding."

He got up and fetched a rhubarb crumble, golden on the top and oozing pink juice, which had been left to heat in the oven. There was also a little jug of warm custard.

"Oh let me do that, Dr Stevens." Esther jumped up to serve it, glad of a distraction.

He gave way and sat back in his chair, smoothing his hands across his face. "Oh for heaven's sake Esther. I spend all day being Dr Stevens, do call me Frank."

Esther knew there was no possibility that she would ever call him Frank. She searched for another topic of conversation.

"Is your work very exhausting?"

"Exhausting?" He glanced up at her briefly. "I don't know. It's all relative I suppose. If you compared my life with that of one of my patients, say a mother of five whose husband is laid up with gas in the lungs and whose child is coughing because the house is so damp and she's having to take on work in the evenings to make ends meet, I suppose my existence might appear pretty leisured. And at least I'm not encumbered with offspring."

What distaste lay in that single word "encumbered"! He disliked children, that was plain, and it did not surprise her in the slightest. She felt genuinely sorry for his patients. Doctors were supposed to be gentle, caring figures but it was impossible to picture crabby Dr Stevens with his abrupt manner ministering tenderly to the sick. Doubtless he would just as be rude and impatient with them as he was with everyone else.

"Excuse me for asking, but exactly what made you become a doctor?"

"You might say that coming from a medical family, I simply suffered a striking lack of imagination."

That didn't really seem to answer her question, but he seemed to be always like that, evasive and mocking, twisting her words.

"Oh. I see."

"I doubt you do." He collected their plates with a clatter and rose from the table. "But enough of that. Thank you very much for joining me. I should be getting on with a report I'm working on, and you're probably wanting your beauty sleep."

She fled upstairs, as fast as was decently possible.

The following day, the morning of the Empire exhibition, she was up at seven. She had decided to lurk in the hall by the umbrella stand, so Dr Stevens would not have to open the door to Alan, but as luck would have it as she came downstairs the doctor was there already, packing his briefcase. He glanced up in surprise.

"You're up early."

"I'm going to the Empire Exhibition. I've been asked to do a report about it. Using my own illustrations."

He paused, with what looked like a bandage in his hand. "I say, that sounds fascinating. Do you have to leave so soon?"

"I wanted to get in as much as possible. Apparently there are far too many exhibits to see all in one day."

"So I heard. You know, I'd rather like to accompany you.

I was planning to go myself. But there's just a little job I have to do first. It's an elderly lady, she only lives round the corner. I'm just dressing her leg, it won't take more than half an hour. What do you say, we go together? "

"Well the thing is, I mean that's very kind of you to offer, but.."

The bell shrilled loudly in the narrow hallway and they both looked at the door to see the shape of Alan adumbrated behind the stained-glass panels.

"You already have an escort."

"It's just Alan Collins. He's the editor of…"

"Forgive me for presuming then." He said shortly. "Have a good day."

Dr Stevens opened the door, greeted Alan peremptorily and ducked round him into the street, pulling his overcoat on as he went. Esther could not help but feel immensely relieved.

"Ouch. You want to be more careful, young man. That hurts."

"Sorry."

"Well just try to be a little gentler if you would."

Of the many joyless tasks which jostled for space in his life, this was proving to be more than usually thankless. Frank Stevens was deeply regretting his generosity in helping an elderly lady in her hour of need. Especially as this old lady had turned out to be particularly ungrateful. He had come across her that week when she was getting off the bus, the stop before his own, and had stumbled and fallen heavily onto the pavement, gashing the shin. He had helped her hobble back to her flat - up four painful flights of stairs - and explained that he was a doctor and could give her leg a quick examination, fully expecting her to refuse because old ladies like this were usually excessively modest. But instead she agreed at once, whipped off her stocking and flopped into a chair with her leg up and what was more, suggested that as he lived so near he could perhaps drop back when the dressing needed replacing. Now, upright and irritable, her leg propped on a footstool, she had already directed him to the kitchen to make her a cup of tea before submitting to antiseptic lotion and a new bandage. He did the job deftly, in a matter of minutes, reminding himself that she might be in pain.

"I think that'll do it. It's a superficial wound, not much more. Keep it elevated but if this bit of swelling continues it would be best to contact your own physician."

"Oh there's no need for that young man. I'll be right as rain in a few days and you can come by again to take it off. Of course if this is all too much trouble for you…"

"No. Of course it's not too much trouble."

Yes it was! It was Saturday! His one free day of the week. The old woman's cat, an overfed Persian, had begun to poke its head in his bag and he shooed the animal off. The old lady didn't like that, either.

"I'd thank you not to speak roughly to him, young man. Tinker is a very timid creature."

That was another thing. Her insistence on calling him "young man". He didn't feel especially young today. He felt old. With a wince of angry embarrassment he thought of Esther, gallivanting off to the Empire Exhibition with her male friend, and himself last night, so rude and abrupt at the dinner table. But then she probably hadn't given him a second thought.

He finished the dressing and rose. He had the rest of the day to do whatever he chose. Then tomorrow was Sunday, and on Sunday, he thought with a slightly sinking feeling, he would do what he always did.

Chapter Thirteen

"Three thousand years of civilisation and they all look the same," said Barrington, as he surveyed the sketch Samuel had just finished illustrating the hundred near-identical shabti servants accompanying the king in his procession to the underworld. They were in the entrance lobby of Barrington House, where eventually Samuel would reproduce the figures in a frieze to run along the top of the majestic atrium. He sat back on his heels and did not answer. "But then," mused Barrington. "I suppose there's not much to choose between them. They're all untrustworthy, the Arabs."

What could Samuel possibly reply? There was nothing unusual about Barrington's views. He had thought the same himself to start with. He recalled his own nervous reading of Baedeker as he journeyed out to Egypt: *The average oriental regards the European traveller as a Croesus and feels justified in pressing upon him with a perpetual demand for bakshish."*

"Intimate acquaintance with orientals is to be avoided, especially with the dragomans who sometimes presume on their opportunity of social intercourse."

Those sentiments were amply echoed in the voices round the Winter Palace Hotel who loved nothing better than disparaging the natives or the gyppies, as all the expatriates called them. He recalled overhearing a group of ladies discussing an Egyptian driver who was suspected of making eyes at the youngest and least ugly of them. Her voice, rich with Home Counties horror.

"I couldn't ever think a gyppie attractive. They look so peculiar. That swarthy skin and darting eyes. I mean they're not *like* us, are they?"

The British did their very best to replicate England in the

harsh Egyptian desert. The women staged gymkhanas, though they used donkeys instead of ponies, and they organised croquet matches, tea parties and charades. At breakfast they ate marmalade, at tea there were Huntley and Palmer biscuits and on Sunday they had roast beef. Few of them bothered to meet real Egyptians, beyond the dragomen and the house servants, and the only Arabic all of them knew was "*inshi*" which meant "be off".

"What about you?" said Barrington, looking down at him. "Did you ever get to know any of the natives personally?"

"Not really," said Samuel, putting his pencils away.

* * *

Given how much he admired Husni, it amazed him all the more that Husni was so curious about him. As they sat together, talking and drinking mint tea, or walked the town after the heat of the day, Husni would drape his arm round Samuel's shoulders in the easy way of Egyptian males. One day Husni took him to the *hamman*, the arab baths, with its smooth black and white marble floor, and domed roof that let in shafts of sunlight through the steam. As they sat side by side, sweating in the scented vapour, Husni questioned him tirelessly about his life, his childhood, his schooling, his parents, and his beliefs.

"So let me get this clear. In England, the father *shakes hands* with his little children? Like so, eh?"

Or "So the *public* school is a *private* school, and not at all open to the public. But your school was a grammar school. Is that good?"

And when Samuel was explaining that most English families were quite unlike the sprawling Egyptian model, and that he himself had no brothers or sisters, a look of consternation crossed Husni's face.

"But every man needs a brother Samuel. Think of me as your brother. Please."

No-one else had ever been that interested in him before and while he relished it, Samuel could not help but laugh at the torrent of questions.

"What's so fascinating about my life? Why should you care about the customs and behaviour of a colonial power that you profess to despise?"

Husni's face grew uncharacteristically grave.

"It's true. But when you have been dominated by a colonial power, you come to see yourself from another's perspective. You no longer know what you are to yourself. How do you think it feels to have you English come here and look at us, and not even us but our past, as though the British empire owns the past, whoever's past it happens to be?"

"Surely Egypt is a great enough civilisation to have its own identity?"

"Perhaps not. Not recently. But the world is changing and ideas are changing too. People like you can help us, Samuel."

"Now you're flattering me again," Samuel smiled, towelling the rivulets of sweat from his back. "Any particular way I can help chart the course of Egyptian civilisation?"

"I'm glad you asked." Husni adopted the same jocularity and pulled his moustache in mock mysterious vein. "Who knows? But perhaps an opportunity will arise."

Samuel laughed and sent a spray of icy water across Husni's smooth torso. But even as they joked, he realised that if ever Husni needed help, he would provide it. He had known him just a matter of months but he felt a connection with him that he had never felt for another human being.

One evening soon afterwards, they wandered away from the tourist area towards the poor, workers' quarter of Luxor. They passed down alleys wide enough for just one man to walk, glimpsing the entrances to dim, cloacal stairways and rooms where lanterns of patterned metal threw a yellow, speckled light. White robed men in sandals, or bare feet, passed silently or disappeared through heavy wooden doors, set with brass grilles. Smells of sandalwood and nutmeg and coffee wafted out on a thin breeze. Rounding a corner they found themselves in a square where a gaggle of men were standing around a speaker, a bearded young man with blazing eyes and a traditional red tarboosh, who stabbed his finger in the air as he spoke, his husky, youthful voice carrying high on the evening air. Though his speech was in incomprehensible to Samuel, his tone and the reciprocal gestures of the crowd clustered tightly around him were all too recognisable. They were agitated, simmering with anger and spoiling for a fight.

"What's happening?"

"Local business," said Husni, drawing him swiftly into the shadow of a shop front.

"No, tell me. I want to know."

"It's a political rally."

"What does he say?"

"Very well then. I shall translate for you. This man here is calling for a Moslem brotherhood," said Husni. "He is opposed to the separation of religion and state. He wants to free his country from the shackles of the West and regain respect for our own culture and history. We says we in Egypt need to close the gap between the idle elite and the impoverished masses and we can only do that if we reject British military control. He asks how dare the British offer us only partial independence? Why should our children grow up under the intolerable yoke of colonialism? He says Egyptians should take to the streets and oust the imperialist oppressors."

"I suppose you support these people Husni?"

"I hope very soon they will be supporting me!" smiled Husni, with the unquestioning confidence Samuel so admired.

He looked at all the tanned faces upturned to hear the speaker's message and for a moment they appeared to merge into one single, featureless mass, each face indiscriminate from the other. He thought of the numberless generations that had passed between these Egyptians and the stylised faces of their ancestors that he saw in the tomb paintings every day. Millennia had passed and yet how unchanged they seemed! Despite the wonders of their ancient civilisation, this dark sea of faces appeared to have no distinguishing characteristics or individuality. As the speaker paused the men began chanting, in harsh, guttural Arabic, their voices rising in unison, and a tremor of anxiety ran through him. He had never seen the locals like this before. Their usual demeanour when working at the dig, or in the hotels, was one of sulky subservience towards the Europeans, or, if one was determined to probe, a brooding resentment. Now he sensed a dark violence ripple through the crowd like a river. The nameless force that motivated them needed no language. He felt suddenly threatened and afraid.

At that moment a face in the crowd turned towards him and there was an angry murmur. A hand pointed him out and the whites of eyes glimmered in the dark. The voices became louder until one shout rose above the rest.

"We need to leave here," said Husni quickly.

"What are they saying?"

"They recognise you from the excavation. They think you are spying on their meeting. They say that British intelligence has packed the town with spies. They are talking of the British tomb-robbers and they want a fight. Go before me and quickly. I will protect you."

He began to run. Casting a look backwards he saw a single face detach itself from the mass. It was Carter's water boy regarding him with his dark, watchful eyes.

They hurried through the shuttered streets until they reached the banks of the Nile and stopped beneath a palm grove.

"They're wrong to call the British tomb-robbers," panted Samuel, attempting to regain some dignity. "Mr Carter is a man of the greatest integrity. He couldn't be more rigorous over the recording of every object that comes from the tomb. If you could see him…..just the way he talks about, and handles these objects. He has the greatest reverence for them. Even if he has taken various things to his home, it's for research purposes only."

Husni grunted sceptically.

"Unauthorised removal of artefacts from the tomb is a crime. It's enough to lose Carter his concession and everything he's worked for. Those treasures were made for Egyptians, not foreigners."

"They were made for the gods, most of them."

"Egyptians have no need of those gods any more, but we do need our history. That is our true inheritance. We are forging a new country here, and we need a past we can be proud of. You agree with me, don't you? From everything we have talked about, I know you agree."

"Well, of course I agree. I just don't hold with your conspiracy theories about Howard Carter."

"That's your choice."

Husni leant closer towards him, so close he could see the flecks of gold in his dark eyes and the sleek bristles of his moustache, and smell the lime cologne he always wore.

"But Carter is friendly to you, isn't he? He invites you to his home?"

Silence seemed to lap in waves about them. The only sound was the faint hiss of the match in the darkness as Husni lit a cigarette and contemplated him.

"Don't be alarmed my friend. I wouldn't want to spoil that relationship. I know Mr Carter's favour means a good deal to you. But you want to help us too, don't you? The next time you have the chance, see if you can see what treasures he has secreted there. Find out what spoils he has sequestered. That's all I ask."

"He has nothing, I promise you."

"Well then. We shall see, won't we?"

Chapter Fourteen

Esther had lost all interest in the tomb. Her feet were sore, she had a headache coming on and entry cost an extra shilling and threepence. She could tell from the low entrance that you would be forced to view the inside crouching down for verisimilitude and as she entered the long white building she remembered how much she hated enclosed spaces.

Inside it was dim yet glittery and after the bright afternoon sunshine outside it took a moment for her eyes to adjust. It was far too crowded for sketching. They joined the crowd of people shuffling slowly through a series of inter-linked rooms and Alan, following her, read out the details from the guidebook in an enthusiastic, Welsh whisper.

"The rooms of the tomb tell the story of the gradual rebirth of the pharaoh," he hissed in her ear. "His funerary pilgrimage would take him on different stages, in which he would attack demons, triumph over evil and cross thresholds. The art portrays the rituals which permit him to enter the other world."

He pointed to a large, dog-like statue, made of varnished black wood with silver claws.

"That's Anubis. He's black because black was the colour of rebirth in ancient Egypt. In the tomb Anubis was there to watch and assist the king's transformation."

Esther stopped before a painting of Anubis with a pair of gold scales. On one side of the scales, beneath a column of hieroglyphics was a canopic jar and on the other what looked like a feather. The tongue of the balance was scrutinised by a dog-headed ape, seated on a pedestal.

"What's Anubis doing here?"

Alan consulted his guidebook. "This drawing shows the Weighing Of The Heart".

"What was that?"

"The Egyptians believed the heart was the seat of reason, will and conscience. After death, the heart would be weighed in the scales against Maat, the feather of truth, to determine whether the soul could proceed to the afterlife. That's the heart there, represented by the canopic jar. It was a dreadful moment. The heart must prove as light as the feather if it was to pass the test, otherwise the soul would go to eternal annihilation. But there was always the problem that your heart might betray you and confess to all the sins in your life. So you did everything you could to keep the secrets of your heart hidden."

"But what could you do?"

"Well, this is ingenious. There was a book - The Egyptian Book of the Dead – which contained magic spells to ensure that the scales would balance by silencing your heart. Apparently the most popular spell was one which calls on your heart never to reveal the crimes of your life. There's a translation of those hieroglyphics - there – *"O my heart, my mother! My heart whereby I came into being! May naught oppose me at my judgement."*

Anyway, sometimes - whatever lengths you went to - it would be in vain."

"Why?"

"Because Thoth - sitting there see above the scales - had the power to see into the heart. He could examine it and find what was hidden. So unless you balanced the evil in your heart with good, you would be found out."

Esther looked into the face of Thoth. She could well believe he struck fear into anyone who had something to hide. Her skin crawled. She gave a tiny shudder and rubbed her arms. "It's freezing in here. Let's go."

"I must say my friend Samuel would be interested in this place," said Alan as they filed out. "He was out at the dig, you know. He's actually been in the real tomb. He worked with Howard Carter. We should have brought him."

Esther fervently wished they had, or indeed that she and

this man Samuel could have swapped places. For most of that day the exhibits that had interested Alan were precisely the ones which had not appealed to Esther. She had been taken with the magnificent dolls' house made by Sir Edwin Lutyens for Queen Mary, towering like a giant wedding cake behind the ropes. It was the work of 2,000 sculptors and craftsmen, its walls hung with paintings by real artists, like Munnings, Paul Nash and Mark Gertler and its library stuffed with tiny works by Hardy, Kipling, Bennett and Conrad, painstakingly rewritten by the authors themselves. Alan, on the other hand, had been fascinated by the working coal mine and spent some time lecturing her on how Britain's million miners were threatened by imports of cheap coal from the continent.

"Isn't the problem to do with inefficiency?" ventured Esther hazily, her only knowledge of the mining industry being drawn from Uncle Frederick's mine, about which she had no intention of telling Alan. But from what she could remember, Uncle Frederick believed that the entire industry needed drastic re-organisation and streamlining, and the miners themselves should have their wages cut.

Alan reacted warmly to this suggestion, as though Esther was keen to begin a debate.

"The miners can't help inefficiency if the mines they work in are dangerous, inadequate and badly co-ordinated," he argued. She didn't reply, but gave a grunt of assent, hoping he would drop it.

They found a bench and Alan went off to buy ice-creams. He looked rather warm in his thick tweed coat and small beads of moisture were visible on his forehead. Esther leant back relishing the soft touch of spring sunshine on her face and when he returned Alan talked some more about the mining crisis, then the Russian situation and then just as Esther was just gazing over at the amusement park he faltered to a halt and said:

"I hope you don't mind me saying you've been an

extremely equable companion Esther."

Equable? What did that mean? Was it a compliment?

"Thank you. I don't mind at all."

He had taken off his glasses and without them his eyes looked naked and slightly pig-like, his pale lashes blinking earnestly in the light. His normally chalky complexion was moist and lightly flushed. "I've really enjoyed your company. It's refreshing to be with someone who's genuinely interested in politics."

"Oh yes. I am. Yes."

"We share a lot of interests."

"I know," agreed Esther.

Faint strains of music drifted over from the bandstand. They were playing Jerusalem. She glanced over at the funfair. She supposed there was no chance at all of interesting Alan in the Flying Machine.

He was trying to loosen his tie. "The thing is….there was something I wanted to communicate to you."

"Oh?" she said in an encouraging tone. Given that this was more than a purely professional outing, she was deeply curious about how it would proceed. She had found Alan's attention flattering and wondered if that meant that she was attracted to him. Was it enough that you respected someone and admired their views?

"I have a proposition to which I was wondering if you might be amenable," Alan continued. "That is to say…a concept I wanted to put to you for your consideration."

He sighed effortfully. The heat was causing a slight odour of unwashed clothes and ancient cooking to rise from him. Esther had never known Alan stuck for words like this. He was always so fluent and passionate. She wondered if it would be rude to resume licking her ice-cream, which was beginning to drip.

"That is to say, though we are partners in a working situation, I hope I might not be misled if.."

Without warning his arm snaked along the back of the

bench and came to rest heavily against her shoulders, like something asleep. She was startled, but quelled her surprise and leant politely against it. It wasn't unexpected after all, and she was excited that for the first time there was an adult man who was demonstrably interested in her.

"If what?"

For a moment, Alan disengaged his arm from her shoulder to fish out a yellowing handkerchief, wiping beads of sweat from his face, before stuffing it back in his pocket and swinging the arm back round again. His small eyes focused on the middle distance as he searched for the precise expression.

"If….you had felt there were ways in which you could answer my needs."

"Well, I'm always keen to help," said Esther, mystified.

At that, Alan seemed relieved. He promptly withdrew his arm and stood up purposefully as though some matter had been resolved. "Well then." He beamed at her, signalling the conversation was over. "I'm so glad we agree."

For the rest of the afternoon, as they continued to get their money's worth at the exhibition, Esther tried to puzzle out exactly what she had agreed with.

Chapter Fifteen

Samuel was looking out at an undulating sea of glitter. From the place he was standing, on a balcony at the Albert Hall, he could see jewels of every kind but most of them were diamonds; in long drop earrings and rivières, in necklaces and tiaras, blazing against white skin, folded into gleaming hair or pressed against pale breasts, the light from the chandeliers glancing off a million tiny facets. An entire mine in Africa must have been emptied to produce the diamonds on display tonight, he thought, though no-one here would give a second's consideration to the hot, dirty beginnings of all this magnificence.

Iris herself was not wearing diamonds but pearls. Like many of the other girls there she was dressed in a white silk toga and a crown of gilded laurel leaves. They were supposed to represent something - the Muses of the British Empire he thought she'd said - but from above they looked simply like a flock of lovely white birds, their calls and chatter rising up out of them, into the air. Surveying them now, he tried to pick out the face of Iris amongst the dense plumage, but in vain.

To look at Samuel himself, tall, clean-shaven, impeccably dressed in a dinner suit and perfectly polished shoes, lighting a cigarette with his silver lighter, it would have been hard to guess that he did not feel utterly at home in this world, or that he had not been born to it. The life he had once inhabited seemed unimaginably far off now. He pictured time stretching far behind him into infinity, like a plane of pure mathematics, and on it the distant figure of his childish self. The boy he was then bore no relation at all to the person he was now.

Yet, for the first time since he left Egypt, the solitude that rose around him like an invisible bank of fog was lifting and it seemed possible that he might step into something new. Though he was not rich or landed, his time in Egypt seemed to have brought him a certain cachet. People clustered round him at social occasions, asking about the excavation as if they might be able to see it afresh through his eyes. His experience was an attribute, like singing or acting or play writing, which marked him out as worthy of honorary membership of this set, while his cool demeanour promised that he would not dream of transgressing their essential social customs.

Could it be possible that Elmer Barrington felt the same? Indeed, over the past few weeks it was almost as if Barrington was encouraging the idea of a relationship between Samuel and his daughter. As they stood waiting for the car that evening, Barrington had passed by on his way out to a dinner with his mistress. Pulling on a pair of smooth, kid gloves he paused and looked at the two of them with a smile of approval, Iris in her white pleated silk with a golden bracelet on her upper arm, Samuel holding her rich, velvet-trimmed evening coat. But Iris just seemed in a hurry to leave, fidgeting impatiently with her pearls, and patting the carefully set whorls of her Grecian-styled hair.

Samuel himself felt a surging sense of excitement. He tried to quell it by reminding himself that Iris's motives were not the normal ones of a girl who embarks on a date with a young man. She had some ulterior plan, he'd been sure of that since the moment she had first mentioned the ball, the only question was what? Yet… each time he looked at her he began to believe it possible that she simply wanted to spend some time with him. Perhaps she had actually invited him for the pleasure of his company. He wasn't such an unpromising escort after all. He was only a few years older than her and had some interesting stories to tell. It wasn't as though he'd spent the past few years working in a bank.

By the time they had arrived that evening, he was almost convinced that the stirrings of interest he had in her were reciprocated. She seemed excited, nervously animated, and took his arm flirtatiously when he offered it, leaning against him in the chill of the evening air. She chattered gaily and when he looked down at her, her skin glowing and the gilded laurel leaves set in her bright hair, she smiled at him secretively, as though they enjoyed some confidence together. As they went up the steps of the Albert Hall into an arena transformed with golden wall-hangings and decorated with great boughs of trembling yellow mimosa, he placed his hand round her waist. It was the first time he had touched her properly, and it was electrifying. Immediately he wanted to run his hands all over her, but there was no more touching until the first dance, when the legitimate press of her body against his left him shocked at the power of his arousal.

Yet for the past hour, since the opening dances, Iris was nowhere to be seen. She had simply vanished. At first perplexed, and then concerned, he had come up to the balcony to search her out among the swell of people below and it was then that she came up behind him softly and put her hands over his eyes.

"So this is where you're lurking!"

He wheeled round, smiling broadly. "I was looking for you."

"Were you? Well here I am." Her cheeks were flushed, and he focused again on the deep, unusual blue of her eyes.

"You vanished."

"No I didn't! I've been here all along." She doodled an invisible hieroglyphic on his shoulder. "Though I'm a little tired actually, so I'm going back."

He frowned in dismay. "We've only been here an hour or two!"

"Well there's no need for you to come. You must stay and enjoy it. Some of my friends rather want to dance with you."

"Nonsense. I don't want to dance with your friends. I'm coming back with you. I'll find the car."

"No!" she spoke quite sharply. She seemed a little agitated.

"It's all right. I insist you stay. I did drag you out tonight, after all."

"I couldn't let you go alone. Besides, I'd much rather be with you."

"Please. Humour me?"

She turned away from him, as if to signal that the matter was closed, then turned back, reached up to take his face between her hands and gave him a slight, playful kiss. Stooping to receive it a tiny buffet of her perfume came eddying towards him on the air. She smelt musky and intoxicating, the imprint of her lips tingling on his face.

"Thank you for coming. I'll see you later."

After that he had drunk three glasses of champagne in quick succession and discovered that not one but several of Iris's friends genuinely did want to dance with him. One on particular, an older girl, traced a red enamelled finger down his cheek with a practised, seductive ease.

"Has Iris abandoned you then?"

"She was tired."

"Well I think it's awfully silly of her to let you out alone."

"I can look after myself."

"Perhaps you'd like to look after me then?"

She claimed him for the rest of the evening, her warm, satin-wrapped body moving against his, stirring senses that were already aflame, so that it was necessary to drink a great deal more champagne to dull the sensation.

It was three o'clock when he finally made his way to the Barringtons' home and into bed. He was deep in his sixth hour of drunken sleep when a maid came into the room to say that Barrington wanted to see him instantly, in his study. Samuel fumbled his clothes on hastily, and descended to find Barrington, purple-faced, still in his dressing gown. He seemed to be trembling with rage.

"What do you mean by this?"

"I'm sorry Sir. I don't know what you mean."

The man was almost choked with anger. He could barely speak. He waved a piece of paper at Samuel, who took it and read.

"*Am in Paris with Bunny. Stop. Perfectly fine. Stop. Staying here so please don't try to find me.*"

Dislocated facts danced but failed to mesh in his brain. Iris and Paris. Bunny. The woman who danced with him last night. Samuel was having trouble connecting the fury directed at him with any of his own actions. He rubbed his eyes. He wanted to sit down but felt it would be unwise.

"Well?" expostulated Barrington.

"Paris? My God. I had no idea."

"You had no idea? You were supposed to be with her. Where were you when this happened?"

"Iris felt tired. She left early."

"And you didn't have the manners to escort her home?"

"She insisted that I stay," he offered, lamely.

Barrington snatched the paper from him, screwed it up and flung it with violence into the fireplace. "She's eloped. With that parasite Bunny Devine. She's ruined. Her reputation is worthless. And you were supposed to be looking after her."

"She...she really wouldn't let me come back with her."

"Wouldn't *let* you?" Barrington's contempt was coruscating. "Wouldn't *let* you?"

"What are you going to do?"

The older man's face contorted with rage. "Me? It's not me. You're the one who're going to do it. You're to leave straight away and fetch the damned girl back."

"How do I go about doing that? I mean I don't have any idea where she's gone."

"Oh, you'll manage." Then he came to stand very close to Samuel as though twisting a knife in his side.

"After all, you don't have very much choice Mr Dux. Given what my friend Violet has told me all about your *resourcefulness*… finding my daughter should be well within your capabilities."

Trying to ignore, for the moment, the alarming implications of Barrington's comment, Samuel marched along the corridor to Iris's bedroom. Even if his first instinct, like Barrington's, had been to jump on the boat train for Paris, a minute's rational reflection caused him to pause. In the room he found a maid was dusting a dressing table crowded with trinkets and perfume bottles. She paused awkwardly when she saw him, and he said: "Do you know the name of Miss Barrington's friend? The tall girl?"

He had seen her with Iris, a great gangly thing, by whose side Iris looked yet more graceful and petite, and perhaps deliberately Iris had never introduced him.

"Miss Vickers, Sir. Dolly Vickers you mean?"

"Yes, that must be it." Barrington had mentioned her father, a collaborator in some short-lived journal he had established. "Where do they live?"

"They're in Brook Street, Sir. Just off the Square. Number 21."

"Thank you."

He picked up his hat, coat and small leather bag and set off through Hyde Park, a grim figure in the fine, green light filtering through the fringed horse chestnut leaves.

Selina Vickers was surveying the ranks of dainty gilt chairs in her drawing room and adjusting those that fell out of line with military precision. That morning she was hosting a meeting of the charity committee she chaired, and she did like to give things that little personal touch before everyone arrived. She was just rounding up the flower arrangements, bullying a few blooms that had drooped like sentries on parade, when Dawson came and told her that a gentleman was asking to see Dolly.

Dolly was out, choosing a dress for the engagement party, and though Selina knew she should have been there too, steering her daughter away from the less flattering cuts she habitually chose, she was secretly relieved her charity had already been pencilled in. When Dolly had come to them, all childish defiance and suppressed excitement, and told them she had got herself engaged to Hector Monroe, Selina was momentarily cautious but Arthur hadn't seen the problem. He called for champagne. The girl was crazy about this chap, the Monroes were a frightfully good family and the son had every chance of becoming a Conservative MP. And just between themselves Dolly could hardly be expected to do much better. If Hector Monroe was what his daughter wanted, then that was what she should have.

Selina sighed. Arthur was at his most obtuse when it came to human relationships. Emotional nuance bored him and complexity made him impatient. He would prefer the pairing of humans to be as simple and straightforward as breeding the horses at Woodstanton. Ultimately Selina she could see there was no point in being sentimental. Dolly had her father's looks, poor girl, but she also had her mother's fortitude. If the thing turned out badly she would simply, as women always did, have to make the best of it.

"Who is it?"

"A Mr Samuel Dux."

Ah, she recognised that name. It was the young fellow Elmer had hired to help with the Egyptian building. Elmer was rather taken with him, she knew. He came recommended by that witch Violet Esterhazy. The young man apparently shared that fascination with Egypt of which Selina had many times, and through many years, borne the conversational brunt.

"Send him in then please."

When Samuel came in he saw a large, buxom woman with a friendly, curious expression.

"I understand you've come to see Dolly. Well you're out of luck, I'm afraid Mr Dux. Was it anything I could help you with?"

"It's not really about Dolly." Samuel glanced perplexedly

at the rows of gold chairs, as though in the abandoned audience room of some minor monarch. "It's about Iris Barrington."

"What about Iris?" Intuitively she felt a sudden quickening of alarm. "Has anything happened to her?"

"No. I mean yes. But nothing dangerous."

"Come here and sit down. Dawson will bring coffee. Tell me what's happened."

Samuel took her through the tale. Though he kept the story brief and factual, without elaborating on Iris's motives, Selina thought she detected a bitter note in his references to the girl he had so carelessly let slip.

"And what is Elmer proposing to do about it?"

"Apparently, as I'm the one who lost her, I'm the one who must go and fetch her back. That's assuming she wants to come back, which it would appear she doesn't."

"I see." That would tally with Elmer's way of doing things. "So what exactly are you planning to do?"

"I'll go, if Mr Barrington wants me to, and relay her father's feelings. The trouble is that Iris has never told me much about herself, so I have absolutely no idea where she would go in Paris or what she might be intending to do. I thought she might have mentioned something to Dolly, which could give me a clue about where she is. Does your daughter know this Bunny Devine?"

"I'm afraid she probably does. He's an art dealer, I think. A perfectly odious man." For a second, just a single second, Selina compared Bunny and Hector in her mind and felt relieved, then she stopped herself.

"I'm not sure what he wants with her."

Selina raised her eyebrows and he felt awkward despite himself. "What I mean, Mrs Vickers, is do you think he wants to marry her?"

"Probably. But Elmer would never give his blessing. He disapproves of Bunny terribly. Didn't you know? Iris would get nothing."

Samuel frowned. He looked pallid and unshaven and his eyes were slightly bloodshot. Selina took pity on him with his unenviable errand. "I'll have a chat with Dolly when she comes back and see if she has any ideas."

From the hall came the sounds of the first guests arriving. Selina paused, torn between her instincts as a hostess and the drama in hand.

"I can see you're feeling awfully cross Mr Dux and this may seem horribly callous to you, but believe me we don't need to worry too much about Iris. She's a tough girl after all that family's been through. But I am just a little surprised at her doing a thing like this. She's not an impulsive person, generally. She's really rather sensible. I wonder if something has happened to upset her?"

And with that she excused herself, leaving Samuel to see himself out and proceed with the unenviable task in hand.

Chapter Sixteen

Iris thought Tippy Pleasance had the same vacant, self-satisfied look as a Siamese cat she had once owned. Not that she had anything to be satisfied about, having caterwauled her way through a variety of numbers from her latest revue, in which, incredibly, she was being promoted as a major new singing talent. But Iris didn't comment on this. For despite her naturally forthright manner, she realised there would be little mileage in pointing out Tippy's shortcomings where Bunny was concerned.

They were in a night-club, (when weren't they in a night-club?), and Tippy's singing had formed the centrepiece of the show. As she slipped off her stool and curtseyed, a tiny creature in a sheath of gold material, which ended just below her bottom, with a skirt made entirely of tassels and a little golden circlet on her shingled hair, there were shouts of appreciation from the audience, interspersed with some raucous French suggestions whose exact meaning Iris couldn't decipher.

Iris was not sure precisely how she had imagined life in Paris, but it certainly wasn't like this. Her current existence bore little resemblance to the picture Bunny had painted of life among the lively expatriate community of American writers and artists who were currently colonising the city. How excitedly he had talked about the crowd who had decamped from Greenwich Village to Paris, swapping Prohibition for jazz, drink and creativity. They lived all around Montparnasse, apparently, and the Dome Café was their spiritual home where they would meet and mingle with the most exciting names in European art. Picasso ate there and Modigliani would wander round café tables offering his work for sale. Georges Braque and André Derain sat in a corner, accepting drinks. They were all artists and intellectuals and everyone lived on their wits and what they could get for their work. They summered down south and spent the rest of the time drinking, fighting and gambling.

Bunny was not a natural member of this colony. For a start, although he liked to drink and gamble, no-one had ever called him an intellectual. It was also hard to picture him as someone who sympathised with the artistic impulse or strove to push back cultural frontiers. For when Bunny looked around him, he saw not art, but opportunity. He had expensive tastes and needed to maintain them. The artists he befriended were highly valued back home, and as far as Bunny was concerned, their friendship was well worth securing. He liked to portray himself as a cultural ambassador, shipping important work from Paris to New York, where it would be rapturously and reverently received, yet his chief, indeed sole interest in Cubism, Dada and Surrealism was its price. Paris was cheap just then, certainly compared to London. Bargains were everywhere. For their part, the French artists tolerated Bunny and allowed him to buy them drinks. He took no offence at their drunken insults, or the way they openly described him as a parasite or mocked his atrocious accent. After a while they even came to like Bunny, because, as Iris had noticed, everyone came to like Bunny.

But it wasn't Bunny, or even the prospect of the artistic life, that had persuaded Iris to come here. It was her father. Not just the thought that eloping might infuriate him, though there was that, but it was something he said to Edwina that finally convinced her to accept Bunny's invitation. Edwina, in a rare moment of solidarity with Iris, had been complaining about the amount of time Barrington spent shut away in his study with Samuel Dux, but he dismissed her crossly.

"That boy is going to be very useful to me."

The remark struck Iris to the core. Why should her father

find a use for complete stranger, when he had never found a use for his own children? In the past she would have talked away her bitterness with Dolly. They would have taken their dogs for a walk through Hyde Park, and sat in the Italian gardens watching the fountains, and talked the whole thing through. But now Dolly was always so busy, whether she was in Selfridges making up the wedding list, or discussing numbers with her mother or seeing the dressmaker, or disputing whether quenelles of plaice followed by pheasant would be right for the wedding breakfast, and Iris knew there was simply no chance of discussing her own unhappiness, while Dolly floated on this cloud of nuptial joy. It was a strain for both of them, so Dolly stopped inviting her and Iris waited impatiently for the night of the Heart of the Empire Ball before slipping away to Bunny's flat.

Besides, once she had made up her mind, the idea of coming out here had been so exciting. It had been perfectly simple to slip away from Samuel Dux and she had not given a moment's thought as to how he would explain her disappearance. Instead they had climbed into Bunny's plane, and flown overnight, looking down on the channel and towards the twinkling lights of the French coast, then motored into Paris at dawn. Iris was so full of adrenaline she was barely aware of being tired as she tried to take in the city, all a blur of colour and scents.

The hotel, The Esperance, was so unlike the grand, marbled hotels she had stayed in on holidays with her family. It was just a tall, shabby townhouse, with peeling paint, set in a row of shops in "the Quarter" as Bunny called Montparnasse. Their room was on the sixth floor, at the top of a musty, airless staircase and inside there was only a washstand, an armoire and a narrow little bed.

"Like it, honey?"

Iris admitted that the faded toile de jouy of the curtains and bedspread looked enchantingly French.

"Glad you came?"

"Ever so."

It was not until that evening, however, when he had settled heavily into bed beside her and pulled the greasy bedspread purposefully up, that he pushed his knee down, forcing her legs apart, shifted his weight on top of her and began clumsily to make love to her. It hurt at first, like it was supposed to. She felt a jolt of pain as he jabbed into her, and she lay very still beneath his thrusts, almost suffocating from the weight of him, his shoulder jammed into her neck and his pink, shiny face labouring above her, until several minutes later he sank heavily onto her arm and simply dozed off.

So that was it then. Or rather it wasn't because Bunny was keen on sex, and boasted that he didn't take much time to recover.

That had been a week ago now. The old concierge, who had frizzy orange curls and little black, fingerless mittens, glanced sourly at their comings and goings but made no comment. Their evenings were spent moving among bistros and cafés like La Coupole, drinking cognac, listening to black jazz bands and chatting to people who seemed to regard her as nothing more than a transient female companion, scarcely worth acknowledging.

Then, that morning, they had had their first row. She had been feeling too sore for sex, and when Bunny tried to wake her she pushed him off.

He sat up affrontedly with his back to her, pulling on his socks.

"What shall we do Bunny?"

"Nothing. I've got a little business to settle."

"Not now. I mean generally. What are we going to do? We can't stay here indefinitely."

He hesitated for a moment, surveying the detritus of the room, then turned to her smiling.

"Funny you should say that honey. I thought we might get

married."

"Married?" She sat up with shock. "You're not serious?"

He smoothed her hair. "Sure I'm serious. You want me to get down on my knees?"

"But why?"

"Why not? Isn't that what your father would want?"

"Why do you care what he wants? Besides, I don't want to get married. I thought…."

"You thought what?"

"That we'd just live here in France and be happy, I suppose."

"On thin air?"

She stiffened slightly. Bunny had always been too well-bred to mention money. He noticed her surprise and continued: "Yes. I mean it darling. Think about it. We can't go on like this forever."

"It's just that…." She wanted to ask what he meant about thin air, but couldn't bring herself to. "You never told me you wanted to marry me before."

"What did you think?"

"I didn't think."

"Well honey, you'd better start thinking." He stood up and pulled on his trousers without looking at her. "It's time you woke up and decided what you want to do."

There was an uncompromising edge to his voice. He gave her a brief kiss, picked up his money from the dressing table and went out.

Iris lay in bed and wished someone would bring her a bowl of hot, milky coffee or at least come and clean up the room, which, in the absence of a regular maid, had lost much of its charm and was littered with empty bottles and cigarette ends and unwashed clothes. In the daylight the pretty wallpaper was stained and peeling. When they had first arrived at the hotel she had endeavoured to enjoy it in the spirit of *nostalgie de boue* but it was a long way from what she was used to.

She wondered if this was how it was supposed to be. Losing her virginity had not been the thrill she had always imagined. Though she complied earnestly enough, she felt not the faintest flicker of desire whenever Bunny's large, fleshy form loomed over her. His mushroomy belly with its slick of sweat reminded her of the sea lions she saw as a little girl at the zoo. Whenever he finished, with the cabbagey fluid trickling down her legs, she couldn't help worrying whether the contraceptive sponges he had procured were entirely effective.

In addition, the gregarious persona he displayed in company deserted him when they were alone. Though not exactly short with her, he tended to be silent and impatient with her keen questions about his business or the artists they had met. She had even suspected he was getting bored with her and yet now here he was proposing marriage.

Why, she wondered, did Bunny care what her father thought? Yet Bunny insisted she send the telegram the moment they arrived assuring her father she was all right. Didn't he realise that her father hated him, and would certainly not help them out with money if she went so far as to marry him? But then why should Bunny care about her father's money? He must have an allowance of his own, mustn't he? Everyone did. From their family. And he had a grand flat in London and a plane and spent most of his time in casinos after all. He couldn't be that short of cash. What on earth did he mean about living on "thin air"? She wished there was someone she could talk to about it, someone who cared about her. She wished she could still talk to Charles.

Almost as soon as she thought of Charles, she shook her head as if physically banishing the picture of him, hauled herself out of bed and stood in her creased cotton night-dress contemplating the same clothes she had worn yesterday. She stretched and peered down at the street outside, which was already busy with shouts and traffic, and the enticing smell of baking caused the saliva to spring into her mouth. She was hungry - that was all. It was hunger that was making her think like this. She would take the last of the francs Bunny had left on the dressing table and buy some croissants.

Perhaps she should marry Bunny anyway. Especially since Dolly's announcement, the idea of marrying had become even more of an active verb to her, something to *do*, like hunting or dancing, something that took up time and thought and kept your mind off the idea of any more substantial occupation. Yet in truth she knew that marrying would not be the answer. For a year now she had been restlessly wondering whether there was any way she could find employment – anything that might occupy her brain and channel her ideas. Often she looked curiously at people heading off to work in offices and thought how satisfying it must be, even when work was not exciting in itself, to feel yourself a cog in some great, grinding machine, a cog whose absence would be noticed, and affect the working of others. How delightful to be a minute capillary in the huge, pulsing body of labour, which blindly strove and expended its effort each day. To be a worker, an income generator, an economically active unit.

Yet finding work would involve returning to London and that would mean going back to her father, who would be unspeakably angry with her. Even if, since the arrival of Samuel Dux, he had taken no interest in her at all.

Samuel Dux. Now she allowed herself to think about him, she felt a pang of regret. He had been so considerate. He so obviously enjoyed going to the ball with her that night and he looked so handsome when he was all dressed up. Against all her expectations, she found herself actually liking his company. But that was then. She bet he was annoyed with her now.

* * *

"Bloody awful isn't she?"

A tall, masculine woman, with a severe Eton crop and a dinner jacket had joined their table. She nodded towards Tippy. "I heard she's only here because she's had a line of real stinkers in London and is afraid another flop would ruin her reputation. Paris is absolutely infested with women like her. The more terrifically vulgar the better."

"She's certainly vulgar."

"And she's so determined to make it here. She's getting in with all the right people. She's actually talking about dancing in a Diaghilev opera. Can you imagine darling? Diaghilev! The airs of the creature! Pigalle would be more her scene."

"I wouldn't know."

The woman looked at Iris curiously.

"You're English, aren't you? I had you down for a yank when I saw you."

Mildly interested Iris said: "Do I look American?"

"Not close up you don't, no. I can see that. But this place is crawling with them. Rich American boys and girls. They come over by the boatload with all their money and their *optimism*.." this word was spat out, like an expletive, "and they have absolutely no idea about Europe at all. They think they'll imbibe some culture and slum it for a while before they go back to Harvard or Connecticut or wherever they came from. We English have history, you see, so we don't tend to be so wholeheartedly *enslaved* by the ways of the French. So what are you here for? You're not a little actress are you?"

"No. I'm just visiting." Iris fiddled with the empty champagne bottle on their little tin table. Bunny, who had set off to find more drink, had been gone a long time. To the sound of raucous cheers from the audience, a bevy of women ran onto the stage and began to dance the can-can. They were bare-chested, apart from the tassels attached to their nipples, and they swung their breasts towards the onlookers in a vigorous manner.

"At last some real action," murmured the woman, giving Iris a sly wink. She offered a cigarette. "Anyway, I hope you're staying for a while darling. There's an awful lot of ladies like me in Paris who like a good time."

Iris looked around distractedly for Bunny, but there was no sign.

"I wonder where Bunny's got to."

"Friend of yours, is he?"

"Sort of."

"Well he's probably with Tippy, darling."

"With Tippy?"

"She has a thirty-minute wait before her next act. She doesn't like sitting in dressing rooms on her own."

"But why would Bunny….?"

The woman sucked at her cigarette and examined her rather dirty nails. "Oh surely you know? When she was in that comedy in London she was only in the first and the last act and he'd take her out to dinner in between. Everyone laughed about it. He went every week of the run and it ran thirty weeks. He's crazy about her. He proposed apparently. Not that she'd settle for him. She's after bigger fish. Why go for a yank who's living on tick when she could net an English lord? Lucky for Bunny he's found some spoilt little heiress to keep him in the style to which he's accustomed…. Hey… what is it sweetheart?"

Iris felt it almost physically, the shock of understanding and the wrench of betrayal. She pushed back the table and ran out into the street.

Chapter Seventeen

What did Samuel understand about women? That was not a question he had ever asked himself or even given even a moment's attention. But since this business with Iris, the most selfish person he had ever met, all he could think was that he knew very little about women, understood nothing and cared even less.

He'd been trudging round Paris for days now, wasting a visit to this beautiful city hunting for a spoilt rich girl and her odious boyfriend. He had visited all the places expatriate Americans frequented with no luck. Each evening he had returned to his hotel and called Barrington, and each evening the old man had responded with a growl of anger to the news that his daughter remained elusive and told him to keep looking.

He didn't need to of course. Samuel told himself he could walk away at any time. The idea of leaving had become even more pressing given the old man's parting comment - *"My friend Violet has told me about your resourcefulness…"* The remark filled him with alarm and he turned it over in his head, assessing its significance. Exactly what had Violet told Barrington about him?

Escaping Barrington would mean finding another job. He supposed there was always short-term work for waiters or *plongeurs* or labourers who were young and fit and willing, even if they lacked references. There was only one thing he was certain of. Whatever he did, he could never go back to Egypt again.

By February 1924 it was more than a year since the first step had been laid bare in the sand and still no one knew what the Little King would look like. Would he have anything resembling a face? And if he did, how far would it have deteriorated? Would the embalmed flesh be merely blurred and out of focus like a grainy photograph, or rotted and destroyed like the faces of those boys they still pulled from the mud in the trenches? Or would it be miraculously preserved, like some kind of ancient saint? Might Tutankhamun still look like himself?

The first steps to finding out had been taken. Samuel hovered uncomfortably at the back of the crowd as with infinite care Howard Carter heaved open the granite lid in front of an invited audience of officials and archaeologists.

It was a sight worth waiting for. As the lid, weighing more than a ton, was hoisted into the air by a complicated system of pulleys and ropes, there were gasps of amazement at the figure revealed. There before them was a beautiful, golden effigy, its impassive face set with a rearing cobra on the forehead, its hands crossed at the breast, holding the jewelled crook and ceremonial flail. No one who saw it would ever forget that blank, feminine gaze and Mona Lisa smile, inlaid with coloured glass and precious stones, turquoise, cornelian, quartz and obsidian, with eyes of argonite and eyelids of lapis lazuli. Around the brow there were wilted olive leaves and beside the mummy a frazzled wreath of flowers, perhaps cast there by the queen he left behind.

Inside that effigy lay more cases and they were certain that eventually, at the very core, they would uncover the mummified body of the king.

But no sooner had this been accomplished than all work was abandoned. The granite lid remained literally in mid air as relations between the Egyptian government and Howard Carter shuddered to a complete halt.

It was the first strike in archaeology and it had been a long time coming. Animosity towards the British had been swelling like an irresistible wave. Following Egypt's unilateral declaration of independence there had been a handful of murders of British citizens and then, in January, the election of the first Nationalist government, led by Said Zaghlul (a man whom some in the British administration had tried hard to have hanged) made anti-British sentiment more popular than ever. Everyone hated the British but in particular, it seemed, they hated Howard Carter. Carter, like a human magnet, appeared to attract resentment. The Egyptian dislike of all things British focused with burning concentration upon his bad-tempered person. He was deluged with arbitrary paperwork from the Ministry of Public Works and new, petty regulations. At every step he met unhelpfulness and procrastination. The time was ripe for someone to pick a row.

The dispute itself was a nonsensical thing. Carter had been planning a private visit for the wives of the resident excavators and various British dignitaries to view the sarcophagus after the official lifting of the granite lid. It hadn't occurred to him that this could be controversial, but no sooner had they heard than the Ministry of Public Works objected to British women having access to this magnificent sight before native Egyptians. They sent a squad of police along to the tomb to ensure the ladies were kept out. Carter, ill and angry, continued to squabble for a few days, until in a fit of fury, he abandoned the work and closed the tomb.

Samuel lingered that evening after the other excavators had made their way back up the Valley, watching Carter slam the metal gates and fasten the padlocks. It was like attempting to shut Pandora's Box, Samuel thought, as if mere steel could contain the tumult he had unleashed from the tomb. Carter himself was unrecognisable from the man he had been a year before. His face was grim as he pocketed the keys and leant against the tomb doors, his eyes closed.

"I do ask myself Mr Dux, what else can go wrong?"

As it turned out, he did not have long to discover.

* * *

Samuel tried to shake off these thoughts as he wandered through the cobbled Parisian streets, past tiny courtyards between the white-shuttered houses with geraniums cascading from their balconies. He told himself he should stay here, in France, and start afresh. He could see Notre Dame and Les Invalides and Montmatre and Pigalle, and all the places he had only read about. He could walk in the Bois de Boulogne, see the ballet, the opera and the Comédie Française.

Besides, the search for Iris was plainly futile. Dolly Vickers had suggested the name of a hotel Bunny once stayed at, but when he went there they were equally keen to track down Mr Devine, who had left without paying his last bill. He had spent four days visiting artists in draughty studios who had sold work to Bunny, and as one remarked over a bottle of good wine (paid for by Samuel) you might as well hunt a needle in a haystack as look for an English girl on the Left Bank nowadays.

The only thing which kept him going in this fruitless search was fury. As well as being angry with Iris he was furious with himself for wasting his time and allowing her to play with him, and to use him so deceptively. He was also angry that he had found her attractive and had been so foolish as to go along with her when everything he knew about her behaviour suggested a supreme disregard for others. Yet even given that he was surprised that she could abandon her father quite so lightly. Not to mention the dog.

It went without saying that Iris had never in her life slept outside before. The next morning her legs were like lead, and every part of her body ached. She had passed a few hours, the bad, dark hours of the night, hunched up on a bench beside the river, with the cold all around her, weighing her down like iron, the air like freezing fingers on her face. At one point it had rained, just a light drizzle, causing her to huddle under the shelter of a bridge. When it grew light she perched on the slimy sides of the river watching the dank, brown Seine slide by, giving off a stench of mould and weeds. It was impossible to imagine fish flicking through that murk. All she could picture was the white, bloated bodies of drowned women being brought up, like in nineteenth century novels. She shivered and pulled her navy velvet evening cloak more tightly round her and carried on with cobble-stubbing feet.

She was numb with fatigue, but her senses, instead of being dulled, were nervously heightened so the sights and sounds of the early morning streets seemed almost bodily assaults. A horse passed by at a lazy walk, its flanks glossy and fat, its breath making clouds, a pile of fresh dung steaming behind it on the road. A man crossed her path with a cartful of colour, orange tulips and scarlet roses blazing in the milky air. The pungent fragrance of soupe a l'ognion leaked from a café door. A little dog trotted by and she felt a pang of anguish for Paw-Paw, who would no doubt be suffering the very untender care of the butler Cairns.

She began to wander through the streets, unsure where she was headed, with a vague idea that she might look for the railway station. After a while she came to a marketplace, Les Halles. Trading was almost over. In one corner a man was being sick against a lamp-post. Around him the market people were cleaning up, sweeping debris, clearing the dying flowers and hauling the last, vermillion haunches of meat marbled with fat, the sacks of potatoes, the cheeses and thick wedges of yellow butter.

The sight of the food made her suddenly, desperately hungry. Across the market place she could see a café, a functional place with tiny, benched booths where some of the traders were taking breakfast. The waiters were setting tables and polishing glasses. She had only three francs with her in her evening bag, and she wasn't quite sure what it would buy. An omelette perhaps, and a brioche. The rest of her money she had left with her belongings in Bunny's hotel and there was no chance she would be going back there.

Chapter Eighteen

Samuel had decided to devote one last morning to his wretched task but in order to leaven the business he was off to inspect some antiquities in the Louvre. He had risen early and made his way through the early morning streets, pretty much at random.

Through the smudged glass of a grubby little café he glanced her, pale as a phantom and without her make-up, years younger. He couldn't even be sure it was her, except he recognised the velvet trimmed evening cloak he had carried for her to the ball. The sight of her sitting there quietly eating a roll produced in him an involuntary gasp. He ran inside.

"Iris?"

She raised her eyes to him momentarily then looked away. "Yes." It came out as a whisper. A susurration, for she had not spoken to anyone else for hours. She did not even look shocked to be discovered. She continued eating her brioche ravenously.

Samuel remained standing over her. He would not sit down. Despite the sheer luck of finding her he felt more, not less infuriated.

"Are you alone?"

"Apparently."

He glanced round suspiciously.

"Where's Devine?"

"I don't know. Or care," she added defiantly. She concentrated on her breakfast, as though theirs was a chance encounter between two casual acquaintances.

His mouth contracted with anger. "Have you any idea….?" He stopped himself and said tersely: "Well anyway you can't stay here. You'd better come back to my hotel." He could telephone from there, he calculated, and let Barrington know that all was well, that Samuel had fulfilled his end of the job. After that, it was not his affair. She hadn't moved so he said: "Are you coming or not?"

She looked up at him as if to argue then when she saw the look in his eyes, said dully, "All right."

They were unaware of the impression they made walking through the Paris streets in silence, the tall, lean young man and the girl in evening dress, for all the world like a pair of lovers who had danced the entire night. Iris was obliged to hurry beside her angry custodian, who strode ahead with his head down and his hands in his pockets, outpacing her. They passed through a small park where the neat grass was intersected with squares of mathematical gravel, beneath an avenue of pollarded planes, to the road where his pension was, a town house with a dusty black door. Inside it was dim and cool with a stone staircase and twisty, wrought iron banister. Samuel marched ahead of her up four flights and stood back, to allow her into his room. He gestured stiffly.

"You'll probably want to wash. You can take a bath if you like."

"Thank you."

She shut the bathroom door firmly behind her and Samuel threw open the shutters, smoked a cigarette and gazed out at the layers of speckled grey rooftops polished by the night's rain. He loosened his collar and tried to relax. He had fulfilled his responsibility quite adequately now. By some miracle he had found the girl and would set about delivering her back to her father, although the first thing to do was to get her to speak to him on the telephone, so that if she objected, or refused to return, Barrington could hardly hold him accountable. If Iris agreed to come back to London with him, there would be her ticket to book, second class it would have to be because that was how he would be travelling and he assumed it would be foolhardy to let her out of his sight. He reckoned he had just enough money left to cover the hotel bill, fares and some food and drink without having to wire Barrington for more.

Though his brain continued rationally making these plans, he felt strangely disinclined to do anything. The room seemed airless and he was filled with an almost unbearable tension, as though his nerves were standing on end. He tried to focus on the clotted white paint on the balcony rails, and through them to the terrace below where an old woman with a huge bust swathed in a floral apron was hanging washing out to dry. As he stubbed the cigarette out on the windowsill he was conscious that his pulse was racing. Behind him, through the flimsy bathroom partition he could hear the gentle splashes and scrubs of Iris in the bath. He could smell the scented steam. After five minutes she poked her head round the door.

"I don't have any clothes. My evening dress isn't very clean."

"You'd better borrow my pyjamas till I can go out and find you some clothes. They're on the radiator in there."

She emerged from the bathroom with the blue and white striped pyjama trousers rolled up on her legs and the sleeves of the jacket turned up. She had combed her wet hair back so that it rested flat on her head, like a boy's. Her cheeks were flushed from the warmth of the bath. The sight of her made him turn away.

She gestured at the trousers. "They're too long."

"They'll do." He squatted down to begin packing his case. He planned for them to be back on the boat that evening.

"You seem terribly cross."

"Do I."

"Are you annoyed with me?"

"Very."

It was the first time she had shown any awareness of his own feelings about this business. Other than that one evening, the evening of the ball, it was the first time she appeared to perceive him as a real person, rather than as some cardboard villain, an imposter in her home, designed to vex her.

Perhaps that was what triggered it, or perhaps it was the sight of her as she stood there in the bedroom, so small and self-composed despite the enforced intimacy of their situation, so indifferent to the effect her near nakedness might have on him, that caused the mounting frustration of the last few days and the ache of sexual deprivation which had lingered in him since their evening at the ball, to rise up. He stood up and gripped her shoulders, meaning to say something more - something about the trouble and inconvenience he had been put to - but in the process he pulled the pyjamas aside and exposed her slight, naked body. He hesitated for a moment, looking. She opened her mouth, to protest perhaps, or speak, but he had stepped so far beyond propriety there was nothing to stop him now and it was too late to go back so he kissed her. Pulling the pyjama jacket off he ran his hand over her breasts and then down the curve of her hip, flat against her bottom, and drew her towards him with one hand, while with the other he unbuttoned his own trousers and stepped out of them. Kneeling down he pulled the trousers from her then lifted her bodily up and plunged her onto the bed with himself on top of her. Her eyes widened, she pushed at him weakly and gasped.

That gasp, that tiny gesture of vulnerability, was all he needed. The anger and annoyance she had stoked in him was transformed into a pure, unambiguous desire. There was nothing he could do to deny it any longer. He kissed her neck and pulled her legs apart beneath him. Pushing himself into her he felt her at first tight, then easing slightly, gripping him. His excitement was so intense that he struggled to prevent himself climaxing too soon. He had wanted to dent that composure, and to show her that she could not do what she had done to him, as though he was a servant, bereft of normal male feeling. But now that he was in her he was flooded with longing for her. He didn't merely want to gratify himself, he wanted her to want him too. Everything he did willed her to respond.

And she did respond. Not that she said anything, but her narrow hips began to move with and not against his thrusts and her small gasps were of desire not distress. She clung to him as he climaxed and afterwards he found fading red crescents that her fingernails had made in the skin of his back.

Afterwards they lay wordlessly, the pleasure and satiety ebbing slowly round their bodies. Her hair stuck to her forehead in damp tendrils and the flush in her cheeks had deepened. As he looked at her, she sat up and leant against the white iron bedstead, hunching her knees protectively to her chest, and pulling his pyjama jacket back onto her. He felt a great tenderness towards her. The smell of himself mixed with her was intensely arousing and almost immediately he wanted to make love to her again, but repressed himself. He wanted to draw her into his arms, but feared such an impulse would be rebuffed. He caught her eye and was surprised to see a tear rolling from it. He stopped it with a finger and licked it up.

"Did I hurt you?"

She shook her head.

"Because I really didn't mean to. Iris, I'm sorry…I…"

"Don't."

She looked away, her face in profile, gazing blankly out into the still air. Watching her, the pleasure began to sour and the immensity of what he had done began to dawn on him, even while he realised how impossible it was to apologise for such a heinous act. What on earth could one say? The etiquette for such situations was unwritten. Which pleasantries could he choose to smooth over his behaviour, and even if she wanted to smooth it over, which seemed unlikely, what could she reply? She could hardly say "It doesn't matter." In every way, it mattered intensely. To have taken advantage like that of a defenceless woman in a hotel bedroom, betraying the coarseness of his nature and the baseness of his social standing, revealed at a stroke the true chasm between them. He saw that now. All the confidence he had had that he could move at will in her world vanished like smoke. His feeling of liberation, that he could leave the events in Egypt behind him, even that Elmer Barrington might look kindly on a relationship with his daughter, was nothing but a delusion. What was it worth, his carefully cultivated self-assurance, if he was incapable of self-restraint? How easy it was to lose control of yourself, to ruin any chances you had. For the second time in his life he felt appalled at himself, and at the nameless energy that had risen from somewhere deep within and wreaked destruction.

He dressed stiffly. He was well aware that they should telephone her father, but for every reason he wanted to put off the intrusion of Elmer Barrington and her London life for as long as he could. He looked over at Iris cautiously. She was still staring into the distance. She had not moved.

"Are you hungry?"

Surprisingly she answered in a tone of light neutrality.

"Starving actually, but I've no money."

"Never mind about that. I have. Why don't you put on that dress and we'll go and find something to eat?"

"It's rather grubby."

"Don't worry. You look fine."

They left the pension and stepped out into the street with Iris seemingly content to go along with him. As they crossed a road he tentatively took her hand and she did not withdraw it. It was warm in the sunshine and was going to be a fine day, the mist of the night's rain rising off the streets. People hurried by purposefully, giving the place an undercurrent of excitement that he had never detected in England. Despite himself, he felt a surge of confidence and a nascent happiness. Whatever she thought of him, Iris could not help but be seduced by her surroundings. Paris would assist his efforts. Whatever she was feeling must be tempered by the sheer beauty of this, the first and perfect city, in itself a whole collection of impressionist paintings. Or to be more precise, it was pointillist. He was aware of the tiniest nuances of leaf and shadow. He felt a lust for detail. They passed a baker's shop filled with patisseries whose labels made them seem more like individual works of art than something one might simply consume -*forêt noire, religieuse, soleil levant, opéra, criolo, charlotte aux fruits exotiques* - and he absorbed them all at a glance. He felt alert as an animal in his surroundings, and fortified by the beauty of everything, from the ribbons of a torn chocolate advertisement blowing on a wall, to the mingled smell of drains and baking rising from the gutter. It was as though his senses had been starved until this point.

Down a side street they debouched unexpectedly into a tiny sloping square, in its centre a couple of benches and an iron drinking fountain of leaping dolphins, and under the plane trees a bar where the chairs were being ranked out on the pavement and a cat with apricot fur sat blinking in the warmth. They sat at a tin table punched with paisley holes and ordered coffee and pear tart. Above them plane leaves formed a dark jigsaw against the sky but Iris's face was caught in a shaft of luminous green. Though she had violet circles beneath her eyes, her beauty was entirely undiminished. She was gorgeous, every part of her. He watched the curve of her lips, and the narrow white fingers running through her hair, with an irrepressible tenderness.

Emboldened, he lit a cigarette.

"Isn't this always how you imagine Paris?"

"I never imagined it at all really."

"But you've been here before?"

"Not Paris, no. I've been to Deauville and Trouville and Honfleur and for holidays down in the south. We had a villa near Cap Ferrat, all very pretty, with terraces covered in bougainvillaea. I hated it there. Most of our holidays I spend squabbling with Edwina. You know, my father's mistress."

She fell silent and gazed at him.

"Why are you looking at me like that?"

"I was thinking how different you are from the other men I know."

Different, was he? More sophisticated, travelled, educated perhaps? She might have meant that, yet somehow he suspected not. Instantly an entire world came to him - a house with tiny rooms and an odour of boiled cabbage, a steel bed, a muddy garden with chickens and the whole of it enclosed by a long, bleak horizon of fields where children were paid to pick out stones. Home. The map at the centre of his being, the dull Jerusalem of his world. He hunched his shoulders defensively.

"How am I different?"

"Oh, in almost every way I can think of."

A boy brought their order and she took a cigarette and relapsed into silence. He felt a creeping fear that perhaps through disgust, or distress at his actions, Iris had become her old guarded self again. Looking at the face just inches away across the tin table top, he found it almost impossible to believe that an hour earlier this girl had been pinioned beneath him, and that indeed there was still a damp trace of himself inside her. The awful mixture of desire and aggression that had ignited within him in the room had changed everything he felt about her. The sight of her beneath him had roused passions he had never experienced before, and certainly not with Violet. But what had it meant to her? It seemed the rupture he had made in her had repaired itself, without a scar. Her composure was restored, like the calm surface of a lake, as if it had never been breached.

He reached out to brush a crumb of pear tart from her mouth and wondered if he even had the licence to touch her again.

"So tell me about what happened to you. What happened with Bunny?"

She took a sip of hot, fragrant coffee and said levelly: "Bunny wants me to marry him."

Her use of the present tense caused a frisson of shock to run through him. He had assumed Iris's boyfriend to be a matter of no importance any more. "You mean he wanted you to marry him. But I assume you wouldn't want to now."

"I don't know really."

Surprise gave his voice a bitter edge. "Perhaps I shouldn't have bothered coming to look for you then."

She raised her eyes. "Why did you come?"

"Your father asked me to fetch you back."

"Oh." She looked away. "By return. Like a parcel!"

She smiled lightly, but something about the melancholy droop of her shoulders revealed to him that Iris did actually care about his motivation. "Your father was very anxious for you to come home."

"I'm sure he was."

"He seems very concerned about you."

"Does he." She looked over the rim of her cup and then conversationally, as though discussing the weather, she remarked: "It was you I wanted to escape actually."

A mouthful of coffee stalled in his throat so he almost choked.

"Me? But why, for God's sake?"

"Oh, my father has been so taken up with you. Always talking about Egypt. He adores you, he's so admiring. Every time I saw you with him, I thought, 'There he goes again. He's trying to replace Charles'."

"Me? Replace your brother? How could I? That's an absurd suggestion."

"I suppose it is in a way. Having Charles there would be the last thing in the world my father would want."

He was shocked. "That's not the impression I got." Barrington had never mentioned his son in more than a few brief sentences, not enough to get any real idea of their relationship, but he reckoned the boy was dead so what could it matter.

"I think he was devastated by your brother's death."

"You don't know anything about it."

"Eight years is quite a time," he said gently.

She looked at him angrily. "What do you know? Have you ever lost anyone you loved?"

For a moment his mind was blank. He couldn't actually imagine anyone he might ever have loved. Who was there? Not his father. There had been Husni, out in Egypt, for whom he had felt strongly. But that was not love. The thought of Violet filled him with nothing but self-disgust. Then he remembered his mother's face, corrugated with care, the cool cheek laid against his when she came to visit in bed at night and whisper her rare endearments - "my little man" - which always seemed chosen to encourage independence and maturity. Her leathery palms, rough as a dog's paw.

"I don't think I've ever loved anyone properly. Except my mother. She died last year while I was out in Egypt. I loved her. But I wouldn't in all honesty say I miss her very much."

"You wouldn't know then."

"Perhaps I wouldn't." He hesitated. "What was your brother like?"

"He….was a very, very decent person. He hated the war. He couldn't bear the idea of killing anyone. Even in defence of king and country. Even from a long way away, with a gun."

"That's understandable."

"Is it? How do you know? You didn't fight in the war. Besides, you don't seem the kind of person who would mind at all."

"Mind what?"

"Killing someone."

For a moment neither of them spoke, then she said: "I didn't mean that rudely, that's just how it seems." She wiped her eye with the back of her hand. "But if you don't mind I'd rather we didn't talk about my brother any more."

"You should. You should talk about him."

"Why?"

Why indeed? What did he know about getting over death?
"Well all I know is that the ancient Egyptians said to speak
the name of the dead is to make them live again. It restores
the breath of life to those who have vanished. Unless the
Ren, the name, was preserved, the person would cease to
exist. So whenever pilgrims passed an Egyptian tomb they
would speak the name of the dead person. If you stopped
talking about the dead, they'd be forgotten. One of the chief
aims of Tutankhamun's enemies was to obliterate his name
from the monuments that commemorated him."

"Oh? Really. I can't see any amount of talk making a
difference to Charles." She gazed at him for a moment
thoughtfully. "Anyway, who would I talk about him to?"

"You could start with me."

"Why would you be interested?"

"Because I'm interested in everything about you."

It was as though his words breached some barrier in her,
a habit of defensiveness long built up which crumbled like
a dusty stone wall under the pressure of feelings so long
suppressed. Here in this foreign square, busy with strangers
involved in their own lives, far from anything familiar, Iris
felt her guard give way. She began to talk of things she had
never told another human being, things she had not even
thought she had words for, and he saw her solitary existence
as it was, filled with craving for her father's affection,
the gap left by her brother and the mother she had barely
known. She told him about Dolly's marriage and her dismay
that her friend was making a terrible mistake, while her
parents did nothing to stop her. She talked about Charles
with his wicked sense of humour, his practical jokes and her
puzzlement that even though her father had never seemed to
like him that much, since the war he could not bear to hear
his son's name mentioned. She told him of her dismay when
he, Samuel, had arrived, and all about eloping with Bunny

in a furious act of defiance. It hadn't mattered that she didn't love Bunny. After all, she had always assumed that any love she found would, like her mother and her brother, vanish like something stolen in the night.

When she grew too sad to talk he amused her with stories from his own childhood and the yearning for adventure that had taken him to Egypt. After that he told her the feelings he had had for her from the moment they met. So began an afternoon that could never be taken from him, whatever was to follow.

They wandered the streets of Paris, fingers linked, talking so much they barely noticed their surroundings. The sheer proximity of Iris inflamed him, he wanted to catch her narrow limbs and fold them in his own, to possess her entirely. Once, when they sat on a bench beside the Seine, he put his arm around her. But although he was hungry for her, he was afraid to halt her tide of confidences. It was as though, now she had found him, she was determined he know everything that had happened to her, sparing no detail.

That evening, as he queued for tickets at the train station, she sat watching him and as he returned she said quietly: "You know a lot about me now. What do you feel?"

He could only answer with a kiss. His heart was wrenched with tenderness and love for her.

Chapter Nineteen

"What shall we do this evening? Cocktails at Rosie Barraclough's or the pictures?"

"Cocktails I think. They're such a great idea. I want to learn how to make as many as possible. Particularly the ones with the American names that bear absolutely no relation to what's in the glass. Gin and orange juice and Vermouth and you call it a Bronx. Or whisky and Vermouth makes a Manhattan. Why is that?" Esther paused, chewing a tendril of hair. "Perhaps we should save the pictures for Monday. I'd like to see *A Woman Of Paris*. It's got Charlie Chaplin in it."

Although it was Saturday morning, neither Esther nor Alice were living like students whose final examinations were just weeks away. Every night there would be a party until the early hours, or heading out to a cheap restaurant or visiting the new club that Alan frequented with his communist friends. Somehow exam results simply seemed less significant to Esther than the expansion of her social life, and Alice, whose talent was acknowledged by all and whose interest in the modern movement was intensifying, also appeared to regard her degree as an irrelevance. Though unlike Esther she had been working hard on the pieces she was submitting for the final exam. One of them was a portrait of Ursula Davis who was to come that afternoon for her latest sitting.

"It'll probably be the last for me in this state," Ursula had warned Alice, "because the baby's due in a fortnight, so I won't want to heave myself up on the bus any more for a while."

As the portrait was entitled *Ursula Expects*, clearly Alice would have to make the most of their time that afternoon.

"You really don't mind if I stay?" said Esther.
Cruelly Alice hesitated.

"Oh, I suppose not. I asked you here didn't I? Just don't talk to her so much that she moves about. She fidgets dreadfully and once she starts talking she's almost impossible to stop."

Esther remained in her usual place, a padded window seat overlooking the street, until she saw below her the unmistakable figure of Ursula striding towards them, coat blowing out in the wind to reveal her abdominal bulge.

"She's coming."

Esther was intrigued by Ursula's pregnancy. She was not possessed of all the technical details of reproduction – she had sneezed at the critical point when her mother was explaining it to her and had been far too embarrassed to ask for a repeat – though she knew all about gestation. She had been eight when the last of her siblings was born, so she remembered her mother's growing bulk, the increasing slowness of her movements and the slight grunt as she tried to bend down. But as for birth itself, all she remembered was the enjoyable routine they followed when a baby's arrival seemed imminent. At that point the children were sent to stay at Aunt Ettie's, a childless household where they would be treated with elaborate indulgence, and the cook, who enjoyed having children to cater for, would make a cake to be consumed on the baby's behalf. Then, when they returned home, there would be a face like a tiny fist in the cot beside their mother's bed, and the miniature features would immediately be analysed and apportioned to various uncles, aunts and grandmothers of the Hartley family.

Ursula seemed far less affected by pregnancy than Esther's mother had been. She emerged at the top of the stairs with a beatific smile.

"Oh Esther. How lovely to see you. I hoped you might be here."

She changed quickly into the orange Japanese silk gown she was wearing for the portrait, liberated the spirals of russet hair, and arranged herself on the velvet sofa, a procedure that involved settling herself on backwards and then swinging her feet over with effort, before gazing westwards with a pensive expression. She shifted around to get comfortable and patted her belly.

"It's not moving so much in there now. No room left, I suppose."

"You look awfully flushed," remarked Alice critically.

"I'm not surprised. The bus was stifling. The engine broke, and we all had to wait for the one behind, so there were twice as many people on board."

"Well, if you could try to sit still..."

"Can I get you a cup of tea?"

Ursula looked at Esther gratefully.

"Please. Then you can tell me what's going on in the world. I've been so cut off."

"Why? Where's Fogerty? Why isn't he keeping you company?" Alice stabbed the canvas belligerently.

"He's been busy. He was having to work much harder after those disappointing notices for his last book and then after he had gone all the way out to New York to address the Methodist Writers of America, some gossip about his private life meant the speech was cancelled."

"So there is a god."

Alice continued to jab at the painting. She was an intense artist, capturing her subjects with broad, full brushstrokes, in scenes that were saturated with rich colour and full sweeps of light.

Esther searched around for a change of subject. "Just think. One day people all over Britain could have Alice Cohen's paintings hanging on their walls."

"I certainly hope not," said Alice.

"Why do you say that?" enquired Ursula.

"I wouldn't want people everywhere to have my paintings. I wouldn't allow it."

"Why the hell not?"

"They wouldn't understand my work. It would be beyond them."

"What *are* you talking about?"

"What did Sickert say? 'Art fades at a breath from the drawing room.' Anyway, more to the point, I wouldn't want people to think they understood it, because that would devalue the work."

"What's that?" Ursula craned round from her rigid position. "Why should people's reactions devalue your work? It has its own worth doesn't it, independent of what people think?"

"I think the viewer contributes to the art."

"Oh come on. Surely you want to be accessible to people. You want your art to touch them."

"Not particularly. Not if they aren't capable of understanding it."

"Have you any idea how absurdly lofty you sound?"

"You're speaking as a writer Ursula. Writers are different. Of course you want as many people as possible to read your work. The more they read, the more books will be printed and the more money you will make. Besides which writing is not so much open to misinterpretation."

"That's plain anti-democratic."

"Is that bad?"

Ursula abandoned all pretence of maintaining her pose. She leaned forward and stared at Alice passionately, the flush mounting in her cheeks.

"I'd say it's fascistic. Why choose ordinary people for your subject matter if you don't want to be appreciated by ordinary people?"

"Because what I have to say isn't ordinary."

"Well I call that utterly silly. What do you think Esther?"

Esther was aware she was being used as a buffer between two confrontational characters. Alice had mentioned several times that Ursula liked a good row, and Alice also thrived on disputation. She had a particular type of blunt delivery, suggesting she was spoiling for a fight and a manner, perhaps unintentional, of implying that her opponent was entirely trivial. Esther was just embarking on her trusted tactic of agreeing with both parties when Ursula gave a little gasp.

"Whatever is the matter?"

"No. It's nothing. I don't know…I felt something peculiar." She shifted and rubbed her back. "Oooh, there it is again. Very sharp."

Alice put down her brush and went quickly over to Ursula. "You don't think….?"

"No, it's nothing." There was a vagueness to her. Somehow she didn't seem to be concentrating on them. Still holding her back with one hand she rose and picked up her bag.

"I'm awfully sorry Alice but I think I'll just get changed and go home."

"Are you sure?"

"Yes. It's nothing. I know it's nothing, the baby's not due for a couple of weeks now. Apparently you do get these twinges beforehand, according to the books I've been reading."

"Well you'll have to take a cab. You can't go back on the bus with pains, twinges or not."

"Oh no. It's all right. I'm fine now."

Then just as she was bending to put on her shoes, Ursula gasped again and leant forward, grasping the sofa back for support. "Gosh, that hurt."

"Drink some tea," offered Esther. "And you should probably lie down."

"At least sit still a minute."

"No," Ursula drained her cup and frowned. "I really think I'd be better off getting home. I will take a cab. But it's stopped now actually."

"Well at least let us come and hail it for you."

Ursula fastened her dress, put on her coat and smiled brightly.

"Oh, it's completely gone. Sorry to give you a scare. Actually Alice I think it was just backache from that excruciating sofa of yours. It's cruel of you to make your sitters suffer."

"What am I going to do about the picture?"

"I'll come back tomorrow if you like."

"All right," smiled Alice grudgingly. "I do just need to get the eyes right. That indignant scowl of yours."

Though Alice's studio was part of her family home, it had a separate entrance to the street, accessed by steep stairs. The women descended in single file, with Esther holding Ursula's bag, but suddenly Ursula stopped and grasped the banister, her face contorted.

"What is it? Is it another pain?"

For at least a minute she didn't speak, but remained gripping the rail, her knuckles white. Then she relaxed and said: "Yes. It's coming in waves. It comes, then it goes away again. Sort of grips you…That one was the most awful…." She slumped down on the stair and wiped sweat from her forehead. Her flush had been replaced by a greyish pallor. "I'll be all right when I get in a cab."

"No you won't. I don't think you're all right. I think we should get help," said Esther.

"There's no-one here," pointed out Alice.

That much was true. Sidonie and her husband were away in the country and the maids had been given the weekend off. Esther was paralysed with indecision. She could ring her mother, who at least was an expert on babies, but the thought of her coming over from Chalcott Street and flapping about uselessly was too horrifying. Not to mention the moral indignation. Besides it was Saturday.

"Oh God. Look what's happened now. What does that mean?" Ursula lifted her skirt to show the white thigh above her stocking where a purplish rivulet of blood trickled.

Crammed in the stairwell they looked at each other in desperation.

"We need a doctor. Esther, what about your doctor?"

"You mean Dr Byng?" Dr Byng was a mumbling, silver-haired physician, who wore a pinstripe suit and had a brass plate with his name and letters on outside his practice in Wimpole Street. "I don't think he works at weekends."

"No. Whatever his name is. Your landlord. The bad-tempered one."

"Dr Stevens. Oh, I couldn't."

"I think….." Ursula was once more rigid with pain. "I think maybe a doctor would be a good idea."

Frank Stevens was savouring the profound pleasure of a Saturday morning on which he would not be attending the clinic. He was sitting down with de Maupassant's *Bel Ami*, part of a scheme he had to read all the classics he had missed as a young man due to studying constantly for medical exams. He had attended the same Oxford college as his father and grandfather before him, and had been destined for the same career path as them too, until his training was interrupted by the war. The war changed everything. He joined the medical unit of the Oxford University Officer Training Corps and in time was assigned through the Royal Army Medical Corps for a bout of training in Essex before being sent out to the front. He remembered the evening the unit had left for Southampton and then on to France. It was a cold night, but as he stood on the freezing deck looking down as the ship's prow cleaved the black water, he had actually been excited, genuinely looking forward to the battle ahead. He worried the war might be over before he caught sight of it. That was not a sensation that lasted long.

The war had changed everything, yet now the idea was that you were to go on as if nothing had happened. The war was an experience that was with him every day, and yet in another way entirely distant and separate, as though it had happened to a different person entirely. The war shattered your sense of self, but the plan was to construct a different identity for yourself and shrug it on like a set of new clothes when the fighting ended. To stand in the bus every morning, pressing companionably next to your fellow passengers, as though you had never stood over another man with a bayonet and run it through his bowels. To hear the crack of fireworks with excitement instead of wanting to throw yourself into the nearest ditch.

The war was also the reason why he was not, like his father and grandfather, maintaining a consultancy in Harley Street, or driving a shiny car, but had instead taken a job in a hospital in the East End and now took the bus every morning to a shabby little clinic in Bethnal Green.

His father couldn't understand it, but he felt comfortable there. The people he saw were overwhelmingly the working poor, the men's illnesses stemming mostly from drink, the women's from malnutrition and bearing too many children. When they came to the clinic they would sit in mute obedience, enduring a pain or clutching a frightened child. Something about the conditions there ensured that Stevens had never acquired the attitude of jovial condescension which so many of his fellow doctors in hospitals cultivated, but had instead become tight-lipped and was generally considered a little terse.

He heard the telephone bell with a pang of disappointment, though he did not consider leaving it to ring.

"Dr Stevens? It's Esther. Esther Hartley."

"You sound out of breath."

"I wonder if you could help me. Well, not me. My friend. Ursula Davis. She's having a baby."

"Well generally her husband would be the right person to speak to…."

"There isn't. I mean she hasn't got a husband."

"I see," he said, not allowing surprise to affect his level professional tone. "Well then Miss Davis will need to see the doctor at whatever nursing home she plans to be confined. Does she have a telephone number to hand?"

In the background Ursula emitted a low moan of pain.

"No. She doesn't. And besides, that's in Crystal Palace, and we think she's having the baby right now."

"We think?"

"My friend Alice. She's here too. Look, could you come?"

"Really, Esther if there is any sort of urgency to this you'll need to telephone an ambulance. I'm not the right person to help you here."

"No. She doesn't want that."

"Well I'm afraid professionally I can't…."

Esther lowered her voice to an anguished whisper. "Dr Stevens. Frank. She's got blood coming out of her and she seems to be in a lot of pain. You're the only doctor we know. Could you come? Please."

He hesitated a moment. "You haven't told me where you are."

He took the address and left the house at a brisk walk, case in one hand, forgetting de Maupassant and trying mentally to brush up on his obstetrics instead.

First babies - he could only assume it was a first baby but with this unmarried friend of Esther's perhaps one should assume nothing - first babies, anyway, tended to take longer to be born. Even as he made his way to Chelsea, Frank Stevens was therefore reassuring himself that there would be several hours in which to get the woman into a hospital or at least into someone else's hands before an actual delivery was needed. Because the fact was, it was a fair while since he had attended his last childbirth. In the neighbourhoods where he operated, the mothers always relied on local wise women or midwives for their births, rather than go to the expense of calling the doctor out. The same woman would often have delivered every child in the street and would perform occasional abortions too when the prospect of another mouth to feed became too much.

From what he could remember the blood Esther had referred to was obviously the show, and this could precede actual delivery by as much as thirty-six hours. The pain did suggest that contractions were underway, but that too was not definitively suggestive of any immediate outcome. He had soothed himself into a state of near calm when he knocked at the smart address he had been given and found the door flung open by Esther, white faced and fearful, and heard from somewhere up above the long, keening wails of a woman in established labour.

"Oh thank you, thank you for coming."

He followed her up the stairs and looked curiously around him. He assumed it was an artist's studio, with enormous canvases stacked against the wall and long picture windows through which a high, pure light poured in. In the centre of the room, the pregnant woman, wearing a theatrically flowing orange robe, was walking in circles supported by another girl, until she came to a rest, moaning, and leant forward over the end of a grubby velvet sofa.

"Are you Dr Stevens?" The large girl held out her hand. She seemed a little more composed than Esther. "It's very kind of you to come out. This is Ursula Davis. She's been like this for, oh, at least an hour."

He knelt down to open his case. "Hello Miss Davis. I'm Dr Stevens. Now could you try to get comfortable because I'm going to need to examine you. Is there anywhere I can wash my hands?"

He stood over the sink as Ursula manoeuvred herself back onto the sofa and then came back to her, his hands running over her so gently, it looked to Esther as though he was barely touching her, before slipping his fingers deftly between her legs.

"Well you seem to be doing very well indeed. I think we may have a baby here in no time at all."

He turned to Esther and Alice and his tone changed sharply.

"Boil water, get me soap and towels. And any carbolic you can find. Quick as you can. And a sheet to put over here."

To Esther, innocent and unprepared, the violence of the birth she was witnessing was horrifying, like standing impotently over somebody being tortured. How could someone feel as much pain as Ursula was plainly feeling and not faint? Was childbirth always as dreadful as this and if so, how could it be that she had simply not known? How was it that the arrival of a child was always painted as a tender, pastel- coloured experience, involving cherubs and other gentle things? With what callous irony was that vision superimposed on this mediaeval chaos of tears and pain?

She had known in a general way of course. People talked of labour pains, and women died in childbirth - but if she had ever thought about it before, she would have imagined it like a tooth extraction - which would hurt intensely, but be over very quickly. Instead, she saw now, women routinely underwent this protracted, horrifying ordeal and there was absolutely nothing one could do about it. You couldn't stop it, or call a halt. How was it that her mother, and whole generations of women before her, had not told this terrible truth rather than keeping it a prim confidence? She pictured the legions of shadowy women, stretching back through history, conspiring to suppress their fearful secret. It seemed like the most terrible conspiracy in the world. In Ursula's moans, she even thought she detected a note of surprise at the amount of pain that was racking her.

In her shock, the relief at seeing Frank Stevens was immense. The sardonic manner he routinely adopted with her had vanished, to be replaced with a brisk professionalism. His face was tense with concentration and concern. For the next half hour she stood mutely by the sofa where Ursula laboured and when he gave orders Esther responded gladly, grateful to be helping. Alice, who seemed far less perturbed by the whole event, stationed herself at Ursula's head, dabbing her brow with a cold flannel as Dr Stevens focused on the birth, uttering a steady stream of muttered encouragement. At one point, when Ursula seemed to have entered another realm of pain and confusion and her eyes rolled wildly round the room, he put a hand up against her cheek and said softly,

"Don't be frightened. It will soon be over."

Meanwhile Esther hung back, awkwardly unwilling to intrude. Then suddenly he grabbed her forward saying 'Just hold her hand would you Esther?' and Ursula clenched her hand so tightly it hurt and at that moment a surprising stream of yellowish cloudy water and mucus gushed from Ursula, soaking the sofa. At the same time the tenor of her groans lowered to an effortful grunt.

"That's right, time to push now. That's very good."

The pushing was a new kind of horror. Ursula's face was white and covered with sweat, flung back against the sofa with her teeth gritted, her legs braced against the end of the sofa with force. It seemed to go on and on, as Ursula strained to expel the enormous thing from her body. It must have been an hour before, from beneath the great white dome of the belly, tight with its blue veins, Esther saw a tiny grey wedge and took seconds to realise it was the crown of a head, whorled with dark spirals of hair, just visible between Ursula's split flesh. In a moment the head was out completely and Esther could see a minute face with eyes screwed up. It turned round to one side.

"Gently now. I don't want you to push. Can you just pant please, blow the air out of your mouth. That's right."

Ursula seemed to gulp air and blew it through her mouth in little rapid pants while Dr Stevens, his hand bigger than the baby's head, probed gently round its neck, as though looking for something. Ursula wailed, gave another almighty push and out of her in a slithering rush came a coiled blueish object covered in blood and white slime.

"Towel Esther."

She handed him a towel and he cleaned the face and eyes.

"Congratulations. A boy."

"Oh." Esther's eyes were brimming with tears. "A boy."

It was silent, so he hoisted the child by its ankles and gave it a tap, producing a tiny, high pitched bleat. Ursula propped herself up and stared at the child, which lay curled on her belly, frowning with its navy eyes open.

Stevens bent down to concentrate on delivering the afterbirth, and then cut the cord and checked the baby over, wiping a fleck of blood from its face. He then wrapped it in the towel and restored it to its mother's arms. Its cries ceased as by chance or instinct it found the breast and began to suckle its first hot drops of milk.

The doctor looked away. He felt most peculiar. Having swabbed the mother with disinfectant solution, he balled up Sidonie's soaked and bloodied towels and tried to concentrate on the clinical details - which were uncomplicated - but all the time he wondered why such a mundane event as a birth should have this curious effect on him. He had attended several more straightforwardly joyful than this one - the arrival of a being, which to judge from its inauspicious social origins would be marked by stigma, not to mention the burden it had brought on its mother, plainly an educated, refined girl. The child was most probably destined for adoption within days, but it was thankfully not his business to discuss that. He walked away to wash his hands and observed the three women, their heads close together, crying and whispering endearments, poring over the boy, stroking the fuzz of fur still on his back and the tiny pouch of the mouth, holding the bent purple feet, marvelling at the length of fingers and toes, let alone their very existence. Stevens saw that his presence, once so urgently required, was now superfluous.

When he packed away his instruments and bent to fasten up his case, he found his fingers were trembling. He must be in a slight state of shock, he thought, down to the unexpectedness of it all, or indeed to this place itself. Since he arrived in the huge, airy room, smelling of paint and turpentine, the sun had sunk so much deeper that space was now replete with exultant colour as the canvases were lit up by shafts of late afternoon light. They were great life sized figures most of them, with flesh so lustrous it might be pulsing with blood. Though the room was long and high, with bare, echoey floorboards, the paintings made it intimate, like a haven from the outside world.

He was reminded suddenly of a church he had visited in Florence, before the war, when he had stepped quite by chance off a dusty street into a cool, hushed space crowded with Renaissance frescos. The place was empty, but for a solitary priest stacking chairs who gave them a harsh, unfriendly stare, but Stevens recalled the sudden joy that rose in him as he gazed round at the beatific Madonnas and their smiling Christs, their colours glowing through the gloom. One in particular he liked. It was scabbed and peeling in places, the dark-eyed Mary shadowed by a penumbra of dirt and the plump baby obscured by a dim veil of soot, but the more he peered, the more it was as though he was seeing the familiar scene for the first time. He had stood there for a long while until his companion, a guide, had protested, trying to hurry him on.

"Please signor, these figures are nothing. Quite ordinary, you understand? There is nothing of any significance here."

The guide was right. They were ordinary, that mother, with her grave, long-nosed renaissance face, and the child on her lap squirming to give the painter a watchful stare. As ordinary as any family.

There was no point in disturbing the girls. Esther had gone to make tea. For a moment more, in Alice's studio, Stevens looked avidly at the pictures, like a person starved of everything they represented, before letting himself quietly out of the door.

Chapter Twenty

To outward eyes at least, Elmer Barrington carried on as if nothing was amiss. Partly this was to prevent Iris's "adventure" drawing unwelcome attention to his business affairs and partly because ignoring pain was knit into his very nature. His days were spent at the building site, or supervising a recent shipment of antiquities he had purchased, and in the evenings he attended the odd dance or society dinner with Edwina Glencoe. Otherwise he dined alone at home. The absence of Iris was not commented upon. Cairns, whose normal demeanour was of a man treading on eggshells, now behaved as if he were picking his way through shards of poisoned glass. Though this attitude of exaggerated caution annoyed his master, it was very hard to articulate Cairns' precise trespass, so Barrington contented himself with complaining loudly about imaginary tarnish on the cutlery and sending back a dish of perfectly respectable fish on the grounds that it was undercooked.

It was with some relief then that Cairns opened the door to Iris at ten o'clock on a Tuesday evening and stood back as she glided into the hall and handed him her coat. She was wearing clothes he did not recognise, and her hair had been newly styled. But she looked pale and distinctly tired by her experience.

Barrington was in his study. Just that afternoon he had had some exquisite granite statues of the lioness deity Sakhmet delivered and he was very pleased with them. He was not one of the big spenders in the antiquities world, far from it, but he prided himself in having people in the right places. People who knew where the pick of the pieces would be and how to get hold of them.

He was entranced by the quality of the pieces, standing almost as proudly perfect as when they were made over three thousand years before, but even they could not take his mind off the irksome business of Iris. Samuel Dux's telephone call from Paris was a measure of reassurance, and had allowed his anger to simmer down into something more like aggrieved annoyance and the persistent reminder that both of his children had resoundingly turned out very differently from the way he had planned.

The inadequacies of Charles had always been apparent. Though the boy had been groomed to take over the business, Barrington knew in himself that it was Iris, not her brother, who had inherited the Barrington traits of ruthlessness and determination while Charles had picked up only his mother's soft sentimentality. He was a gentle boy, with a dislike of confrontation and a penchant for animals. He was always fashioning splints for injured rabbits, or feeding doomed fledglings with a pipette. He recoiled from any kind of aggression. God knows how he had suffered at the front.

Iris however, had always had an eye for getting what she wanted and it was that which frustrated him about her. For what Iris should most obviously get - a good marriage to a well placed family, if not aristocracy - she seemed in no hurry to acquire. Granted, she would inherit everything that Elmer Barrington had built up in his life. She would be a rich woman in her own right, with property in London and the country and in the south of France, not to mention something back in Chicago. But that was standing still. Capitalism was about multiplying assets, using what you had, rather than simply letting it stagnate.

Now, owing to her wilful and silly behaviour, the odds on building on her inheritance with a good marriage seemed longer than ever. Edwina had assured him that very few people had wind of the episode, but that only meant it would spread like measles once the season started. Having a reputation as a bolter before she had even married did not bode well.

He recalled Samuel Dux's tone on the telephone. The boy had sounded angry and curt. He evidently had a mind of his own. After all, despite Barrington's rage, it had not been entirely Samuel's fault that the girl had eloped that evening. Barrington hoped that this would not mean the boy would try to evade him by seeking employment elsewhere. He had already needed to drop a little hint, to apply a little pressure, which could have scared him off, so it was all the more essential that he should now press ahead swiftly with the other matter.

He stiffened and put a hand on his back where it hurt him. He wished his wife were still here. It was at times like these that he missed her most. After all, it was a woman who should be dealing with girls, not a father, and Edwina had never been able to share this kind of worry with him. Apart from anything else, she was far too intimidated by him. It had been so long now, he couldn't properly remember Margaret's face.

Even as he was thinking this he heard the slam of the door and walked into the hall to see the image of his dead wife pallid and tight-lipped, taking off her coat. Iris busied herself with a bag and avoided his eyes. The sight of her, and her mother's ghost in her, robbed him of all he had planned to say. He put his hands on her shoulders, forced her to look at him and in a voice of stone said: "Go to bed now Iris. I'll speak to you in the morning."

In the event it was Selina Vickers who got in first. She had heard, God knows how, though probably through the servants, that Iris had returned the previous evening and took it upon herself to drive round in the morning without telephoning beforehand. Selina believed there were times when Elmer needed a woman's help and that silly fool Edwina who had no family and no expertise in anything except couture and hair crimping and bridge, was certainly not going to provide that. Having barged her way in and sent Cairns off for coffee she found Elmer poring over some enormous statues, which looked far too large for the room.

"They're rather big, aren't they?"

"So they should be at the price I paid."

She could see that Elmer was having one of his bad days by the poker-straight demeanour he adopted, one arm on the mantelpiece, the other on his back. Without preamble she plumped herself down and said: "Well, thank God she's come back."

"I'm supposed to be thankful am I? I suppose you're going to tell me to treat her gently. Tell her well done for coming home."

"She's young, Elmer, and without a mother. Be patient with her. After all, nobody knows about it."

"You know about it."

"But you can trust me."

"That fellow Samuel Dux knows about it. He was the one who had to fetch her back."

"He seemed a rather sensible chap to me. Certainly not the type to gossip."

"It'll be the talk of every silly women's gathering by lunchtime."

"Trust me, Elmer. It's as good as forgotten. Let's be realistic, plenty of young women have escapades like this nowadays. I'm sorry to say it, but it's a fact of life, and I don't think anyone is so shocked by it. She hasn't gone and married Bunny has she?"

"No. Though the fellow did me the courtesy of sending me a telegram informing me he was planning to marry my daughter, it appears that his plans were thwarted."

"Well thank God for that. Dreadful man. Just be glad she came to her senses. We can't all choose whom our daughters love, unfortunately."

"Oh, so I should just relax and wait around for her to run off with the next numbskull who thinks he would like to share her inheritance?"

Selina fixed a cigarette in her holder and waited until the maid who had brought coffee had left the room.

"No. Not quite. Listen to me, Elmer. Iris needs an occupation. A job even. She's got a brain in that pretty head of hers. Had you ever thought of having her in the business?"

"Nah. She's smart, I'll give you that, but the girl has no judgement."

Selina had to admit that Iris had shown a shocking lack of judgement in her choice of Bunny Devine, but she was not to be put off.

"I happen to think she could be a real asset to you."

"No, Charles would have taken over the business. It's not the thing for a girl."

The ability of poor Charles to run a business had been much overestimated, Selina thought. It was just one of the ways Elmer failed to face reality about his children. She exhaled smoke through dark crimson lips.

"Let me speak candidly, Elmer. Iris is not like Dolly. Dolly could spend all her time riding horses and hunting and playing tennis and be as happy as Larry. Iris needs something to do. She's crying out for some sort of occupation. A few years ago she'd have been a VAD or something. We all did an awful lot in the war. It's a great pity people expect women just to sit around now doing crochet until they're married. Had you thought of letting her help out at this building project of yours? I don't know…" she searched her mind for some suitably feminine occupation, "helping with the decorating or something? You were telling me how much there is yet to do. Sybil Colefax might give her a few pointers."

"Decorating?" Elmer's face appeared thunderous for one moment, as though she had suggested tricking out his new building in chintz. Then he sighed and smiled.

"You're right, Selina. That could be just the thing. Though not the Colefax woman. Can't stand her."

"Who were you thinking of then?"

He stared into his coffee cup. "Woman called Celia

Urquart. She's very innovative I understand…."

Very vulgar, was Selina's private assessment, but she understood exactly why Elmer had suggested her. Celia Urquart, though nowhere near so well known as Sybil Colefax and a frightful arriviste to boot was a chum of Edwina Glencoe, who was always trying to inveigle Elmer into employing her friends. Celia was a divorcée who ran around with a raffish set of photographers, stage people and journalists. She had been a model or an actress Selina recalled, before alighting on design to make a living.

"Well if you think Celia's up to it…"

"If she's not, I'll soon know."

As she made her way to the door he cleared his throat and said "Selina. I want you to know I value your advice. Thank you."

Chapter Twenty-one

London was launching into a sparkling summer. The white of the stucco terraces gleamed against a high blue sky. Late magnolias, with petals like fine porcelain, flourished in the gardens of Eaton Square and the grass in Hyde Park was a luminous green, as though lit from within. The season was well underway – Ascot, Henley and Lords stood like skittles in Society's calendar and everyone prepared to tackle them with gusto before decamping to Scotland in August.

But for Iris, time was suspended. Since returning from Paris she had found herself together with Samuel, yet still, frustratingly, apart. By day he was at Barrington House, and in the evening, Iris's father was there too, his heavy presence permeating every corner of the house. His little eyes would follow them whenever they left the room. He seemed to be watching Samuel even more acutely than usual. There was barely any chance for them to talk and they were obliged to sustain themselves with snatched moments of intimacy. Occasionally Samuel brushed against her in the cool vault of the hall, and once, in an unlit corridor, pressed his lips against the shadowy dip of her clavicle. A couple of times she slipped into his room – Charles' room – to embrace him, and when she did she found the happiness which had once imbued that room seeped back like great shafts of sunlight. Because they had agreed to keep their secret, Samuel barely spoke to her publicly, and when he did his manner was reserved and polite. But now Iris saw the wry lift of his mouth, and his every comment seemed freighted with double meaning.

The most harmless of enquiries, "Can I pour you some tea?", for example, or "Will you be out tonight?" seemed to vibrate with sexual tension. When he spoke her name it brought a tinge to her cheeks and made the blood run faster in her veins.

The problem was, they could not tell anyone. Neither of them doubted that if Iris's father knew what had happened, he would do everything in his power to prevent them meeting. So they agreed that until Samuel found somewhere else to live, Iris should carry on as she always did. Which meant that Samuel was obliged to look on dispassionately when an escort with a yellow Rolls Royce arrived to collect her for dinner at the Cavendish Hotel, or the ballet or the opera, or when she glided out to the theatre dressed in a shift of aquamarine sequins that hugged her slight figure and made the light shimmer and ripple around her.

The chance for a conversation came quite unexpectedly. Elmer Barrington had decided that he needed to have his portrait painted, to hang in the entrance foyer of Barrington House. Given that the rest of his grand project was absolutely of the moment, he had rejected the usual list of artists patronised by society circles, who would reproduce him conventionally in flattering, soft-edged oils, in favour of a controversial new painter, fresh out of art school and much talked of in society circles. This choice was typical of Barrington. His artistic acumen was rarely wrong, and this painter specialised in bold, unorthodox portraits, with dramatic colour and odd, incidental details. To add to the originality, she was a woman.

Barrington was planning to have himself immortalised surrounded by a number of his most precious possessions, so that Saturday Cairns and the manservant had been roped in to transporting these pieces into the morning room, where their master was planning to arrange himself beside his eclectic hoard. There he would sit, surrounded by his Etruscan vases and his Ming plates, his head of Rameses the Second and his statue of Venus, a triumphant, latter day Napoleon, amid the strewn treasures of conquered empires.

Samuel had no idea of this when he came down on Saturday morning to find the coming and going of elaborately wrapped antiquities in the hall and Cairns with a pained expression, trapped like an Egyptian slave beneath the head of Rameses as the doorbell sounded.

"Don't worry Cairns. I'll answer it."

He opened the door to a bohemian figure in a light coat patterned with a melange of orange and mauve spirals, and a necklace of dangling pearls. She thrust a bold hand towards him.

"Hello. I'm Alice Cohen."

"Oh hello," said Samuel distractedly.

"The painter."

"I think it must be Mr Barrington you want. He's in the morning room."

Once Alice Cohen was safely ensconced with Barrington, Samuel sought out Iris straight away.

They walked to the gates of Kensington Gardens and headed for the boating pond, where the nannies like a flock of starlings in their black uniforms parked their perambulators and chatted. Standing in the dappled shade of an oak tree they watched the gulls diving and disputing as a child scattered crumbs like confetti in the air.

It was a perfect July morning. The air was clear and the banks of rose beds perfumed the air. A bee droned past them, heavy with pollen, and dust drifted like diamonds in the sunlight slanting down through the canopy of leaves. Standing there, so close together, Samuel felt an almost unbearable attraction to Iris, but he couldn't kiss her. People didn't kiss in the park. Instead he took her hand, trying to channel the whole of his excitement into that slender point of contact.

"I hope that portrait painter keeps him sitting there for hours," he said.

"I hope he proves unusually difficult to *capture*," she laughed.

"I can't bear it much longer, Iris. Not being able to be with you properly."

"I know."

"If your father finds out…"

"*When* my father finds out…."

"When he finds out about us. And if he doesn't agree, which he won't, I'll need to move out and find another job. That won't be a problem for me. But will you be strong enough to defy him?"

"How can you doubt me?" she whispered, squeezing his hand in fierce response.

He looked down at her, glowing with happiness in her yellow pleated skirt and a knitted cardigan, the light glancing onto her face and making her squint at him, and he could hardly believe that she loved him. He thought of the time in the Paris hotel – their one time together - with something approaching pain because he craved her so much. He imagined her body bare and undulating beneath him and the slight cushion of her pursed lips, offering herself up to him for his possession. Her legs wrapped around him. Her breasts pressed against him. Excitement trembled up within him.

Above them a blackbird broke into song, sending its high, clear notes ecstatically into the air. He wanted to preserve this moment for ever, because he knew that the time had come for him to risk losing it all.

But how could he ever expect her to understand?

"Before that, Iris, there's something I need to tell you."

"Do you? Say it then."

"No," he said hastily. "Not here. Not now. It will take a little time. Perhaps tonight?"

"I was going out with Dolly, but…"

"Go then. I'll wait in the library until you come in. Try not to let your father hear you come in."

What did Samuel have to say to her? Iris thought – no, she was certain – that she knew, and she smiled at his hesitation. Could he possibly believe, even for a moment, that she would say no?

"Tonight then."

To fill the time and stop the same thoughts circling round and round in his mind, he arranged to see Alan. They were to meet in a club, some kind of hang-out for artists, where Alan was hoping to persuade some man to provide sketches for his magazine.

"It's called Nefertiti's. It's an interesting place. A friend of mine put me on to it. Apparently Augustus John goes there and Epstein. Anyway this chap I'm meeting was in the Artists' Rifles out at Ypres. He kept a lot of sketches of trench life and I want to use some of them to go with my special issue."

Nefertiti's was in a square north of Soho, in the midst of a drab frontage of Georgian houses, sooty and unkempt. On the way up the stairs Samuel passed a woman in a mangy fur stole being pursued by a man carrying a live bird of prey on his arm. In a high attic room with bare floorboards and simple wooden tables and chairs, he found Alan sitting with a girl in a pink hat. He had never seen Alan with a girl before.

"Samuel! I'd like you to meet Esther Hartley. She's…"

"I work with Alan," she said quickly. She had a frank smile and curious brown eyes. This must be the girlfriend then. Samuel thought she seemed pleased, almost relieved, to see him.

"I've been telling Esther all about your experiences out in Egypt," said Alan, "and your hard luck having to live with Elmer Barrington."

"So interesting," said Esther, leaning towards him and cupping her face in her hands. "Being at the excavation I mean. We saw the exhibition at Wembley but it can't have been anything like the real thing."

"I'm sure it's not. Did you enjoy it?"

"Be careful, he's the expert," laughed Alan. "He spends all

day reproducing those things."

"It sounds dreadfully rude to say this," Esther made a wry little grimace, as though the admission might offend him. "But I found it rather disturbing. When you look at those faces, those Egyptian faces, I always think there's something so haunting about them. Something I don't understand. Their world seems so alien to me. And dreadfully harsh. When I see pictures of those treasures, I can't help thinking of all the poor slaves who had to build the tombs and paint the walls and cart around those huge blocks of stone. Thousands of people who just happened to be slaves and it was as though their life was nothing, whereas the life of a Pharaoh was infinitely important."

"So what's changed?" scoffed Alan.

"I know I sound naïve and I'm not expressing it properly," she appealed to Samuel, her large brown eyes willing him to understand her, "But when I look at those ancient faces, I don't feel admiration or wonder or excitement. I just feel fear. They look so unforgiving, so judgemental. Didn't you feel that Samuel? Even for a moment?"

He hesitated, so she laughed awkwardly at her own outburst. "Oh forget it. Perhaps I'm being silly. And that's not to say that I don't feel terribly sorry for that poor boy."

Samuel's eyes jerked up.

"What boy?"

"The young king, of course," she mused. "I saw his death mask - at the exhibition you know – and he looked so beautiful, and so sad. All that gold, all those treasures, he had everything the world could offer and what good did it do him? He still died far too young."

"Ah," interrupted Alan. "This looks like our man!"

The artist was an abrupt northerner wearing an army greatcoat, grey flannel trousers with visible holes and a torn shirt. He had dark, rumpled hair, full lips and a wide, almost arrogant stare. He shook hands with Alan, nodded at Esther and Samuel, then squatted down on the floor and opened a portfolio of work.

It was full of stark, melancholy trench landscapes, harsh, geometric forms with stumps of trees rearing up in the foreground and charcoal drawings of towns reduced to rubble, the facades of houses still standing like the tracery of a ruined abbey. There were portraits of the soldiers themselves, bandaged and damaged, bent and shuffling.

"My God," said Alan reverently. "They're even better than I'd been told." He began outlining the magazine's payment rates but the artist rocked back on his haunches and closed the portfolio up.

"They're not for sale," he said shortly. "I won't sell them."

"But I thought….."

"Why would I profit from other men's despair? I don't see myself as an artist anymore. I'm just a messenger."

Dismayed, Alan embarked on a defence of his magazine's purpose and his idea for a special issue, devoted to the wounded men who had been left behind after the war.

"We're trying to force people to think about the hidden legacy of the war," he said coaxingly. "And these are very powerful drawings. When you see these mens' faces….." The artist interrupted him.

"What I mean is," he spelt out slowly. "You can print them for free. If I took money for these pictures I'd be just another war profiteer. Leeching off my dead comrades. I had some toff in here the other day, trying to buy my work. He was trying to flatter me. Kept talking about how I was going to get famous. How my work was undervalued. What does that mean? Does he think art is the same as pork bellies, or barrels of oil? Something just to buy and sell? That has a value you can measure? All it told me was that he knew nothing at all. The man was an idiot. I sent him away."

At this point, some of the artist's friends joined the table and they set off in a discussion about the war, and the generation of greedy old men who had profited from it.

Alan maintained that the new socialism was in grave danger

of failing.

"Even with our new economic order, who has the power? Who controls the means of production? My fear is if Mr Ramsay MacDonald does not strengthen this tottering government of his, then it will be the same men who held the power before the war. Baldwin and his crew."

"Capitalists!"

"Every last one of them! A generation of spongers, feeding off the dead."

The conversation rose and fell around him but Samuel did not participate. His mouth was dry with nerves and his mind kept returning to his meeting with Iris later that evening. How would she react when she heard what he had to tell her?

They had agreed to keep their secret while Samuel remained living under Barrington's roof, but he feared the true nature of their relationship may prove impossible to conceal. She had almost given them away that morning when she touched his hand beneath the breakfast table, only luckily her father was helping himself to scrambled eggs and his back was turned. But Barrington would find out soon enough, that was certain, and Samuel worried what would happen when he did. It was becoming hard to ignore his growing sense of unease about Elmer Barrington. Violet had told the old man something, that much was certain. All the more reason then for him to gather his courage and explain to Iris what had happened.

Barrington. At that moment it was as if his thoughts had actually been articulated for he clearly heard the name "Barrington" spoken aloud.

It was Alan, leaning towards his group of listeners with a gleam in his eye.

"And then there's Elmer Barrington, the sugar millionaire. The tycoon who's building a temple to himself in the City of London. There goes another war profiteer! I've been looking into him. Between ourselves we'll soon be hearing a lot more about him!"

What on earth was Alan talking about? Samuel was about to ask him, but thought the better of it. The idea that Barrington had been some kind of war profiteer was no doubt another of the obscure conspiracies that Alan liked to collect. It was typical of his melodramatic streak. Yet Samuel felt a rising panic that they should even be discussing his employer like this. If Barrington were to discover that he and his friends spent their spare time publicly disparaging him, would he ever look favourably on a relationship between Samuel and his daughter?

Bidding Esther a polite good night, and with a curt nod to Alan, he marched out into the Soho night.

By the time he got back to Belgravia it was after nine and the house was quiet. He guessed Iris had not yet returned. In the darkened library a fire burned low in the grate, throwing a red glow onto the chesterfield and rich Persian rugs. Samuel went over to the large sofa table which was laid out with *Country Life, The Tatler*, and *Art and Archaeology* as well as all the daily newspapers. He selected a paper, then sat beneath a brass reading lamp, glancing in desultory fashion at a report about the Prince of Wales breaking his collarbone in a steeplechase near Leighton Buzzard. After a few minutes he heard the door shut softly and he looked up, but the dark figure coming towards him across the rug with a waft of cigar smoke was not Iris. For a moment there was no sound but the soft clunk of coal shifting in the grate.

"I trust you're feeling satisfied with yourself," said Barrington.

"Forgive me?" Samuel held his hand up to shield his eyes from the light, but Barrington's face remained in shadow. He felt a surge of panic. For an irrational second he wondered if Barrington could be referring to Samuel's discussion at the club that evening, but reassured himself it would be impossible.

"Satisfied with what?"

"With those figures of course," said Barrington, rocking backwards on his heels, as though pleased to have discomfited him.

The previous day Samuel had finished the likenesses of the wall paintings found in the tomb, in which the dead king, accompanied by his Ka, embraces the god Osiris. They were to adorn two huge decorative screens for the Barrington House dining room.

"Ah. Thank you."

"And the hieroglyphics are a triumph," Barrington waved his cigar expansively. "Though what with the decline in this country's culture and education I doubt anyone will be able to read them fifty years from now."

"Well the fascination with Egyptology has lasted thousands of years, so I suppose it might linger a little longer."

"I hope you're right. But whatever happens, I'm grateful to you. It was a smart idea of Violet Esterhazy to recommend you."

Violet. The way Barrington spoke her name gave him a jolt of alarm. Samuel wanted to stand up but Barrington remained looming above him, with uncomfortable closeness. Then he came even nearer.

"In fact, on the subject of Violet, there's another little job I'd like you to undertake."

"Oh…"

"It's a delicate job."

"What is it?"

Barrington turned his back suddenly and walked across the room to trickle some whisky into two crystal glasses. He was thinking how serendipitous it was that this negotiating tool had just fallen into his lap. He had waited all this time for some infallible way to get a hold over the boy, some way to ensure he did exactly what he wanted, and then just that morning he had noticed Iris and the boy touching hands beneath the breakfast table. What a piece of luck! Business was like that sometimes.

He handed a glass to Samuel with a smile.

"You like my daughter, don't you?"

Samuel took the opportunity to move slightly away.

"Er yes, I would say I liked her. Yes."

"It's more than that, I fancy."

Samuel felt the blood rise up to his face, the rush of fear. He lifted the glass to his lips, then lowered it because his hand was shaking.

"I don't…um.."

"You fancy yourself "in love" with her perhaps?"

Samuel remained silent.

"And that she, perhaps, is in love with you?"

Samuel's every nerve was tensed, willing Iris not to walk in at that moment.

"Oh yes," said Barrington quietly. "What an opportunity! A young heiress, at a vulnerable stage in her life, with an apparent need to rebel from her father. You valiantly rescue her from a scandalous episode abroad and in an instant are transformed into her saviour. You must have thought her easy prey, Mr Dux. You must have thought she had fallen at your feet! Though you are perhaps unaware of the precise terms of her inheritance."

"I have no idea of her inheritance!" said Samuel angrily.

"Evidently not. Because you will find that even her mother's money is controlled by me, and that without my consent to her marriage she will have nothing. She will be…I think the technical word is…*destitute*."

"I am not and never have been interested in Iris's money!"

"Oh, let us drop the pretence Mr Dux. Let us talk to each other as men of the world. Iris is not the kind of girl who knows what it is to live without money. You will never find Iris wringing out her washing in some squalid tenement. She will not be cooking your supper in a little thatched cottage with hens in the yard. Iris could not even boil an egg. And I

214

have no desire for my only daughter to live that way either. I'm not sure there is any need."

Samuel made to get up and walk out but Barrington laid a detaining hand on his shoulder and continued in the same pleasant, conversational tone.

"I would never normally have contemplated ….what shall we call it?… a *tendresse*, between Iris and a man like you. But the more I have heard about you, the more I have come to admire you. I like a man who knows how to get on in life. It reminds me of myself. I like people who know how to seize opportunities when they present themselves. And from the accounts I've heard, that's what you do. Care for a smoke?"

Barrington passed a silver cigarette case and proffered a glass lighter.

"I mentioned our friend Violet. She was close to you, wasn't she?"

"We were friends," said Samuel, carefully.

"Yes 'friends', that's right. And she mentioned to me that you might have something I'd like."

Samuel could not read his expression.

"I don't know what you mean."

"I think you do."

"I'm afraid you've lost me."

Barrington's tone continued levelly. "Well let me make it clearer. You don't think I employed you just for nothing, do you? Just for a few designs and the benefit of your so-called 'professional expertise'?"

"I thought…."

"I employed you because our mutual friend Violet told me how resourceful you had been out in Egypt. And how you have in your possession something I would find rather interesting."

Comprehension, miserable and leaden, was beginning to dawn on Samuel.

Barrington leant back casually and waved his hand. "And I

would love to see it."

"If you mean what I think you mean, then I'm afraid Violet misled you."

"I doubt it."

"Well, you see I couldn't….. I mean I don't even know where it is."

"Don't know where it is? That's not true. Is it, boy? You disappeared with it. You've got it hidden somewhere haven't you? It's the pick of the pieces, the very best of the lot, I've heard. The greatest treasure of the burial chamber."

Samuel was silent. Then he whispered: "I promise you it's not possible. It's not in this country. It's in Egypt. It's long gone."

"Then find it."

"I don't know that I could. I have no idea where it is."

"If you know it's in Egypt, I want you to go back there. I'll pay you."

"I can never go back to Egypt. You don't understand."

"I think I do." Barrington's tone had modulated into a menacing growl. "Look at it this way, Mr Dux. I want something from you, and you want something of mine. You know what I want. And I'm prepared to pay handsomely for it. I've had a package of £200 placed in your room. If you get the piece, I give you my word, you will have what you want too. But if you don't, then……well then I'm afraid that my family and I will not welcome your presence as we have thus far. In fact, things could become pretty difficult for you."

Barrington crossed the room and rested one puffy hand on the head of one of the 3000 year old lionesses. Watching the priceless artefact beneath that huge fist Samuel understood how his slender chances of happiness lay entirely in Barrington's unscrupulous hands.

"And one more thing. You will leave first thing tomorrow and there is to be no contact of any kind with my daughter until you return. No letters, no meetings. Not a word. Do I make myself clear? Do we have a bargain?"

Samuel did not reply.

"Good then. I see that we do."

Chapter Twenty-two

Iris had never before been an early riser, but the next morning when she heard the delicate chink that signalled a maid bringing her cup of tea in bed, she awoke with a surge of happiness. She had the same euphoric lag between feeling and thought she remembered as a child, when you woke up excitedly at birthdays or Christmas, without knowing exactly why.

As the maid pulled open the heavy silk curtains and the light streamed into her room, glinting off the mirror and the silver brushes on her dressing table, she had thought that that was exactly like her life. Samuel had opened a window and the light had blazed in.

"I feel like my life has started again," she had whispered to him yesterday, at breakfast time.

It amazed her that she had known him, without really seeing him. As she luxuriated in the warmth of her bed, she dwelt again on the moment she had seen Samuel properly. It was when he stood over her at the café that terrible morning. His face had transfixed her. She had never seen him like that before - his jaw clenched, his sage green eyes burning with anger - and she realised that although she had scarcely considered him until that moment, though his feelings had barely registered in her life, yet her own behaviour had offended him deeply. He hadn't harangued her, as her father would have done, or criticised or complained. Instead he'd been perfectly controlled, right up until that moment in the hotel, when he had turned to her with a kind of passionate rage, and made love to her.

She ran that scene over in her mind and it still had the power to make her flesh prickle. When she went back to his hotel that morning, she had been thinking of nothing but her own misery and Bunny and the prospect of an abject return to London. But what Samuel did blotted all that out of her mind.

He took hold of her and forced her to see him afresh. The reddish hair on his chest, the pale, freckled skin of his shoulders, the urgency of his love-making and the alarming groan he uttered at the moment of climax. Until Bunny, she had never seen a man naked before, if one didn't count statues of David and that sort of thing, and Samuel was very different from Bunny indeed. That was what she had meant when she told Samuel he was different from the other men she knew. There was something about him that felt utterly foreign to her. His build was wiry and thin, so unlike the broad shouldered ease of the type of men she mixed with, who were confident in their breeding and their attractiveness, secure and rich. Samuel's body came from stock which had had to work for a living, had grafted and gone hungry. At least, that was how it felt to her and his love-making was the more intense for it. Remembering his body pounding against her, with the faintest acid tang of sweat, stirred her so much she felt dazed with desire for him. Desire for Samuel was something she would never have anticipated, but now she had experienced it, she yearned for the touch of his flesh. Just the memory of it was enough to make her flushed and sexually alert. She pictured herself moving into the circle of his arms. She felt again the slippage of clothes until they were face to face, his rough hair against her smooth skin, his muscled arms, which were strong enough to crush or at least detain her, only supporting her, his hands in her hair and her fingers running down the ridges of his back.

And now he had something to say to her, and she knew just what it would be.

It was strange that he should not have been there the night before. She had gone to the library as they arranged, but there was no sign of him, only her father, swirling a whisky round in his glass, smiling to himself at some remembered incident of the day.

She got out of bed, dressed quickly and went down to breakfast, but again there was no-one but her father, finishing off a kipper. When he saw her he smoothed his palms across the white nap of the tablecloth and cleared his throat as though he had something unpleasant to say.

"I was wondering Iris. Whether you might like a little occupation. Something to fill your days?"

"Perhaps," she said cautiously.

"You've often said you would like to be more involved in the business. I thought you might like to come and work for a while…at Barrington House."

Where Samuel worked! Side by side. With the chance of seeing him all day too. Had her father read her mind?

"I'd love to!" she said, perhaps a little too quickly.

She could start, her father added, just by watching what was going on, and later perhaps she would like to talk about interior decoration with a Mrs Urquhart, who had kindly agreed to advise on wallpaper and interior furnishing fabrics.

So at nine o'clock sharp she set off for the site in the smooth gleam of her father's Bentley and was taken up to the little architect's office. The architect seemed enthusiastic about the idea that she should be joining Mrs Urquart in the decorating scheme, but Mrs Urquart was finishing off a nine-bedroom house in Buckinghamshire and keen though she was to advise on Barrington House and in the process give Iris Barrington a little rudimentary instruction, she could not start immediately. Perhaps until then Iris would like to take a look around.

Keeping an eye out for Samuel, Iris began to reconnoitre the building, roaming from floor to floor, to see for the first time the monument on which her father had spent so much time and money.

The main work was in place, and Barrington House was scheduled to open in November. Now was the time when the fine details of the design were being perfected. The cornices and the scrolling, the metallic work of the lifts, the carving of the woodwork, the mosaic on the lobby floor. Iris walked round the gleaming halls, with their jazzy details and Egyptian influences that were so subtle and delicate, gazing at the marble and wood cut in bold, streamlined curves like some fabulous ocean liner, the surfaces sleek as racing cars, the mirrored elevators like little shining caves. She observed the opulent touches of onyx and silver leaf, the inlaid wood finishes and the glittery, beautiful mouldings. Whether in ebony or lacquer, marble or mirror, everything shone, every surface presented your own reflection glamorously back to you. There was something about the style that seemed at once new and very old, both modern and eternal. Iris began to understand her father's passion for this building. It was perfect in every detail, and perfection was a quality he held in high regard.

But though she wandered the building high and low, she could not see Samuel. That evening, he did not return to the house and when she looked in the morning his bed was untouched. There was no sign of him the following day either. At the end of the third day she said she needed a walk and returned to Kensington Gardens, but he did not appear. She loitered beneath the same oak tree, smoking fretfully, for an hour, before walking home.

With rising panic, Iris questioned Mr Holmes, but he could offer no answer. Samuel seemed to have vanished into thin air. She searched her room and his in case he had left a note, but found nothing. She had no idea where he had gone or when he would be returning, and her casual inquiries to her father were met with ambiguous replies.

Left alone, she tortured herself with possibilities. She had been so certain that Samuel was about to ask her to marry him. And now, he had disappeared without a word. Had he had second thoughts about her behaviour in Paris? Had she scared him off with the vehemence of her response?

What else could have caused him to change his mind? Had she found the man to whom she could unburden herself completely, a man who could talk without judging or condemning her, only to have him disappear without a word of warning and with no idea if he ever intended to return?

Chapter Twenty-three

He was an appealing little baby with a shock of feathery black hair and a quizzical expression. Ursula sat with him in her lap, tracing his tiny snub features with her finger.

"Don't you think he looks the absolute image of William?"

"No," said Alice. "He may be small, but he's not fat or ugly."

"Has William seen him yet?" said Esther.

"Oh yes. We thought we'd have the baby fostered, rather than adopted, so that I could see him, and when I do, Fogerty suggested he call me Auntie. So he doesn't know I'm his mother, you see. Fogerty's mother, who comes here quite often, already refers to me as Auntie."

"What a horrible idea," said Alice. "What does your mother think?"

Ursula gave a wry laugh. "I wouldn't know. There's not a chance of her coming down. Even though he's her first grandchild. Unofficially, of course. I wrote, but I've heard nothing back."

"Have you sorted out the foster parents then?"

She paused and looked at the baby. "I haven't really had a moment."

During the pregnancy, Fogerty's mother, a formidable septuagenarian dressed in unvarying black, had devoted a lot of time to what she called "Ursula's problem". She had contacted a number of adoption agencies and women had come round, proposing that the child should be taken away and placed with a decent family, who could love it and give it exactly what it needed. It would be selfish, Mrs Fogerty explained, not to want the best for her child. Mrs Fogerty plainly wanted the best for *her* child, given that William's own hypocrisy in the affair went entirely unmentioned. With unflagging energy the old Mrs Fogerty entrenched herself in

Ursula's front room and stuck to her guns. How did Ursula think a child could live with the stigma of illegitimacy? How could she compound her own wickedness with the sheer selfishness of trying to keep the child and depriving it of …(at this she gave a disdainful glance around the gloomy front room).. a decent home. What about her future husband, her future children. How could this be fair on them?

At one point a nun was brought round, who ran a home for unmarried mothers and could find a place for Ursula. The nun was worse, harsher and more unpleasant than the agency ladies, and she attempted to introduce an element of psychological authority to the situation. She knew from long experience that the best thing for mother and child alike was that baby should be taken away as soon as it was born, before the mother had time or inclination to become involved with it. And that would be it, and Ursula could get on with her life, and she would forget all about it. She really would.

Though she summoned the strength to reject the offer of purdah in a home for fallen women, Ursula had submitted to these lectures in the bovine placidity brought on by pregnancy. As well as the hormones, sheer exhaustion and creeping immobility had kept her moored to the armchair and prevented her from jumping up and showing her unwanted visitors the door. She listened to them with cool detachment and told herself she found them amusing. One day she would put them in a novel. But gradually the combination of her own poverty and the apocalyptic predictions from well-meaning women depressed her and eroded any vague confidence she had about keeping the child. How could she doubt that they knew what was best? Besides, she had not actually wanted a baby any more than she wanted to keep a camel in the back yard. To Ursula her writing had always been the most important thing in her life.

Until now that was. Now, through the fog of exhaustion, she realised she was becoming passionately attached to her child. So when eventually old Mrs Fogerty proposed the idea of fostering, Ursula pictured a kindly, childless couple, running a farm perhaps, surrounded by kittens and puppies, and a lovely farmhouse to which she, "Auntie Ursula", would make visits at weekends and exhaustedly she agreed to the plan.

None of these complications were apparent to Alice and Esther as they made their way to visit her ten days after the birth. The house was quite some way out of London and the trip there took two changes of bus. Ursula's house was a tiny one up one down, so narrow, Esther thought, it looked almost like a doll's house and far too poky to accommodate their grand, glamorous friend. But when Ursula flung open the door she was beaming reassuringly and enveloped them both in emotional hugs. She had her hair loose around her and wore a grubby linen overshirt with damp patches across the front, yet otherwise she seemed quite her normal self.

"Come in straight away and see him," she said, imperiously.

The baby was tucked up in a high blue pram. He was pinker and more rounded than he had appeared on the day of his birth and opened his eyes to observe them. They cooed over the child reverently, both too scared to hold him until Ursula scooped him up and plumped him into their arms.

"Look after him while I make you some tea," she commanded.

"Isn't there anyone here?" asked Esther. Her mother had always had a monthly nurse when the babies were born.

"Oh no. We prefer it by ourselves."

"I do admire you, coping on your own. Doesn't he wake a lot in the night?"

"Oh, he's a pretty good sleeper."

Alice looked critically round the drab parlour with its shabby furniture, worn carpet and basket of fading lilies exuding a morgue-like smell. "Has Fogerty been to visit?"

"Of course."

"Where is he now?"

"He's lecturing. But his mother dropped in. And very kindly made me a meal while she was here."

"So what did he say? Is he planning to leave his wife for you?"

Ursula came back into the room with a laden tea tray and Esther jumped up to take it.

"No, he's not going to leave her, Alice. I told you. Fogerty doesn't see conventional marriage as important for the future of human relationships. And nor do I."

She went off again to put the white roses Esther had brought in some water. The girls followed her into a dank kitchenette looking out on a concreted yard.

"What does he believe in?" said Alice, allowing her finger to travel along the table, collecting a frill of dust.

"Well, if you really want to know, he believes that we share a passionate, essential love, which is probably deeper than any other love we will find. But that doesn't mean that each of us shouldn't experience what he calls contingent relationships with others. That way we will both remain free, and our relationship will not be polluted by possessiveness."

Alice laughed. "The man's a sadist. He's insane."

"How conventional you sound," replied Ursula levelly.

"He probably thinks Ursula's independent enough to cope."

"Thank you Esther. He does. And I agree with him. He believes that if women are ever going to produce the same masterpieces as men, they must be given the same freedoms as men. To have the freedom to create we need freedom of experience."

"So this is freedom of experience then?" said Alice, helping herself to another biscuit.

"Absolutely."

"It seems horribly *furtive* to me. And when are you going to get time for these contingent relationships?"

"Oh, when I've got my life back on track. It's not at the top of my mind just now." She mopped her brow. "Gosh, it's close in here."

"How are you feeling?" asked Esther, noticing that Ursula looked both pallid and hot at the same time.

"Oh fine. Practically back to normal."

The baby began to squall, and Esther picked him up and rocked him awkwardly.

"No, here." Ursula adjusted the position, so that he was comfortable in the crook of Esther's arm. She laughed. "I'm learning fast."

When Alice and Esther had finally gone, Ursula sank back into her armchair and closed her eyes. Dusk slid across the room, but still she sat there in the gloom, unmoving. They could not know what it had cost her to appear normal and cheerful after the nights she had spent. Nothing could have prepared her for this. Life since the baby had arrived was an awful blur of exhaustion and pain. The third day had been the worst, when the baby seemed to cease his almost continuous sleep and cry more lustily, and her breasts became rock hard and sore, a state she knew from her books meant the milk coming in, but suckling him became agony. She tensed with pain when she put him to the breast, and something about that made him pull away and cry all the harder. She wept while he tried to suck and watched her tears splash uselessly onto his crimson cheeks. Knowing that she was the sole thing keeping him alive was a ghastly responsibility. She wondered if he would die. She tried putting him in the pram and rocking it but he would not sleep unless he was by her side, nudging and shifting occasionally, and her own sleep when it came was no more than a light doze, alert in case she should roll or crush him in the bed. It had been two days before he had seemed to feed properly, though the pain of feeding him still made her tense up before it subsided.

At the same time melancholy settled on her like a rock. She scarcely moved from the bed. She wept all the time. She felt like an animal in a cave, only stirring for her most basic needs. Fogerty had not visited, though he had sent the basket of flowers now wilting before the fireplace. When Mrs Fogerty came she had been visibly shocked and suggested the child take a bottle, but Mrs Fogerty neither had an infant bottle, nor infant milk, and made no move to procure them. She saw Mrs Fogerty's little eyes calculating whether she need involve herself out of common humanity, or whether bringing supplies of milk and bread for Ursula, and promising another visit, would be enough. In the event it was the woman next door, unable to avoid the baby's cries through the paper thin walls, who had knocked with a chicken pie she had cooked for Ursula "while her husband was away" and stayed cradling the baby while Ursula washed for the first time in days.

Ursula knew she should engage a nurse, but she didn't have the energy to go about it. Or the time, between washing the nappies and delivering the endless feeds. The more depressed she became, the less she even wanted to venture from the house. Labouring up to the parade that morning to buy a quarter pound of tea, sugar and biscuits for her friends' visit, pushing the weighty pram, had been like a trek up the Himalayas. Now, to make things worse, she felt as if she was coming down with a bad cold. Her face prickled with sweat. She was feverish and light-headed. On top of everything else! What bad timing!

She looked down at the baby and thought how strange it was that hell and heaven could so closely co-exist. She had thought about the baby while she was carrying him, and responded to his random kicks and squirms, but the child inside her had never been more than an extension of herself. She had looked up childbirth in *Harmsworth's Household Encyclopaedia* and found that the process would require mackintosh sheets, drawsheets, abdominal binders, sanitary napkins, cotton wool, linen thread, narrow tape, safety pins, nailbrush, Vaseline and scissors. But diligently assembling these accessories, which in the event she had not needed, had not made the baby's actual existence any more convincing.

Now when she picked him up and held the perfection of his two feet in her hands, she could not imagine ever being parted from him. She looked at his palms, lined like freshly unfurling leaves, and the slack parting of his lips when he fell asleep from the breast with a trickle of her milk coming from the corner of his mouth. She felt the dense, pearly flesh, the irresistible nape of his neck with its tiny cleft, and the weight of the head laid quietly against her shoulder and she knew, even if she did not feel, that there could be no greater joy than this.

* * *

"How's the baby by the way?"
Frank Stevens had offered Esther dinner again. He detained her in the hall and made the suggestion in an offhand, slightly weary tone which, combined with the fact that dinner was to be cod in parsley sauce, made his invitation completely resistible.

This time, fortunately, Esther had been able to decline on the grounds of needing an evening to study for her history of art exam. When Dr Stevens pointed out that the next day was Saturday, she explained that it was going to take her all weekend to get her knowledge up to scratch.

"Oh, the baby's adorable. We've just been to see him actually. Ursula says she can never thank you enough for your help."

"Am I right in supposing the child's to be adopted?"

"I think Ursula's decided to find foster parents for him. Though I don't know how she'll go about it."

"They sort these things out at the nursing home usually. Is

she out yet?"

"She was never in one actually. She's at home."

"With a nurse?"

"Well no. She's looking after herself."

"Looking after herself? But her mother surely, or a maid….?"

"She's on her own in fact."

"There's someone to cook and clean?"

"Not really."

"Is she under a doctor?"

"She didn't mention it." Esther was beginning to feel badly ignorant. "I suppose I should have asked."

"You probably know very little about it," he said dismissively. "How did she seem?"

"Not too well. Sort of flushed, I suppose. She said she felt hot."

He remembered the feeling he had had after the child was delivered. The anxious wonderment on the faces of the three women, clustered around the baby, the studio hung around with pictures, the disorientating smell of turpentine, and the sense that he was intimately involved, almost complicit, in that intense, secretive experience.

"I tell you what, Esther. Why don't you give your friend a call and tell her that we'll be coming to visit her tomorrow morning? I'm sure your history of art won't suffer from a few distractions. If you're really concerned I'll question you on the way."

"I didn't know you knew anything about history of art."

"Then it will be instructive to see just how far you have underestimated me," he said, with just the trace of a smile.

Esther telephoned several times that evening, but there was no reply, so she told Frank Stevens that his visit would not be necessary.

"Why don't we go, just in case," he said, having mentally already given up his Saturday reading.

Esther was hesitant. "It's a long way to go if we're not certain she'll be in."

"But I was looking forward to you instructing me in the history of art," he remarked, and she couldn't tell if he was joking.

They sat on the top deck of the bus together, the wind ruffling their hair. It was a glorious, cloudless day, and Dr Stevens had changed into his Saturday clothes, which seemed to be a lighter, shabbier version of his working suits, just a soft-collared shirt, flannel trousers and a moss coloured tweed jacket which looked as if it had seen better days. Esther felt overdressed beside him, wearing a green velour cloche and a brown dress, which Alice had convinced her to buy because it was supposedly exactly the same shade as her eyes.

Despite a lingering sense of gratitude towards him since the day of the baby's birth, Dr Stevens still struck Esther as an entirely formidable figure, with his dry, deadpan delivery, which meant she was never certain whether he was serious or not. She wondered how old he was. Her father had always referred to him as "old Frank Stevens" but he could only be about half her father's age. She still had no real idea how the two men came to be friends.

"How did you meet my father?"

"We got to know each other in the war."

"Were you in his regiment?"

"Yes. I was a medical officer."

"But how exactly did you know him? I mean my father was never injured, was he?"

John Hartley had spent his war at regimental headquarters, well away from the front.

"No. In fact we only knew each other briefly during the war. But we kept in touch afterwards. I have a lot of respect for your father…..Now then. You've been learning up on History of Art have you?"

Esther had been nervous about the idea of him quizzing

her, but it seemed that he must have been teasing, because he was far more interested in her talking about her own enthusiasms. He asked some probing questions about the modernists, the Surrealists and the Dadaists, as well as the New Movement and the London Group. She found herself talking freely, about Jacob Epstein and about the excitement of Cubism, which had influenced everything from fashion to design.

"So what is its influence?"

"It's taught people to see things differently. When it began, it was as though the whole language of art changed. Things were more immediate, I suppose. People started to draw their sensations, rather than just representing what they saw."

"It changed ideas too," Stevens added. "In every sphere, social, scientific, as well as artistic. It's an exciting time Esther. I envy you."

"You envy me. Why?"

"I always fancied the idea of being an artist. I knew what I wanted to paint, it would have been in the Post-Impressionist style I suppose, another Gaugin or Cezanne. I could see it all in my head, but my hands wouldn't do what I told them. Though that never seemed a problem in my surgery examinations," he added.

"Well, I shouldn't envy me. I'm not a remotely accomplished artist, nothing like Alice for example."

"Mmm. Her work did look pretty original."

"Besides, the idea of my ever making a living from art seems highly unlikely."

"Why? Don't you want to earn your own living?"

She blushed. "Oh yes. Don't misunderstand me. I do. But I'm not sure that an artist is what I want to be. I don't think I've found that out yet."

"Why go to art school then?"

"Oh I don't know. It wasn't even my idea. There didn't seem much choice. You know, I think it was easier in the war, for women, anyway. There were proper jobs at least."

She faltered to a halt, aware of the way he was studying her. Why was he looking at her in that way? He wasn't even looking at her – he was *observing* her, the way you would some kind of biological specimen staked out on a slide. A thing you might examine dispassionately, out of entirely scientific curiosity. He probably didn't mean it that way, he was being perfectly friendly to her after all, but she wriggled in her seat, like an insect on a pin, wanting to be free of his gaze.

They reached Ursula's house and rang the bell but stood waiting for a long time on the step.

"So she is out."

"I doubt it," said Stevens shortly, and sure enough a reedy cry started and there was the sound of someone clumping down the stairs.

Ursula looked much worse than the previous day. Her face was scarlet and her clothes dishevelled. Her hand was shaking as she held it out.

"Esther! You've come back! What a surprise! I'm afraid I'm feeling a little seedy… I've a horrid cold. Oh and Dr Stevens! You'd better come in."

She showed them into the front room, which looked if anything more depressing than on Esther's previous visit.

"I just wanted to see the little lad I delivered the other day," said Dr Stevens evenly. "And perhaps I should take a look at you at the same time. Esther, perhaps you could watch the baby."

He took Ursula gently by the arm and led her back to her bedroom while Esther sat in the front room watching the plump, contented baby as he dozed in his cot, his little arms flung out to each side as though surrendering to the overwhelming power of sleep.

Ten minutes later Stevens came down and was bidding Ursula farewell, and to Esther's astonishment promising to make a return visit the following weekend.

"Let's walk for a little, shall we?" he said.

There was a park at the end of the road, with a brass band playing at the bandstand. Nearby there was an outdoor café next to a rose garden, so they sat outside in the weak sunlight and had cheese rolls and ginger beer. The shouts of children echoed in the air.

"It was jolly lucky I saw your friend today."

"Was it a bad cold then?"

"It's not a cold at all. She has an infection of the breast, mastitis. I've given her something for it, showed her how to massage it and cool the breast down. I advised her to continue breast feeding the child but the important thing is that a nurse is engaged. I'm going to arrange that myself."

"But can she….? I mean I know nurses can charge quite a lot."

"We'll sort that out later."

The whole idea of breasts becoming infected was new to Esther, as was their treatment. Dr Stevens did not seem to notice her silence. He appeared quite animated.

"It's quite astonishing that she had planned to have a child with absolutely no help. One would assume she could afford to engage a nurse? I mean, she looks as though she's of good family. She graduated from Cambridge, she said."

"I'm not sure how much money she has. She's estranged from her family and she's a writer. I don't think she can earn much of her own."

"What about the father of the child then? Is he known of? Where is he?"

"Do you really want to know?"

"Why else would I ask?"

So Esther told Frank Stevens all about Ursula, and her novel, and the subsequent estrangement from her family. Then about William Fogerty, and his theory that he and Ursula should continue their relationship unconstrained by bourgeois conventions of monogamy or possessiveness. Stevens was fascinated. The whole affair and the mileu in which it arose was a universe away from the people he spent his daily life with at the clinic in Bethnal Green. Though he had seen his share of girls trapped in the snare of unmarried pregnancy, they were always terrified, or ashamed, or bent on ensuring that the father be made to accept his responsibilities in the form of swift wedlock. Esther and Ursula's breezy acceptance of the situation, with their bohemian talk of free relationships would be unknown amongst his patients. Those families, with their strict mores of family honour and shame, operated within another code of ethics entirely. As he listened to her, something in him hankered for the kind of world in which Ursula and Esther lived and he discerned that hankering and resented it.

If he had taken another path after Oxford, if it had not been for the war, then his life might have been entirely different. He too might live among those rarified, artistic types who considered themselves in the vanguard of human evolution, able to condescend to the vast mass of humanity. He too would have the leisure to read the latest books, see plays, and pronounce airily on the dullness of bourgeois convention instead of being exhausted by an inexorable and unchanging burden of work. With an edge of bitterness he said:

"Your friends are very different from the people I work with."

"How?"

"Where I work, a girl like Ursula would never be permitted to exist in such a situation."

"I should think she's very glad that she is 'permitted' to live in the way she wants," said Esther indignantly. "Free from other people's interference."

He looked at her coldly. "You misunderstand me. What I mean is, Ursula wouldn't be abandoned. Either the father would be forced to take his responsibilities or if he didn't then at least the woman would be looked after. The community around her would pitch in wherever they could.

A girl in my clinic wouldn't find herself alone, isolated like that with a new-born baby, miles from anyone she knew. The working classes would give her plenty of what you call interference and what I would call help."

"Are you saying you disapprove of Ursula's situation?"
"Yes."
He was about to emphasise that it was the situation, not the girl herself, that provoked his disapproval, but he did not get the chance.
"Well I think it's typical that a man should disapprove," she responded hotly. "Actually I admire Ursula. I think she's incredibly brave. I'd say it's other people's attitudes that need changing and it's up to intellectuals like Ursula to take the first step in changing them."

"Intellectuals?"
"Yes. You see Ursula's not like the girls in your clinic. I don't mean she's better or anything, I just mean she has the intellect to rise above the hypocrisy of other people."

The only way Esther could have known the emotion this statement provoked in Frank Stevens was to observe the slight tightening of his jaw as he tapped a cigarette out of its packet and cupped his hand to light it. But there was no missing the iciness of his scorn when he spoke.

"Do you really think life is like a novel, Esther? Can you really not see the difficulties of having an illegitimate child? Do you imagine for a moment that your *intellectual* friend – though she may be oceans apart from the girls in my clinic - will manage simply splendidly on her own, a happy little family of two, rather than being the target of vicious prejudice for the next eighteen years, trapped in miserable poverty, cut off from her family and decent people and unlikely ever to marry or realise the potential of her privileged education? Let alone what will happen to the child."

Esther glared back at him defiantly. She was tired of being condescended to by someone who constantly implied that she was empty-headed and looked at her in such a superior way. Until a few months ago she would have been quite unused to arguing with a grown man, but now she had met Alan, who always wanted to hear her views, and never implied she was immature of ill-informed. At that moment all the recent changes in her life, the excitement of new friends, fresh ideas, and her passionate admiration for Ursula, came together in a rush.

"If that's the case then it's the fault of society, not Ursula. Why shouldn't she believe in free love? How can society change if women allow themselves to be governed by outdated prejudices?"

"Free love? Can't you see that's just thoughtless romantic claptrap made up to trick silly girls who don't have the sense they were born with?"

"Well you would say that." Esther remembered something Ursula had said. "But I'd say it's just the first challenge to a society which has so far been run entirely for the convenience of men."

Stevens stood up and sighed, stubbing his cigarette savagely in the tin ashtray.

"I do wonder just what equips you to pronounce on society Esther."

"What does that mean?"

"Well, you know nothing and you've been nowhere. You've hardly even lived at all." He pulled his arms into his shabby jacket. "Shall we go?"

They walked in silence to the bus stop, Esther's face burning with hurt and indignation. When the number 221 arrived it was crowded so they shared a seat, keeping a few stiff inches of space between them, and travelled back all the way to Waverley Gardens without exchanging another word.

Chapter Twenty-four

Samuel had never expected to see this place again. Yet as soon as he stepped off the train and inhaled the choking, sand-filled air, it was as if the events of the past few months had never happened. The Winter Palace hotel was a reddish building in balustraded, colonial style, a place of comfortable, shabby splendour where the Egyptians affected not to mind the way that their guests, ensconced at marble-topped tables in the cool entrance hall, spent their time openly disparaging the local food and culture and issuing curt instructions to the waiters in loud, decelerated English.

He had his dinner out on the terrace looking across the creeping brown river to the west bank. The beds were planted with garish flowers which gave off an overpowering scent and were tended constantly by white-robed gardeners. From the ballroom came the sound of a pianist playing the Tutankhamun rag. Out of season, in the blistering heat of the Egyptian summer, the place was less crowded than he remembered it but there were still groups of loud-voiced Americans in the billiards room and walking among the palms in the exotic garden. Most of them, he knew, had come up by boat from Cairo to "do" the temples of Amun-Min and Karnak and then take in Tut's tomb.

He sat in a corner, watchfully. The journey had been ten frustrating days – he had taken the boat to Dunkirk, then gone by rail to Paris, where he had boarded a slow train with wooden seats which progressed in fits and starts the length of France, deep between the pine forests and the distant hills, with boys bringing coffee at the platforms. Another sleepy train took him through Italy to a boat which sailed along the Dalmatian coast. They docked at Alexandria, where he took another train, staring out of juddering, dust-clouded windows, alongside peasants carrying packages and baskets of vegetables and spices, down to Luxor. At any other time, he would have relished the sights and colour but this time it had been exhausting.

On top of the fatigue of the journey, he felt weak with trepidation and a sick, dragging sense of dread. Not just that he might be recognised, though there was a good chance of that here - there were plenty of people from the dig who frequented this hotel, even out of season - but for the enormity of the task ahead of him. He had been stupid even to attempt it.

He went to bed, but despite his bone-aching tiredness, could not fall asleep. As he lay between the crisp, linen sheets, waiting to drop down into unconsciousness, his mind returned restlessly to England again. It had been only a few months since he left Egypt, just long enough for his skin to turn pale, yet in that time his soul had flared up into life. His thoughts were like feet of rope paid out, mooring him to the place where Iris was.

All he had was the tiny clutch of images of her from that day in Paris and he fed on them, half afraid to wear them out. He felt for them repeatedly, like a pocketful of pebbles. In his mind his hands travelled over her body like an endless land he could never see enough of. He thought of her breasts, high and small, the peach stone nipple puckered beneath his touch, the pocket of shadow at the top of her inner thigh and the tiny slope of her belly as she sat. As devotedly as a parent poring over the diminutive details of a child, he dwelt on the perfection of her features - the narrow white feet with their net of veins, and the nape of the neck with its appalling vulnerability, bared by her short hair. She was the first woman who had ever meant anything to him and he realised that he had never wanted anything with the intensity he now felt.

Yet at this moment she probably had no idea where he was. It agonised him to think that despite their snatched moments of intimacy in her father's house, and all his protestations, she must think he had abandoned her entirely. He had not even left a note for her, or a message of any kind. He felt a dreadful pang of loss. The pleasure he felt on that day in Paris may never return. And this mission of his was doomed from the outset. He thought of happiness, like a face peering in through the window of his life, before passing nonchalantly by.

He rose early the next day but the heat had risen before him, towering up ahead of him like a wall. As he made his way through stalls selling boxes and trinkets with mother of pearl inlay, ivory cigarette holders, plates decorated with badly executed hieroglyphics, rows of gold necklaces, heaps of scarlet and yellow confectionery piled high and barrows full of fruit, he was assailed by a crowd of urchin boys dancing around him. "You want a guide?" "See very good art?" "See tombs, Sir?" "Clean boots, pliss?" "You want carpet? Gold? You tell me Sir." Having almost forgotten the European technique of striding rapidly through the boys, like a cloud of flies, he hesitated for a while, as though actually considering their offers, which made them doubly hard to shake off when he finally decided on his direction. He would go and take another look at the tomb.

Beyond the town he made his way along the Nile banks, past fields of sugar cane, cotton, wheat and clover, and settlements where beneath the palms and sycamores buffaloes were working waterwheels, urged on by men armed with sticks. Along the sand shallows of the Nile, where farmers were growing tomatoes and marrows, he found a felucca, with patched triangular sails and flat white seat cushions, and was ferried west to the bank of the dead. There was a guide with camels waiting to take visitors up the winding road to the valley. The animals rolled their eyes and shifted foam-flecked jaws. Samuel disliked camels - the rolling, primordial gait they had threw their rider around and made one ache in a different way from donkeys - but there was no choice, so he was hoisted up and the beast

lurched to its feet, was whacked from behind with a cane
and swayed reluctantly off. As he began the tortuous climb
up the winding path, the fields below them were heaving
and wavering in the heat. Already the sun was sharp as a
knife, its white glare glancing off the cliff sides. Within him
the anxiety was physical, like a hand gripping his heart. It
was impossible now to avoid what he had tried to keep shut
away at the back of his mind – the last day he had spoken to
Howard Carter.

*   *   *

The day after Carter closed the tomb, there was a concerted
attempt to distract him from his worries. The Lythgoes were
planning a dinner in the evening and during the day there
was a picnic to Medinet Habu. The great memorial temple
of Rameses III was a favourite with the British, and they
often saddled up for the two mile journey towards the Nile
to see the massive inscribed walls of its temple complex and
sketch or paint in the fronded shade of the date palms and
pomegranate trees. That day their group included Samuel,
Violet and Arthur Mace, who was collaborating with Carter
on a book about the find. They kept up a cheerful banter but
despite their best efforts Carter sat despondently, brooding
on his plans to sue the Egyptian authorities for their actions.
He was dressed as properly as ever – three piece suit, bowtie
and trilby – but he hadn't slept and looked as if he had spent
the night in his clothes.

It was an exquisite day, the warm, dry heat of Egypt at its
best, and the clear, sharp light seemed to shimmer off the
immense walls of the temple and raise the carved reliefs. As
they ate their picnic of figs, pears, pate and tinned sardines
with flat, Egyptian bread, a group of black clad local women
approached the fetid, green lake beside the temple, and
began to wade in. They watched with curiosity as one by
one each woman, still in her flowing gelabiya, immersed

herself entirely, before coming up again with barely a splutter.

"A rather unorthodox place for a bathe," commented Violet.

"That's the sacred lake," said Mace. "One of the most holy sites in Thebes. It's supposedly the birthplace of the very first gods. Those women are taking part in a fertility rite. They believe its waters have magical properties."

"Well I hope it's worth it. I shouldn't fancy it. Looks an absolute breeding ground for disease."

They continued eating and watching the ritual for a while until Violet said,

"I say. I think one of them might be in trouble."

The last of the women, a girl of perhaps 17, had followed her predecessors and sunk into the lake. The sluggish waters closed over her with barely a ripple, and the surface restored itself like a dull, implacable metal mirroring the sky. For almost a minute, there was no further movement. The little group looked on first curiously then anxiously, for signs that the girl would emerge.

"You don't think…?" said Violet.

With rising alarm, Samuel began to take his jacket off.

There was now no sign that anything had ever penetrated the brackish waters of the sacred lake.

"I wonder how deep it goes?"

He began to calculate where he should dive in, and if so how he would see anything in the aquaeous gloom beneath. He pictured himself breaking the stagnant surface, the weeds catching and choking him in the mud beneath and fish flickering between the rushes. He saw himself with tearing lungs hauling the dead weight of the drowned girl.

He rose from the table and ran towards the lake. Just as he was about to jump in there was a splash and the girl emerged vertically as if she had propelled herself like a jubilant diver right from the bed of the lake. Streams of water slid off her slender body, and beneath the soaked cotton her breasts stood clearly out. Her hair was plastered black about her shoulders, and as she shook it the sun glanced off the spray of drops, turning them to shards of silver. She looked as if she had received some ecstatic baptism in the dank waters of the lake. As she rose, the girl looked directly into his eyes and smiled, her face alight with joy.

Relieved and slightly sheepish, Samuel returned to the table. "That's a dangerous habit," he grumbled.

"Whatever ritual it is, it looks like it worked," said Mace, laughing.

"They do love their magic, don't they?" said Violet indulgently. "They all believe in it. I mean Egyptians call magicians the way we might call a plumber. My servant had a magician in just the other day to deal with an *afrit* which he said had escaped from the cemetery and was haunting his house!"

"You sound surprised," said Mace, "but you shouldn't. Egypt is the mother of magic, after all. The first necromancers and scorcerers came from here. Think of the Magi in the bible, or the Pharaoh's magicians who duelled with Aaron and turned their wands into snakes. The Egyptians are famous amongst Arabs for their magic. Europeans have come here for centuries searching for their secret texts. They call it Heka. It's part of their religion. In fact religion and magic are indivisible to the Egyptians. And the way they see it, it's as potent now as it ever was. Isn't that so, Howard?"

Carter, who had been watching the whole episode silently, turned savagely away.

"Heka! Magic. It's all a load of nonsensical superstition." Mace glanced at Samuel and rolled his eyes. Violet laughed lightly and poured everyone tea from her flask. But Samuel was amazed. Like any professional Egyptologist Carter was respectful of the ancient traditions and he had never been heard to utter anything disparaging about Egyptian culture. But then presumably he had his reasons for disliking the locals, just at that moment.

Shortly afterwards Violet, Mace and the others departed to examine the inscribed reliefs of Rameses III defeating the Sea Peoples, leaving the two of them alone.

"So it's nonsensical superstition. Is that what you think?" said Samuel softly.

Carter's face was inscrutable in the shadow of his felt hat. Then he took a scrap of paper from the inside pocket of his jacket.

"Can you read that?" He pushed the scrap of paper towards Samuel. He recognised it. It was the column of hieroglyphs, an arm, an ibis, a setting sun, the small canopic jar.

"I'm sorry. I'm afraid my knowledge of hieroglyphs is still far from adequate. I can make out the ab, and the Ibis. That's Thoth, isn't it?…. Is this a coffin text? The one you were asking me about?"

"In a way."

Carter's face was like a mask, the whites of his eyes were filmy, impenetrable.

"Well I give up," said Samuel, handing the paper back to him. "I can't do any better than that. Tell me. What does it say?"

"It doesn't matter," said Carter, folding the paper away.

* * *

By the time he reached the Valley it was almost midday and the place was deserted. The gates were still locked. Beside the steel door a slouched guard opened one eye, lizard-like, extended a hand, then withdrew it again as Samuel remained silently staring ahead of him for several minutes. Other than the possibility of baksheesh, the guard did not care what the tourist wanted. He assumed, like all the rest, he wanted to see the tomb and contemplate the magnificent beauty of the ancient King's burial place. In fact, Samuel couldn't have been less interested in all that. All he was wondering was how on earth he was going to find Husni.

Chapter Twenty-five

"Yes Miss? Can I help you?"

Esther, who had dropped home unannounced, was amused to find herself unrecognised by the new maid, a plain woman with a wall eye who had been hired by her mother after a long, irritating trawl. Mrs Hartley, who had been driven to her wits' end by the shortage of domestic servants, had had to take out an advertisement in *The Times* offering two pounds ten a week plus keep and even then had been obliged to interview all kinds of unsuitable applicants, the current employment situation having lent them the most tremendous airs and graces.

Esther laughed. "I live here actually. Or rather I did."

The maid hurried away, indignant rather than abashed, and Esther stood in the hall for a second, breathing in the familiar fragrance of polish and dusty carpets and something baking in the basement kitchen. The sounds of a disagreement between her two younger sisters floated down from upstairs.

"I did *not* say you could keep it. I said I was *lending* it to you. For a single evening. Now give it back you *utterly* selfish girl."

"Mummy?"

Her mother's head was bent over her desk, writing letters, a task she regarded with little joy. Esther caught a distinct flash of alarm in her eyes.

"Esther! Is everything all right?"

Was it alarm at the idea that her daughter might be returning to claim space in the crush that was Chalcott Street?

"Don't worry. Everything's fine. I'm not back to stay."

Esther's mother looked relieved. She rose but did not kiss her. She disapproved of unnecessary displays of affection.

"Well this is your home. And it's very nice to see you. Now just let me finish this letter then we can have some tea and you can tell me all about how your exams went."

"Is Dad here?"

"Somewhere I think," Mrs Hartley said vaguely, returning to her letter. "I'm sure I heard him come in. Go and ask him if he'd like some tea."

Esther knocked at the study door.

"Daddy?" She opened the door gently.

"Goodness. What are you doing here?"

Her father was sunk in an armchair, slumped in a position of profound relaxation, a pair of pince nez balanced on his nose. From the maroon cover Esther could see he was reading his favourite book, *The Decline And Fall Of The Roman Empire*. He rose and patted her shoulder awkwardly.

"Come back for some home comforts? Need a bath or something?"

"The flat does have hot water, you know."

"Glad to hear it. I trust Frank's looking after you."

She perched on the arm of a chair, and looked round at the familiar room, the walls an indeterminate crimson, hung with hunting prints and lined wall to ceiling with books.

"He's not really looking after me. He doesn't need to. Anyway, we don't encounter each other that often."

"Keeps himself to himself does he?"

"I think he's very busy."

Her father grunted. "That sounds like Frank."

There was no way of telling her father how difficult things had become at Waverley Gardens. Every day when she made her way downstairs, Esther was tense as a cat, worrying about whether she would bump into him. Since the day they had been to see Ursula, after his stinging words and the awful silence on the journey back, they had exchanged barely a word. She had seen his back, disappearing into his rooms and heard him moving about in the evenings but there

246

had been no more offers to dinner, no more enduring stilted conversation and staring at the murky Victorian landscapes. Perhaps, she thought, it was better that way.

After the first shock of their row had subsided, she began to wonder whether she had offended him, she knew she must have, but after a while, when she had gone over and over the conversation in her head, she convinced herself that the fault, if it had been hers, was far too minor to merit such treatment, and she became indignant. Again and again she heard his accusation in her head. *"You know nothing and you've been nowhere. You've hardly even lived at all."* Even before he had been difficult, always wrong-footing her and making her feel foolish. Now she began to wonder how long she could go on living in this atmosphere. No one flourished in a state of perpetual unease and Esther, who hated confrontation, found it almost intolerable. It gave her headaches.

"Dad, how exactly did you meet Dr Stevens?"

"We've known each other for some time now. I put him up for my club."

"Yes I know, but how did you meet?"

"Has he been talking about that to you then?"

"Not at all, actually. I was just curious." Gingerly she added: "Was it in the war?"

Esther's father never talked about the war. No-one in the family ever asked him about it. It wasn't done. A closed chapter.

Her father regarded her momentarily, placed a leather bookmark in his book and laid it down beside his chair. "You're inordinately inquisitive today. Trying to puzzle Frank out are you?"

She flicked a lock of hair from her eyes and swung her foot restlessly. "I just wondered."

"Frank's a complex sort of chap."

"Is he?"

"Strikes me that way. I wouldn't normally say this, but if

you're really determined to get to the bottom of him then you could try asking him about the war yourself."

* * *

Frank Stevens took another cigarette. He knew all the arguments, about how tobacco soothed the throat and cleaned out the lungs, but he was still convinced that in some way it might actually be bad for health. After all it was impossible in his clinic to ignore the ragged coughs and the desperate, rattling wheezes that accompanied the really heavy smokers. Could cigarettes be the cause, as well as seeming to offer them some respite? He suspected so, but the thought only interested him in an entirely theoretical way. Though he saw plenty of them, diseases of the chest were not his speciality and besides, when one felt the relaxing pleasure as the smoke curled down the throat and insinuated itself into the bloodstream, it was impossible to think something so universally comforting might do one serious harm. And even if it could, when people had gone through a war, there were more important things to dwell on than the hypothetical health risks of everyday comforts.

He tilted the brass lamp so that a skein of smoke twisted up though the pool of light, but his eyes kept lifting off the page, into the middle distance. He was trying to read a new work on psychoanalysis but was finding it hard to concentrate. His own consciousness, he supposed, was waiting for the slam of the door that signified that his tenant had returned for the night. She was out very late this time. He had no idea where. Really, it had proved more trouble than it was worth, having a tenant in. Perhaps he should ask her to go. Having another person here was a distraction, when what he really needed after a day at the clinic was relaxation.

He had always viewed this house as his sanctuary. In the six years he had lived here, it had been an escape from the misery and the hopelessness that he saw in his working day. He'd had a death yesterday - a twelve-year old boy who had perished predictably of pneumonia. He recalled the wasted body, the dark, feverish eyes, roving unfocused round the room before he lapsed into unconsciousness and the dreadful wailing of the mother. He had seen a lot of deaths, but they still had the power to affect him.

Most of what he saw however was mundane rather than moving - ulcers, suppurations, aches and growths - and every morning they would be waiting for him without fail, the wretched and the truculent, the aching and the insane, like a pack of dogs wanting a piece out of him, craving a chunk of his time.

Perhaps this interest he had in psychoanalysis was an antidote to that relentless stress on the physical body and its decrepitude, even though reading Freud, it was almost impossible to imagine the theories about dreams and attachments and complexes could possibly apply to his wretched patients. "An archaeologist of the mind" was what Freud called himself apparently. The man was mad keen on collecting Egyptian antiquities, people said his consulting room was crammed with rows of tiny little figures from past civilisations, because, he said, what archaeologists did was pretty like his own work. By which he meant burrowing into the past, uncovering what has been buried, and analysing the way art is used to express human desires, even desires which lie beneath the conscious mind.

Stevens's thoughts returned to his tenant. That remark Esther had made about the girls at his clinic. How different they were from her intellectual friend Ursula. As though Esther, with her sheltered life and art school friends, could have any idea of the existence his patients struggled through. A fresh irritation ran through him every time he thought of it.

And yet - he stubbed out his cigarette and finally laid the book aside, abandoning himself to his thoughts - why exactly had that conversation annoyed him so intensely? Why had that ignorant comparison between Ursula and his patient enraged him? Why should he have reacted so strongly, so that even days later the poor girl was obliged to creep about for fear of encountering him and his flinty displeasure? For the first time he forced himself to consider whether he had judged her unfairly. Was Esther, so gauche and unformed, really expressing condescension towards the people he worked with? Or was his real objection that Esther inhabited a different realm, a bright, colourful, stimulating, frivolous world, wholly unconnected with the life he lived, and he was jealous of it? Perhaps, if he was honest with himself, that was the case. Well then, if she was so committed to those political beliefs of hers, maybe she should come and visit his clinic. If she was so keen to change the world, it might help if she saw something of it first.

* * *

"We don't *have* to talk about the future of revolutionary socialism," said Alice, coaxingly.

She and her parents had been invited to join a house party in Suffolk arranged by Mrs Webb and they had extended an invitation to Esther. The venue was to be Godstone Court, home of Mr and Mrs Ronald Silverstein, a branch of the banking family who had decided to ally themselves and a good chunk of their money with the Socialist cause. Alice was desperately keen for her friend to come, to leaven the assortment of older, duller guests. Esther, though she had time on her hands now that the exams were over, felt mildly intimidated.

"Do come. It'll be so dreary without you," Alice made a face. "Just imagine me discussing the world economic crisis with Flaky Ellison."

'Flaky', a Cambridge economist revered in academic circles

for his work on the collapse of capitalism, was famous to Alice and Esther for the collapse of his personal hygiene.

"It sounds rather daunting."

"Oh, don't say that. We can just roam about the countryside and paint and paint and paint. There are some fabulous views near there."

"Couldn't you take Alan? He'd be in seventh heaven. He never stops thinking about the future of socialism and the new world order and the need for world revolution."

"Well the thing about Alan," said Alice cautiously, "is that he's a little too far left for most of the people there. Whereas they'll absolutely love you."

"I don't see why," objected Esther, slightly put out at the suggestion of inoffensive mediocrity in her political views. "The other reason you must come is, I want to paint you."

"You can paint me any time."

"No. Properly I mean. I've wanted to for ages. I want to do a life study." "All right then. Thank you."

She lay back on the grass. They were in the Cohens' garden, a small, sun-speckled space with high trellis fences over which honeysuckle, clematis and jasmine had been allowed to run riot. Beside them the pursed buds of a white rambling rose slowly unfurled and the beds were a tangle of pastel colour opening up to the sun. The only sound was the low drone of bees visiting hebe and lavender, their furry bodies carrying little knapsacks of pollen. In the light, perfumed air Esther felt suspended and inviolate. She wanted to stay cocooned in the chrysalis of the present against the great rush of tomorrow. She closed her eyes in the sun and saw against her lids a spangled map of red.

The end of the examinations had left Esther with a degree, but precious little else to equip her for a working life. She had no idea what she wanted to do, or if she would be able to do it. Alice, by contrast, had no doubts about her future. All she wanted and intended to do was paint, and her canvases were already attracting enough attention for that to seem a most promising livelihood. The finished canvas of *Ursula Expects* had been displayed on the wall of Sidonie's drawing room, and once they had got over the shock of the subject, with its dispassionate pose and unforgiving flesh, the rich and powerful friends of the Cohens had begun clamouring to sit for Alice. So rapidly had her reputation spread that she had even been commissioned to paint a well-known business tycoon, who wanted a portrait for his new office building.

"A businessman?" said Esther, incredulously. "That's not your sort of thing at all Alice. I thought that kind of official portrait was everything you detest. Won't he just want something terribly polite that hides his double chins?"

"Well," said Alice. "You're right. That is exactly what I thought at first. I'd vowed to myself that I would never undertake any kind of commission that involved painting fat, old men in a flattering light. Men like that don't want to be portrayed, they want to be camouflaged.

But I went along to meet him, just out of curiosity, and I had a revelation. I thought of all those Renaissance artists who painted the Borgias and the Medicis and the wicked cardinals and I realised it doesn't matter who you paint, because art doesn't lie. It tells the truth. Kings and rulers have always patronised art after all, as far back as the Egyptian pharaohs. But that doesn't mean they can control it."

"Does this unfortunate man have any idea what you're thinking?" laughed Esther.

"I hope not. When I went to visit him he said he wanted to be painted surrounded by all the valuable antiquities he had collected. It was unbelievably vulgar. There was heaps of Egyptian stuff and probably because of that, the thought just popped into my head of Ozymandias, you know; *"the wrinkled lip and sneer of cold command"* so I'm going to do a painting on that theme. The idea that it's not the businessmen of the world who live on, it's the artists."

"But at least the businessmen pay while they *are* alive," said Esther, enviously.

She herself faced no such tide of potential employers. Her only salvation was Alan, who seemed willing to commission as many cartoons as she wanted. At least he had been her salvation until that morning, when something had happened which made the idea of leaving London for a while doubly attractive.

She had been to the office, where he was trying ineffectually to fix on the wall a large poster depicting a red flag circling a globe inscribed 'Workers Of All Lands Unite'. It kept collapsing back and enveloping him in such a comic way that Esther had to stifle her laughter while he talked.

"Don't laugh. I'm having a frustrating morning Esther. I've been trying to track down my friend Samuel in connection with a piece I'm writing, but he seems to have vanished without trace. No-one seems to have the faintest idea where he's gone. Very aggravating. Anyhow, don't stand there laughing. Give me a hand with this."

Esther stretched up to hold the poster in place as Alan searched for tacks.

"Perhaps you would like to write us another piece Esther."

"You know, I'm not sure I'm meant to be a journalist."

"Whyever not?" he stopped and looked at her, surprised. "You observe things, you're aware of injustices, you've all the makings of a journalist. I've always thought of you - if you don't mind me saying this - as someone who's not timid, as so many women of your class are."

He returned with the tacks and stretched up beside her. In the sudden closeness she smelt the sharp, vinegary odour of sweat on him and thought how thin he was. His trousers hung loose, anchored only by his braces. He continued to speak with his back turned.

"Not that I mind about your class. Not at all. I don't hold it against you."

He turned to face her, pushing his spectacles back up his

nose.

"In fact, as I said before, I think we have a lot in common. A political philosophy, most importantly of course, and when two people share a great passion - a great political passion - then I suppose it's only natural there will be a physical attraction too."

In his pale, ascetic face, two spots of colour burned.

"I know you feel the same. After what you said about meeting my needs."

She took a casual step backwards and crossed her arms over her chest. "Actually Alan……."

Alan had abandoned the poster. He stood awkwardly, hitching up his trousers. The tips of his protruding ears were reddening.

"The fact is, it feels unnatural and indeed wrong to have to suppress what is a purely natural, chemical….attraction towards a woman…by which I mean you, Esther, and given that we are of the same mind…"

In a sudden movement, before she could get away, he had sort of darted towards her, gripping her tightly to him, and started kissing her. For someone so slightly built he was surprisingly strong. His little red beard scratched against her face, and the lithe, insistent muscle of his tongue thrust into her mouth. Their teeth clashed. For a moment she could hardly breathe and thought she might suffocate. There was the powerful, musty smell of unwashed clothes and instead of the expected excitement, the flush of rapture she had read about which accompanied one's first kiss, Esther felt nothing but a galloping panic. She pulled herself from his grasp, gasping for breath.

"It's so hot in here."

"The window won't open."

She looked round desperately at the window, as though hoping to jump out of it.

"Can't you fix it with something? The hammer? I'm sure the sash just needs a strong knock."

He was still holding her shoulders.

"Forget about the window Esther. It doesn't matter. What matters is this. I've believed for some time that our relationship should become more physical." She had to prevent herself flinching but he was looking at her earnestly. All the forcefulness which he generally applied to the political cowardice of the west and its refusal to commit to communism was now being trained on her.

"You see," he continued. "I think two people should be honest with each other and not ashamed of their natural impulses. Sex is a basic bodily function, like eating or going to the lavatory. We all go to the lavatory, don't we? Well sex is the same, there's nothing mystical or sacred about it. Yet our society has a kind of prurient fear of it, based on the need to maintain a rigid social hierarchy. It's up to people like us, who see things more clearly, to ignore outmoded social customs, especially when they're simply designed to oppress women.

You do like me don't you?"

"Yes. Yes of course."

And she did like him, or at least she admired him, and did genuinely want to become the person he thought she was, the serious, untrivial woman who had broken free of the hypocrisies of her class. She had liked his compliments, the flattering, flirtatious banter, and the idea of being respected, as well as desired. But how had they jumped so suddenly from that situation to this? Was enjoying flattery – provoking it even – just one step away from this grim business of bodily functions?

"Then surely you're not bourgeois enough to object to taking a lover? After what we agreed?"

Blushing furiously she hunted hopelessly for an excuse.

"I didn't …I mean I don't really think…."

He attempted a light-hearted smile. "Well please do think then. Because the fact is I've been thinking about nothing else."

She snatched up her jacket and edged out of the office, clattering down the stairs as fast as was decently possible.

Chapter Twenty-six

Celia Urquart had a complexion the exact colour and consistency of a hard boiled egg, an asset she attributed to extreme avoidance of the sun's rays. She had a figure like a drainpipe and wore clothes by Poiret, Schiaparelli and Chanel beneath a long coat trimmed with white fur and a hat large enough to keep her skin in complete shade. Her hair was of a black generally unseen in the human species, her nails were scarlet and her lips vermilion. But her heart was pure gold.

Celia had been briefed by her friend Edwina on the ghastliness she would face in taking Iris under her wing, but she had taken Edwina's advice with a pinch of salt. Edwina was extremely beautiful and she could be very amusing but she would not be anyone's choice of a sympathetic maternal figure to a poor, motherless girl.

"She's an absolute fright, darling," Edwina had confided, flicking her fingers through her ringlets and turning her face aside to puff out little clouds of smoke. "Honestly the devil in disguise. She has simply set her face against me marrying her father and she utterly delights in thwarting me."

Celia rather liked the sound of Iris.

Though she took no offence at all at being called in solely to cope with Iris, she had assumed this meant the girl had expressed some interest in the decorating arts. But on their first meeting she found no sign of it. Iris trailed a few steps behind as they toured round Barrington House and appeared distracted as they scrutinised the exquisite architectural details and Celia took photographs. She did not respond when Celia discussed ziggurat motifs for the penthouse, and volunteered nothing when she began to murmur experimentally about fruitwood veneers and *verre églomisé*. Yet Celia remained unfazed. Not only was she genuinely thrilled at the spectacular interior of the building

- far more sumptuous and exciting than suggested by the rather forbidding exterior - but Iris's silence only aroused her raging interest in human relationships.

"Tell you what my love," she said, perching a cigarette on her lip as she pulled on her coat. "Why don't we go back to my HQ and look through some samples to show your papa?"

"All right," conceded Iris neutrally.

When Celia opened the door of her shop, a narrow cupboard in Mayfair with a flat above, and called: "Where are you, my little abandoned babies?" Iris did not turn a hair. But she seemed to come alive a little more when Celia's dachshunds "madly yappy, poor little darlings" arrived in a sea of hysterical, trembling fur at their feet. The girl sat on one of the dainty gilt chairs reserved for clients, smoking Celia's cigarettes. She had a striking face with high cheekbones and wide blue eyes, set in that extraordinarily pale complexion – ivory was it, or alabaster? – either way, Celia couldn't help but like beautiful things. Patiently, carefully, with some gingernut biscuits, copious cups of tea and several jokes at Edwina's expense, Celia drew her out.

"You know, it really is the most exquisite building," breathed Celia.

"I suppose."

"You must be terrifically proud."

"Why?"

"Of having such a thing bearing your name."

"It's nothing to do with me though, is it?"

"It could be. Your father seems keen for you to be involved."

"In the decoration yes. Anything so I don't try to interest myself in his business. That's what I'd really like to do."

"And what would that involve?"

"Deciding what to buy and sell, helping things grow, watching the markets. I mean I know the building is beautiful, but what I'd really like to do is develop a market -

you know, find something that isn't being properly exploited and make it work. That's what business people do isn't it? It's what my father does, or at least I think it is. The trouble is, he never talks about his business and he certainly doesn't like anyone interfering with it."

"Well I think that's awfully clever of you. But I don't suppose he has any idea you're thinking like that."

"Oh he does. He's never spoken to me about what he does. I think because it was meant for Charles. He was the one who was supposed to take over."

"I see." Celia paused from riffling a pile of chenille swatches. "Well as a businesswoman myself I do completely sympathise. Of course you want to get involved. But I think you're giving up hope far too soon. You see, Iris, the thing about men - and that category includes your father - is that they need to think things are their own idea."

Celia was well schooled in this concept. She was quite used to congratulating her male clients for repeating suggestions she had just inserted into their heads. Women were cannier - they were far more likely to know what they wanted.

Iris looked baffled. "What does that mean?"

"It means that your father needs to believe that you do actually know all about these economic things - banking and money markets and financial conditions and so on."

"But I don't."

"You don't now, but I'm sure I could find someone who could teach you."

Iris was intrigued. She had never had anyone like this to talk to. Someone who seemed to understand, without judging. Who was spiky, yet sympathetic, but not sententious or repressed. Celia's voice alone, surprisingly deep and drawling, promoted a sense of worldliness and unshockability. In her most private imaginings, she thought that her mother might perhaps have taken on such a role, if she had lived, and yet the nearest thing she had to a mother,

Mrs Vickers, kind and sensible though she was, was hardly the sort one would want to confide in.

Celia was not anyone's mother, though she was quite old enough. Threads of grey could be discerned at the centre parting of her ebony hair and her dramatic lipstick feathered into tiny little lines around her generous mouth. The skin on her neck formed horizontal pleats which she kept stroking upwards, as though they might be encouraged to disappear. The admirers who dropped in to the shop to see her, who always behaved with charming courtesy towards Iris, had to be as least as old as her father. Yet Iris felt she had found a friend.

For her part Celia was fascinated, but she was also patient. Observing Iris as she fingered her way through some of the sketches that Celia had made, she knew that there was more to her unhappiness than plain discontent with her family role. The girl looked absolutely stricken at times, almost desolate. But it was not until a few days later, enjoying a pink gin and some silverskin onions with Edwina in her flat just behind the Dorchester, that the first clue emerged. Celia had remarked, warily, on Iris's moodiness.

"Don't you know why? Oh Celia dear, it is absolutely hush hush and Elmer would simply murder me if he knew I was telling you, but you might as well know, because practically everyone else does. She's lovesick. She eloped to Paris."

"No! Who with?"

"Bunny Devine. You know, the American art dealer fellow. You met him at Vince's. Anyway, they eloped together and Elmer had to send someone to fetch her back."

"Who did he send?"

"Oh I can't remember," sighed Edwina, fiddling with a diamond clasp in her hair. "Some chap he has working for him."

"And is she still in love with Bunny?"

"Who knows? But one does rather hope not given that Bunny himself is head over heels with Tippy Pleasance.

He's made quite a fool of himself over her."

"Poor Iris."

"Well yes. But the chief thing is, Elmer is absolutely convinced that it will wreck her chances of a decent marriage if people find out."

"Then we'd better not tell them."

"Quite," said Edwina, getting up quickly and edging into her minuscule bathroom, with its salmon pink basin and chrome fittings. "Now I'd better get going or I'm going to be fearfully late and Elmer will be horrid to me all evening."

"Bunny Devine?" Iris's blue eyes were full of a contempt quite at odds with the loveliness of her face. "If I never saw him again it would be too soon."

"Well I'm glad about that at least."

Against her own normal practice Celia was giving Iris lunch in a little café near the shop - a cigarette for herself and a chop and vegetables followed by rice pudding for Iris. Celia had insisted that Iris ate something and was surprised by the voraciousness of her appetite.

"I just thought…"

"You mean you heard, because everyone is talking about it. As if I cared."

"So it's not Bunny who is making you unhappy?"

"Did I say I was unhappy?"

"Do give me credit for having eyes in my head darling."

"Is it that obvious?"

"Not to most people, no." It would be beyond the ability of most people to imagine that a girl could be simultaneously as beautiful, well-dressed and monied as Iris and also be miserable. "Why don't you tell me?"

So Iris told Celia everything, beginning with the arrival of Samuel Dux in their house, and omitting almost nothing, including the rudeness of her behaviour towards him and what had passed between them when Samuel came to find her. But there were some parts of their encounter that she could not confide in Celia, no matter how worldly she was. How could she explain the intense sexual arousal Samuel had provoked in her, the foreign feel of his body and the rush of passion beneath his controlled exterior? Sometimes she had to force herself to think of his face and his eyes, because otherwise her mind would fill with images of his body against hers, his lips pressed to hers and the burning excitement that aroused. Fingers linked surreptitiously in the hall of her father's house, swift kisses exchanged when they found themselves alone, his extraordinary scent of hot male skin which could only be detected close up. His tenderness. Then his disappearance a few days later, without a word.

"It's been three weeks now and I've heard nothing. I thought. He told me,…I mean I really had got the impression he genuinely felt something for me. I just…. don't understand."

Looking at the girl, Celia did not understand either.

"I expect he did feel something for you. When one senses that one is usually right. Might he have gone for a holiday? Or to visit his family?"

"I don't know. He hasn't got a family. He just left. He vanished. He's left some….things at our house which might mean he's coming back. But Cairns doesn't know and there's no-one else I could ask."

"Except your father. And I can see you might not want to raise it with him."

"Exactly. My father would guess immediately why I was asking. And he would never countenance any kind of relationship with someone…well someone who came from.."

"Humble origins darling?"

Celia raised an elegantly plucked eyebrow signalling that exquisitely refined though she now was, she also remained the daughter of a civil servant and a dress maker from Shepperton.

"Not that I care."

"Of course not."

"The thing is, Celia. I've begun to think that it's me. That this sort of thing is what is meant to happen to me. That all the people I love or trust will just vanish, without saying goodbye. When my mother died I was sent away to stay with the Vickers because she was ill and needed some rest and when I came back, she just wasn't there. For years I just felt my mother had disappeared and there was still a chance that she might come back. Then there was Charles."

"But this is different."

"Of course. I know that. But it feels a little bit the same somehow. Just being left with no explanation. My mother and Charles didn't get the chance but I still don't see why anyone who cared about you would want to disappear without a word."

Iris rested her forehead momentarily on her fist, so that Celia should not see the glint of tears in her eyes. The gesture stirred Celia, who although she did not know of this Samuel Dux, determined to find out as much as she could.

Chapter Twenty-seven

It had been another exhausting day at the clinic. As Stevens trudged through the East End streets he occupied himself by ticking off all the local industries in terms of the specific maladies they produced for him to cure. There were the sweatshops where seamstresses sat at machines all day, ruining their sight and acquiring prematurely arthritic hands, as well as hacking coughs from all the fabric dust and tailor's chalk they inhaled. Then there was the laundry, where the damp humidity induced bronchitis and respiratory infections as did the foul, dusty air at the saw-mills. Heaving barrels at the brewery wrecked the back. Working at the glue factory blistered the skin. Only the dockers, who spent their days lugging cargo off ships into the cavernous riverside warehouses had any chance of good health, and that was because they were strong and muscular. But then all too often they would be crushed by a falling load.

By a row of little terraced houses he passed a gang of children out late in the streets playing a game involving a rope and a tin can. Soot hung in the air, and he knew that when he got home he would find his collar and cuffs laced with grime. A tiny child stumbled towards him, no more than a year and a half old he calculated, with a fat fist extended, offering him a stone, and he would have taken it from her but before he could accept it a sister grabbed her away. "Don't bother the gentleman."

It was a balmy evening, with the light low and slanting in the west. As the warm air slid over him he felt intensely aware of his body, still strong and full of potential. He thought of his physique the way he had studied anatomy drawings, the muscles dovetailed and interlocked, smoothly bunching and spreading under the skin. Contracting and extending in antagonistic movement. He pictured his own brain, with its intricate ripples and rifts and the pulsing purse of gristle that was his heart. He was fit for his age, with all the walking he did, and unlike those he ministered to he was in good physical shape, yet he lacked something which his patients, with their excessive families and sprawling relations unthinkingly possessed. What he craved, he realised, was touch. Not just any touch but the simple sensation of another human being who was giving, rather than receiving comfort.

For a moment he saw himself, as if from above. A well-dressed, middle-class man heading home, because he rarely had the appetite or the energy for his club nowadays. To a home which was too large for him, with a housekeeper who would have prepared one of her wholesome, solid meals, chops or a roast, bread and butter pudding, toad in the hole, summer pudding, and then would have withdrawn quietly, tactfully, leaving him to the delight of his own company and a stack of books to read. A home whose solitude had become surreally complicated by a great, welling, awkwardness of his own devising.

He shook off his self-pity with disgust. How was it that he'd let a single comment, a flicker of injured feeling, grow to such a palpable presence in the house? Why was he so offended that a girl like Esther should be ignorant of these slum quarters of London? He really must take her to see the clinic. She was twenty-one after all. No younger than some of the women he had worked alongside in the war.

He thought of the nurses at the casualty clearing station, holding the stumps of amputees to pour on a solution of Eusol and Peroxide, staunching pus from wounds, administering aspirin to men in excruciating pain, applying bandages and dressings to deranged soldiers who lashed out, imaging themselves still in the thick of battle. If those girls could bear such sights, then Esther could too.

Stevens had just made up his mind to broach the subject when to his surprise, early the next morning, Esther herself sought him out. As she came through the door and he felt of flood of relief. She was wearing a pretty chiffon with a geometric pattern of blue and green which made her look uncharacteristically sophisticated, and a faint floral perfume.

"Esther! Have you had breakfast? Would you like a cup of tea?"

"Oh. Yes, thank you."

He found a willow pattern cup and she watched him pour for her, finding it curious to see him engaged in such domestic detail. She had been so nervous about seeing him, though she knew she would have to let him know she was going away for two weeks. Yet he didn't seem angry any more.

"I wondered if I could have a word with you."

Stevens was going to say sorry, but he realised it would be hard to articulate exactly what he was sorry for. Instead he said:

"Yes, actually I wanted to mention something too. I wondered if you might like to see my clinic? I've been meaning to suggest it for some time, but there've been a lot of TB cases, so it's not been the best time to visit. But they're falling off now so if you'd be at all interested…."

Mercifully, she did not flinch.

"Well thank you. I would really like to. That would be kind of you. But I came to tell you I'm going away for a couple of weeks. In case you wondered where I was."

"Oh? Going on holiday?"

"Sort of. It's a house party in Suffolk. Near the sea. There's a whole group of artists and musicians going and the idea is to paint and play music and talk about politics."

"How delightful."

"Oh I'm sure it'll be terribly dreary. I don't have any thoughts at all about the future of socialism which is what most of them want to discuss, apparently."

"Come, come," He summoned a playful tone. "No views on the decline of Mr MacDonald? No ideas on the direction of Russian communism? Inflation in Germany? No thoughts on the breakdown of liberal bourgeois society?"

"Nope. At least hardly any."

"Then you'll have to stick to Cubism and the state of modern poetry. Or better still keep quiet and look superior."

She laughed, and shifted awkwardly, draining her tea cup.

For a moment Stevens contemplated the idea of two weeks by the sea in the company of artists and intellectuals, engaging in high-minded debate and painting the scenery. The idea seemed inexpressibly wonderful to him. Yet the thought of Esther there, laughing and joking with her friends, aroused the familiar sensation in him. A kind of envious resentment.

Turning his back to her, he summoned his professional dismissiveness.

"Well I'd better get on then. Thank you for letting me know. Have a marvellous time."

Chapter Twenty-eight

Samuel began to wonder if Husni might be avoiding him. He had searched for him for several days without success. He had visited his office, a regional branch of the Ministry of the Interior, where he heard that Husni had been given some newly created post, but every time he made the journey, it appeared that he had just missed him. Mr Al-Khalid was away just then. He had left his desk and no one knew when he would be back. Samuel tried again at noon when the midsummer sun was harsh and the streets deserted, save a few palm trees, leaking black shadows on the ground. But still he was politely rebuffed. Perhaps he could try another day. Given the Egyptian approach to time, as something infinitely plentiful, infinitely elastic, Samuel realised he could be in the country another month before he set eyes on Husni. Obviously he needed to take more direct action.

He set out that evening. He had forgotten the precise address, but once he had entered the quarter his feet infallibly found their way through the warren of narrow, dirt streets, mediaeval, almost biblical in aspect, where camels and donkeys poked their heads from makeshift stables and behind the latticed windows veiled women could be seen hastening from task to task. The little courtyard was shut off from the street by a wrought iron door. He rang the bell experimentally and smelt from somewhere within a faint, familiar smell of hashish.

"Samuel! My friend. This is an unexpected surprise. What brings you here?"

It was hard to miss the glimmer of hostility masked quickly by a diplomatic smile. But even harder not to see how much Husni had changed. In the space of only a year, he looked dramatically different. His fine, handsome face had aged ten years, the cheeks were hollowed and the whites of his eyes tinged with yellow. His voice had lost its edge of urgent passion and as they embraced Samuel felt the ribs beneath the skin. He could not help noticing how shabby his clothes were and where once his shirt had strained robustly against his belly, now it hung loose. His gaze, once so direct and forthright, now avoided Samuel's eyes,

He ushered Samuel onto a terrace and they sat on kelim-covered cushions taking coffee. Husni offered him the sheeshah, pungent, with spicy smoke, and he himself seemed to gulp at it, drawing greedy breaths. A servant circled silently, lighting kerosene lamps. Above them the vast Egyptian sky bristled with stars and all around were the sounds of the night, bats fluttering in the trees, the grass rustling as a snake passed by. Eventually Husni stirred himself to speech.

"So what brings you back here now? There's no excavation at the moment. Your Mr Carter has run away to America. He's making a thousand pounds a lecture, I heard."

"Very nice for him."

"And how's London? Have they got over their enthusiasm for ancient Egypt yet? I suppose fashion has moved on."

"Quite the opposite. They're still immensely interested. I'm finding myself quite a popular figure at parties."

"Nothing new there."

"No. I mean it. Since Lord Carnarvon's death, there's an added fascination. They're certain it's A Sign."

Unlike Samuel, Husni had always mocked those soothsayers who liked to see signs and messages in the discovery of the tomb. He always said it was time for Egyptians to stop musing on magical powers and start focusing on political power instead. The ancient superstitions were all part of a culture that was keeping Egypt in the past, rather than looking to the future. The incident with the canary had made him laugh out loud. Just before the Earl's death, Howard Carter had returned to his house to find his pet canary dead in the mouth of a coiled cobra. Natives immediately said that the cobra, the sacred symbol of Egyptian monarchy, had wrought its revenge on the Englishman. Then there was the case of a French professor, La Fleur, who accepted an invitation from Carter to see round the tomb and straight afterwards returned to his hotel room and fell down dead.

"The fact that he had been suffering from influenza was obviously irrelevant!" Husni had said, triumphantly.

But Husni was no longer in a joking mood. His reliable geniality appeared to have dissipated, just as the old intimacy between them, that unspoken electric current of feeling, seemed to have stiffened and died. How could it be, Samuel wondered, that a year ago this man had been his dearest friend? Now Husni stared into the distance completely detached, his eyes hooded and brooding. Then he said:

"I'll never understand you British. You're a nation that has seen so much of its own suffering and destruction, that's been through the most horrifying war the world has ever seen and lost millions of your own sons and yet you're transfixed by a single young man who died ..what...? three thousand years ago."

He fell silent again, allowing tendrils of fragrant smoke to curl and fray in the evening breeze. After a while he stretched his legs and talked listlessly about the political process he was engaged in, how difficult it was to defeat the forces of bureaucracy. How perhaps there was no point in bothering.

"Yet something tells me you've not come all the way back from England out of concern for the future of the Egyptian state. Or even for the sake of our friendship. Am I right? Why've you really come to see me?"

Now that it had come to it, Samuel hesitated. "It's hard to know where to start."

"I'm listening."

"Impossible really. I hardly know why I'm here."

"Well come on. Don't keep me in suspense, man."

"What I want....I mean, I have a request which you're going to find very strange. I don't know if you could possibly help me. A year ago, I brought you something. You must remember?"

"How could I forget?"

The night when Samuel had arrived with the parcel, bundled in a copy of the local paper, which fell open on the desk before them. Husni's delight. So eager to display it he didn't even comment on the linen wrappings, ripped and mottled with rusty blotches the colour of dried blood. Their embrace and Husni's effusive gratitude on behalf of the Egyptian nation.

Without looking at him Samuel said, "I want it back."

Onto the table he placed a wallet. From it he drew out a small brown brick of notes. Two hundred pounds, held together with a rubber band. He stood it up on its end.

"I can pay."

"You want to buy it?"

"It's not for me. Not directly."

"For some museum then?"

"A private collector."

Husni's eyes were hard, and his tone hostile. "What makes you think it's for sale?"

"Wait. Please don't be appalled." Samuel reached out a hand to Husni's arm and for a second he looked intently at him, willing him to understand.

"Believe me Husni, I wish to God I had never seen it in my life, and even more that I should never have to see it again. I can hardly bear to think of it without feeling sick. For the past year I have done everything I could not to remember it, not for a second to let its image creep into my mind. If I could I would have banished it from my dreams. I have tried to comfort myself by thinking how many thousands of miles of land and sea it is away from me, in another country, another continent even. I have taken consolation from the fact that it has been locked in some deep vault, and that there were no circumstances I could conceive of which would mean I would ever have to set eyes on it again. Until now...."

"And now?"

"Now, there is something I want even more. Something... *someone*....who is so important to me, that I would do anything in my power for her."

Eagerly, his words tripping over themselves, he told Husni about Iris and Barrington and the pact that had brought him here.

"So you see I have to have it. It's as simple as that. If I don't return with the piece, I won't see her again."

Husni took a pull on his hookah and looked at him with a glimmer of interest. "This woman, Iris, what is she like?"

How could he describe the face that was imprinted on his mind? Especially to Husni, with whom he had never discussed women.

"She's very beautiful..."

"Does she have feelings for you in return?"

"I think so."

"Why could you not simply elope together with this woman, if she feels the same for you?"

"It's hard to explain. It's not so easy. She occupies a different world from me."

"A member of the English upper classes, you mean. Like our friend Violet."

"No! No! She's not at all like Violet."

"All right my friend. Calm down."

Now that he was expressing what had been on his mind for so long, his eyes gleamed with excitement.

"You may think all English are the same but in fact their stratifications and hierarchies are as precise as if they were cast in stone. Iris is different both from Violet and from me. She's born to wealth and comfort. Her life and expectations are unlike anything I could offer her. Or anything I even know. I have friends at home - friends like you - who talk about changing the established order and whenever I listen to them discussing the class barriers, how every class has no idea of the way the others live and how that situation will be resolved with the coming of socialist revolution...."

"As it will.."

"No. Whenever I listen to them I just laugh because no revolution would be enough to connect Iris's social position with my own. It's an impossible situation. I come from a tiny village in the countryside. My father was a printer. Her father is a millionaire. She's utterly unattainable to me. As distant from me as if she lived on Venus."

"But not so unattainable that she can't be bought."

"I can see you're angry....I shouldn't have come. This is useless. I knew this would be a pointless exercise. I knew there would be no chance of getting it back again."

Abruptly Husni rose and gestured. His face, which had been so hostile, seemed transformed into something like resignation.

"Do you want to see it?"

Samuel felt the shock like something physical. A jolt of alarm, and then pure, elemental fear. He gripped the arms of the wicker chair, as though for support.

"It's here?"

"Yes. You can see it if you like."

He could not summon the words to reply. He could only, weakly, nod his head.

"Follow me."

Shaking with nerves, Samuel followed Husni back into the house. They passed along a tiled corridor, and down a dim passage to a studded, wooden door. Husni reached for a key on a chain round his belt and unlocked it, then passed into what looked like a black void.

It was a steep stairwell, reeking of damp and mildew. Husni groped beside him and brought up a lantern which he lit, and descended some steps and after a second's hesitation, Samuel went after him.

Though he had come here with this express intention, his heart was pounding with the prospect of seeing it again. He remembered, with a crushing sense of déjà vu, the night they entered the burial chamber. He felt again the chill crawling on the flesh, the sour choke of dust at the back of the throat and the darkness blanketing the eyes as they groped their way by the thin beam of Carter's torch. Again his head flooded with heart-pounding claustrophobia and beneath it a sense of intrusion, of violation, as they squeezed their way deeper into the cramped space. And then the terror when something nameless and formless seemed to rise up before him in that place of vacancy. The moment he knew for certain he had been brushed by the dark, swift wing of death.

"Here it is."

They had reached a tiny, bricked cellar. In the middle, on a table, stood a plain wooden wine case upended, its lid on hinges. Husni opened it and with the lantern splashed a pool of yellow light.

And there it was. To see it again was most extraordinary. The first rush of excitement was almost as great as when he had first set eyes on it. For a second he felt a flare of pure rapture as the thing before him meshed with the image that had been seared on his retina. It was even more perfect, he realised, than the idea of itself. It was a sight, after all, intended only for the eyes of the divine.

It was a statue of a young man, a delicate thing, no more than a foot high, made of pure gold. The left leg, according to convention, was placed ahead of the right. The lobes of the ears were pierced. The face was gorgeous in its tranquillity, and the whole of it, nose and cheekbones and brow, chiselled so precisely that the eye unconsciously searched for a single deviation that might have lessened its perfection. The eyebrows, eyelids and kohl marks were made of gold, the white of the eye fashioned from crystalline limestone and the pupil obsidian. A broad collar was suspended from the neck with a pectoral embodying a winged scarab and gilded bracelets were on each arm and wrist. The face was serene, yet curiously judgemental. The body was poised in movement, and from the right hand were suspended a pair of scales. And along the pedestal, a row of hieroglyphs - an arm, a canopic, an ibis, a setting sun. Husni gazed at it, pensively.

"The Weighing Of The Heart. The moment the heart is weighed after death to determine entry to the afterlife. Does the heart's good outweigh its evil deeds, or do the scales refuse to balance?"

For Samuel, seeing the statue again brought everything back. He was filled with an intense sadness and a poignancy so deep his eyes filmed over with tears. Yet the face seemed to exert a peculiar forcefield of its own, making it hard to tear his eyes from it. Turning away he said:

"I thought it would be in a bank or a museum vault by now."

Husni gave an almost imperceptible shrug.

"How could that be? How could I possibly go through with my plan? All my ideas about asserting the rights of the Egyptian nation to the treasures from their own tombs, unveiling this symbol of Carter's treachery and demanding all his stolen goods to be returned? My plan to have Carter and his thieving held up to public view. After what happened, how could I have let this be seen?"

Samuel glanced round the cellar. Almost in a whisper he said:

"You did ask."

"I don't deny it. I wanted something. A piece like this to publicise yet another tawdry episode in the British rape of Egypt. And now I hate the sight of it."

"Or is it still here, Husni, because you just can't bear to let it go?"

Husni was staring at the statue. Samuel thought he might react with fury, but instead he murmured:

"You're right. I could hardly bear to be apart from it."
With an almost visible shudder he wrenched his eyes from it and turned to face Samuel. His voice was low and intense.

"Almost as soon as you brought this statue to me, I felt an overwhelming need to keep it utterly to myself. I didn't want anyone to see it. Of course after what had happened, it was inevitable that it should remain a secret for a while, yet I dreaded the day when I would eventually have to give it up.

"At first I rationalised this feeling by saying that I didn't want them to do with this object what they have done with everything else. Copy it, patent it, turn its image into a million dreadful wallpapers or lamp stands or ashtrays. I didn't want to see a hundred of it down in the market every morning. I hated the idea that something so ancient should overnight become modern - a popular piece, a fashion item, corrupted by the present."

"But the fact was, I thought this was the most beautiful thing I had ever seen. Nothing else in life could match it. I craved to be with it. I spent many hours, here in this cellar, simply looking at it, and I could hardly bear for it to be out of my sight. It somehow both attracted me and repelled me, like two sides of a strong magnet. And it felt like my soul was being torn apart in the process.

"After a time the effect it had on me was becoming plain to others. I became distracted and depressed. I stopped seeing my family, and my friends stopped calling, or if they did they found me incommunicative and inhospitable. My work no longer interested me, and I gave up attending meetings. My colleagues complained that I lacked commitment to my job and my comrades in the movement blamed my lethargy on the indolence of power. But that was not the cause. The truth was that this face had begun to weigh on me in my dreams, speaking of dark things to come. I would wake in a wracking sweat, trembling and shouting out. I knew its history but now it was the future that I dreaded. What more did it have in store for me? I would ask it that question, night after night."

"Then to my great surprise, I learned you had returned to Egypt and were looking for me. I knew exactly what it was you wanted and for your sake, Samuel, I avoided seeing you for as long as I could. I dearly hoped you would give up the search and return to England. I didn't want to give the statue up. And I didn't want you to have it either my dear friend. Yet, while the idea of losing it terrified me, the idea of keeping it scared me even more."

In the gloomy light of the cellar Husni looked desolate. His once confident, laughing features were sharpened by the bones beneath. Between them the statue seemed to burn with its own peculiar light.

"So will you sell it to me?"

"No."

For a moment Husni laid a fingertip on the figure's head. He gave a great, shuddering sigh. Then he said:

"I will give it to you though. It's not mine to sell. And besides, its price has already been too high."

With elaborate care he began to wrap the piece in its stained linen shroud. After several minutes he replaced it gently in its box and carried the box up the steps in his arms, as tenderly as a sleeping baby.

At the door Samuel tried to take it from him and for a moment Husni held onto it, before, with force of will, relinquishing the box into Samuel's waiting arms. Even then he barred the doorway, his eyes huge and staring in his cadaverous face.

"I used to joke about the curse Samuel. That foolish idea that something malign may have stretched dark wings and flown out of the tomb when its doors were breached. But if you really want to know, I think there's something in it after all."

"Husni. Please."

"No, listen to me. First your Howard Carter disappears in frustration, before he has even set eyes on the face of the mummy. Then my dream of a better nation has become corrupted, all my plans thwarted by my people's….. ineptitude, their inefficiency and their squabbling. And I myself - you saw at once how changed I am, though your damned British manners forbid you to mention it! I am skin and bones. I sicken by the day and the bloodsucking doctors have no idea what is wrong with me. It's not a tumour, they say, not malaria or any other kind of illness they recognise. They conclude it must be some kind of foreign disease, contracted through my habit of associating with our European friends. That means nothing. I myself think it is a disease of the soul. I no longer have any ambition or energy for change. I feel the lifeblood ebbing out of me."

"Don't say that Husni. You're a young man."

He ignored this remark, as if he had not heard it.

"And then there's you my friend. We both know what curse has been laid on you."

"I don't believe in the curse," said Samuel stoically, automatically, the way an agnostic recites the creed, as though by repetition something might become true.

Husni looked at him wearily.

"You say that because that is what everything in your culture has taught you to believe. That is the rational, the enlightened attitude that centuries of Western thought have taught you to uphold. You can't explain something, you can't measure it, or see it, therefore to you, it must not exist. You can marvel at the beauty of these totemic objects, but deny them the other powers their creators gave them. So! Refusing to believe something can save you from it, can it? Well, I shall refuse to believe in death then! Perhaps that will save me!"

He gave a vicious smile, took Samuel's arm and clutched it, a little too tightly. His bony fingers were shaking.

"How can you deny this is a cursed thing? You have seen that it carries a terrible power. You Samuel, of all people, should know that."

Chapter Twenty-nine

"Was the house party fun?"

No actually, it wasn't fun at all, thought Esther. Not one bit of fun.

"Yes, thank you."

It had been very hot. The back of her Aertex shirt was damp with sweat. Someone was supposed to have met them at the station but must have forgotten, so while they were standing in the little shop, buying an ice-cream and thinking what to do, Alice had befriended an old man with a tweed jacket and a walrus moustache and somehow bullied him into giving them a lift in his car. His manner had been both lecherous and condescending, "Can't abandon two young ladies in this heat. Where are we off to then?", but when told it was Godstone Court he gave a little sniff and his manner turned distinctly cooler. Still, Alice had installed herself comfortably in the front seat, so Esther had no choice but to climb in the back.

"Staying with Mrs Silverstein are we? I've heard her gatherings get very political."

"Oh, we're just hoping to do some painting," said Alice demurely. "Just some of the lovely views you have round here."

The idea of women and landscape seemed to mollify him. Watercolours seemed an unlikely revolutionary tool. Nonetheless, he still disapproved.

"They keep a pretty full house at this time of year. Always a lot of folk up from London. Bolsheviks, or what have you. Tramping around."

The image of local crops being ground underfoot by negligent communists made Esther snort with suppressed laughter.

"Oh, I don't think they'll be doing much tramping," said

Alice airily. "Some of them are so old it's as much as they can do to shuffle."

They rattled on in silence until the driver drew up outside a pair of tall gates.

"Well I suppose I should say enjoy yourselves, whatever you have planned."

"Thank you so much," said Alice, and as they walked off he craned his head to see if any other attractive young women were secured behind the large, black, shiny gates.

The house itself was curious. Jacobean redbrick outside and inside a strong smell of dog and mildew. All the doors seemed to be concealed in dark panelling and led out onto small winding corridors. The hall was entirely empty. No-one appeared to greet them and as Alice's parents were not due to arrive until the following day, there was absolutely no one Esther knew. She followed Alice, who led her upstairs to a pretty attic bedroom and flung her case down on the counterpane. This must be where they were intended to sleep and if it wasn't Alice didn't care because the view was so wonderful, she said, craning out of the window from where meadows rolled and heaved towards the sea. Then she turned suddenly towards Esther and said with unusual intensity, "I'm so glad you came."

"So what did you talk about?" asked Frank Stevens.

"Revolutionary socialism of course."

"Of course." He had been kneeling on the floor, busying himself with the controls of his new wireless when she stuck her head round the door. He still had his back to her.

"And were all the comrades your age?"

"All horribly middle-aged I'm afraid…" She stopped herself. "Not that…"

"Not that there's anything wrong with being middle-aged you mean? Or not that middle-age is horrible?"

His sat back on his heels and looked at her with a wry smile. A tuft of hair stuck up from the crown of his head.

"What I meant was I didn't seem to have much in common with most of them."

In fact there had been scarcely anyone their age, except for a stringy man with oiled, carrot-red hair and poached-egg eyes behind steel glasses. He was down from Cambridge and was infatuated with Alice. He trailed around after them, offering to carry her easel, and seemed likely to spoil the entire two weeks until Alice was intentionally rude to him to make him go away. She was good like that with men, Esther thought. She never seemed to mind hurting their feelings. Esther had been brought up to think the gentlest rebuff could pierce the male psyche like a poisoned arrow.

Yet even Alice's undivided company could not alleviate the ghastliness of the occasion. The food was dire. The family was militantly vegetarian and alongside piles of cabbage and carrots, ate hunks of lumpy brown bread that tasted of sawdust with every meal. People talked about politics with furious intensity. They called the Prime Minister a criminal and a class traitor. They quarrelled irritably about Russia, discussing the revolution in proprietorial terms, as if it was something they had personally arranged for the benefit of the Russian people. Then someone formally objected to them even talking about Russia because it was divisive, on the grounds that it was impossible to get the radical left to utter a word of doubt about the revolution, it was like a religion to them, whereas other people were questioning the whole direction of the revolution after Lenin. Everyone's opinion was simultaneously sought and aggressively rejected. Everyone took umbrage. One of the main points of contention seemed to be not what people said, but how they were labelled. There seemed to be infinitesimal yet crucial divisions between revolutionary socialism, communism and Labourites. Esther genuinely wanted to decide where she stood, but the way they discussed it only made it more, rather than less obfuscating.

When they strayed from politics, things were even worse.

The Silversteins had a convention in which after dinner all their guests would take turn to speak or perform or in some way entertain each other. Being "fun" or "amusing" was an important requirement, and being a "bore" the ultimate faux pas. Some people acted out little scenes they had written themselves and others composed satirical poems. Alice, who was a confident pianist, played *Rhapsody in Blue*, whose glorious, jumpy rhythms miraculously silenced the loud jangle of voices among the guests, inducing at least for a moment a blessed calm.

"And how are you going to entertain us?"

Esther's inquisitor had a strangely long tongue, which seemed to loll out of his mouth, and a high pitched drawl. He lounged back in his seat as he peered at her, folding his legs over like a stick insect and allowing his etiolated arms to trail down. Looking at him, with his gimlet eyes, a stripe of saliva glistening on his beard, the answer came to her in a flash.

"I'll draw you, if you like."

"Great idea," said Alice, amused. "But she's a cruel cartoonist Edgar, so be warned!"

The cartoons had been her salvation. After that she found herself studying her fellow guests covertly, deciding which one should be sketched each night. No matter how much she exaggerated noses or bulges of fat or drooping jowls, no one appeared offended. Though they delighted in mockery of each other, they appeared blind to their own shortcomings and several begged Esther to sign her sketches. Her picture of Edgar Portnoy, with his shrivelled arachnid limbs, was seized by Mrs Silverstein and framed.

"It may be unkind Edgar," she crowed, "but she has you to a T."

Alice, on the contrary, produced just one painting during the entire fortnight. Her life study showed Esther at once innocent and sexual, hands on hips, and her head tossed back. When she was finally allowed to look at it, Esther gasped. The dark brown cropped hair, pale skin and slightly titled nose, she recognised at once, but the casual, sensual abandon of the pose was so unlike her. It was as though Alice had found something inside her, a kind of exultant freedom, that she had never known herself. She looked quickly away, embarrassed.

Seeing that Frank Stevens was still absorbed with his wireless, she sank down in a nearby chair.

"It's good to be home." She didn't register that it was the first time she had referred to Waverley Gardens as home but Stevens noticed it. He replaced the wireless on the mantelpiece and picked up his bag. He was late, as ever.

"What are you doing tomorrow?"

"Nothing."

"Come with me then."

"Where to?"

"You said you might like to see where I work. If you're still keen be ready at eight. Though I warn you, you won't meet many revolutionary socialists."

The consulting room was painted bottle green and stank so strongly of disinfectant that it made Esther's eyes water. Outside, rows of patients sat impassively down the tiled corridor, some clutching bottles and medications, others clinging to their children, staring ahead. Her presence seemed to arouse absolutely no interest in them. Presumably they thought Esther, in her tailored jacket and round collared blouse, was just another middle-class professional, most probably the lady from the Health board or some other expert.

One by one they were called in to see Dr Stevens, hope, fear and resignation mingled in their faces. He wasted no pleasantries on them, but she could see that he was popular. He was gruff, certainly, but he didn't have that air she had noticed in other doctors of treating the sick as though they were naughty children rather than genuinely unwell. He seemed to accord them a certain respect and in some cases it was obvious that was all he could offer them. The first patient, a middle-aged man, came in guided in by his wife and sat mutely by while she described his symptoms and how he had never been the same since the gas in the trenches. Stevens said the only thing for him was rest. After him came a brewery labourer, with a fever and racking cough. Stevens sent him off with a bottle of pink medicament.

"What did you give him? Will it cure him?"

"Not at all. It's utterly useless."

"But why ….?"

"I don't have the drugs to cure him. And something is better than nothing. People like to feel they're doing something for themselves and sometimes just that feeling alone can help their condition."

The day went on. Esther sat on a chair in the corner of the room. After a while she listened to the consultations only in snatches.

"Feels a bit liverish, she does, keeps yawning."

"It's a bilious feeling I 'ave doctor. But it's making me breathless."

"My husband tells me it's only a nervous cough."

"Practically 'ad to carry 'im 'ere doctor."

They didn't even stop for lunch, though a kind, russet-headed nurse darted in several times with cups of tea, and at one point gave Esther a cigarette which took the edge off her appetite. So it was with distinct relief that around five o'clock she saw Stevens packing up his briefcase for the end of the afternoon. She was feeling almost faint with hunger.

"Are we going now?"

"Not quite yet. I need to make a house call. You'd better come too. It's only round the corner."

He set off through the narrow streets at a brisk pace and she struggled to keep up.

"Do you get called out often?"

"Not really. It's a shilling to call me out, so most people have to be desperate. It's almost always a child. But we've got an older man this time. Father of five. Fish porter at Billingsgate."

"What's he suffering from?"

"I don't know yet but it's a chest disease usually. Pneumonia. Might be diptheria. And is it any surprise?" He waved his hand at the houses as they passed, the narrow terraces bisected by cloacal alleyways. "Look at these places. They're riddled with damp and infestation. They have nothing but brick WCs in the yard. People wash at the public baths. They share a pump for drinking water. No wonder diseases spread. After the war everyone said they would build homes fit for heroes, but it certainly hasn't happened round here."

When they arrived at the house Stevens stood by to let Esther enter first and she stepped straight from the street into the tiny front room. It was papered in a faded floral, so the walls seemed clotted with flowers, and the table was covered in newspaper. Every surface was stacked with the family's possessions. Through a door to the scullery she glimpsed a large copper boiling, giving off clouds of steam and around the door peered a couple of filthy children, giggling and shy. In a brass bed pushed to the corner of the room lay Dr Stevens's patient and next to him a table bearing a clear bottle with a red wax cork labelled Fenning's Fever Mixture. The man was a shocking sight. He looked like a skeleton with a thin coat of flesh. His breath was rasping from his lungs and his face was waxy. His eyes were red circles and the hair stuck to his scalp with sweat. When he saw them he struggled up on one elbow, his face beaded with perspiration, and hacked into a grey rag.

The room was unbearably hot and stuffy. Esther tried not to intrude, but in the tiny space it was impossible to pretend she could not hear Stevens's consultation. He held a hushed conversation with the wife, before turning to the man and prodding his chest.

"So Mr Ramshaw. You're feeling bad?"

"It's not that bad, doctor, I keep telling her. It's just a winter cough."

"Winter? It's summer now."

"I've always had a dicky chest. Always had coughs." He broke off for a lengthy demonstration.

"I don't think that sounds like a winter cough. There's blood in that sputum." He peered at the rag in the man's hand. "My fear is that you have tuberculosis. Consumption, you know? Do you understand what that is? We'll have to have you into hospital to be tested. And if that's the case, you might need to go into an isolation ward and have absolute rest."

"That's impossible doctor. If I rest who'll keep the kids?"

"Who'll keep the kids if you die?"

Did he really need to be so harsh, Esther wondered, with the children just the other side of the door? She was trying to edge away from the fire blazing beside her in the grate. How could they bear it so hot and airless in here? The whole place smelt terrible, of sweat and damp clothes and cabbage and urine, and when she tried not breathing through her nose she had a great rush of nausea. Suddenly her early start and the lack of food came together and she felt herself sway. The walls of the room rushed towards her and she clutched at the door for support.

"Esther." Stevens's arm was beneath hers before she could fall. He circled her waist and took her weight. "Sit down."

"I'm so sorry. I'm just a bit hot." She saw the faces of the family, even the man in the bed, turned towards her blank and uncomprehending.

"Why don't you wait outside for a moment?"

"Yes. Thank you. I will."

Being in the cool air outside refreshed her and she felt her swimming head return to normal, though her face burned with embarrassment. To faint in such a place, when Dr

Stevens was attending to a genuinely sick man. When he emerged a few minutes later he gave her a brief, searching glance.

"Does this sort of thing happen a lot?"

"No! No not at all. I'm so sorry. I've never fainted. I think it was just…I mean...it was very hot in there."

"Hmm. They were probably using up every lump of coal they could get their hands on in the mistaken belief it would make the man any better."

"Do you think he'll recover?"

"Probably not. Not unless he takes himself off to a sanatorium, which I think you'll agree seems unlikely."

"What will he live on?"

"Credit, to start with. The kindness of neighbours, for a while, plus anything his wife can earn. They probably eat no more than bread and lard as it is. If he doesn't get better in a few weeks, Billingsgate won't keep a job open for him."

"Can't you do anything for him?"

That was obviously the wrong question.

"*Do* anything? You mean invent a cure for tuberculosis or re-order our social structure so that people can afford to go into hospital when they need to and still have their families properly looked after? I'm not sure it's in my power but perhaps your socialist friends have an answer to that."

"Perhaps they do. You don't need to be so fierce. I was only asking."

They walked up the road in silence and halted at the bus stop, where Stevens leant against a hoarding advertising Walls' Ice Cream. Just the sight of it made her mouth water.

"Don't you get awfully hungry? I mean not eating all day?"

He looked at her briefly then laughed. "Poor girl. We missed lunch. Then I wonder why you feel faint. Low blood sugar." For the first time that day his face relaxed a little. "We were unusually busy today. Normally I dash out to a corner café with one of the other doctors. That one there actually, is one of our favourites."

Across the road she saw the lighted windows of a café
and inside huge etched mirrors on the gleaming tiled walls.
Uniformed waitresses glided between the marble table-tops.
A mingled fragrance of cooking vegetables and fried fish
hung in the air.

"In fact, I vote we have something straight away. It's a real
East End place here. Pie and mash, jellied eels, all the local
delicacies. D'you like that kind of thing?"

"It sounds wonderful."

In the event they had steak and kidney pudding, which
they drank with tea followed by stewed fruit and custard.
The food revived both of them and he watched her as
she ate, neatly and quickly, her eyes wandering round the
immaculate little restaurant. She caught him looking at her
and said: "Do you know, I think even Mrs Bennett could
learn something from this place."

"I'd like to see you try persuading Mrs Bennett to served
jellied eels. Or bagels."

They laughed.

"You feel better now then?"

"Much. I told you, I've never fainted before."

"Perhaps it shocked you. Seeing what you did today."

"No," she lied. "I'd like to come again. It's been…" she
searched for an appropriate phrase, "enlightening."

His tone changed. "This communist stuff you and your
friends talk about. Are you really convinced by it? Do you
think it could make any difference to the conditions round
here?"

"I think so. It seems the fairest way."

"The way they're doing it in Russia?"

She chewed her pudding. "Mmmm."

"There's a couple of people I know who've been out there
and they say it's more like a dictatorship. They seem to
think the revolutionists are ignoring basic human rights."

"I've heard that too." Some of the people at the house party had argued about that. "But even if it's true, that's not what communism is supposed to be about."

"What is it *supposed* to be about then?"

"Safeguarding the interests of the vast mass of people."

"The working classes?"

"Uh-huh."

He looked as though considering her answer seriously, then said:

"Yes, I suppose that sort of cant is the thing I hate most about it. The "working classes", the "middle classes". That way they have of lumping people together as masses. I can't stand it. I'd rather see people as individuals. All this stuff about class war depersonalises people, it makes out they can't do anything of their own free will because they're controlled, like robots, by social and economic forces. It's a philosophy of hate. Those Bolsheviks preach class war and hatred rather than the consolidation we desperately need."

"That's not true."

Esther thought of everything she had heard about the struggle between bloated capitalism and labour, about the proletarian revolution and how vital it was for the working class to seize power if it was ever to abolish social divisions. True, she'd always thought the brutal demarcations which Alan portrayed seemed a little too black and white. Society seemed far more complex to her, made up of a huge number of social layers. God knows her mother was able to detect the most infinite nuances of social status just by what hat a person was wearing, or whether they talked about sitting rooms or drawing rooms or looking glasses or mirrors.

"What I think," she persevered, "is that it's more about breaking down rigid barriers. So the social order isn't set in stone."

"No more rich man in his castle, poor man at his gate. That kind of thing?"

"Exactly. Which is only the message of Christianity after all."

"I see." He lit a cigarette and waved the match out. "And you believe in that too I suppose?"

To Esther, the kind of person who believed in the lyrics of popular songs, the notion of God had always been unprovocative and benign. It seemed entirely natural to her that He should exist, and that He should find himself most comfortably at home in the Church of England.

"Of course."

"Of course? You make it sound so simple. I thought all communists were atheists."

"Well not this one."

"Lucky you," he said lightly.

"Are you saying you don't …..have faith?"

"Faith in what?" As he talked he watched the movement of her mouth, the minute dark hairs on the top of her lip, as though he were studying her beneath a microscope.

"In God of course."

"Oh God." He shrugged and stirred sugar into his tea. Then he laughed, a short, joyless bark. "Sorry, but no."

How could he explain? She had talked of cubism teaching people to see things differently but for most people, ordinary people, it wasn't art, it was the war that did that. After the war the only thing he had felt was absolute desolation and futility. The God of his childhood - the one in the hymn books and the Bible, the one he prayed to when pets died - had no shape and significance for him any more.

"Not after the war, at any rate."

Esther knew not to talk about the war. Not ever to mention it. Even though she remembered her father telling her that it might be good to ask Stevens about it.

"Did it matter to you? Losing your faith?"

He reflected for a moment. "It's a good question. Losing faith is a dangerous thing. People often say when people cease to believe in God, they don't believe in nothing, they believe in anything. Like communism for instance."

"What do you believe in then?"

"I'm not sure. But to my mind the only system that seems to offer any certainty or improvement in our lot is not religion or politics but science."

They left the restaurant and walked through the streets. This area was entirely new to her. They passed the open door of a pub and caught a waft of beer and tobacco, and the hot press of damp bodies. A blast of noise, and the smell of sick. A group of children were picking scraps from dustbins in an alley. They walked along streets of terraced houses and she peered in, hungry for a glimpse of worlds she didn't know.

It was late when they arrived home. The hall was dim as they entered. Light from the street lamp outside filtered through the stained glass of the door and fell in jewelled colours on her face. Stevens, who had reached for the light switch, noticed it and stood with his arm resting against the wall, looking down at her. She smelt the faint steaming of damp from his tweed coat and could see a map of tiny lines etched round his eyes.

"Tell me about your time in the war."

She didn't know why she said it. Her father's advice, or her accursed need to fill every space with speech. He started as if he had been stung then said with exasperation:

"Esther.......Why do you ask these things? The war is hardly something I feel like talking about. Not now, at any rate."

He let his hand fall, then in a gentler tone wished her goodnight before going into his sitting room and shutting the door behind him. After he had gone she stood for a moment in the unlit hall with a curious sensation of dreadfully dampening excitement, like a firework inside her fizzling out, a feeling she had not felt before and could not quite put a name to.

Chapter Thirty

"I should have her worries darling."

Celia Urquart was nipping round the director's suite of Barrington House, pins in her mouth, tucking the drapes of a curtain into expert folds, as though she were arranging a bridal dress. Iris sat at the monumental walnut desk, doodling on the jotter with a perfectly sharpened pencil. She was telling Celia about the disaster that was Dolly's marriage. It was only a few months since the wedding but already Hector Monroe was passing the days in an alcoholic haze and treating Dolly with a kind of vicious resentment, even as he made his way through her money. His latest purchase had been a type 35 two litre Bugatti racer in aubergine with cream leather seats, which he said was vital if he was to pursue a racing career. When Dolly suggested that he should perhaps settle his debts at the casino first, he had turned on her and slapped her across the face, leaving a purple bruise. Dolly had had to pretend she had fallen off her horse in Richmond Park.

But Celia was not concentrating properly on Dolly's predicament. There was so much to do before the official opening of the building, on which day a phalanx of important guests and newspapermen would be invited in to inspect its splendour. Such was Elmer Barrington's pride in his creation - which in his grandiloquent way he had dubbed "an important addition to London's architecture" - he wanted to show it off as widely as possible. So on the opening night there would be a big party. But according to Edwina, from whom Celia had secured this information, Elmer was being utterly eccentric about the guest list for the event.

"He doesn't just want to invite our usual crowd Celia, he wants to invite arty people - you know, the sort you go around with."

"How enlightened of him."

"Is it? I don't know. I don't seem to understand Elmer these days. He's so grumpy. I think it's something about his business, he was complaining about people poking their noses into his affairs, but I haven't the first idea what he meant. Anyway, he says the building is a work of art and he wants it to be culturally appreciated, though why our usual friends couldn't do that is a mystery to me. And the worst of it is, he's asked me to suggest the guests - you know art writers and critics and that sort of thing. People who do magazines. *Tatler, Bystander, Vogue*, newspaper chaps. But I simply haven't a clue about these people. They aren't my type."

"Want me to suggest a few names?"

"Oh could you Celia?" Edwina turned her famously limpid eyes to her friend. "He seems to think I know everybody, but I know you, which is just as good."

Celia rather relished the idea of composing a guest list of prominent writers and artists to share in Elmer's pride. And she had to admit, he had a lot to be proud of. Every detail had been meticulously observed. She had rarely worked for a client who was so keen to spare no expense. In this room there were silky suede sofas the size of horses' flanks, giant lacquered vases and immaculate Egyptian rugs. Most of the rooms, though they were to be used as offices, were panelled in oak or decorated with moulded gold lacquered screens. Along the soft green corridors stood huge chesterfields the colour of conkers, with plump swells and cleavages along their tightly buttoned backs. In Barrington's own office was a stone fireplace which had been shipped from a sixteenth-century French château. Even the lavatories boasted lotus shaped mirrors and exquisite geometric basins. Everything about Barrington House was rich and expensive, a great cathedral of mammon enclosing a soft cocoon of wealth.

She looked over indulgently to where the dachshunds were curled on Iris's feet and then at the girl herself.

"Don't do that! Who wants a jotter that somebody's scrawled on for heaven's sake?"

Iris glanced at Celia, trim and birdlike as she darted round the room, and thought how she was going to miss her. Celia had not just taken charge of her days, but in her efforts to help her forget Samuel, she had also opened up her own social life to Iris, taking her out to parties and clubs and dinners and introducing her to friends who seemed just as relaxed and generous as Celia herself. They were artists mostly, she explained, painters, out of work actors, a few journalists who drank a lot and a couple of older, courteous men whom Celia described as her admirers, and might have been lovers too.

One of these men was called Peregrine Percy, a fat ex-stockbroker with a crimson drinker's nose who lived in St John's Wood. He had been instructed by Celia to talk about stocks and shares, the way the City worked, what made the money markets go up and down and how they could be influenced by international affairs as much as the doings of domestic governments. That was Celia's way of helping, and Iris for her part soaked up the information keenly. Peregrine had even taken her to the Stock Exchange and they had stood up in the public gallery, watching the pinstriped insects throng beneath them. Whatever people said about Iris's father, he told her, as a businessman and manufacturer, he was on the side of getting the country onto its feet, injecting fresh blood into it.

"Peregrine says we're enjoying an unprecedented economic boom. He says capitalism has decided that the middle classes were meant to be rich."

"Glad to hear it," remarked Celia. "Though I hadn't noticed much of an economic boom in my neck of the woods."

"You got the contract here, didn't you? My father said this is the most prestigious building project of the year. And you've done it so wonderfully, once everyone's seen what you can do, the commissions will come flooding in."

"That's a very flattering show of confidence. And I'll believe you, though millions wouldn't."

"I'll recommend you to all my friends."

"Now we're talking."

"No, I mean it. Tell me Celia - how do you currently go about securing work?"

"Just contacts, darling. And little jobs like the one you very kindly fixed with Dolly Monroe." Celia had been hired to decorate several rooms at Dolly's new house.

"Exactly. But what about people who don't know you?"

"Not sure I follow sweetheart."

"The thing is Celia, I've been thinking of something. Everyone wants their house done in the modern style, and all my friends will be desperate to have you, but not everyone can afford to have Celia Urquart personally come and decorate for them. Had you ever thought of manufacturing your designs? Sort of en masse? And making everything people might want, textiles, accessories, furniture but all with your own imprint on them? You know, Celia Urquhart paints, wallpapers and fabrics. Cushions, curtains, counterpanes and lamp shades, everything the modern home might need. You could sell them in Selfridges!"

"Wildly flattering darling, but to be honest I wouldn't have the first idea how to go about it."

"If you wouldn't, I might."

Iris knew she was never going to match Celia's passion for the substance of her trade - the trims and fabrics, paint effects and finishes, the hand-blocked wallpaper. Celia had a particular eye - a way of making things look fresh, modern and exciting - that Iris lacked. She only had to look at a room to be thinking of screens and lacquered Chinese furniture or soft floral chintzes and faux panelling with a faded Samarkand rug. She had done Dolly's morning room with book-filled alcoves either side of the fireplace and painted panels of rustic scenes. Pictures of the work she had done in Mildred Hutton's drawing room - a carpet fractured with intersecting diamonds of aquamarine and pale green, matched by soft moss green patterns on the chairs, crystal figures by Lalique and clean lines of silver, steel and glass in the art moderne style - had aroused huge admiration when they were published in *Vogue.*

Yet Iris had her own kind of vision.

"What I think is that talent like yours deserves to be exploited better. And not just in little commissions like doing up Dolly's house."

"Well I'm at your disposal then. I have no objections at all to you setting me up in a business empire darling," said Celia lightly.

But at the same time a thought occurred to her. She had heard a lot of talk about a big exhibition coming up in Paris next year – the *Exposition Internationale Des Arts Decoratifs et Industriels Modernes* - to showcase the new style. If she and Iris were to set up any kind of design business, it was obvious they should attend this exhibition, yet even before that they could visit the antique shops and flea markets there and take some ideas back to Britain. A little foreign trip would be just the thing to help Iris forget the elusive Samuel Dux. Too bad then that her selfish father would almost certainly prevent her going.

Quite by chance it was Edwina who solved this problem. The crux of the issue was Edwina's holiday. It was just a few days late in the season that she and Elmer were planning in Cap Ferrat, with a group of friends, but Edwina had been discussing the trip with tedious enthusiasm for weeks. Until one day she telephoned Celia in the shop in outraged tones.

"The most appalling crisis. He wants to take Iris with us."

"Oh dear," said Celia mildly, stroking a dachshund. "And you think she might be a bit of a gooseberry, I suppose."

"Worse than a gooseberry, Celia. Far worse. And pricklier than a gooseberry too. Well you *know* the girl. Think of her moping around the pool with a face like a wet Wednesday, spoiling everyone's fun. It's awful. I simply can't bear it."

"Have you told him how you feel?"

"Don't be mad. And anyway, he would never be persuaded. Elmer's convinced she'll get up to something silly again if she's left on her own for a second."

"What about that Mrs Vickers?"

"They're shooting."

"Oh dear."

"No, it's absolutely not 'oh dear'," snapped Edwina in the steely way Celia recognised. "*You've* got to do something about it."

"Me?"

"Yes you. The girl is your charge after all. You said you were fond of her, though I can't imagine why. Can't you tell Elmer she's needed urgently for the decoration?"

"The decoration's finished now. He knows that. We've only a few details left to attend to."

"Well you'll have to think of something. I'm not having my holiday ruined. I need the rest after all the exhaustion of planning Elmer's party."

Celia smiled at the thought. Though Edwina knew the names of every flower and every fine wine to be offered at the opening party, she knew almost nothing of the guests. Celia had given her friend a list of appropriate writers, journalists and artists who might subsequently disseminate cultured opinions on the building and Edwina had obediently sent out hand-written invitations.

"Well I do have a thought about Iris. If you could be relied upon to tell Elmer just what I say."

For the first time in a long while Elmer Barrington looked up from his dyspeptic survey of the morning's newspaper to address his daughter at the breakfast table. He had not forgiven Iris for the Bunny episode, which had marked her down as silly and unworthy of him. Moreover, he had not completely adjusted to the notion of a daughter who was no longer his innocent child, but a sexually experienced, unmarried woman. The glaring taint of her sexuality despoiled her like an ugly crack on a Grecian vase. Now, there was something else she was fooling about with. The previous night Edwina had been telling him some rambling story about his daughter and Celia Urquart setting up in business together, but he had not been listening properly. He never listened to Edwina's conversation if he could possibly help it, because it depressed him.

"Edwina tells me you want to be one of these lady decorators? Like Sybil Colefax? Selling curtains to your friends?"

Though her father had not directed a word at her for weeks, Iris sipped her tea coolly before replying.

"No actually. It's much more than that. I want to start a business. In interior design. With Celia as our chief designer. I think there's a real market out there."

"There aren't too many projects like Barrington House, I assure you."

"I know. I'm talking about commercial design. It's a blossoming area. It's no good just being small scale. That's amateurish. Securing commissions from people you've met at dinner who think they don't need to pay you until years later. We want to be taken seriously. We want our own manufacturers making our own designs."

"I see."

This turn of events rather appealed to him. Any fresh business venture got him excited, but there was something about Iris's interest in the aesthetic side of things which especially pleased him. When he tried to fathom it, he realised it was because in that she resembled himself. She appreciated beautiful things. Even if she was the soul of her mother to look at, something of himself endured within her.

That led him to recall the old gratification he would have when he discussed their children with Margaret, back in the days when they were still children and one could have ambitions for them. Since those ambitions had had to be so categorically abandoned, the idea of his daughter selling anything came as an unexpected surprise. Particularly given that the only market he had ever expected her to sell in was the matrimonial one.

He rose from the table and brushed crumbs off his trousers onto the floor.

"Well I'm glad you've found something to occupy yourself. We should discuss it further. Perhaps I might be able to advance some small investment. And while we are talking, there is something I need to tell you Iris. It's about our former friend Mr Dux."

The shock wiped the smile off his daughter's features, confirming everything he had suspected. He watched the colour drain from her face as he came and stood over her, carefully weighing his words.

"He's coming back tomorrow, so I think it's right I tell you this first. I'm sorry to have to say this but there is something pretty dreadful you need to know about that young man. I'm not going to shield you from the truth, but I'm afraid you're going to find it rather shocking, my dear."

Chapter Thirty-One

Good doctor though he was, the prospect of draining an infected abscess did not often put Frank Stevens in a genial mood. Rarely did he move with a spring in his step towards an elderly patient who wanted to discuss, in the most circumlocutory fashion, chronic constipation. But that day he felt a lightness of spirit that even his staff noticed. He refused to admit even to himself that this change in humour was prompted entirely by the prospect of an evening at an art exhibition in Soho.

He remembered Alice Cohen from the day of Miles' birth. A large, bosomy girl with a forceful air, wearing very bright clothes, deliberately eccentric. The exhibition was entirely of her paintings, apparently, and he had been rather surprised to be invited. He had prevailed on a fellow doctor to cover his patients and although he would be tired and hungry and know virtually no one, Esther would be there and Alice Cohen had suggested on her card that the thing would be highly informal - just a crowd of art students.

The address he had been given was far outside his usual ambit. It was a place called Nefertiti's, situated in a dingy sidestreet north of Soho. It was already packed when he arrived, a writhing press of bright chatter. Someone handed him a glass of wine, someone else offered a bowl of salted almonds, but no-one asked who he was, or how he came to be there. There was no sign of Esther, so he began inching around, scrutinising the paintings with a solemn air, until to his immense relief Ursula Davis approached.

Through the crowds of admiring guests, Alice drew Esther to one side.

"I think Ursula's rather taken a shine to your Dr Stevens."

"Frank? What on earth is he doing here?"

"I invited him. Don't be cross, I was playing Cupid. Look

over there."

There in the corner stood Stevens and Ursula, heads bent together, chatting animatedly.

"You did that without telling me."

"I did it for Ursula's sake, and it looks like it's working too."

"Ursula wouldn't be interested in Frank Stevens!"

"Why not? Ursula claims he has a brilliant mind. Apparently he's good company once he relaxes. And on top of that, he's told her he loves children. He's been ever so attentive to little Miles."

"Has he?" Esther looked at Stevens wonderingly.

"Yes. He's visited her a couple of times, and paid for her nursing care. He plays with the baby like it's his own, which it might as well be, for all she sees of Fogerty."

"But…" Esther faltered, looking over at Frank. She felt a stab of dismay, which she could not account for. "Ursula wouldn't be interested."

"Wouldn't she? You never know what might happen. Given time. And what a blessing it would be if it got the loathsome Fogerty out of her life. I bet Dr Stevens doesn't believe in contingent relationships."

"We can't just stand here talking. We're supposed to be admiring Alice's pictures. They are excellent, aren't they? Go on. I'll look this way, you look that."

Stevens wandered away from Ursula to give the canvases his full attention. He felt a warm, dreamy sense of well being, here in this glittering room, being plied with champagne and surrounded by intellectual conversation. It was as though he was entering new territory, moving in a mileu he had only heard about. To one side of him there was an animated argument about the new pictures promised by Hollywood, and how hearing the actors talking would debase the cinematic experience. To the other an art critic was pontificating loudly that Alice's "underlying sense of geometry reflects the legacy of cubism coupled with a fluent naturalism". By his left shoulder two young men were discussing in intimate detail the affairs of a sexually voracious acquaintance. Stevens hovered hungrily, wanting to eavesdrop on it all.

As he stood, he focused on the work before him, a marvellous painting, which had gathered a small, admiring crowd. It was stirringly erotic, a huge, life-sized portrait of a naked girl, standing confidently to one side with her head cocked and her hands resting on her hips. Alice had painted her brown eyes looking up to the viewer with a challenging air, as though she was fully aware of the exquisite voluptuousness of her body and pleased with the way the light caressed and moulded her body's curves. Everything about her - the creamy skin, the rose pink nipples and the dark pubic shadow above her crossed leg - exuded sexuality. She was provocative, proud of herself and unashamed. The picture was stunning but it took a few moments before Stevens realised that the face looked very like….indeed it was… Esther Hartley.

The shock went through him like an electric charge. Esther! The girl he had known since she was thirteen years old. She had not been a particularly attractive child, just an indifferent, lanky, giggling thing with freckles, and even now she remained the child of his friend, whom he had taken into his guardianship and whose moral welfare he had attempted to protect, because it was what her father would want. The young woman whose company had been such a distraction for him, and whose immature ideas about religion and socialism he had hoped in time to set right. And here she was, provocatively naked in a way that stirred in him an intense sexual response.

His cheeks flamed. He turned quickly away from the picture as if physically struck, and as luck had it his gaze fell immediately on Esther herself, standing nearby, talking to an intense young man, without a trace of shame. When she saw him she ducked beneath the man's arm, and smiled at him cautiously.

Stevens could barely summon words to his mouth. He felt himself contract with embarrassment.

"I have to go," he said stiffly.

"But you've only just got here."

"Well I'm sorry. I have a patient. You'll have to make your own way home."

"What do you mean? Of course I'll make my own way home. But.."

Esther cast a desperate glance around her, then followed Stevens to the door and out into the street. He kept glancing away, as though he did not want to look at her.

"Is there anything wrong?"

He voice was hoarse, as though his mouth refused to articulate.

"That painting."

"You don't like it then."

"No," he said hastily. "It's not that. It's not to my taste, but..."

"But … ?"

Finally he faced her fully, pulling her to one side as though someone may overhear their conversation.

"I'm amazed at you Esther. Don't you mind half of London gawping at you?"

She laughed lightly. "Alice would be awfully pleased if she thought half of London was looking."

He fought for words. "Would she indeed?"

His nerves were humming, jangling, his thoughts conflicting like electric messages crackling along a wire. He attempted to collect himself.

"I'm just surprised you would want to be displayed like that."

"*Displayed?* You make it sound…pornographic or something."

"What if your father or mother were to see?"

"Well they won't," she said, folding her arms. "And if they did I wouldn't care a bit. It's art. It's not as if it's just been invented. It's been going on since the Renaissance. Anyway, why should you mind? You're a doctor. You've seen hundreds of naked bodies."

He shook his head, finding it momentarily impossible to connect anything about his patients' scarred and suffering flesh with the erotic vision he had just encountered.

"I think you might regret this later."

"I'm old enough to know what I'm doing thank you."

For some seconds they remained motionless on the pavement staring at each other, the chatter and laughter of the party drifting out on the evening air.

"I say. Is everything all right?"

It was Alan. He came and put a tentative hand on Esther's arm which she immediately shrugged off. But it had the effect of breaking the confrontation.

"I'll say goodnight then."

Stevens turned away, a formal figure hurrying along the busy Soho street, where people chattered to each other as they climbed into their cars, on their way to a casual, carefree evening out.

Chapter Thirty-two

It was hard to imagine that the place had all been rubble and brickwork a year before. Barrington House looked as if it had been there forever. Above its neighbouring buildings it rose, towering from a broader base with succeeding echelons stepped and telescoping to a pyramid at the top. Outside it appeared solid, classical and elegant, its black mirrored glass facade, marble columns and gold finials suggesting modernity and antiquity exquisitely harnessed. Inside, its limestone and marble interior was discreetly and expensively inlaid with ornamental motifs. Everywhere one looked was gleaming wood and lustrous metal wrought in simple shapes - geometrical angles, curves and circles, elegant and clean outlines. The colours were orange, violet, emerald, gold and silver and an intense, shocking, cobalt blue. Everything was of one accord. There were no mixed references, or if there were, they meshed with beautiful allusiveness, as harmonious as life itself.

That night every window glowed with lights. Almost everyone Edwina had invited came to the party. There was jazz and champagne but the beauty of the building made people unnaturally respectful. Awed by their surroundings, the guests moved with a heightened grace and hush, fingering the carved wood and indented stone, tracing the scalloped metal around the lift shaft, as though they were in a mediaeval church. Some even took notes.

Celia was surrounded and bathed in congratulations. Elmer Barrington himself strode beaming amongst his guests, even if privately he was already dreaming of his next project - a magnificent country house with a grotto and Italianate garden. A photographer approached him, a little, shabby, fawning man who aroused immediate irritation, but Barrington only smiled and waved the man over to his centrepiece.

It stood in the middle of the lobby on a raised dais, within a glass case. The diminutive figure inside, entirely dwarfed by the great hall, seemed at first glance to be quite undeserving of its position. At least, that was the opinion of most people before they approached it for closer inspection. But when they did they found a beauty and simplicity which outweighed entirely its surroundings.

It was a young man holding a pair of golden scales. His body was poised in movement, one foot stepping confidently forward, and the face was exquisitely detailed. Around his neck he wore a broad collar with a dangling necklace featuring a winged scarab. His arms and wrists were circled with gilded bracelets. Beneath it on a brass plaque were the words *"The Weighing Of The Heart. 18th dynasty."*

Since his return the previous day, when he had handed the statue to the architect, Holmes, Samuel had not had the chance to speak to Elmer Barrington. There had been no word of thanks or gratitude for his providing, against all the odds, the spectacular centrepiece for Barrington House, which had returned to Britain in an old wine box wrapped in a towel at the bottom of his luggage. Not that Samuel cared. He was overwhelmingly relieved to be rid of the statue. He consciously avoided setting eyes on it. Besides, it was Iris he was longing to see.

Frustratingly, he had not yet been able to track her down. She was not at home. He had lingered all day at Barrington House, but she was nowhere to be seen. And now, at the party there was no sign of her either. Where on earth could she be? He had spent most of the evening circling in search of her, batting off attempts at conversation from well-meaning guests eager to praise his work and flatter his artistic skills. Finally he ran into Alan Collins, who had been invited on behalf of his magazine.

"Pretty magnificent for an engine-house of capitalism," Alan commented cheerfully, waving a glass of champagne. "I'm going to track down Barrington himself in a while, get some comments for my article. I've been trying to get him on the telephone all day."

Samuel barely heard him. He was unable to engage with anyone as his eyes continually scanned the room. His every fibre ached for Iris. He was bewildered by her absence, and the exhaustion of the journey was compounded by his state of nervous tension. After another hour of drinking and searching for her face in the crowd, he left the party around midnight, empty and frustrated.

The following morning, he came down to breakfast to find the dining room deserted. That was not unusual. Elmer Barrington was a man of enormous energy, who often rose early, even after a night of partying, and Samuel was quite accustomed to eating his meal in solitude.

But after he had selected a plateful of bacon and devilled eggs and poured himself some tea, a maid entered with a letter for him. He recognised the hand immediately. It was Iris.

The note was short.

"Dear Samuel,

I am writing to say that it is best we do not see each other again. I am sure you will understand. I have gone away and would be glad if you had moved from my father's house by the time I return. My father is in complete agreement. Please do not try to contact me.

Iris."

He jumped to his feet, and dashed out of the room, staring wildly around him as if Iris might be waiting in the hall. Finding no-one he rushed up the stairs to find Cairns in his room, folding clothes.

"What the hell are you doing Cairns?"

"I'm sorry Sir. I've taken the precaution of beginning your

packing. Mr Barrington would prefer it if you left at once."
He ran down the stairs to Barrington's office but the startled
maid told him he had gone out. Grabbing his coat, he hailed
a taxi cab and headed into the City. But when he reached
Barrington House the owner was not to be found. For a
while he walked around London, from the City all the way
to Bloomsbury, past the British Museum, down Shaftesbury
Avenue, then through to St James' Park. He paced the grid
of streets like a cage, imprisoned by his own uncertainty.
After a few hours he returned to the house to find the great
black door closed firmly against him. His frantic knocking
was answered by an anxious looking Cairns.

"What is this Cairns? What on earth is the matter?"

"I'm afraid I've been asked not to admit you Mr Dux."

Behind him, Samuel glimpsed Barrington striding down the
hall. Pushing Cairns to one side he forced his way into the
hall.

"Mr Barrington! Sir! If this is about Iris. I can explain.
There's no need to react like this."

Barrington's expression was as impassive as the statues he
surrounded himself with.

"It's nothing to do with Iris, Dux, as you well know."

"Then I need to know. I've done everything you've asked.
How have I offended?"

Barrington's great bulk came towards him. His voice was a
low growl.

"Don't insult me Dux. I don't want any dealings with a man
like you. All I want is you out of my house. Now."

Samuel shook off Cairns' hand, with which he was plucking
beseechingly at his sleeve.

"Sir, whatever you or Iris have been told about me, I swear
to God it's not how it seems. Who has levelled accusations
against me?"

Barrington appeared to splutter with anger.

"Don't make me engage in this undignified debate. Get out
of my house now."

So saying he turned on his heel and disappeared down the hall, while Cairns manoeuvred Samuel's ancient, stained suitcase out onto the front step.

Chapter Thirty-three

Ursula had taken new rooms. She would no longer be hidden away, she would be defiantly, gloriously in the heart of London. The flat itself was nothing grand - just a basement, with a tiny kitchen and scullery, a front room heated by an ancient gas fire, with dingy sash windows that were stuck, and a bedroom she shared with Miles. But to her it was freedom. Already she had lightened the flat's drabness with a few touches - some pretty, printed curtains, a worn Turkish rug, a bunch of late roses plunged in a jug on the desk and along the bookcase copies of *Little Lives* with its light blue binding next to T.S. Eliot, Katharine Mansfield and D.H Lawrence. Best of all, she was at work on her next novel.

   Justification through work. That was the one thing her mother had taught her. Ursula recalled the matriarch of her childhood, her tall figure erect and unbending as though Protestantism ran like steel through her bones. Work was your salvation. Work got you through. She thought of her mother's face, the grim stripe of a mouth, furrows carved in the brow and a complexion as scrubbed as the kitchen table in the family's squat Victorian home.

   Yet through the door that morning had come a letter from her mother, which despite its customarily frigid tone, constituted a serious relaxation in her outlook. Not that one would have known straight away, because reading it was like walking into a play during the second act, with no reference at all to the events which had precipitated two years of silence between them. Instead it began with a workaday round-up of family life which dwelt almost entirely on her sisters' academic progress, some detail of an aunt who had moved to Shropshire with her second husband, before in the third paragraph, the single, almost casual line:

"Your father and I have decided we should be happy to see the child next time you visit".

Next visit! And with Miles too! Both ideas made Ursula laugh out loud, yet she did not entirely dismiss it. She had no special desire to see her mother again or re-enter the force-field of her disapproval, nor would she ever expose Miles to any more provincial prejudice than she could help, but somehow she couldn't help thinking it would be nice for him to have some family, other than herself and a few well-intentioned friends.

She looked down at the child in question, sitting before the fireplace, unaware that his very self, bashing energetically on the brickwork with a soon-to-be-broken clay jar in which Ursula had stashed some wooden animals, constituted a moral misdemeanour. Then he caught her eyes upon him and tried to move towards her. He could not yet crawl, but sat forward as though on the starting blocks, rocking himself forward until he began to cry with frustration. When this happened Ursula sighed, put away the letter and crouched down on the rug with him. She looked at his fat pink face, crumpled with tears, and wondered how she could adore it when it so resembled his father's fat pink face, which she would not be seeing for some time.

She had guessed that her decision not to have Miles fostered would scarcely delight Fogerty, but the extremity of his reaction had taken her quite by surprise. He had, after all, just published a book whose heroine, an unmarried mother, rose triumphantly above the barbs and prejudices of society. *The Sphinx* had been hailed as his most acute work to date. While a few of the more reactionary publications - what he called "the dregs of the middle-class literary establishment"- had been scandalised by his subject-matter, elsewhere it had been praised for its unsentimental, clear-eyed detail of motherhood, including scenes of the heroine breast-feeding and enjoying a sexual relationship.

The writing was daring, "startling in its honesty" said the Times Literary Supplement, which Fogerty had thoughtfully brought round for her to read.

It was that night that Ursula admitted to Fogerty that she intended to keep Miles. To her dismay, the author of *The Sphinx* was appalled. She thought of him, spluttering and purpling as he stood in that front room in his cream waistcoat and heavy silver watch chain (he was attending a party later in the evening) alternating between threats and cajolery. His objections centred mainly on the cost - how would she afford Miles' clothes, food, shoes and education if she was unable to work? And how could she expect to work with a child in the house? She needn't talk of nannies. Nannies cost money, money that Fogerty with four other children of his own to support, could scarcely be expected to provide.

Fortunately, a couple of days after that acrimonious evening, she had been lucky enough to come across some new work. A new publishing company, established in one of the grander houses nearby, had offered her a job reading manuscripts, preparing sales copy and soliciting quotes for new novels. It was mindless stuff but it would keep her and Miles going and pay for a girl to come in and look after him while she was out.

The only thing missing now was company. Miles was engrossing of course, but no-one could really consider babies endlessly stimulating. She did wish Frank Stevens would come again. She'd been thinking of him a lot recently. She had sent him a note with her new address, but he'd not been to visit. With a twinge of disappointment she told herself not to dwell on him. Life was hard and no-one could be depended on, let alone men. She took up her manuscript again and stiffened herself. There was more of her mother in her than she would ever realise. Work was the only thing one could rely on.

Chapter Thirty-four

Esther had not seen Frank for days. He seemed deliberately to leave the house before she got up. She knew this was down to his shock over the picture and wondered, with slight trepidation, if he would discuss it with her father. She began to see the issue through his eyes, and to feel embarrassed, before chiding herself indignantly.

"How could he be so shocked at a portrait of me naked? I mean he sees nudity every day. What kind of doctor can he be if he can't take the sight of the human body?"

She was in a cab with Alice, travelling across London to deliver a painting so large it required two people to carry it. The purchaser was a restaurant owner who was well-known as a patron of famous artists and liked diners to admire his acquisitions. Alice was so excited to be bought by him she would have given him the painting for nothing. Indeed she would have paid to have him take it. As it was she would receive £20.

She was no help at all with Esther's problem. She seemed pleased, if anything, to think that one of her works had produced such a powerful effect.

"Nudes have historically aroused strong reactions," she noted casually.

"But I don't think it's nudes in general. I mean I'm sure he likes Botticelli."

"Perhaps it's because he's a friend of the family, he feels it's improper in some way."

"Surely not."

"Well he's a man and there's no telling with men. Their moral sense is entirely askew. They thrive on contradictions. Anyway, I know it's not my style he objects to. He admired the picture I did of Ursula - he told me."

"Perhaps that's because he admires Ursula."

"Oh he does, definitely."

"You really think so?"

"Yes. And it's a match made in heaven."

Esther stared dismally out of the window. "Why?"

"Oh they're both so cerebral, so other-worldly. Not like you and me, because we're artists and we live through our senses. They've lost the ability to react instinctively."

"Ursula reacted pretty instinctively with William Fogerty."

"Well yes, I suppose so. But she's rid of him now, and good for her. Have you seen his latest novel? It's all about Ursula. And utterly ersatz. Horribly sentimental. What a hypocrite that man is."

The streets outside were glistening in the morning sunshine, the window boxes flickered with the little crimson flames of autumn cyclamen, burning against the earth. Even if she was an artistic person in touch with her senses, Esther felt a pall of depression sink over her.

"Look," said Alice. "If it bothers you so much talk to him about it?"

"I just can't."

"Well frankly I agree. Given he's such a dry old stick, there probably is no point. Actually Esther, I've talked to the family about it and I've been meaning to ask for some time. Why don't you come and live with me? There's a spare room in the studio annexe."

"I couldn't."

"Why ever not? I won't charge you rent. And we could have such fun. And I promise I won't lecture you about disreputable conduct. In fact, I'll positively encourage it. The more parties and life modelling, the better. You can move in straight away."

"Oh, I don't know… I'd have to give a month's notice."

"No you won't. He'll probably be delighted to have his house back to himself again. No more immoral young women. And you won't ever have to see him again."

Esther thought of the shock in Frank Stevens's face as he

left the art gallery that evening. "I suppose you're right. He probably would prefer it if I moved out as soon as possible."

* * *

"It represents, we are bold enough to say, the apogee of the mode Egyptienne. Those who said Nile Style was over spoke too soon. Barrington House is a triumph. It is the new face of Britain, a triumphant synthesis of the old with the new, and a glorious addition to our City. Now I hear the Barrington family has another kind of partnership to celebrate. Miss Iris Barrington, the lovely daughter of Elmer Barrington, is to form a new company, Antika, with Mrs Celia Urquart, whose talented designs are currently sought after in all the best homes."

Celia sat across the white, linen tablecloth, glasses perched on her nose, reading the paper out loud in a way which could only be described as ostentatious. Since Iris had turned up at her flat two nights ago, insisting that she be allowed to stay, but refusing to discuss the reason for her crisis, Celia had been driven to distraction trying to cheer the girl up.

"I think we should go out for lunch. There's a piece in The Daily Express diary which calls for a celebration and I simply have to be seen reading it in a public place."

The place she had chosen, The Eiffel Tower, was Celia's favourite restaurant. Indeed it was more than a restaurant, it was like a cross between a café and a club, with a regular clientele of writers and artists, many of whose paintings hung on its burgundy walls. It had a casual charm quite unlike other London restaurants and its customers would find themselves charged on a variable scale, according to how they got on with the patron. Celia got on exceptionally well. Rudolph had an eye for a pretty girl and she had been meaning to introduce him to Iris, particularly as their partnership was announced, but now was evidently not the time.

Iris sat like someone in a trance, twisting her spoon so that it reflected two different versions of herself, one round and moon-faced, one severe and etiolated. She wore a suit of dove grey wool with a frosting of fur around the collar that made her complexion appear paler and more translucent than ever. Her eyes were red from crying. She had barely slept the night before, and did not even pretend any interest in the newspaper piece.

Just then the proprietor, Rudolph, bustled up.

"Rudolph darling. The food is delicious as ever. May I introduce my new partner, Iris Barrington?"

Iris had been staring at a painting of a recumbent figure that hung above Celia's head, a beautiful nude with flesh like marble. Rudolph grasped Iris's hand, stooped and kissed it.

"I see you are admiring my latest acquisition Madmoiselle? We have just this moment hung it and I am giving the artist some lunch. A young lady called Alice Cohen who I think will be a very famous painter one day. May I introduce you?"

Before Iris could decline he had crossed the room and returned with a woman.

"Miss Alice Cohen, Miss Urqhuart, Miss Barrington."

Iris looked up dully at a large beaming woman with untidy hair and a scarlet velvet coat. She seemed familiar.

"I've been to your house, actually," said Alice.

"Have you?" said Iris indifferently.

"I've been painting your father."

Iris regarded her with faint gratitude. The only thing that had remotely interested her about her father's portrait was that it meant him being closeted away for hours during the sittings.

"How is it going?"

"Almost finished now."

"Well good luck with it." Iris felt the tears brimming and turned her head to one side again. Awkwardly Alice withdrew. Not the best of introductions, Celia sighed.

She began to outline the numerous tasks that awaited them when they returned to the office that afternoon, but then stopped midflow. She fitted another cigarette into the amber holder and leaned back.

"It's Samuel, isn't it?"

She had Iris's attention at last. She continued.

"He was there last night, Iris. Looking everywhere for you. But you didn't want to come. Why?"

At this, Iris leaned forward and stared searchingly into her eyes, as though she might hold the answer to some impossible riddle.

"I've got a question, Celia. A very important question."

Celia had lived a tough life and she had picked up a lot of worldly wisdom in the process, but when it came to profound questions, she was not entirely confident.

"Go ahead."

"If you'd learned, Celia, that someone had done something terrible - the worst thing a person could do - could you still love them? What I mean is, if you love someone already, can you go on loving them, despite what they've done?"

Celia relaxed and smiled.

"Oh, that's easy. Of course you can."

Chapter Thirty-five

Dawn slid in like a note under the door. Stevens had woken an hour earlier, as was increasingly his habit, from a bad dream. His heart racing, his breath tearing in his throat, he had tried to leave the dream but the paralysis of sleep drew him back in. Back to where the ground was cratered with shell holes and he sheltered in a trench shaking with fear. Rats which ate men's faces ran over him. One man, lying half dead beside him, had the whole lower half of his face blown off, leaving a gaping hole. To his other side was a corpse, whose skin, stretched over the swollen, rotting flesh, was already a mottled indigo. He shook himself out of sleep and allowed memory to disgorge the disordered horror of his dreams.

The casualty clearing station was set several miles behind the line between the village of Saulty and the base at La Bellevue. From there the 16th Motor Ambulance Company shipped men who were too ill to return to the trenches to the waiting trains at Warlincourt Halte. Though it was no more than a cluster of tents and huts, the CCS was sufficiently well-equipped to perform amputations and operations on serious wounds, as well as dealing with shrapnel injuries, compound fractures, nervous disorders, skin diseases and infections. It was the job of the medical officers to decide if the men could be patched up, or were simply too badly injured to be dealt with and needed sending to a base hospital. Though the unit could hold up to a thousand casualties at a time, since the opening of the battle of the Somme the work had been overwhelming. Stevens was on duty for sixteen or seventeen hours at a time, mostly with boys whose legs had been blown off or hastily amputated at the front-line. He was numb in the face of it. Numb when men arrived screaming as their stumps bumped against the stretcher, numb when he treated them with aspirin alone because a morphine injection would render them instantly unconscious and more likely to die. Numb from fatigue and with no idea what lay beyond the end of each day.

He had not, initially, been posted at the CCS. Until a few weeks ago he had been a medical officer at the front, tending the wounded and deciding who should be sent back for treatment further behind the lines. The battalion had been thrown into it quite suddenly. Two days after arriving at the front they had received orders to take part in an assault the following day, starting at 4.20 am. The preparation for the attack didn't go well. The guides failed to turn up, and while waiting for fresh guides, they were caught in German shelling which caused casualties. Eventually the guides arrived but they only had the vaguest idea of the route which meant the battalion reached the jumping off trenches with only minutes to spare.

The attack started under heavy German bombardment of the trenches and no-mans-land. Machine gun fire pinned down the battalion and ahead of them, across the broken desert of clay mounds and craters, the dead from a previous assault, who had fallen days earlier, still lay on the ground bloated and putrid. Some of them had crawled into shell-holes and curled up to die. One lay in the arms of a German soldier, gripped together in a deadly wrestle as they were cut down. Others, as they lay dying, had placed their own bibles across their chests.
 Even then, before they went over, they had no idea of the ferocity they were about to face. Once they had fixed bayonets and were waved up over the top, they found themselves walking into a hail of bullets and shells. The air was filled with the vicious spit of gunfire and tussocks of turf sprang into the air from where they had been hit. They

could feel the wind of the shells as they passed over. Men went down like corn being scythed. Wire caught and tripped them up everywhere they went, but they stumbled on, bravely disentangling themselves, as though the wire was no more than a bramble. Those who were trapped were certain to be targeted by snipers if they moved. Stevens found himself tending the injured in the open under heavy fire, in view of the Germans. As day turned to night he searched for wounded men on the ground in front of the enemy's lines, and with a party of volunteers, made forays to rescue others from shell holes close to the enemy trench.

The following few days were spent digging their dead comrades out of the trenches and tramping along the duckboards carrying bodies down the line. Even when they were confined to the trench, there remained decomposing bodies everywhere around them. This waiting, being forced to remain immobile, listening out always for the dull thud and whistle of the shells, had a curious effect on some men. While many, especially the conscripted ones, who didn't want to be there and had not volunteered, were shaking like leaves, unable to fix bayonets, or even hold their rifles, others developed a different reaction. They progressed through fear, a healthy animal terror, to a sort of callous disregard for their own safety. Their nerves were gone.

Stevens had heard about shell shock. He had seen it before a few times but by the time of the Somme, he knew there were hundreds more cases. From what he understood the shock manifested itself in different ways. Some men seemed blind or deaf, or developed curious twisted gaits, as if their entire body had gone into protesting spasm. Some went mute or stuttered, in dramatic demonstration of the requirement to repress their anger and fear. Some said it was "hysteria" – the kind of thing women might suffer from - and to many officers, even medical men, just accepting the idea of a neurotic casualty blew a hole in the entire discipline of war. But to Stevens it seemed as if the only logical response to war was to go mad. The turmoil in these men's minds was only a reflection of the dark tumult of no man's land.

Therefore, when some of his own men began to show signs of shock, he refused to return them to the front. Instead he made arrangements for them to be sent to base hospitals miles behind the line.

Within days this policy towards those men whose nerves had gone came to the notice of the battalion's higher authorities and Stevens found himself suddenly and without explanation redeployed behind the lines. He didn't complain, but nor did he desist from diagnosing those, like the young officer who appeared before him that day at the CCS, who were clearly suffering from traumatic neurosis.

The boy was waiting for him as he walked back from the operating theatre. As he ducked under the greasy flap of the tent he found the boy - he looked too young to be called a man - sitting on an iron bed as a nurse dressed a cut on his head. He had fair hair and widely spaced blue eyes and although filthy, with a torn uniform, he appeared otherwise unwounded and was staring about himself with manic, nervous energy.

The nurse said the boy's problems began when a shell landed near him and buried him alive. The following day, when his company had come under repeated heavy shelling, he had, apparently "gone off his head with terror, shrieking and crying." He was sweating and shaking, calling out. He thought the trees were sending out their roots to snare him, or that the moonlight was raking into his eyes. He swore he was being pursued. The next day he had gone absent from his company and was missing for two days before being apprehended by military police, who brought him to the CCS, reporting that he had been found dazed and unable to remember his own name.

Swiftly Stevens noted all the usual neurotic attributes - high pulse rate, tremors, legs shaking spasmodically – and began the process of organising for the young officer to be transported back to the base hospital and from there aboard a hospital ship to England.

The next day the man had vanished and in the turbulence of his work, Stevens did not give him another thought. Nor would he have done had another doctor not commented. "Did you hear about that subaltern? He's going for a court martial. Looks like they're going to shoot him for desertion."

Stevens lay in bed, his body still leaden with fatigue. At least now at six o'clock, the coming of light meant it was finally acceptable to get up and join the waking world. To rejoin those who had slept through all the perils and dangers of the night, as said the prayer book in which he no longer believed. He could testify for the perils and dangers though. He knew them only too well.

His thoughts returned to Esther. She was still in the flat now, though she might as well not be. The more he thought about her, the less he saw her, and he knew she had been avoiding him since his outburst the other evening. He thought again of the picture at the gallery, and of Esther's face as he heard his own voice again in his head, mean and prudish.

"It's not to my taste."

That picture was, though, to his taste. As she was. So why could he not say that? Why could he not admit the effect that her presence had had in his life? How she had pervaded his life, so subtly and completely, like the trail of perfume that remained after her when she left the house, dispelling the odour of books and dead plants.

More and more she had come to occupy his thoughts. In his anxiety to repress his desire for her he had dwelt critically on the deficiencies of youth. Her immaturity, her flippancy, the gusts of silly laughter that emanated from her flat in the evenings. Her fainting fit on his house visit, unable to bear the stench and the sight of real life. He compared her with her friend Ursula, so mature and well-read, but it made no difference. He tried to remember her the way he had first seen her in her father's drawing room - an unprepossessing thirteen year old of no conceivable interest whatsoever, conventionally dressed with her hair held across her forehead in a slide. He thought of her facile adherence to Communism - the first political creed presented to her - without any appreciation of its realities.

Again and again he had tried to list her faults to himself like some grim trial judge sentencing in absentia, yet now he had become her advocate. Those admissions of ignorance, weren't they a sign of intelligence? Her willingness to please, which he had so readily taken as signs of a weak personality, did that not merely make her more honest and endearing? That pre-pubescent girl had evolved into a woman whose every feature, from her small, straight nose and slightly crooked teeth, to the swell of her breasts and hips, exuded a potent sexual attraction which Alice Cohen had clearly felt, and so, he finally admitted, did he.

He forced himself to get up and wash and shave, yet as he regarded his body, still hard and fit but the legs narrow, the hands beginning to crinkle with age, he wondered why he held out any hope. She could not possibly be interested in a man like him.

Sunday morning was, even for an unbeliever, a time of small ceremonies. The slow pouring of the water into the basin for shaving. The making of tea and toast and the leisurely consumption of it. The possibility of a second round of toast, if one could be bothered to make it. He was just heading for the kitchen when Esther came downstairs.

She started at the sight of him. "Oh."

"You look surprised."

"No. I'm not. Not at all. It's just… I haven't seen you in

the house for days now."

"I do still live here." Shaking the peremptory tone from his voice he added: "Would you like some tea?" expecting her of course to refuse and was surprised when she looked at him thoughtfully and said:

"Yes, thank you. We ought to talk."

As he walked off to the kitchen her words struck him with alarm. He stood waiting for the kettle to boil and wondering what she meant by that. They *ought* to talk, did they? Why did they need to talk? They'd coped quite well without talking for some days now. What on earth could they need to talk about? Then as he stood there, he had the sudden intuition that she was going to say something important - she was going to say, he realised in a flash, that she was moving away, because his hostility and coldness had finally outweighed their own frail friendship.

She was leaving. So there would be no chance to see her and no reason to meet at all, except on infrequent occasions at her father's house, when she might shake his hand awkwardly and he would ask after the progress of her career like some ancient uncle, or worse, be required to meet her fiancé. And then, as time seemed to unravel in front of him, he saw himself attending her wedding - far back in the pews - and later having fleeting encounters with her children, a slumbering infant, a recalcitrant toddler, a boy who might like to be a doctor one day, so could he give advice. He thought of Esther's slender body, making love, pregnant, giving birth, becoming rounder and softer with the years, without ever having been his, and a sense of dread overcame him at the missed opportunity and he felt his life closing in over him once again. He had taken so long to recognise what he wanted, and now it was slipping away from him.

He splashed the boiling water into the teapot and carried the tray back to the dining room, searching his mind for anything to forestall her announcement.

"I'm going to visit someone this afternoon. Someone your

father knew."

She had been gazing dreamily out into the garden but turned and regarded him with some surprise.

"My father?"

"More than knew, in fact. Your father saved his life actually."

He told her about the young officer and how he had disappeared, only to be assigned to undergo a court martial and face being shot for desertion. "I realised at once I needed to see this man's commanding officer. It was his only chance and it turned out to be a piece of great good fortune."

"Why?"

"Because the Commanding Officer happened to be your father."

"Ah. So that was how you met."

"Yes. That's how we met. And the good fortune was that your father is an intelligent man. He's old fashioned in many respects, but in other ways he can be quite forward thinking. He was one of the few top brass to realise that neurasthenia was a genuine condition which could and should be treated by trained psychiatrists."

"You mean he recognised that those men had gone mad?"

"Depends what you call mad. If you consider that war is an aberration from civilised standards in which men are encouraged to behave sadistically then by that token those who refuse to participate are not mad. They're more sane than the rest of us. Anyhow, your father agreed to see me and I was able to show him that this boy's behaviour conformed absolutely to the condition of neurasthenia. Your father was prepared to listen to me and to agree that he should be sent home for treatment."

"So he let the man go."

"Yes, he arranged for him to be taken back to England and be given a course of therapy at a special hospital for officers called Palace Green in Kensington. It was a combination of psychiatry and drugs, quite a novel one. When other cases of shellshock came up later, your father asked me for reports so I kept in touch with him, and that was how I came to know your family. And I have had a great respect for him ever since."

"And was the man cured?"

"Well no. Not exactly. In fact not at all."

"Is he still mad?"

"His condition changed over time. In some ways it got worse. He still had moments of terror about the trees and the dark and being afraid of his surroundings, but other things developed. He became suicidal. And one of the more difficult things for people to cope with were episodes in which he became…. rather crude."

He thought of the hushed wards, the thin disapproving lips of the nurses, and the boy, his eyes glinting with manic energy, throwing out sexual invitations to the women who passed him, slipping sly innuendoes to the ladies who brought him food. It was the unpredictability of these episodes that made them so awkward. One day he would be shaking a little, and demoralised, but otherwise lucid, then on another day the frail carapace of social conformity would be shattered by a volley of sexual excess, ravings fuelled by all the vigour and appetite of a healthy young man. Whenever he witnessed these outbursts Stevens felt himself becoming more upright and proper, as if to compensate for the boy's obscene imaginings. That was, until the potassium bromide slowed him down and then he would become dull and quiet. Then it was possible to have a conversation with him, most of it concerning his hopes of a job. Generally Frank was his only visitor, so what had begun out of sheer compassion, the occasional visit after the war, continued and solidified into habit.

"Where is he now?"

"In a sanatorium just outside London. For the meanwhile at least. A place where they care for people like him. I tend to visit him every Sunday."

At that moment he realised what he would ask of her and how important her answer would be. He felt a tenderness, almost compassion for her, and at the same time a desperate determination to join the two halves of his life together.

"You know, I'd rather like you to meet him."

Though nervous, Esther was aware of Frank watching her for the flicker of her response. She remained entirely composed.

"I'm not doing much this afternoon. I could come with you then, if you like."

Chapter Thirty-six

From the grim November day when Cairns handed Samuel
his luggage on the doorstep, just eight months after he had
first set foot in the house, he moved into Alan Collins's
flat. He had nowhere else to go. The room was much as
he remembered it, a cramped space crowded with books
and a bed of excruciating hardness. On the little stripped
wooden desk were a couple of books with stained cloth
covers, a complete Shakespeare and *Das Kapital*, and down
the narrow, uncarpeted stairs was a small bathroom. In
the evenings, more for the companionship than any actual
interest, he went with Alan to rallies about democracy and
workers' rights and the crisis represented by the election of
a new Conservative government. By day, he walked round
London, his steps travelling the blank pavements like the
questions winding fruitlessly round his mind. All he could
think of was Iris. How he could find her, and explain to her.
He wrote, only to find his letters returned unopened. Several
times he would stand in the square until the afternoon
drained of light, hoping for her to emerge and jump into the
cars of friends, or linger in the shadows for the chance to see
her return home, gliding across the luminous pool of street
light. Images of her slipping her clothes off in the high,
narrow Paris room, of her body released and resting beside
him, ran constantly through his mind.

But Iris did not appear. Nor did Barrington seem much
in residence. The tall, white house acquired a shuttered,
deserted air, the great drawing room curtains closed on the
first floor.

For days he haunted the square, while birds huddled in the
trees and shook their feathers like grey thoughts brooding in
a brain. If it rained he sat in the soft yellow fug of a Lyons
corner house, watching the fat tears of condensation slide

down the window face, stretching out a single pot of tea. He began to smoke and could not stop himself. His mood oscillated between frustration and despair.

One day, under a dull, heavy, blotting paper sky, he found himself wandering down the embankment, past the patched and leprous plane trees, along where the Thames ran, sluggish and glimmering with oil, up through the City of London. From habit his steps took him right to the entrance of Barrington House. He stood before it, impervious to its monumental splendour, the great stone doorway carved with Egyptian figures, and the huge burnished bronze doors, etched with decorations copied from the tomb. Through the upper windows, chandeliers hanging from ceilings of pale green and gold lit the friezes he had helped to paint. He could see from here the tiny, jewel like figures, the birds, the animals and the gods, frozen in their ancient procession. The opulence and sheer perfection of Barrington's vision was so completely realised that it put the surrounding buildings to shame. Yet Samuel could only look on the building with a sense of foreboding. He knew what it contained.

At that moment the heavy bronze doors opened, and with a shudder the image seemed to leap from his mind's eye directly into his line of sight.

The Weighing Of The Heart.

That figure he had held, whose face he had been the first to see for three thousand years, gazed out from its pedestal at the centre of the foyer right at him.

And there on the London pavement, time telescoped. The street tumbled and fell away from beneath him. Again the smell came to him, the dank, sour breath of the tomb, and his flesh puckered with the sudden chill. Looking at the golden scales he was filled once more with that sense of crushing inevitability. In the terrifying, impersonal gaze of that statue he saw again the faces of the Egyptian crowd, as ancient and impassive as the ones he had sketched from the walls of the tomb. He felt the alien, incomprehensible power, an inexorable force of judgement more ancient than anything in the bible, as vast and merciless as the will which caused pyramids to be built and tombs to be dug. He felt the weight of that civilisation which allowed its rulers infinite treasures but accorded its masses nothing. There was no compassion in that gaze, or mercy. It did not speak of any modern god. It issued only judgment for what he had done. It told him that he did not deserve happiness. He knew now that finding Iris and then losing her again was all he could ever have hoped for.

It might be that they lived in the same city, that they walked the same streets, he might follow her activities in the gossip columns or one day see her wedding pictures in *The Tatler.* He might catch sight of her at a first night, or at a party, and she might in return give him a cold, uninterested glance. But that was all. They might come a few feet from each other, but in reality there would be an infinity between them. Never again would their intimacy return – their two lives, which had once briefly touched and knit tightly together, would now unravel far away from each other, like cold planets unlocked from their ellipses, spinning away into the night.

Almost in a daze he made his way back, bought a bottle of milk and a loaf of bread and let himself into Alan's house.

The only consolation he could think of was drink. To drink until his senses were entirely blurred and all thoughts of Iris drowned in a swirl of consciousness. There was a particular pub, on the corner of Windmill Street and Charlotte Street, which had sawdust on the floor and a friendly dog and he took to sitting there night after night, fondling the soft ears of the spaniel and listening to the songs of the drinkers round the piano while the alcohol soaked into his brain, detaching his thoughts from his feelings and bringing his whirring mind slowly to a halt.

One evening, coming out of the warm, beery, atmosphere

of the pub he walked slap into a freezing fog, and shuddering from the combined effects of alcohol and cold, he hurried around the corner to Nefertiti's, the nightclub Alan occasionally frequented. Its licence allowed it to stay open late at night and it was used as a watering hole by musicians, writers and artists who found 11 o'clock too early to retire and wanted a meal of bread and cheese to soak up the quantities of alcohol they had consumed.

The place was packed that night. A crowd had assembled to listen to a jazz band, assembled on the tiny stage in the corner. Samuel forced himself through the heaving, jiggling press of bodies and headed for the corner where he had sat with Alan, thinking vaguely that his friend might be there. But there was only a woman sitting on her own, rolling a cigarette. She was wearing a scarlet coat and a beret from which copper spirals of hair escaped. Samuel vaguely thought he recognised her and being uninhibitedly drunk, he lurched up and plumped himself down at the table opposite her.

"You're the painter, aren't you? Alice Cohen? You painted Barrington."

Alice appeared entirely unruffled by this drunken intrusion. She regarded Samuel thoughtfully, then offered him a roll-up.

"What a surprise! Samuel Dux. The archaeologist. The man who brought the statue."

"You remember me then."

"Of course. You're the guilty man."

Though his wits were dulled by alcohol, he was instantly alert.

"Guilty. Of what? What are you accusing me of?"

She raised an eyebrow.

"Nothing serious. I was just being facetious. What I meant was, you're the one I blame for the change in Elmer Barrington."

"I don't understand. Has he changed?"

"I think so. Though it's hard to explain how." She regarded Samuel pensively and twirled a curl of hair in her fingers.

"Try then. I'm listening. I've got all night."

Alice shot him another curious look, and then decided he was not too drunk to talk to.

"It's an odd story. If you wait for me to get another drink, I'll tell you."

Samuel took the hint and went impatiently in search of gin and vermouth. Once he had finally extracted two glasses from the barman, Alice carried on.

"When I first met Barrington – that morning at his home - he was everything I expected. A wealthy, arrogant man, who regarded a portrait of himself as a necessary statement of his achievements in life. In Barrington's case his achievements included his antiquities. He was so proud of them. He absolutely believed that the possession of them was an attribute of his own personality, that their splendour somehow made him splendid, rather than just rich.

"Anyway, the morning I first met him I got to his house to find he had arranged all these priceless vases and busts and plates and pieces in one enormous, vulgar display. Then he sat himself down in the midst of them and commanded me to paint him. It was going to be marvellous. I had an idea about the Shelley poem *Ozymandias,* so I got going and over the weeks we were progressing very well. In fact I had nearly finished when you turned up with that statue and spoiled everything."

"What do you mean?" Samuel whispered.

"Once he acquired that little statue, it had the most curious effect on him. Barrington immediately changed his mind about the portrait. Everything else, all the other ornaments had to go – it must be only the statue depicted with him. Our sittings would take place at Barrington House with the object on a pedestal and himself standing next to it. Well, you might say that was absolutely maddening for the artist, but to tell the truth I didn't mind in the slightest. I'd always been terrified of stepping on one of those beastly Ming vases or smashing something hideously valuable into smithereens, and I can't deny that the statue is very, very beautiful. So I started the picture all over again. This time I was under pressure of time because I've got a lot of commissions lined up. So it was all the more frustrating that Barrington began to change."

"He changed? How has he changed? Physically you mean?"

"The look of him, I suppose. The essence of him began – just very subtly – to alter. Somehow, to him, this statue wasn't just another possession, it was more like a devotional object. He spent so long looking at it that his entire demeanour was different. Then he began to talk about having it moved from public display because he didn't want other people seeing it. It's only a small object but he seemed *craven* before it. Almost,,,,and I don't know how to explain this without seeming theatrical…. but it's as though he is *haunted* by it."

Samuel was utterly sober now. "You're right."

"I'm right?"

"It does sound theatrical. It's just a statue."

"I'm not certain. But what I do know is, since he's had it, Barrington's become terrifically gloomy. He's lost that wonderful, bombastic self-assurance which made me want to paint him in the first place. That obese, mediaeval pope look. There's something broken about him. Then again…" she paused, with a curious eye on Samuel. "Perhaps he's just depressed about the daughter."

At the mention of Iris, the music and the laughter of the people in the room around them fell away. Samuel leaned closer.

"What about the daughter? Have you seen Iris?"

"All I know is that she has left home. Barrington never discussed that with me of course. He never talks much at all. But she was beautiful, wasn't she? She really would make a lovely portrait."

Just to hear her name was astonishingly potent. A minute ago, when Alice was discussing the statue, Samuel had felt the urge to stop up his ears. Either that or escape from the club as fast as he could into the freezing night to blot the image out. But now he wanted to keep Alice there, like the Ancient Mariner, and talk on and on, about Iris.

"Please tell me. Did you see her?"

"I'm not going to be much help to you. We were introduced in a restaurant just recently but she didn't say much."

"How did she seem?"

Alice deliberated. Analysing the emotion in a face was part of her professional skill and she took the question completely seriously.

"If you really want my opinion, she looked like someone had broken her heart."

So Iris was heart-broken. The sensation of relief was alternately sobering and euphoric. That Iris should be not indifferent, not coolly dismissive, but distraught, gave him fresh hope. Yet it also inspired other feelings in him, of shame and fierce compassion, that she should be suffering because of what he had done.

He walked home through the freezing streets and spent a rough night, tossing restlessly, unable to sleep. Images of Barrington, and the statue, and the heart-broken Iris, churned endlessly in his brain. At the back of his mind a question hung, but he could not recall what it was. He rose late the next day and put his head under the cold tap to clear the fog that remained, but it still eluded him.

As he came down the stairs he saw the letter on the mat. For a second his heart jumped in his chest, but although the neat, looping handwriting looked most definitely feminine, he could tell at a glance that it was not from Iris. Curiously he tore it open, and when he had read it twice through, hurriedly pulled on his coat and left the house.

He made his way through Bloomsbury to the offices of *The Watching World*. He had never been there before and was bemused, given Alan's grandiloquent description of his enterprise, to find only a tatty attic, decorated with revolutionary posters, and grimy windows giving out onto the rain flecked sky. Alan was alone, bending over a large desk, checking proofs. He looked round with a start.

"My lodger! It's not often I see you in daylight hours."

Samuel looked around him.

"Where's your assistant? Esther?"

"She seems to have abandoned me."

"That's a shame. I liked her."

"Did you? I found her a little mercurial actually. Not entirely suited to journalism. Anyway, what brings you here? It's a little early for lunch?"

"There was something I had to ask you…."

"You know," Alan straightened up. "I think it's about time you saw this. Our special issue - the one I told you about. *The Forgotten*. A tribute to the war wounded. Kipling's done us a piece! Take a look."

Privately Samuel thought anything about the war wounded was unlikely to become a big seller. People wanted to forget all that now. He recalled his days at the Horrocks's house, with the poor, maimed men shuffling around, and Lady Horrocks saying in her brisk, upper class tones: *"A lot of them would really be far better off if they were dead, you know."*

He began leafing dully through the magazine Alan thrust into his hands, then he laid it aside.

"Alan, there was something I came to ask you. It's been bothering me. The other night…at the opening of Barrington House. You mentioned you were trying to contact Elmer Barrington? You've written something about him, haven't you? Something I might want to know."

"Who have you been talking to?"

"It doesn't matter."

"Oh well, I suppose you were going to find out sooner or later," Alan stood before him, hands in pockets, with a decidedly self-satisfied expression.

"Go on then," said Samuel.

"You remember me mentioning that that there was something about him that was about to emerge, something rather discreditable?"

Samuel tried to remember exactly what Alan had said. The other night at Nefertiti's. Something about war profiteering, wasn't it?

"Well that's where you come in."

"Me?"

"Yes, you see I'd been trying to get hold of Barrington for some time to answer my questions. Telephoning and writing letters, but he was lying low. In the end, I decided to tell him I was a friend of yours and that you'd helped me with some very valuable information."

"My God, Alan! What were you thinking of? And besides, I don't have any valuable information."

"I know. But you see, I did. Because I discovered something about Barrington that was very interesting indeed. That shows him in a very poor light."

Samuel could barely focus on what Alan was saying. Events began to fit together in his mind.

"So that's why he turned me out of his house! Because you said you were a friend of mine. He must have thought I was trying to….blackmail him or something. Why on earth didn't you tell me?"

"Terribly sorry about that. I couldn't you see. I couldn't have him finding out what I was writing and trying to stop the magazine."

"You didn't trust me!"

Alan took no notice of his friend's distress. He seemed delighted with his discovery.

"Sorry if I put you in a spot Samuel. But the man's a rascal, and you said your job with him was coming to an end. Anyway, now we've gone to press you might as well see what I discovered. It came up when I was doing my research." He gestured at the magazine. "Take a look!"

Samuel re-opened the magazine in a daze. As he expected, it was a depressing sight. There were photographs of hospital wards with row on row of beds, where dull-eyed men stared into space, men with horrible injuries, amputees. Pictures of upright young, officers, turned a conventional three quarters to face the camera for their official photographs and then the same men later, maimed and crumpled by the war. He leafed through the pages without really seeing them.

"I don't understand how this has anything to do with Elmer Barrington."

"Well you wouldn't. Unless you look carefully." Alan pointed to a photograph and the caption underneath. "There! It's a complete co-incidence. I was quite amazed myself when I made the connection."

Samuel looked at the page and stood for a while, letting its meaning sink in, piecing together, like the archaeologist he had once been, the fragmentary images that came into his mind.

He thought of burying and unburying. He thought of the human urge to hide and the equally ancient urge to excavate what others tried to keep hidden. He thought of the blank green surface of the sacred lake in Egypt, and the girl who sank beneath it, of the dark lawns upon which Iris and her friends danced, as immaculate as the war graves with their jumble of bones beneath. And he thought of Iris's brother Charles, the gentle, sad-eyed boy, with his room which remained exactly as it was, all his books untouched, as though he had not properly left, even though he had never come back.

Chapter Thirty-seven

There was no way of telling, from the first sight of the nursing home, what could lie within. It looked like a friendly, red-brick place which might have been a girls' school or the country seat of some sprawling local family, swelled by horses and dogs. The lawn was broad and well tended, with an ancient fir at the centre, its trunk girdled by a wooden seat. On the outskirts of the grounds, before the landscape receded into woodland of oak and beech, was a steep grassy slope which seemed to bank in the residents like a natural fence. The sky was flooded with low, generous afternoon light which glittered off the yellowing trees.

"Its not an asylum or anything, don't worry. They don't have bars on the windows."

The inside hall was pleasant and panelled, with a portrait of the Prince of Wales and various framed landscapes which she guessed had been painted by the patients, or inmates or whatever they were. It could have been a real home, but for the few telling institutional touches - a cork noticeboard fluttering with messages, the faint odour of catering. The atmosphere was casual. Someone passed by carrying a pot of tea on a tray. A telephone began to ring. No one stopped them or asked them what they wanted.

"Now then," his voice had a deliberately casual tone, as if they were on some routine afternoon outing. "He's just down here usually."

What had she feared? A madman, a monster? A creature restrained by a chain? Instead there was a long corridor, walls papered in an ornate pattern, made shiny beneath repeated layers of conker brown paint. They passed opened doors through which she glimpsed desks and a nurse in uniform and from which came sour, alien smells, of disinfectant, cleaning fluid and cooking. At the end of the corridor they came into a room, where perhaps twenty men sat. Great shafts of sunlight came through the high mullioned windows, showing up the smears and slicing through the rising coils of cigarette smoke. But for the high number in wheelchairs, it could almost have been a university common room. Most of them were young - in their twenties or thirties it seemed - reading, playing cards and chess. She felt their curious gaze upon her as she passed.

"He'll be jolly glad to see a fresh face."

He looked normal from behind. But when he turned her first impression was how much older than his age he appeared. He had a fine-featured, wide face and might have been handsome but he was cadaverously thin and his sandy hair was liberally threaded with grey. He wore a tweed jacket, fraying and patched on the elbows. The book he put down, she noticed, was a New Testament Commentary.

"Hello Charles. I've brought a friend of mine to see you." Esther was surprised to see Frank kiss him on the cheek. She had never seen men kiss before.

Charles seized her hand and pumped it with alacrity.

"I say. I wasn't expecting visitors. I don't count Frank in that."

He smiled broadly and motioned Esther to a seat. There was a jerky quality to his movements. Up close he had a sour smell, of sweat and unwashed clothing.

"Always glad to meet a friend of Frank's," he said, in a way which made Esther wonder whether any other friends of Frank's had ever in fact been produced.

Frank sat down and shot a packet of cigarettes across the table to Charles, who immediately lit up. "How's the chess?"

"Oh, don't talk to me about that. That fellow over there is unbeatable. He spent two years in a prisoner of war camp playing with twigs and pieces of stone and reckoned he's worked out every defence that's mathematically possible."

He cast an apologetic glance at Esther. "But why should I mind when I'm practically the raffia basket champion of southern Britain?"

Frank chuckled softly and Charles drew a letter from the inside pocket of his jacket.

"As it happens, I've just received something frightfully interesting."

It turned out to be not particularly interesting at all, something to do with his army pension, from what Esther could gather. Someone brought them fiercely strong tea and as she drank it she looked around her at the patients in their armchairs or at tables, some playing cards, others sitting with visitors, or talking in a perfectly animated way, to themselves.

She was relieved when Charles suggested they walk in the garden, even if their progress round the grounds was slowed to a crawl by him explaining the history of the house to her in enormous detail. They walked down gravelled paths, past slightly listing, mossy statues, and banks of straggling, leggy lavender, with Frank, who must have heard Charles' story a hundred times before, strolling behind them, his hands in his pockets. They turned through the sunken garden and admired the fountain statue of a truculent cupid wrestling with a stern faced Father Time, and then made their way out into the woodland, along a tiny stagnant stream. Eventually Esther, exhausted by Charles' narrative technique, hung back at a little Chinese bridge watching a cloud of gnats.

"Had enough?" said Frank in her ear.

"No. Not at all. I was just looking."

"I say, we'd better be off now. Don't want to miss our bus."

Charles barely seemed to mind. He saw them to the gate, bid an effusive farewell, then walked quickly, jerkily, away.

The bus shuddered comfortably beneath them as it pulled away.

"Thank you for coming."

"I enjoyed it."

"You were very calm with him Esther. Very relaxed and friendly. I'm grateful. I wanted you to meet him and know about him. And luckily he was on good form today. What did you think?"

"I liked him."

"The place is ghastly though, isn't it? I've got to get him out of there soon. He's like an old man, and he's not much older than you."

Esther felt herself slowly recovering from the shock as the bus bore them through tunnels of trees, gliding further and further away through the green evening light.

"There were just so many of them. And they were so young, most of them. What is wrong with them all?"

"So many?" He gave a dry laugh. "You can't have seen more than thirty. There are thousands and thousands of young men like that. Stuck in sanatoria and special military hospitals up and down this country. Ruined by shell-shock. Sitting there with injuries which no one can see and no one really knows how to treat. They frighten us, and we don't know how to deal with them, so we shut them away and try to forget, and in the meantime they moulder and rot their lives away. You don't know the half of it."

"I do know about them actually. Alan – the editor of my magazine – has been visiting some of these places. He's been meeting and photographing some of the men. He's done a whole issue about it. Kipling wrote for us."

"Really? Well I'm glad." He looked at her with interest. "So you'll understand why I'm so determined to get Charles out."

"But what about his family? Why can't they help? Why does it have to be you?"

"Oh, his family." Frank gave a savage little laugh. He remembered a meeting with Charles' father, looking down at his son as though he were   a half-shot rabbit, jerking and limping and needing to be finished off.

"Well his father does see him sometimes, but the impression I get is that they don't really want to know. The fact is, he was misinformed. First of all he was told that his son was missing in action, which pretty much means dead. I think everyone back home must have assumed that he was dead. Then they were told that Charles had been shot for cowardice – that must have been a tremendous shock I accept – and after it emerged that he had been reprieved, I think it was hard for the father to adjust. He certainly doesn't want him back home. He doesn't think it would be 'appropriate'. He's told himself Charles is too badly damaged to cope so he tidies him away down here, and just hopes everyone will forget about him."

"You mean he's told people his own son is dead?"

"I don't know what he's said. But in any case, I'm going to find somewhere for Charles. The longer he stays cooped up in that place, the more he will become institutionalised. You noticed, he barely asked you anything about yourself at all. That's partly because he's afraid to show any interest in a woman, but it's also because he's becoming so self centred."

"Why does he tremble all the time?"

"Oh, that's just the drugs."

"Does he still need them?"

"He'll need them for a long time. They stop him trying to kill himself."

"Oh. Of course. Though he seemed so cheerful."

"Rather manic perhaps. But anyway, in the long run, I want him to see a psychiatrist again, rather than keeping him doped up with drugs."

They were almost alone on the bus, apart from an elderly lady several rows behind, but Frank did not seem to mind anyone overhearing him.

"What I don't understand, Frank, is why you come. I mean, he's not a relation or anything."

"I have my reasons. And besides, no-one else does."

"How often do you visit?"

"I try to come every week."

"What do you talk about?"

"Everything. We argue about God. That's one of our favourites. Charles still believes."

"That's good."

"Yes I think it's rather good too. On the question of religion as a tranquilliser, I happen to agree with your friend Marx."

"I never said…."

"No. I know you don't. But I happen to think it's important to have something to hold onto. God must have his uses, even if he's never been any use to me."

He smiled at her - a wry, deprecating smile - and at that precise moment it was as if she had never seen him before. Before her was a face she had known and forgotten almost half her life, and had certainly never looked at. Frank Stevens. A friend of her father. His features, which had been blurred by familiarity, and were now sharp and new. She saw his high forehead and the glint of stubble on the cheek. His eyes, which she had thought as dull as grey stones in a stream, were flecked with amber and gleamed with humorous intelligence. It was as though she had put on a pair of spectacles, so that everything sprang swiftly and sharply into focus. She looked quickly away, so he shouldn't glimpse the surge of emotion she was experiencing. The effect of being with him was both exciting and chastening. Somehow she began to perceive things differently, as though her world had been washed of its bright colours and for the first time she glimpsed the sober shape of things beneath.

It was dusk by the time the bus came up through Kensington. There had been a shower of rain.

"If we get off here, then we'll just have to cross the park. Is that all right for you?"

"Yes, I'd like a walk."

The city's soft rumble was close by, the shops and buildings, the trams and buses all lit up in the twilight air, yet walking through Hyde Park Esther felt they were entirely alone, with the rest of the world merely flickering on the fringes of vision as they moved through pools of darkness, their faces violet in shadow. The vegetation seemed lush and swollen from the recent shower, exuding an earthy, sexual smell of decay. They passed a bank of giant rhubarb with thrusting, veiny stems, and she brushed it, scattering raindrops from its heavy leaves onto her neck.

"I'm very grateful to you for coming today."

"Oh, it was nothing. I wanted to."

"No, Esther, it wasn't nothing. It's a hard thing to confront. I find it very difficult. You asked me why I visit Charles…."

He hesitated momentarily.

"The thing is….madness, mental incapacity of any sort, is the thing I've always feared most. It runs in my family, you see. There've always been stories of great uncles and others relations further back who've done themselves in, or been shut away, and we just accepted it. Then I had a brother, a younger brother called Victor, and he killed himself."

She gasped. "Oh I'm sorry. I never knew."

"No reason you should. He would have been the same age as Charles, if he'd lived. I suppose by visiting Charles…"

He paused, as if to draw breath, but his silence continued so long, with just the sound of their feet crunching on the path, that she assumed he had stopped short of any further revelation. Then he said:.

"We're cursed with it in my family. Depression. Or melancholia as they used to call it. Whatever name you use can't begin to describe the dreadful thing it is. It creeps up on you slowly, and seeps over your life like oil, making everything black and worthless. You tell yourself it's self-indulgence and that if you ignore it, it'll go away, but it doesn't."

"So you know what it's like."

"Yes. A few years ago I even went so far as to see a psychiatrist myself. After the war." He forced a bright smile.

"There. I've never told anyone else that."

"What happened?"

"I fired him. He asked too many personal questions."

She frowned. "Don't joke."

"I discovered very rapidly that the talking cure wasn't for me."

"Yet you recommend it for others."

"Yes. There you have me again, I'm afraid Esther. One of my many hypocrisies."

He fell silent. Dark trees reared up, then were swallowed behind them. She longed to keep on walking like that, talking, barely able to see his face but feeling him beside her, the soft brush of his coat, and her face tingling in the chill wind. As they reached the periphery of the park and turned down Bayswater Road it began to drizzle, the rain fingering through her jacket and causing her blouse to stick to her chest. They quickened their pace to reach Waverley Gardens, where the plane trees offered some shelter.

Once inside the house she hesitated.

"It seems a long time since lunch. I expect you're famished."

"I suppose so," she said, though she was surprised to find she wasn't in the least hungry.

"Let me cook for you. Unless you don't want to risk my cooking?"

"Of course I do!"

"Come in here then."

He took her hand and led her into his sitting room, lighting the green desk lamp, which threw a warm glow across the jumble of books and papers. She saw a photograph of a young man, whom she guessed to be Victor, and an old couple standing by a car. She tried to focus on the spines of the books. *Gray's Anatomy. Psychoanalysis And The Unconscious.* A battered leather Tolstoy. George Eliot. Balzac.

"Let me take your coat." He helped her off with it and she

noticed that his hands, his big wide hands, were shaking slightly. He didn't move away but stood there, looking at her intently.

"Esther. You mentioned you had something to talk over with me."

"Oh yes. I did."

"If I were to guess - after my little explosion the other day - I'd guess you were going to tell me you want to move out."

"Yes."

"Do you know that I'd hate that?"

She could barely speak. Her senses were acutely alert. There was so little space between them, assent seemed the only gesture possible.

"Yes."

"Then before you do, can I tell you what I want?"

"Yes."

He moved towards her and collected her hair in his palms, feeling the weight of it like a cornucopia of treasure in his hands. Cupping her face he bent down and kissed her, holding himself back, allowing himself to savour the touch of the lips he had seen and wanted for so long. As he allowed his hand to caress her, to sweep down across her shoulder to her breast, the portrait of her passed through his mind and he felt her imagined body becoming real, like beauty becoming flesh. And it was a beauty so much more perfect in the flesh than in the mind. The beauty of the sexual response, the unspoken conspiracy of muscles and nerves that moved her towards him, with its old, instinctive urgency. He brought an arm round her back to draw her closer to him. For a moment he thought of his bed, chaste counterpaned and chill beneath the skin, and an image flashed into his mind of themselves naked upon it. The idea seemed more than just exciting. It seemed inevitable. He began to ease the blouse she was wearing from her shoulders. She moved her body hard against his and he knew it was reciprocation, rather than protest. The movement made him urgently aroused and to slow himself he tried to re-picture the anatomy he was caressing in its latinate forms: thorax, sternum, ribs, peculiar ribs, the costal cartilages, clavicle, scapula, spine. He started on the cranial nerves - olfactory, optic, motor oculi, trochlear, trifacial, abducent, facial, auditory - but it was no good. She would not turn into words for him. His senses were flooded with her.

They drew apart for a moment, looking at each other. Her face was already reddened by his kisses. His expression was so serious she might have been intimidated once, but now she felt as though they were having an intense conversation, which just happened to be unspoken.

"When?" was all he asked.

She took his hand. "Here. Now."

Chapter Thirty-eight

"1925 is going to be a new beginning. It's going to be a wonderful time for us!"

Celia was guiding Iris among the shops and workshops preparing for the forthcoming Paris Exhibition. Everything about this modern style, the furniture, decoration, sculptures and china, the luxurious materials and the mass produced designs, seemed to proclaim their separation from the past and herald a new era. Everywhere was a swirl of colours, crowding in on the eye, stimulating, jangling and frivolous. It was all rich velvets and hard jewel-like surfaces which made the light bend and skim and dazzle.

Already there was more demand for Celia's designs than they could possibly fulfil. There was a little lamp-stand she'd designed, brass with two recumbent sphinxes at the base and a lotus design round the top, which was proving very popular. Then some Louis XVI chairs. And a hand-blocked wallpaper with golden pyramids. Not to mention the textiles - the curtain material with fauns dancing through a writhing, leafy forest and the beautiful velvets and chenilles. The time had never been so ripe for such an idea. In smart circles, having one's home done up was now like getting a new spring wardrobe, or even like buying that season's best-selling book, just another way of keeping up with fashion. Shabby country houses that had made do with dull cream for decades had recently became hot-houses of experimentation. Decoration was not just about repairing the ravages of time - it was all about ideas and a means of personal expression.

They had been here for weeks now. Celia was in her element, drawing little sketches in her notebook and discussing supply and prices, but Iris remained silent as she turned things over and over in her mind. At times she felt so numb it was a relief to have the art probe at her senses with its sharp, glittery edges.

Her feet hurt that day. They had walked all round the city, visiting galleries and junk shops. Celia wanted to visit the studio of Madame Vionnet, the couturière, before they ate that evening so Iris set off back for the hotel alone. It was dusk by the time she approached the street of shuttered houses, and entered the dim, stone hallway. She saw no-one, though there was a distant sound of doors banging, a scent of cooking and a screech of laughter. Slowly she trudged up the stairs.

Her room was plain and tranquil. There was an armoire, a dressing table with a mirror and a simple chest of drawers, then to one side a tiny bathroom. Her plan was to take off her shoes and lie perfectly still on the little hard bed with its white iron bedstead and allow the tears to slope silently down her face. She would open the window and let the sounds and smells of the city drift in as the light faded and the clamour of the day receded. Then she would take a bath and dress carefully for the evening.

That was what she was planning until she shut the door behind her and saw him there, sitting on the bed, that same high bed, looking expectantly towards her. She froze and the breath caught in her throat. For a second she didn't know whether he was actually there, or just a figment of her imagination. The air between them seemed to swim slightly, like liquid.

"How did you find me?" she whispered.

"Dolly told me," he said.

"Dolly?"

"Yes. She said you'd come to Paris. And I thought to myself, if Iris was looking for a very charming hotel in Paris, she might just remember this one."

"But how did you get in?"

"I told them I was your husband, of course."

She looked away.

"Celia couldn't understand why I wanted us to stay here.

A cheap, dingy little fleapit, she called it. Though now she's
decided there's something *echt* about it."

"Where is she now?"

"She's out spending all the money we've saved. We've
been buying things all day. The stuff here is amazing."
He took a step towards her but she shrank away from him.
"Please don't."

She sat down on the rickety chair by the dresser,
straightened her narrow shoulders and looked at him
with resolve. Her hair was pinned back from her face by
a tortoiseshell clip and she wore new kid-leather shoes,
silk stockings and a round collared blouse that made her
look rather chic and French. She sat very still. There were
shadows of sadness beneath her eyes and her hands lay in
her lap like something dead. Very quietly she said:

"My father told me what you did. The worst thing anyone
could do. Is it true?"

He held her gaze. "It's true."

She gave the tiniest shudder.

"So he was right about that at least. Though he was wrong
in every
other respect. He thought I would be so horrified. He
thought it would be enough to kill any feelings I had for
you. Actually though, I'm not sure I care at all any more."

"I was going to tell you that night Iris! That was what I had
to say to you. I was going to explain."

"Explain?" She arched an eyebrow with disdain. "Can you
explain such a thing? Anyway. I don't want you to explain.
Not now. I just want you to go away."

This steeliness, from a face he loved, was terrible to him.
He tried hard to be controlled, to match her control, but
her face had closed like a shutter. While every instinct in
him yearned to reach out and touch her, it would not have
surprised him to find that her flesh had hardened too, like
marble. For comfort he reminded himself of Alice Cohen's
words : *She looked as if someone had broken her heart.*

"Please….I'm sorry Iris."

Her eyes flickered upwards and for a moment he thought there was a chance she might relent. Then she seemed to have made a decision.

"All right. I will do this for you, even though you never did it for me. *I* will explain."

She got up from the chair and went over to the window sill. For a while she didn't speak. She seemed to be watching a cat passing soft-footed along the adjacent roof, arching its back in the weak sunlight. Below them was the sound of a car horn and loud, French disputing voices. Then, with her back still turned, she said:

"I can't deny that it was a shock, finding out what you had done. I minded very much that you hadn't told me, I really thought we had told each other everything…. But that wasn't why I went. I went because you left me without a word."

"I had no choice….."

"No choice?" There was an edge of contempt in her voice. "No choice? Did you think for a second what that was like for me? Did your imagination stretch so far as to wonder what it would be like for me, left without any explanation, no letter or note? Not even a telephone call from someone I had just learned to trust? Left to imagine for months on end, with no-one prepared to tell me where you had gone? Did that occur to you?"

"Of course it did."

"Yet you let me suffer it. You went off on your errand and could not be bothered to enlighten me. Not a letter or a call. You left me hoping, like some silly girl!"

"Your father insisted. He said he would disinherit you if I contacted you in any way. I wouldn't want that for you. If I spoke to you before I came back with the statue, he said you would be left destitute and you would never have another penny from him."

She gave a proud little shrug. "He was right about that at

least. I don't want to live with him any more. I won't take his money. I can earn my own. I have a business now. It's called Antika. We're already starting to make profits." She softly, almost beseechingly, she added: "I *told* you I would stand up to my father. Don't you remember? That day in Kensington Gardens?"

"Yes."

At the thought of that day he came instinctively towards her and put one hand on her thin shoulder, but she shook him off.

"Twice in my life it's happened before. People I've loved have vanished without trace. First my mother, and then my brother. They had no choice of course, they died. But you did. You vanished just like them, without saying goodbye. So this time, when it happened, I decided I would not shut myself up and cry. I decided I must take control of my life and make sure that I won't ever be left again. That's why I came to Paris."

She turned away again and all he could see was the whiteness of her knuckles as she gripped the windowsill, watching the indigo clouds massing against the Parisian dusk.

"Iris, I will go. If that's what you want. But before I do, there's something you need to know. It's about your brother."

"My brother?" She glanced round dully and he could see the track of a single tear on her face. "What has any of this got to do with Charles?"

There was no way to prepare her.

"Charles is alive, Iris. And I know where he is."

Chapter Thirty-nine

The long corridor echoed with the efficient step of nurses and distant, muffled voices. They tried to make it as much like a home here as possible, he could see that, with the vases of flowers, the chintz curtains, the roomy armchairs and the paintings on the wall. Only the faint institutional odour of carbolic gave it away.

He sat on a bench, staring down at the tessellations of the blood red tiles on the floor, and tried to distract himself by working out the interior angles of the burnished polygons. On such calculations, an ancient maths teacher had told him once at school, the entire Egyptian civilisation was founded. Without geometry the pyramids wouldn't exist. Pattern and angle, rigour and precision, this was Egyptian art's way of expressing the divine. Perhaps that was why he had found refuge in that art, when human life was so full of evasions and elisions and so rarely ran true.

He wondered what was going on behind the firmly closed door. Iris had said she wanted to be alone with Charles to start with. There were so many years to fill, and although the brother she thought dead had been brought back for her, she was aware that he was far from the brother she knew. Would she be shocked by his appearance? It was eight years since they had met. Would he be deranged, or even remember his sister?

Just then a woman came and sat next to him on the bench. Glancing up he saw that it was Esther Hartley.

"Hello Samuel." She extended a hand. "You got my letter then."

He held onto her hand for a moment. "Esther. I'm very grateful to you. And Iris is too. More than you can imagine."

"Don't be. Alan was so determined to keep it a secret until

the magazine came out. He didn't want you to forewarn Mr Barrington, so he told you he was writing something else."

"War profiteering?"

"I think that was it. Did you see the report in the newspapers?"

Samuel pointed to a copy of *The Daily Telegraph* on the bench beside him. Halfway down page three was a photograph of Elmer Barrington and another of Charles alongside the headline*: "The Sorrowful Tale Of The Tycoon And the Son He Said Had Died, by A J McIlroy."*

"When I found out about Charles I just thought it was terribly unfair of Alan not to warn you. It might be fearfully awkward for you when it did come out, given that Mr Barrington is your employer."

"*Was* my employer."

"So you've left your job too!"

She had pretty teeth when she smiled, very slightly crossed at the front, and her mouth had a pronounced cupid's bow.

"Alan probably told you I've left the magazine. I decided I'd rather make myself useful here. I think I'd like to study medicine but until I can find out about training, a friend of mine, a doctor, fixed this for me. Not that they trust me with anything remotely medical of course. I've never even done first aid. I'm just helping with the patients, reading to them sometimes, pushing round the trolley…there's rather a lot to do actually. Mostly I've just been talking to them, at least the ones you can talk to. Some of them, well, there's not much point…."

She tailed off and they both looked at the door.

"I'm sorry for your friend. It must have been a terrific shock. Is it really true she had been told her brother was dead?"

"Her father thought it was better that way. But I'm worried now, that Charles might be much more…damaged….than she's expecting."

"Don't worry too much. I've met him and I know having his sister back will make a great difference to him."

A woman with a trolley containing an enormous urn of tea and stacks of green china cups was beckoning from the end of the corridor.

"Oops! I'm wanted again. I'd better give a hand. I expect I'll see you then, if you're going to be visiting Charles. If there's anything I can do, just ask!"

She smiled again and walked away.

Celia Urquhart's flat was an exquisitely decorated bower above her shop in Mayfair, decorated with ribbons and striped pink and purple wallpaper printed with gold fleur de lys. It also came with two tiny, disgruntled dogs.

"Celia says I can use it for as long as I need," said Iris as she unlocked the door that evening. "She won't tell me but I know she's staying with a new boyfriend."

She put down her case, turned on the lamps and in the surge of soft light, looked around her. The sitting room was tiny, just big enough for Celia's vermillion sofa and a big armchair. There was a mantelpiece with her china decorations along it, a venetian mirror, and a stack of magazines. Off to one side was a bedroom, cluttered with Celia's panoply of make-up and dresses, then a cupboard of a bathroom and a miniscule kitchenette. Iris explored her new living space in a daze, still trying to digest the events that had overtaken her.

"I've got something else for you." Samuel held out the envelope containing £200. "Your father gave it to me, but in the event I didn't need it, so it seems appropriate that you should have it. Until you decide what to do."

He placed it on the table. Now that he had seen her to the flat, there was no more reason for him to stay.

"Well. I'd better go."

She watched him as he went to the door, then he lingered a moment. After days of purposeful behaviour, he found himself hesitant, aware that this was a moment which could determine the course of his life. His throat was dry with desire as he tried to articulate the words to plead his case. What could he say? *"I will be always be glad for that time we had together."* That sounded like a resignation letter. He stiffened himself to focus on her face, the bright blue eyes. "Iris....I don't want to go. I want to be with you. I want our lives together."

For a moment she stood where she was, then she rushed towards him and placed her arms around him. He closed his eyes and felt her hair on his cheek and her soft body press up against his own and with a moan he began kissing her convulsively on her lips and her eyes, gripping her small frame to his body, savouring the soft transfer of their breath. She reached up her arms to his neck, standing on tiptoe, and kissed him with her opened mouth, an acquiescence which provoked him to greater intensity. She was crying and her tears seeped down between their lips onto his tongue and she felt herself trembling as he began to move against her, caressing her beneath her fine woollen skirt, feeling the slippery silk of her stockings and suspender belt, her satin shift and underclothes. He slipped off her blouse and saw again the sprinkling of freckles at the base of her throat and a flush rising up from her chest. He reached his hand to caress the small, smooth breasts below and felt her press herself into his palm. She was breathing harder. He loosened all of her clothes until they dropped one by one to the floor and he felt her skin again, all over, every part of her. She stood before him naked while he covered her in kisses, kneeling down and touching her briefly between the legs, and feeling the faintest, reciprocal shiver, before he rose and put her fingers to the buckle of his belt.

Afterwards, she gazed into his face on the pillow beside her. "I never stopped loving you, despite what you did. And you brought my brother back to me. You brought him back from the dead. Whatever else you've done, to me that outweighs anything."

Chapter Forty

Christmas was approaching and the shop windows were lit like jewels along the street with displays of teas, coffees and sweets, or hats, silk stoles and scarves. Pedestrians jostled on the pavement and the roads were busy with vehicles. It was not yet five, but the lamps glowed against the wintry dusk. Glistening baubles decked the Christmas trees in every department store. Decorations were underway in the great London houses where the friends of Iris thronged to parties and dinners and balls. There was a general air of excited anticipation which no bitter wind or bone-grey sky could diminish.

As he made his way up the steps of the British Musuem, and passed beneath the imposing portico of Portland stone, Samuel could not help remembering his early days in London when he had ventured here for relaxation and escape, drawn by a growing interest in the ancient Egyptians. It felt strange to be back now, heading again for the Antiquities department.

The young man at the desk was new.

"I was wondering. Could I possibly see Dr Wallis Budge?"

"You've just missed him I'm afraid."

"Well then, could you tell me when he'll be back?"

"What I meant was, he's just retired. There's a new keeper now. Was it anything I could help with?"

"Oh. No, It was just….I've been out in the Valley of Kings. I wanted to ask Dr Budge about something he had written."

"Well in that case," mention of Samuel's experience brought the familiar note of respect to the young man's voice. "We do have the complete collection of his works, which is not inconsiderable. You're very welcome to take a look."

He led Samuel into a room filled with glass fronted bookcases and motioned towards one.

"Here's the key to the cabinets. I'll leave you to it."

It was dim in the room, the long, oak table illuminated only by green shaded lamps. The fustiness of scholarship and old leather and mildewed paper filled the air. Samuel turned the key in the lock and began to look through the glass cabinets. He pulled out draws to find papyri, tomb texts and demotic writings. He scanned lines of ornate script, trying to decipher the cursive hieroglyphs and dense columns of symbols, black with detail, illustrated with tiny, coloured creatures. There were parts of the yellowed Papyrus of Ani, the most complete version of the Book of the Dead, written for the royal scribe Ani, and brought from Thebes by Wallis Budge. It lay here preserved under glass, with all the elaborate incantations, rituals, spells and words of power needed by Ani after death written out with exquisite artistry. Here were the magical formulae he would need to protect himself on the long journey to the kingdom of Osiris, a road infested with the powers of evil.

Dr Budge must have devoted decades to collecting, deciphering and decoding all these tomb texts, funerary spells and litanies, yet despite the reams of material, still Samuel could not find what he was searching for. He racked his brain to remember what Carter had talked about. Something Budge had written concerning Egyptian Magic. But what?

He leafed through books, dozens of them. There were commentaries on the Egyptian language, on customs and ancient fetishes. There were descriptions of magical rituals and funeral ceremonies. Then, at last, he found what he was looking for.

"From time immemorial the Egyptian people believed that every statue and every figure possessed an indwelling spirit. Statues to which magical powers had been imparted by means of the performance of certain symbolic ceremonies and the recital of certain words of power could be employed to do both good and evil. In some cases these figures have

been known to drive men out of their senses and to strike terror into them."

As he read, the air in the room around him felt cold. He reminded himself that he was standing in the heart of enlightened, modern, twentieth century London. A city of cars and trains and aeroplanes. Of cough medicines and cinemas and psychoanalysis. A place that had progressed three thousand years from the primitive rituals and spells of dust-ridden Egypt. Yet as he stood there in the distinguished depths of the British Museum, the hoots and rumble of traffic, the hum of shoppers, the sheer, civilised ordinariness of a December afternoon fell away, and the same premonitory sense came over him – the feeling he had before – of inescapable destiny. He sensed it around him, pressing close enough to reach into his chest and clutch at his heart. He saw again the young girl at Medinet Habu rising from the sacred lake, he saw the water boy, he saw the golden face in the tomb. The blood sang in his ears. He read on.

"Some archaeologists have been fortunate enough to find statues and idols with words of power carved into them revealing a series of interesting charms and magical formulae. The most potent by far of these spells would invoke the aid of Thoth, the god believed to have written the Book of the Dead. Ancient Egyptians would beseech Thoth on behalf of their dead and place them under the protection of his almightly spells."

The sweat prickled on his skin. A tide of nausea rose in his throat. He knew now what he knew he would find.

"A list of such potent spells, curses and coffin texts has been compiled by the Cairo Musuem."

The Cairo Museum? He paused for a moment, until it came to him. His encounter with Carter on that darkened Cairo street corner the night Lord Carnarvon died.

"I needed to consult a man in the Cairo Museum about some coffin texts. There was something I needed to

understand."

Now he knew what it was. Out of the page before him one line stood out, the tiny, dense hieroglyphs etched like fire in his mind. A canopic jar, a setting sun, an ibis, an arm. It was the same line of symbols on the scrap of paper which Carter had carried with him. It was the writing on the statue's pedestal. All it said was:

"Fear Thoth, Lord of Magic, who sees every heart."

Chapter Forty-one

Other than the slightest upward flicker of an eyelid, Cairns gave no sign at all that he was surprised to see Iris after so many weeks. But as she walked into the hall of her former home, Iris knew he was pleased. It might be because the old man had known her all her life, and had no children of his own. Or perhaps he was just relieved at the thought that she was returning home and he would no longer have to care for the neurotic Paw Paw. Either way he would soon be disappointed.

Cairns continued to hover annoyingly as she looked about her.

"You don't need to take my coat. Where's my father?"

"Mr Barrington is in the morning room. He's…that is, is he expecting you, Miss Iris?"

"I don't need an appointment to see my own father, Cairns," said Iris, her brisk manner concealing her apprehension as she marched across the hall.

Every day for the past week, she had visited the sanatorium and sat by Charles' side, her hand in his, talking quietly, calmly, while he stared back at her with his wide blue eyes as though she, rather than he, was the apparition raised from the dead. And every day she had rehearsed this confrontation with their father in her mind. But now that she was in the same house as him, the entire brave, angry speech she had planned deserted her, and she knew it would be impossible to stop her voice from trembling. Her face was flushed with emotion as she pushed open the door and peered into the gloom.

Sometimes, as he had sat there in recent days, alone with his antiquities, Elmer Barrington was filled with a sense of incredulity at the assumptions of his former self. How had the young man who came over to England three decades ago, possessed of so much energy and presumption, ever thought it necessary to attend so many soirées and dinners? Why had it ever been important to own a number of race horses, or to possess so many properties or build his own monument? Why had it mattered to meet members of Parliament and Lords, to be chauffeured around London in his Bentley, to be pictured in the newspapers, talked about and admired? Or to do business and make meaningless amounts of money? Why had he ever cared what people thought about himself, or his family?

It was dark in the morning room. He had managed to persuade that fool Cairns to stop lighting lamps all the time. Why should he need light? After all, the glow of the fire was enough. He liked the way that the flickering beams glanced off the statue, deepening its gleam, bringing out its golden depths, so it seemed almost to burn with its own mysterious warmth. He had studied the way it changed throughout the day. In the frank morning light the piece looked harder and sleeker, more metallic, whereas the mellow afternoon sunbeams seemed to mould and shimmer around it, burnishing it to perfection. But he thought he liked it best by firelight. Then it became most alive.

It was hard to take his eyes off such a lovely thing. To consider it better he had pushed the other pieces to the edges of the room, leaving the statue in splendid isolation. Generally he wished that he could be entirely alone with it. It had a peculiar, penetrating gaze, as though it could see everything he was thinking, or had ever thought. He found it very difficult not to look at it, and frankly, did not see why he should resist. What else was worth looking at, when he had this?

Yet it would be wrong to say the statue gave him pleasure. He longed for it certainly, and wanted to be near it, yet it filled him not with pleasure, but infinite sadness. How irrational it was to desire a thing so much, when it brought so much pain. It was as though everything bad in his life, every shortcoming, was brought before him and he was obliged to see it afresh.

In these lonely hours he had been forced to think properly, for the first time, about Charles. He had looked into the depths of his bombastic self, into his very blood and bones, and felt unfamiliar stirrings of shame and regret. He cared little for his place in society. Society's approval could be bought as easily as it was taken away. Or for his ruined hopes as a public man. His fraudulent business dealings, like the profiteering in the war, when he had been able to rack up the price of sugar at a time of shortage, did not oppress him in the slightest. But the thought of his treatment of Charles lay like lead within him.

There was a noise in the room. Someone had come in. It was Cairns presumably, bringing his dinner on a tray. He had taken to having all his meals here with the statue because it was far more convenient, though he was increasingly bored by food, no matter how many little delicacies Cairns tried to trick him with. He sustained himself with brandy and water. When he glanced round though, he noticed it was not Cairns, but a woman in the doorway. Not Edwina, obviously. She had absented herself the very day Cairns had brought the newspaper, carefully ironed and folded, revealing the story of his son. For a moment he thought it was his dead wife Margaret, looking enticingly pretty in a swinging, red coat, which set off her milky blonde hair, until he realised it was his daughter, Iris. He forced himself to look at her.

"Daddy. I've come to talk about Charles."

That seemed reasonable. After all, that was what the rest of the world was talking about.

"What do you want to know?" His voice cracked after days of silence.

"How can you possibly ask that?" She seemed very emotional. Her voice was trembling. "What do you think I want to know? I want you to explain why you allowed me to believe my only brother was dead!"

He moved his eyes from Iris back to the statue again, but when he looked at it now, its beautiful face seemed to change. In fact, now he came to think of it, it looked strangely like his son.

"You want to know about Charles?"

"I want to know *everything* that happened. Everything you should have told me before."

He cleared his throat and began to speak.

"At first, they said Charles was missing. I just assumed that was the end. Missing always meant dead, you see. It never meant just *missing*. But very soon afterwards, just as everyone was saying how sorry they were, and sending letters and so on, and as they were all hearing that their own sons were going missing and being killed, we got the news that Charles was alive. Only there was some kind of disgrace involved. A sort of cowardice. Apparently Charles deserted rather than do battle. According to the military chaps, our son was a coward, he was up for court martial and there was every chance they were going to execute him."

As he spoke he stared into the middle distance and for a moment it seemed to Iris that he was not addressing her but the ghost of his dead wife.

"Anyhow, no sooner had I discovered this and begun to make enquiries than someone intervened and he was reprieved. You can imagine how pleased I was. I actually welcomed the fact that he was to be sent back to Britain for treatment. But any relief I might have allowed myself to feel was short lived because it soon became apparent that the boy was a wreck. An excuse for a human being. This was not the son I had. This boy had lost his senses. He was raving like a madman. He needed constant nursing and would never live any sort of independent life. When I did visit him he barely recognised me. Given that everyone thought he was dead already, I decided to keep it private."

Iris gasped. "You mean you tidied Charles away and just let everyone assume that he had died?"

Barrington remained in his armchair, his huge figure huddled forward, gazing at the statue on the table before him. The only sign of his inner tension was the way he clenched and unclenched his hands. Then he said, hoarsely, "You don't understand. I had to protect you. He wasn't the brother you knew."

"Why did you assume I needed protection? He was still my brother!"

He did not answer. The rage and bluster that were so much a part of him had gone. The titanic self-assurance had dwindled and the mountainous man she had known was shrunk to his shadow. Iris felt tears come to her eyes, though whether for Charles, her father or herself, she was not sure.

"Anyway," she continued. "I want Charles to leave the sanitorium and have some kind of independent life. I've discussed it with his friend, Dr Stevens, and he agrees with me. He's going to help me find somewhere."

As if to emphasise her disgust she added:

"He certainly won't want to come back here."

Barrington only nodded.

Iris waited for a response, and seeing that none was forthcoming, she pursed her lips, then turned to leave.

"Iris. Wait." It was a croak, which seemed to come with effort. "I want to give you something."

At this encounter with his daughter, his heart had given a final jerk of feeling. She was the one person in his life whom he loved deeply despite himself.

"It's worth a lot. Priceless in fact. Only…."

He had betrayed her brother, but he couldn't bear to betray her.

"Only, you must promise to sell it. I don't want you to keep it. Sell it, and take the money for Charles. I already provide for him, but if this Dr Stevens is so keen to find somewhere for him, the extra money might help."

He rose, turned to busy himself on a far table, then placed the box in her hands. As she took it, he felt the lightening of an immense weight. He bent to kiss her, then crossed the room and switched on the light.

After Samuel left the museum he hurried back to the flat, his mind racing ahead to the thought of Iris waiting for him. It had only been a week now, but each morning she had woken and looked at him with shining eyes and each evening when he returned to the flat, clattered up the steps and pushed open the door to the tiny sitting room, she had been there waiting for him. Every day he would draw her down into bed, to spend the evening hours tenderly rediscovering each other, as if to make up for the months they had been apart.

But that afternoon she was nowhere to be seen. He waited, with mounting anxiety, as dusk passed into night, wondering where she could be. Perhaps she had been delayed at the sanatorium with Charles, or was visiting a friend, or seeing Celia about more designs for Antika. Maybe she was consoling Dolly Monroe, whose marriage had broken up and her husband gone to live in the south of France. There were no end of explanations for Iris's absence. Yet he was possessed of an irrational fear that something else hung over them and threatened their precarious happiness. Something that he had no power to resist.

At last he heard a slow tread on the stair and raced to the door with relief. Iris entered pensively carrying a bulky leather bag and sank down onto the sofa. She stared bleakly ahead.

"I went to see my father."

"But why, Iris? Was that wise?"

"I wanted to see how he explained denying my brother to

me for all these years. To see if he could explain."

"And could he?"

She looked at him with troubled eyes.

"He tried. But I was shocked, Samuel. I think the whole episode has had a terrible effect on him. He didn't ask me anything about myself at all. When I said I wanted Charles to leave the sanitorium and to have some kind of independent life, he just nodded. Then as I was leaving, he gave me something. He said I was to sell it to help buy a house for Charles."

Even before she reached down into the leather Gladstone bag by her side, felt for the bulky parcel wrapped in brown paper and brought it out onto her lap, he knew. He knew as she firmly, delicately, unpeeled the linen strips, blotched with rusty stains the colour of old blood. He knew as the lamp light glinted off its perfect lineaments, that there before him, in his lover's hands, was the sight he had hoped to forget forever.

Iris held up the statue and examined it.

"My father said you stole this. That you killed a man just to get hold of it."

Samuel gasped. "Is that what he told you?"

She looked at him and he saw what she had thought, and that she had resolved to love him in spite of it. And he wondered why it had taken him so long to explain.

"It's hard to express how insignificant you feel under the Egyptian sky. It's so vast you sense your life is no more than a flicker of light between two oceans of darkness. When you stand in the valley you can almost feel the world turn beneath you. You picture yourself clinging to the earth's curve and it's like you're nothing at all. The seconds of your life pass like grains in a sandstorm. So if you're given a chance to make your own little mark on Egyptian history – to right a wrong that has been done to those people and restore a tiny part of the treasure that's been stolen from them – well, you take it.

"Howard Carter's house was at Elwat el-Diban near the entrance to the Valley of the Kings. I knew Carter was out that night, over to the Metropolitan House for dinner with the Burtons and the Lythgoes. Those dinners always went on late and afterwards there were cards or mah jong or party games.

"As luck would have it, I ran into Carter's favourite Arab lad, the water boy who had discovered the tomb steps. He was a handsome boy with black curly hair who looked rather young for his years. He'd taken a liking to me, I think, at least he was always tagging along behind me like an annoying little brother, bombarding me with questions and never knowing when to stop.

"What is the House of Commons?"

"Have you seen Big Ben?"

"Have you met the famous Charlie Chaplin?"

"Have you seen snow?"

"One day, Mr Carter promise, he will take me to England. We will ride in a taxi cab. Perhaps we will meet the king."

So when I saw him my heart sank, but luckily he seemed to be going elsewhere. He just said 'Good Evening' in his rather careful English and went straight on past.

"It was dim inside Carter's house. The lamps were unlit and the shutters were down against the heat of the day. The stone walls were cool to the touch. But I knew the house very well and I could grope my way quite easily in the darkness. My plan, as much as I had one, was to find the Wishing Cup that Carter had already shown me and leave with it discreetly, then head back to Luxor to give it to my Egyptian friend Husni. I saw it as some tiny, token reparation for the way we British had ransacked his land.

"I already knew the route to Carter's study at the back of the house, and I was treading softly, trying to make no noise, even though I knew Abdel Al the servant was out and I was alone. The door was unlocked and I went straight to the cupboard where Carter had kept the cup, but when I tried the handle it was locked. That was maddening. I remember looking around for a key, rummaging in the desk drawers. Carter always kept his desktop starkly tidy, so there was just an inkwell and his diary lying open, ready to be completed for the day and a couple of photographs of old people, Carter's parents I assumed, and one of Lady Evelyn and her father Lord Carnarvon, standing by a train. Otherwise, he had no ornaments and there was no sign of any other treasures. Frustrated, I began to hunt through the chest of drawers without even knowing what I was looking for, then right at the back of the bottom drawer, I found a parcel.

"I picked it out it and was surprised to find it was incredibly heavy. My fingers were shaking so much I had to discipline myself to remember the professional delicacy we had been taught for handling objects in the tomb. I even heard Carter's voice in my head saying: "The lightness of a feather, lad, the lightness of a feather!"

The parcel was wrapped in linen. From touch alone, I thought I could detect a pair of figures tightly shrouded. With extreme care I unwrapped them, and held one of the figures up. In my shock I almost dropped it again, because it was something I had seen once before, just for a split second, but had never forgotten. I had seen it one night in the burial chamber. It was the statue you're holding now.

Because of its weight I knew at once it must be made of pure gold, and it was far more beautiful than the companion piece, so finely wrought, almost as if it had been made by a different craftsman altogether. There was a line of hieroglyphs around the pedestal which I couldn't read. It had the most amazing effect on me. I found it almost physically difficult to draw my eyes away from it.

But at the same time I knew then that this was not just something Carter had taken to inspect, with every intention of returning. This was not some object for his research, He had taken it that first night in the burial chamber and he had mentioned it to no-one. Only Lord Carnarvon knew about it, and Carter had refused to give it up. That was what they had argued about. I guessed Carter couldn't bear to part with it.

"But it wasn't his to keep! It belonged to the Egyptian people and I felt a wave of anger on their behalf. Everything Husni had told me was right. They were being ruthlessly exploited by excavators who refused to accept that these treasures were their heritage. I was motivated by sheer, indignant rage and also perhaps by the need to make some kind of gesture. To set things right.

Anyway. I decided to take it.

The days may be hot in the Valley but the evening chill can penetrate to the bone, so I'd taken a thick jacket and I realised it would be quite easy to hide the thing beneath the folds of material. I began to wrap it up, carefully, back in its linen shroud.

"It was at that point that I sensed a presence in the room. There was a flicker behind me, like a rustle of air, and when I turned I saw the boy. He must have crept in while my back was turned. I could barely see him in the gloom, but I could tell he was agitated. He kept gesturing to my jacket with an agonised expression. His whole body was trembling and I realised that he was terrified too.

"Please. Sir. Mr Carter say nothing must be taken."

I spoke as firmly and formally as I could.

"I don't know what you mean boy."

But he wasn't going to give up.

"Sir. It was a mistake, I am sure. The statue."

"What statue?"

Bravely, he kept challenging me.

"There Sir. The gold."

He was making a high keening sound and pointing wildly. I was terrified someone would hear. I had the statue on Carter's desk and kept on with my wrapping – trying to be as careful as I could, though I was so nervous my fingers almost wouldn't work.

"Then suddenly, quite unexpectedly, I felt a thud on my back. The boy had started hitting me, pulling at my clothes, dragging me by the arm, trying to reach the statue. I fended him off with one arm, but he didn't give up. By then something had overtaken me, I'd seen the figure and I was possessed of a determination to have it. I couldn't bear to fail. I couldn't let Husni down.

"I turned to face him and could see from his eyes that he was frightened of me, yet he still wrestled bravely to grab this heavy gold figure. I grappled with him, and all I remember is holding the statue high above our heads, like some trophy we had both won, and pushing him with my other hand, so he lost his footing and staggered backwards. And then, though I absolutely didn't mean to hurt him, somehow the statue slipped out of my grip and crashed down onto his skull. He went down hard onto the tiled floor, and lay flat out.

"At first I thought he was feigning. I knelt down beside him and hauled him up by the shoulders. I realised though I had seen him so often I didn't actually know his name so I whispered in his ear "Boy! Wake up boy!" He sank back in my arms, then suddenly he jerked up and clutched me round the neck. A moment later, just as quickly he folded back into my arms as if he was exhausted. His face was visibly paling and there was blood bubbling from his nostrils. I cradled him against my chest as though I was his father and he was my child, and I was trying to console him for some little injury he'd suffered.

"Eventually I let him back down onto the floor. He twitched slightly, and a trickle of blood came from the gash on his head onto the tiles. Then he opened his eyes and said: "Mr Carter?" And after that he just lay there as though he'd gone to sleep, except his eyes were still open.

"I felt strangely paralysed. It was an accident, no more. I told myself the boy had spied on me and followed me and brought it on himself. I had been attacked and he had only himself to blame. For a moment I just knelt there stunned, peering down at him. To my astonishment the statue, though it was such a delicate thing, was entirely undamaged so I swabbed the blood up from the tiles with the linen shroud, wrapped the statue back up, and put it in my jacket. Then I heaved the boy up over my shoulder. At that point I was almost beside myself with fear. My throat was so tight I could hardly breathe. I suppose some kind of animal instinct got me out of the house in the darkness, and propelled by the horror of what had just happened, I made my way to the mountain path.

"The mountains there are flinty. They're full of fissures and faults – that's the very quality that makes them the perfect place for building tombs. Anyway, there was a steep path which cut down the mountain face. We never took it. It was narrow and winding and usually only the more experienced Arabs went that way. But I carried the boy along there, cautiously, until I came to a spot where the cliff face fell away dramatically from the edge of the path. There was a sheer drop. I stopped for a moment, put the body down, and it rolled forward, scattering the gravel, tumbling down the hill like that game we all used to play when we were children. Eventually it came to rest against a boulder twenty yards down the rock face. His neck was bent backwards, his face was gaping up at the night.

"Compared with the clarity of that memory, everything that followed still seems blurred and indistinct. I ran back down and raised the alarm. Everyone was supportive and kind. They all said it was understandable that I should have taken the narrower path if the boy was accompanying me. People were always saying that path was dangerous, especially in the dark. I explained he had wanted to stop off for some reason at Carter's house while I had waited outside. They said it was an accident that had been waiting to happen. The boy's body was taken back to his family, and as the others clustered round me sympathetically, I began to freeze over with the horror of what I had done.

"I took the statue to Husni the next night and he was so pleased with it, I couldn't bear to tell him what had happened, though I knew he would find out soon enough."

"Did anyone else discover?" Iris asked.

"Violet Esterhazy knew, somehow. She was quite used to procuring illicit treasures for European collectors and I suspect she herself had secured some items from the tomb, which she had sold on to a dealer in Cairo. She must have assumed my motives were as unscrupulous or as nakedly commercial as her own. Anyway, she had her sources of intelligence and she was convinced I had stolen something priceless. She didn't know what, but she heard it was the best treasure of the tomb. She told your father and that was why he brought me to England."

"What about Howard Carter?"

"I'm not sure what he believed. Carter was in a difficult position after all. He was the only one who knew the statue was there in the first place. All I know is, he visited the boy's family and gave them money. A few days later he said that since the problems with the authorities, there was no more work for me on the dig. Not that he told me this directly. He never actually spoke to me again."

"And you Samuel. What did you feel?"

"I forbade myself to feel. I thought if I didn't give them expression, my emotions might wither. If I buried my memories, they might fade. I damped down my feelings so much I assumed I might actually be incapable of love. I wanted a new life in which I had not been responsible for the death of a boy. I tried so hard not to feel guilt, that eventually I couldn't feel anything at all. Until I met you."

Now, looking at the statue in Iris's hands, the golden figure seemed smaller than he remembered it. Its dark potency had dwindled. The symbols on its pedestal had dulled. Its gaze was no longer piercing and intense but seemed to have filmed over, like a mask. The inhuman quality it once seemed to possess had receded to the ancient time from which it came, leaving only a young man of exquisite beauty, offering up his golden scales.

Then he understood. Those scales spoke of death certainly - death was only a step away, the slip of a hand away, a heartbeat away - yet the balance did not just give judgment, but hope. Whatever ill deed had weighed down his life, there was still the chance of good to equal it.

Although he had left the Valley, and for some time believed he had put it all behind him, in a way he had always been there. The guilt of the boy's death would always be with him. That face would forever weigh down his heart. Whoever he held close in his life, his arms would always be full of that boy's embrace. The heaviness of death never lessened, but now, through love, he had found a way to balance it.

Acknowledgements

There is a wealth of literature about Howard Carter's amazing discovery in the Valley of the Kings and among those I found most useful for my research were T.G.H James's Howard Carter: The Path To Tutankhamun and the diaries of Howard Carter himself. Of those documenting the Tutmania craze of the 1920s, Christopher Frayling's The Face of Tutankhmen was a fascinating study and Anthony Sattin's Lifting The Veil is an excellent account of British society in Egypt.

The publication of this book in England would not have happened without Simon Carr, to whom I owe enormous gratitude for his entrepreneurial skills, collaboration and enthusiasm. I am also grateful to Greville Edwards for his superb design.
Many thanks also to the brilliant and generous Clare Conville and to Emma Howard for her editing.

Finally, this book is dedicated to Philip Kerr, in gratitude for his unfailing love, encouragement and support.